Between a Mother and Her Child

ELIZABETH NOBLE

PENGUIN BOOKS

PENGUIN BOOKS

Published by the Penguin Group
Penguin Books Ltd, 80 Strand, London WC2R ORL, England
Penguin Group (USA) Inc., 375 Hudson Street, New York, New York 10014, USA
Penguin Group (Canada), 90 Eglinton Avenue East, Suite 700, Toronto, Ontario, Canada M4P 2Y3
(a division of Pearson Penguin Canada Inc.)
Penguin Ireland, 25 St Stephen's Green, Dublin 2, Ireland
(a division of Penguin Books Ltd)
Penguin Group (Australia), 250 Camberwell Road,
Camberwell, Victoria 3124, Australia (a division of Pearson Australia Group Pty Ltd)
Penguin Books India Pvt Ltd, 11 Community Centre, Panchsheel Park, New Delhi – 110 017, India
Penguin Group (NZ), 67 Apollo Drive, Rosedale, Auckland 0632, New Zealand
(a division of Pearson New Zealand Ltd)
Penguin Books (South Africa) (Pty) Ltd, Block D, Rosebank Office Park, 181 Jan Smuts Avenue,
Parktown North, Gauteng 2193, South Africa

Penguin Books Ltd, Registered Offices: 80 Strand, London WC2R ORL, England

www.penguin.com

First published by Michael Joseph 2012
Published in Penguin Books 2012
001

Typeset by Palimpsest Book Production Limited, Falkirk, Stirlingshire
Printed in England by Clays Ltd, St Ives plc

ISBN: 978–0–141–04312–8

www.greenpenguin.co.uk

Penguin Books is committed to a sustainable
future for our business, our readers and our planet.
This book is made from Forest Stewardship
Council™ certified paper.

ALWAYS LEARNING   PEARSON

For my dear friends Clare Bowron and Catherine Holmes, because they are both extraordinary mothers.

And, of course, for my own lovely mum, Sandy.

'He who has a why to live can bear almost any how'

Friedrich Nietzsche

'Hope is the thing with feathers
That perches in the soul,
And sings the tune without the words,
And never stops at all'

Emily Dickinson

Prologue

Maggie

The dream, the one she had dreamt most nights for many, many months, always started out the same way. She sometimes thought she started dreaming it before she was even asleep. Willed herself into it, in some twisted, masochistic way. Sometimes it could even seem comforting, when it began, when it started. Familiar and warm, sound muffled, the world far away. She wondered if she thought, each time, that it might end differently. But it never did. Like an amnesiac, as though each night was the first, she forgot that the gentle, soothing start inevitably gave way to something much darker.

When she'd been a young girl, back in Australia, she and her brother and sister had often slept, on hot summer nights, on the family's ancient deck boat. It was their thing. Their mum had kept some old sleeping bags and pillows on board, the faint scent of mildew mingling with her fabric softener on worn cotton pillowcases, utterly comfortable and familiar. The gentle rocking, small waves lapping against the hull, had been her favourite way to fall asleep. Her childhood lullaby.

In the dream, she was swimming. It had always been her favourite thing to do. It had always been what she did best. Her dad had called her Goldie. It made no sense to people – Maggie's hair was espresso dark – unless you knew that it was short for Goldfish. Because she swam like one, he said.

She loved to swim. In the dream, right at the start, she clearly felt the surge of joy she was familiar with in water. Strong, confident, able. Her arms moving forward, the backs of her hands together, fingers stretching, arms straight. Then pushing her arms apart, feeling herself moving forward. Her lungs were relaxed. She could feel all her muscles, in her shoulders and her back, in her thighs, moving the way she wanted them to, at her command, the way they had been taught, and how she had practised, over the days and weeks and months of her adolescence, in the perfect rhythm. The water around her was the mythical turquoise-aqua clear of her childhood, cool and refreshing, with rays of the bright sunshine on the surface shining through the shallows and dappling on the wet sand below her. She was perfectly happy here. She was perfect, here.

But then, without warning, the sunshine receded, not gradually, but at once, as though a light switch had been suddenly flicked off. The water became darker, and became agitated, not moving with its age-old ebb and flow. Now it was no longer clear, and she couldn't see her hands in front of her face. She wanted to come to the surface – she knew she had to, but she couldn't. She wasn't even sure, after a few moments, which way the surface was – above her or below – only that she couldn't get there. It was the feeling you got when a wave dumped you, body surfing on Manly or on Bondi: total disorientation. Her lungs were tense and rigid, and panic was rising in her chest. Her limbs, the same arms and legs that had been moving in their perfect dance, were flailing now, ungainly and ugly. She was in pain, and she was afraid. So, so afraid. And she couldn't break the surface . . .

Kate

Kate Miller felt, every day, like she was fading out and away. Echoing around, getting fainter and fainter. The world, with all its sights, sounds and people, was getting further and further away. And what scared her the most about it – this process of becoming invisible – was how strangely comfortable it felt; how familiar and unthreatening. It was like life was being lived on the surface of a pond, and she was sinking towards the dark, silty bottom. People said, didn't they, that drowning was soothing, almost peaceful: how ridiculous that was, when surely you should be fighting for breath, terrified, panicking. Apparently not – you read about some sort of surrender, some sense of peace, and almost hallucinatory happiness. And this was the same. Kate knew she should fight this feeling, this sapping apathy. But something about it, she realized sadly, suited her.

There were days when she didn't leave the house. Her home, this place – it was safe and it didn't challenge her. She knew every inch – everything in it. She slept poorly at night, but often drifted off as dawn broke and slept until ten. Waking so late, it felt as though the day had started without her and the energy to catch up sometimes – often – deserted her. She'd lost weight, though she had been slim enough before. The loss didn't suit her, but cooking for one held no appeal, whatever Delia Smith might have to say on the subject, and anyway, she didn't look at her shape much – she dressed without mirrors, and without variety. Most days the phone didn't ring, and she didn't dial.

It seemed to Kate, when she thought about it, and she thought about almost nothing else these days, that in her sixty-plus years of life, she'd been two distinct and very different people. There was the woman she had been, had allowed herself to be, for most of her adult life, and that woman lived her life in quiet black and white; and there was woman she had been for the last ten or fifteen years, before she lost him, who had basked in glorious Technicolor for all of that time. How quickly she had gone back to black and white. How weak she must be. And how she hated herself for it.

Chapter One

November 2006

When she couldn't sleep, which was often, Maggie had learnt that lying damply, tossing in the hot, crumpled sheets of her too big bed, was the worst thing she could do. She didn't want to take pills, though she had them, hidden in the back of the medicine cabinet, a slender amber pot of blue lozenge-shaped pills, not one missing, all pushed down with a cotton wool ball, the label facing the back of the cupboard, like she was ashamed she had even been prescribed them. She couldn't read then, or watch television. Her daughter Aly, who knew how it was, though they seldom talked about it, had joined LoveFilm with her mother's name and credit card details, and optimistically lined up epic boxed series of DVDs – *The West Wing, Rome, 24, Grey's Anatomy*, alongside the older, black and white film collection that Maggie had treasured for years – the Cary Grant and Jimmy Stewart and Katharine Hepburn films she knew by heart but that Aly didn't consider constituted entertainment. But Maggie couldn't always concentrate, couldn't follow even the simplest stories she knew best. She needed to move, and not to think. If she'd lived alone, she might have run, hard and fast, the way she hadn't done for years, concentrating only on putting one leg in front of the other and on controlling the screaming pain in her lungs, though she knew it wasn't a sensible thing to do in west London in the middle of the night. But she didn't live alone, and she couldn't do that.

So she did housework, and laundry, and ironing. In the middle of the night. Her home was cleaner than it had ever been. Not that it mattered to her, particularly. Maggie had always been quite laid back about that. More laid back than her husband, Bill, ever had been, certainly. She had accused him, more than once, and not entirely jokingly, of being borderline OCD. Bill would square off a pile of magazines and newspapers on the coffee table (if he wasn't, in fact, consigning them to the recycling) and dry dishes left to drain on the counter. He couldn't really relax if jobs like this weren't done. These were not things that had ever worried Maggie. She'd grown up in comfortable chaos – her mum had kept newspapers until she'd read every word, and since she worked hard, that often took weeks, and they teetered in piles on every available surface. It was clean, her childhood home, but it was almost never tidy. Mess was her natural habitat, she supposed. It was one of the differences between them that had once been endearing, but, across the years of their marriage, had become less a cute contrast and more a wearisome irritation. Sand in the pearl shell.

But the cleaning was almost therapeutic now. She could go into a room and make it different. Achieve something. Fix something. Focus on something real, however mundane. And it was hard work physically. She usually gave up on sleep around 2 or 3 a.m. Then cleaned for two or three hours. Then went back to bed, falling exhausted on to the same crumpled sheets, not noticing them this time. It meant that getting up at 7.30 a.m. to see Stan and Aly off to school nearly killed her every morning, the alarm she had to keep on the dresser across from her bed rousing her from the deepest, furthest away sleep she ever got these days. She would swing her legs out of bed the second she heard it, sitting with her head bowed like a disorientated drunk, willing herself to come around.

She never let herself go back to bed after she'd waved them off, though sometimes – usually – she ached to. Somehow that felt like a slippery slope to her, and the idea of it frightened her. She wouldn't be *that* woman. She showered and dressed, dried her hair and put on make-up, something she'd learnt to do without ever really looking herself in the eye, and got on with things. She often napped in the afternoons, in front of *Midsomer Murders*, on the deep denim sofa in the sitting room, but she was dressed when she did it, damn it.

It was a new routine, and she hated it, but it was a routine, at least, and there was some strange comfort in that. For a long time, there'd been no routine at all, because they'd all been so very lost, disorientated, like in the dream.

On the top landing, Aly's door was firmly shut, but Maggie turned the handle silently, braver in the dark night than she sometimes felt in the day, and opened it enough for the pendant on the landing to bathe her daughter's face in a shaft of soft light. Aly's face had hardly changed at all since she was a baby. Her rounded nose, her full lips, the slightly chubby cheeks she so hated – they were all the features of her baby face. The eyes, closed now in deep sleep, were her father's clear bright celadon green. Aly wore her hair long, like every other teenage girl Maggie could think of, and it lay in heavy, wavy layers across her pillow, a dirty dark blonde. Aly would be pleased with how she looked lying there, if she could see. A sleeping beauty. Maggie marvelled, as she had all Aly's life, that this child had come from her. Her own coarse curls were so brown they were almost black. Her skin was olive. Her eyes were a deep, dark hazel brown, like a Labrador, Bill used to say.

From a distance they looked chocolate brown, but up close you could see slivers of amber and emerald and tawny yellow in them. Aly frowned and shifted a little in her sleep, and Maggie closed the door gently. She did this most nights. She and Aly were so out of sync in their waking lives that she needed this contact. Asleep, Aly couldn't argue with her, couldn't make that particular face she seemed to reserve exclusively for her mother, didn't make Maggie feel like she was getting everything wrong.

Along the hall, Stan's door, proudly marked as such with a US car licence plate from the state of New York that bore the name Stanley, was wide open. Stan lay spread-eagled diagonally across his bed, the duvet kicked back and half on to the floor. Stan's left hand was down his pyjama bottoms in the position of comfort he had been assuming all his life, and his pyjama top had ridden up so that ten inches of belly were exposed. Maggie smiled and went in, stubbing her toe on a rogue piece of Lego and swearing under her breath. She pulled him around carefully, smoothing his top down and covering his soft skin. She kissed his cheek and lingered for a moment, loving the smell of him, and almost envying the regular, peaceful sound of his breathing. She touched his hair. If it grew, then those would be her dark curls, but by mutual agreement, she and Stan kept it close-cropped, and it was like stroking an animal's pelt. A sudden tear rolled down her cheek, her sternum contracting in a momentary dull pain. That happened, these days, all the time. Maggie barely noticed.

Her babies were asleep. They were safe, and they were here, and they were sleeping. It brought her a kind of peace, for a while at least.

Maggie tucked him in again, and got on with her labours. She kept a small cleaning kit in each of the bathrooms. It saved making too much noise going up and down the stairs. She cleaned the bathrooms the most. She kept old T-shirts of Bill's, yellowed at the armpits and stretched at the neck, as cloths and rubbed at the tiles until they gleamed. She scrubbed at the grout and polished the taps. Replaced damp towels from the floor with fresh, clean ones from the airing cupboard on the landing outside her bedroom. Neither of the kids appeared to understand the concept of a towel rail, however often she explained it to them.

It was a beautiful house, and she loved it clean as she had loved it messy. She had lived in it for almost fifteen years. Aly had been a toddler when they'd moved in, and Stan was born five years later, just as she and Bill had finally finished renovating. A grand and imposing Victorian end-of-terrace villa, it sprawled over four floors. She remembered standing at the bottom of the flight of steps that led up to the big dark-blue front door, the day the estate agent had taken her and Bill to see it for the first time, struggling to imagine that a place this lovely, this big, could actually be her home. Their home. Bill was a risk taker then. He'd squeezed her shoulder and said he'd done the sums and they could afford it, and even though she knew he'd done the sums he wanted to do, not the sums he probably should have done, she didn't press him because she suddenly, desperately wanted to be the woman who lived here. She wanted to sit in an armchair with the children playing on the rug around her in the vast bay window on the upper-ground floor and wait for him to come home at night.

It had been in a state, of course, with peeling William Morris wallpaper and sticky carpets. Even Bill couldn't have made the numbers work on a property already renovated, not in those days, even in a postcode that was more up and coming than already established. But the rooms had been big, with unbelievably high ceilings, and, thank God, all the period details intact – big marble fireplaces and deep, gracious coving, ceiling roses and picture rails. The agent had banged the doors authoritatively and declared them 'heavy, solid, almost certainly original'.

There were two huge reception rooms on the ground floor, and four smaller rooms in the basement, which was dark, and had a single, solid door that led out into the surprising, overgrown sixty-foot garden. On the first floor there were three bedrooms and a bathroom, and on the top floor, three more bedrooms. As she had slowly climbed each staircase, with Aly wriggling and chattering on her hip, wandering from floor to floor, Maggie had fallen more and more in love with the house. Finally, years after she'd left her home in Australia, Maggie had the strange and marvellous feeling that she was home again. Bill and the agent were brainstorming the possible renovation and tapping walls in a manly way. Maggie had been uncharacteristically quiet. When Bill had whispered in her ear, anxious and unable to read her, 'What do you think?', she had smiled broadly, then buried her face in Aly's delicious scented neck, and giggled. 'I think you better buy it right now, 'cos I'm not leaving . . .'

And she hadn't.

It had been hard work. They'd laboured in the house while the neighbourhood around them also became more respectable and smart, and while Bill's property-development business thrived and made sense at first of the sum, and then light work of the mortgage, and while their children grew and played in the garden. They'd stripped all the gruesome wallpaper and pulled up the carpets. At first, that and fresh paint was all they could manage. Then they'd gone room by room, adding curtains, and furniture. A family bathroom with the clawfoot bath that was everywhere that year. And at last the kitchen. They'd taken the back off the basement and installed a vast and fashionable family kitchen/diner down there, with stainless-steel appliances and a seamless white Corian work surface, although Maggie had insisted on a huge old pine kitchen table and mismatched chairs that she'd found at a reclamation yard to stop the place feeling what she would describe to Bill, her nose wrinkled in distaste, as 'too cataloguey'. There were floor-to-ceiling glass doors that opened all the way back on clever hinges and slides on warm sunny days. Bill always told people he had to get as much fresh air and sunlight as he could in for his Aussie wife, but it was as much for him as for her. They'd put in a master en suite and a small new top-floor bathroom, and decorated everywhere in a warm palette of greens and neutrals, Maggie sneaking a splash of orange and pink in where she thought she could get away with it.

They'd been crazy stupid happy doing that house. Exhausted a lot of the time. There were a million memories in the fabric of the building. Aly riding a trike around a big empty room, a tiny hard hat rakish on her head. Bill, his five o'clock shadow scratching the side of her neck, sliding his hands down the insides of her painting dungarees, desperate to distract her from finishing just one more wall. They'd all laid a handprint in poured concrete and she'd scratched their names under each palm imprint. Heights were scratched into the kitchen doorframe. Bill had filled the foyer with blue balloons the day they'd brought Stan home from the hospital. There was a raised bed in the back garden, made with reclaimed railway sleepers Bill had found, where she'd taught the children to plant seeds and they'd grown tomatoes and lettuces and carrots. She'd loved doing it – every minute of every day of it, she'd loved how it all looked when she was finished – cool and comfortable and lived in, lived in by her happy family, and she'd loved her life. Then.

She loved it still. Several redecorations later, and however many times she climbed that flight of steps and put her key in the lock. In the late nineties, Bill had tried hard to persuade her to move. They could have something much grander now, he told her. The mortgage that had once been terrifying had long been paid off – Bill had been lucky, and he was good at what he did – astute investments and imaginative projects in great areas had made him wealthy far quicker than Maggie would have imagined possible, though Bill had always had a professional confidence that some might think bordered on arrogance. Bill's father, before he died, had crowed that he'd been right all along – Bill hadn't needed university with his head for business and property, it would have been a waste of time, he said. He'd been Maggie's ally – Bill's mother had never entirely forgiven Maggie for 'holding Bill back', though until recently Maggie had never understood what she was supposed to have been holding him back from. Bill wanted to move; he felt he'd earnt it. He had a shopping list of things he wanted – garaging for his car, a garden big enough for a pool . . . he brought home details of behemoths in Primrose Hill and Hampstead. Tried to enlist the children in his master plan with promises of en suite bathrooms and tennis courts – but all in vain. Maggie was rooted here, and she refused to budge. This was their home. It had driven a small wedge – not injurious, necessarily, but irritating, like a splinter – between them. Bill accused her of not enjoying his money, and thereby tarnishing his own enjoyment of his success. Maggie had tried to ignore the feeling that Bill's wanting to move was somehow a betrayal of how happy they'd been here. Somehow an indication that none of it was as precious, as memorable, to him as it was to her. The kind of thought that seeps into a marriage and is never really expressed, because it seems so small, at first. But maybe it's the start of a slight fraying around the edges. A few threads, coming loose. So small a fault at the start that you shake your head and dismiss your own pessimism. But it's a start.

It almost amused her, the cleanliness of the house now. It was ironic that Bill didn't live here any more to see it.

Downstairs now, Maggie boiled the kettle in the gleaming kitchen, and put a teabag in a mug. For a while, after everything, she'd abandoned the strong 'builder's tea' she'd drunk ever since she came to England and switched to what Bill called 'weirdy beardy' tea – chamomile and nettle and fennel and such. Teas she might have smirked at, if she hadn't been so desperate for tranquillity and for sleep that she'd try anything. She'd almost been relieved, though, when they hadn't worked – hadn't kept her asleep or slowed her racing pulse – and she'd been able to switch back. They tasted so awful. She drank too much tea, she knew. Drank tea like an Englishwoman – all day long, as refreshment, as therapy, because boiling the kettle was something to do to break up the hours. But frankly she didn't care about her tannin levels, or her caffeine intake. There were worse addictions to have, and she'd avoided those – painkillers, antidepressants, too much Pinot noir in front of the TV, even. She checked her watch, though she didn't really need to. She didn't have to figure out the time difference – after all these years, she still ran two clocks in her brain. It was 4 a.m. here, so it was three o'clock in the afternoon there, eleven hours ahead. She took the phone from its cradle, picked up her mug of tea and curled up on the sofa, pulling an embroidered Union Jack pillow into the small of her back.

Her younger sister, more than 10,000 miles away, was on speed dial and it only took twenty seconds to get to her. She was #2, after Bill's office at #1. Not for the first time, as she pushed the button, Maggie thought maybe she needed to change that now. Olivia picked up on the fourth ring.

'Slacking off on the housework, sis?' They'd always done that – segued straight into conversation, as though they were in the next room from each other and had broken off only for a moment.

'Tea break. Time for one yourself?'

'Good idea. Hold on.' Maggie could hear the sound of a door closing – Liv's office door – and a technical beep, like she'd closed a computer screen. This was Liv's ritual. She was making time for Maggie. She always did.

'Tell me all about it?'

It was what Maggie always said. Olivia knew that what it meant was 'talk to me, talk at me, let me lose myself for a moment in your life so far away . . .' She knew to talk.

'Work, weather or Scott?'

'You have to ask?'

'Well, I had a long, dull meeting with the partners this morning, and now I've got this report to finish . . .'

'Scott. I meant Scott, you dufus.' Maggie almost laughed.

'Ah . . . Scott . . .'

Scott was her younger sister's boyfriend. The first one, so far as Maggie knew, and Maggie knew everything, who was getting really serious . . .

Maggie was thirty-eight years old. Olivia was eight years younger. She was their parents' bonus baby, born on their own mother's forty-fifth birthday. Maggie had loved Olivia passionately and unconditionally since the first moment she'd seen her, lying in a Perspex cot beside their mother's hospital bed in Sydney. Olivia had been born with a full head of glossy hair that curled at the ends just like her big sister's had, before the curl travelled resolutely up to the roots, and a reflux issue that meant she threw up almost everything she had ingested for the first nine months of her life. Maggie didn't care. She had never tired of washing and dressing Olivia. She was almost proprietary about her, rushing home from school to take over from her mother, who, more tired than she had thought she would be this time around, was happy to hand her over. Their father worked long and often unsocial hours, and wasn't entirely baby friendly when he was around, preferring his children once they could walk, talk and swim; their big brother, Tom, was totally uninterested, so Maggie had often had Olivia completely to herself.

She'd taught her to walk, and she'd taught her to swim. Olivia's first word was a slurred approximation of Maggie's name. The two of them had always shared a bedroom, and often, in those early years, a narrow single bed, Olivia climbing in to snuggle into Maggie's warmth whenever she woke in the night and sometimes before she'd even slept.

Leaving Olivia in Australia had been, at the time, the hardest thing Maggie had ever done. She had been eighteen – Olivia barely eleven, angry and hurt that her sister was deserting her to go so very far away. Over the years, Bill had joked that the phone bills and the airline tickets he'd had to pay for were a very high price for his foreign, exotic flower of a wife. As she got a little older, Olivia flew unaccompanied minor as often as she could: Christmas and New Year, the long Australian school summer holiday. Maggie's parents hated the flight – they'd come at first, once a year or so, but that had dwindled eventually. They preferred Maggie to visit them, anxious for her children to spend time in Australia. Tom made no secret of his dislike of England, with its grey skies and long winters, and his vague disdain for Bill had been another barrier to a close ongoing relationship. When he'd married a woman neither Liv nor Maggie could stick for more than an hour or so at a time, they'd grown further apart – their virtual estrangement a stark contrast to the bond between the sisters. Olivia was the most steadfast member of Maggie's family. Maggie had hoped Olivia might follow her and make a permanent home in England, but she'd had to acknowledge that Olivia, as much as they loved each other, was somehow just more Australian. England didn't suit her as much. And Olivia had known it too, although one summer in her late teens she had fallen in love with a burly hockey player from the club where Bill played, and tried to convince herself she could stay. They broke up and she went home. And there she had stayed.

Always 'the brainy one', although truly she was the one who had had the most opportunity, or at least hadn't blown it like Maggie had, Olivia had read business studies at the University of New South Wales, in Sydney, gaining a first-class degree 'without really breaking a sweat', Maggie would declare proudly. She was working on an MBA now, sponsored by the large insurance company she'd worked for since graduation. The sullen eleven-year-old with wild hair had grown into a groomed, sleek and smart young woman. Maggie was beyond proud of her sister, and still as protective as she had been all those years ago, despite the miles between them and the creeping knowledge that Liv scarcely needed looking after as much as she herself did now. Distance notwithstanding, they were as close as they had ever been. Closer now, if that were possible, in the last couple of years. Olivia had been entirely constant since Maggie's life had started to go so spectacularly wrong – perpetually available to her sister whatever was going on in her own life. And constancy was a great thing. There had been weeks, maybe months, when Maggie had refused to answer the phone or been monosyllabic and uncommunicative when she did, but Liv had never wavered. She called every day, for ages, and when Maggie didn't talk to her, she just carried on detailing the minutiae of her own life, her tone light and bright, knowing that Maggie was listening, even if she wasn't responding.

Maggie had never met Scott, though. She'd last been in Sydney the previous Easter, stopping there for ten days or so, staying with their dad – widowed eight years earlier when their mum, a lifelong non-smoker, had died quickly and violently of lung cancer – before she took the kids north to Hamilton Island. He and Olivia had been seeing each other then, but he'd been in Tokyo on a business trip. Maggie had pretended to be offended, called him Olivia's imaginary boyfriend, and Olivia had made light of it, but Maggie knew from her sister's face that it was serious and that she was a little sad they hadn't met. She knew Olivia wanted to look at this man she might love through the gently refracting lens of her sister's eye.

She'd seen pictures of a tall, good-looking guy with an easy smile, and spoken to him on the phone, though that had been strangely frustrating, as awkward as talking to Liv was easy. It was only when she was talking to her sister that she forgot that slightly stilting time delay and occasional echo on the line. She liked to see people's faces when she was talking to them. Without that, no conversation felt easy. With Scott, their mutual keenness – hers to like him, him to have her like him – made it odd and unnatural.

'He wants us to move in together.' Olivia laughed, a high, excited, happy sound.

'You're kidding me? Really?'

'No. He asked me last night.'

'Wow. Move in, not get married?'

'Well . . . ?'

'Well . . . what?'

'Oh Mags . . .'

'Oh Liv.' Maggie was teasing her, but only gently.

Liv apparently hadn't noticed anyway. 'He made this lovely, lovely speech. Honestly, he was so sweet my knees were buckling, and I was sitting down. He said . . . oh, he said the greatest, sexiest, most romantic, wonderful things anyone ever said to me . . .'

Maggie waited, holding her breath. Olivia's excitement was contagious, but, for her, always with a twist. Her sternum ached again, and unconsciously she tapped herself lightly on the part that hurt.

'He said he wanted to marry me. He said that was absolutely what he saw in our future. That he already couldn't imagine his life without me. Didn't want to. He said when he proposed, he wanted it to be perfect. He wants to meet you first, sis. He knows about us, he really gets it. He'll ask Dad, I'm sure; he's that kind of guy. But he knows it's really you he has to impress . . .'

'And shacking up with my baby sister is the way to do that, right?'

Olivia laughed again. 'You're awful, Mags! You really are. Shacking up! He said he couldn't bear not to wake up with me every morning, and he was getting fed up with carrying his jockeys around town in his briefcase.'

'That old chestnut. Which episode of *Sex and the City* did he get that line from?'

'Yes, that old chestnut. He doesn't watch *Sex and the City*.'

'And you fell for it, did you?'

'Hook, line and bloody sinker.' Olivia laughed. 'Oh shit, Maggie, I'm so happy I might explode.'

Maggie loved so many things about Olivia it was hard to say what she loved best, but it might just be that Olivia didn't try and shield her sister from her own joy, like other people might. She understood that the two things – her joy and Maggie's misery – weren't related, and that Maggie didn't want to be protected from it. She already felt everything, so let her feel this too.

'I'm glad, Livvy.'

'I know. I know you are.'

'Are you going to do it straight away? Before you come here?'

'I can't see why not. *Carpe* the *diem*, right?'

'That's my philosophy.' Hadn't it always been? Liv hesitated for just a second.

'He wants to come with me, at Christmas.'

'Oh.' Of course. He had to come, didn't he? How else could they meet? She hadn't thought it through fast enough . . .

Olivia carried on, quickly, sensing what Maggie was thinking. 'But not for the whole time. I mean, I'm taking a long break, right?' Olivia was arriving on the 15th, and staying for almost four weeks. Officially, she was on a study break from work. Unofficially, Maggie knew she was coming to look after her. And she couldn't wait. The nearer the time got, the more desperate she felt. She would drive to Heathrow to pick Olivia up, and she'd heave a huge sigh of relief that her sister was finally here. Then she'd let her sleep for fourteen hours, and just knowing that Olivia was in the house, was here at last, would be like a salve. She hated the sudden stab of jealousy she felt because it made her feel mean – but Scott had her all the time, didn't he? Scott had her on the other side of the world. She wanted her to herself.

'And he is meant to be with his parents, of course. The whole lot.' Scott came, Maggie knew, from an improbably large farming family in Queensland, outside of Brisbane.

'But he thought he'd maybe come between Christmas and New Year, and stay for a week. The day after Boxing Day until New Year's Day, maybe. Would that be okay?' Olivia spoke slowly and clearly. She knew exactly what she was saying – she must have rehearsed saying this, Maggie realized. And she needed Maggie to know that she knew.

Maggie took a deep breath. 'Of course. It would be great. Stan and Aly will be thrilled.'

'And you?'

Maggie made herself sound light and warm. 'Of course. I can share you – for a while. I've got to meet this man, right, if he's going to be my new brother-in-law?'

'So when does Bill have the kids? Did you sort it all out yet?'

'Before Christmas. He's bringing them back Christmas morning.' God, she dreaded that. The handover was the absolute worst part. There was no way of finessing it, or making it appear as anything other than what it was – two parents splitting their children and their children's hearts in half on a weekly or fortnightly basis. However hard they worked at it, however committed they were to making it as easy for the kids as it possibly could be, and however civilized, that moment was still the hardest.

'Then odd days, between then and New Year's. He'll have Stan on his own a bit – Aly has all kinds of plans with her mates, as usual. Stan's trying to talk Bill into taking him skiing, but I don't know if he's sorted anything out . . .'

'How do you feel about that?'

'I hope he does. Stan loves the snow.'

'And you hate it, right?'

'Bingo.'

'So that works?'

'That works. You and me. Then you, me and the kids. Then you, me, the kids and Scott.'

'He says he wants to be in Trafalgar Square for the New Year's Eve hoopla.'

'Why?' Maggie's tone was incredulous. She couldn't think of anything worse than a drunken scrum on a freezing damp night.

'God knows. I suppose he's seen it on the telly or something . . .' Olivia giggled. 'Let's talk him out of it.'

'You're on. That could only be a huge disappointment, after a lifetime of celebrating it in Sydney Harbour . . .'

'He spent most of his first years celebrating it on a farm in the middle of nowhere. They probably sheared a sheep or two to ring in the New Year.'

'You might have to lose the disdain for rural life if you're going to hitch your wagon to this guy's horse, Liv.'

'No way. He's getting a city girl. He knows that.'

'You sure he's not planning to drag you back to the homestead, get you pregnant once a year for the next decade?'

She heard her sister shiver, then laugh.

'I can't wait for you to be here, Livvy.'

'Me too. Three weeks and I'll be there . . .' After a pause, Liv's voice grew suddenly serious. 'How are you doing?'

Maggie shrugged, though she knew the gesture did not translate on the phone.

'You know. I'm okay. I'm fine.'

'That's the banned word.'

Olivia had banned 'fine' ages ago. But 'fine' was a bad

habit, hard to shake. 'Fine', she could have pointed out, was also exactly what almost everyone else who asked wanted to hear, after the initial interest and support.

'Sorry.'

''S okay. You hanging in?'

'By my fingernails.' Maggie tried to keep her tone light, and Liv responded in kind, though neither of them believed each other.

'What you got going on, apart from the bloody spring cleaning?' No one but Liv knew about Maggie's nocturnal habit. For the sister who'd grown up in Maggie's messy tip of a bedroom, it still seemed bizarre. For all the kids knew, or noticed, a team of pixies slipped in each night and did it all.

Maggie took a quick stock. 'Aly's got the wretched exams, of course. I'm actually having lunch with Bill this week to talk it over.'

'Is that okay?'

'You know it is, Livvy.' She and Bill could still talk about the kids, almost like they always had, with the crucial difference that one of them no longer lived with Aly and Stan and didn't see them every day. She was determined that would not change. She did not withhold information. She did not do PR for their father, negative or positive. But she had never shut him out. She never would.

'And then Stan is determined that we decorate for Christmas on December 1st, so the tree can drop all its damn needles by Christmas Eve, and this year he is also determined we must hike around in the mud at a Christmas-tree farm and cut the wretched thing down ourselves.'

Stan was too young and too oblivious to realize that selecting the tree, wielding the axe and tying the tree to the top of the car was definitely what Maggie would have considered Bill's domain. So she would do it, though she would dread it.

'Sounds ghastly.' Liv hated the cold.

'It'll be . . .'

'Don't.' Olivia's voice, mock strict, was strident down the phone. She knew Maggie had been about to use the banned word.

Maggie laughed, stifling a yawn. 'It'll be . . . an adventure.'

'You yawning?'

'Yep. Think the second rest shift might be on.'

'Charming. You've rung me, on the other side of the world, so I can talk you to sleep. I'm human Mogadon. I'm a lullaby made flesh . . .'

'Pretty much.'

'I love you, Mags.' She hadn't always been so sentimental. Hadn't always said out loud the things she felt that she knew were understood. That was new.

'I love you too. Livvy? I'm really, really pleased for you. Honest. I can't wait to meet him.'

'I'll be there soon.'

Not soon enough. The moment Liv had hung up, Maggie's heart sank. She put her mug in the shiny sink and climbed the two flights of stairs to her bedroom. She stood in the doorway, staring at the bed. It was a little more than seven foot wide – the biggest bed she had ever seen. Sheets for it had to be specially made. Bill had had it made for them, the year Stan was born. He said he wanted a bed they could all sleep in without being uncomfortable. All watch a black and white film on the vast wall-mounted television, or read books and newspapers on a Sunday morning. You could get lost in a bed that big, and Maggie felt lost in it every night now. She needed to get rid of it. She said that at least once a day, usually while she was making it, but she hadn't done anything about it. She nodded her head decisively. She would. She must. She would talk to Bill about it when they had lunch this week. Then she walked to the foot, put her arms out to the sides, and fell forward, like a bungee jumper, her breath forced out of her lungs as she fell on the mattress, eyes already closed.

It was hot a couple of hours later, when Olivia stepped out of her office on to the street. Bright and sunny and still very hot. She pulled the sunglasses she'd had on the top of her head down, feeling her eyes start to water as they squinted at the yellow light. Maggie would be asleep now. She hoped. Like those clocks hotels kept in their foyers, showing the time in New York, Tokyo, London, she automatically thought in two time zones. Whatever she was doing, at any time of the day, she knew what time it was in London – what Maggie might most likely be doing. Now, now she should be sleeping. There was something like relief in knowing that. Maggie was unlikely to call for the next few hours. And she no longer called so much during Liv's night. She had done, fairly regularly, at first. But she didn't any more. Liv had said she could, and she didn't mind, she truly didn't, but it had been exhausting. Even on the nights when Maggie hadn't called, her voice breaking and quiet, her Australian accent more pronounced in grief than it had been for years, Liv slept lightly, fitfully, waiting for the ring. Liv wasn't sure whether it was because she no longer needed to, or because she knew how much those calls frightened and worried Liv, or maybe even because of Scott – because these days more often than not Liv was in bed with him.

That made little difference to Liv. If anything, she worried more. Once it was the phone ringing that woke her. Now it was quite often the silence. The not ringing. Either way, she was often sitting propped on pillows thinking about her sister in the middle of the night.

Scott had helped. God, how he had helped. Sometimes he slept through her wakefulness, and she lay on her side, watching him. The rhythmic rise and fall of his chest. The odd twitch of his eye or his lips as he dreamt. It made her calm, watching him. Sometimes he woke too, sensing her beside him. They didn't speak. He knew and so there was no need. Then he would pull her in towards him, holding her tightly. Quite often he would make love to her then, silent and gentle and slow, as though in a dream, sometimes not even quite fully awake. They had a lot – really, a lot – of lights-on, eyes-wide-open, aerobic-work-out, *Kama Sutra*-style sex the rest of the time, but those times, in the middle of the night, in the silent darkness, those meant the most to her, because what it so eloquently told her was how well he understood her, and how willing he was to give her what he knew she needed. It was a huge part of how and why she loved him.

She remembered telling him about Maggie and Bill, and their story. Horribly early in their relationship. Too soon, probably. No, definitely. It was their fourth date. She'd been out with a lot of men, but Scott had made a huge impact. It wasn't just that he was gorgeous, though he definitely was. They'd kissed, open-mouthed and hot under the collar, against the wall outside her apartment, at the end of the third date, but that was as far as things had gone. And then she was crying into her tapas. And she wasn't a pretty crier – this she knew to be true. That he hadn't run screaming for the hills was to his eternal credit.

And here he was, leaning against a bike rack, his tie already loosened and his jacket over his shoulder. She smiled at him, and he walked towards her. He often met her outside the office these days; he worked a few streets away. He slid his arms around her waist possessively and kissed her deeply, wonderfully oblivious to the commuters milling around them. She let him kiss her and she kissed him back, the sun strong on her upturned face, and gratefully let Maggie slip gently to the back of her mind.

school years. He had always spoken with a lisp – Maggie and Bill had hours of home video of what they had thought of as Stan's charming mixed-up sounds – eating a bowl of 'bisghetti' and pointing at 'aminals' in the zoo, eyes wide with fascination and delight as an 'ambliance' passed, its siren blaring. His kindergarten teacher wasn't overly concerned about his reluctance to learn the alphabet letters in order when she mentioned it to them on their first parents' evenings, balanced on tiny plastic chairs in Stan's classroom – cue more videos of the whole family insanely warbling the alphabet song. And everyone who noticed his handwriting found it easy to attribute it to Bill's own lousy script that still – well into adulthood – scrawled illegibly across the page. Stan liked to be read to far more than he liked to read, and he was hard to resist when he looked at you, big-eyed, and begged for the sound of your voice. Aly read to him, and listened to him read, impatiently finishing his sentences. Maggie had always been mildly repulsed by the pushy mothers at the school gate who boasted about their children's achievements. These witches in Boden, stirring a heady brew of comparison and judgement on one another, saw the developmental milestones in the big red books the NHS provided to all newborns as targets to be smashed, raced past, utterly determined to portray their ordinary – albeit beloved – offspring as extraordinary. The inner-city middle-class mother was often a species to be feared, so far as Maggie was concerned. She wanted happy children. Full stop. But by the middle years of primary school, as the children's reading took off – book titles written on colourful leaves on a giant poster-painted reading tree on the wall of the class – questions were being asked, and before long, to her initial horror and eventual resignation, her happy boy Stan was being tested and subsequently diagnosed by the age of seven. The school – at round-table meetings in the head's office, with plates of biscuits and weak tea – were quick to assure Maggie that they could cope. Stan wasn't severely dyslexic, they said, and they had systems in place to help manage it.

The dyspraxia wasn't picked up as easily: the systems for dealing with it were not quite so slick. Maggie found it hard to forgive herself for not noticing it sooner, determined as she had been to celebrate Stan for the lad he was. The two conditions often overlapped in children. She was an expert now. She'd read the books. Stan was the latest of her children to walk – happy to shuffle on his padded bottom until he was almost twenty months old. More video. Aly pulling him up and placing his arms on the sofa cushions, then backing away from him on her knees, beckoning and cooing to him. Stan would chuckle animatedly, sit down, and move crabwise to his sister, who would be torn between delight and reproach. 'No, no, Stan. You're supposed to walk.' And he did. Eventually. He stood up and walked the length of the kitchen to tumultuous applause a couple of months before his second birthday, and then promptly fell, hitting his head on the corner of the open dishwasher door – the cut required two stitches. That dash to the casualty department was the first of several over his toddlerhood and early childhood. Stan fell often. When he was three, he broke his arm falling down the stairs. At four, he put his hand through a pane of glass on holiday, and by six years old, he'd had several sets of stitches, a handful of X-rays and an assortment of bandages and casts, all documented in the family photograph albums. Maggie had made a shadow-box display of his first fracture – the X-ray, the hospital bracelet and the carefully preserved removed cast, with bright marker-pen writings and drawings all over it, alongside a photograph of a proud Stan taken while he was still encased in the plaster cast. He showed no inclination to tie his own shoelaces or fasten his buttons. No one noticed – Stan was his big sister Aly's living doll. She dressed him and fed him as though he belonged to her, and if anyone noticed that those skills didn't come easily to Stan, they might have smiled benignly at Aly and reflected, if they thought about it at all, that it would all come eventually. Stan was a happy, energetic, loving little boy. Perfectly normal.

Except that he wasn't. Not quite and not really. His clumsiness became more pronounced – and once the children began playing organized sports at school his issues with timing and balance were apparent. Bill went to watch him play football – one of the first matches – and felt bad when he saw how hard it appeared to be for Stan to kick, and pass. He remonstrated with himself, saying he hadn't played enough kickabout with him in the garden. For a few weeks, he had Stan out there in all weathers, trying to be patient and helpful. Eventually he came, dark-faced, to Maggie, and said he thought it was something more. It had been another of the small splinters, niggling away under the skin of their marriage. Maggie had felt, up until that point, unsupported by Bill. She felt he'd shaken off her anxieties, unwilling to face the same reality she was trying to. He'd made her feel, more than once, neurotic, obsessive. She remembered shouting at his retreating back once – the whispery shout of a mother with young children – did he think she had Munchausen syndrome by proxy? Did he think she was making it up? Why would she *do* that? Along with the relief, the day he came to her and said he saw what she saw, at last, came an accusing voice. Why hadn't he seen it sooner? Why hadn't he trusted her, listened to her?

By the time he was eight and half, their beloved Stan had two names attached to his own, at school, at the GP's, in their own heads. Dyslexic and dyspraxic. Endless meetings, endless testing. Endless Googling and reading and research-ing. Everyone assured them he could cope. He could absolutely remain in mainstream education. He was not severely afflicted. He would be capable of GCSEs, A levels, university even – a normal, meaningful life. It wasn't that bad. They spent enough time in alien environments, anx-iously looking around at other children, other families, to know that was true. In their sensible, public selves. In pri-vate, Maggie and Bill struggled.

It was one of a dozen, a hundred, a thousand ways that they struggled sometimes. Mostly little things – small discon-nects, tiny cracks. It wasn't the huge things that were the most dangerous. It was the accruing of all the little things. Most of the time, you ignored them. You were married, you were struggling to build a life, a family, a career, a bank bal-ance that didn't send panic coursing through your veins. You told yourself it was okay – that you still wanted the same things from life, that you loved each other and your children and that nothing was worth more than they were, than this was. You told yourself that it was normal, that everyone felt like this sometimes. That you were basically the same two people you'd been when you'd started this journey, and that would mean everything would be all right. And you hoped it was true.

And Stan struggled. He understood his diagnoses. He could explain, in an adult tone that made Maggie sad, what was wrong with how his brain worked when he looked at let-ters and when he tried to catch a ball. But for him, the knowledge was not power. At school, he became more and more withdrawn, a quieter, greyer version of the little boy he had once been. Bill once heard Maggie on the phone to Liv saying that it seemed like someone had taken Stan's fuse out. He didn't shine brightly any more. The physicality of what he was dealing with was much worse for him than the academic implications. In the classroom, with a sensitive teacher, no one needed to know. At home, Maggie worked with him relentlessly. Plenty of boys in his class did badly in tests and gave wrong answers when they were called on in front of their peers. Academic success was not a great barometer of popularity for eight- and nine-year-old boys. On the sports field, it was much, much harder, and it was here that the bullying started. It began with name calling – borne out of the other boys' frustration that Stan couldn't do what they could all do. Exclusion followed. They ignored him. And then they started to be physical with him. At first, he didn't tell his parents. When one of the children took his lunch and he reported it to a teacher, Bill and Maggie were called in, the teacher telling them she was concerned that Stan was becoming isolated – eating alone, wandering the edges of the playground at lunchtime, always on the periphery. Driving home from that meeting, more details spilt out of Stan, and he cried embarrassed, angry tears in the back of the car.

It got worse. Stan didn't want to go to school – he invented maladies and wheedled at his mother to let him stay at home with her. There were days when she wasn't strong enough to make him go in, and she kept him at home – although the pompous head (and Bill – co-conspirators, Maggie called them) strenuously disapproved – taking him to Tesco's, and the swimming pool and the park. She simply didn't want him somewhere where he was so unhappy. On days when he went in, she sometimes sat worrying for hours about what was happening to him. The children were smart – they tortured him in subtle ways that were hard to punish. If they'd punched him and broken his nose, the school could perhaps have dealt with it more easily and effectively. This was harder to tackle, and she became increasingly frustrated with their political correctness and their assertions that 'bullying was the subject of many classroom discussions' and that 'what was important was giving the child the skills to help themselves . . .' What was important, it seemed to her, was making it bloody well stop. She made herself a thorn in the side of the staff, phoning the class teacher and the headmaster regularly. Now there were no biscuits at the meetings they had at school. At home, she raged to Bill, unable to sleep because she was so angry, and so frightened. Outwardly, she did what she could to help. She launched a charm offensive with the mothers she'd previously avoided. Went to organized coffees and lunches she didn't want to go to, in the hopes of making connections that might help Stan. But nothing worked. In the year he turned nine, Stan wasn't invited to a single birthday party, or to anyone's house to play. He was pretty much invisible to his peer group. And even to her, at home, he was fading before her eyes – a little boy with worried eyes and little self-belief.

In the end, the decision to move him wasn't that hard. It was enough. Maggie convinced Bill that the problem could not be fixed by leaving Stan where he was. He needed a change. He needed to be somewhere where he wasn't out of the ordinary. He needed a new ordinary. She found Chamberlain House on the web and went to visit without telling anyone, and she loved the place at once. Another mother – one whose child would be in the same class as Stan – came in and gave her a tour. She described her own daughter's experience without guile or pretence, and Maggie felt instantly comforted. The school was based in an old Georgian manor house, though outbuildings had been added by the Victorians, and more recently, when the building was converted to a school in the early eighties, by Viola Schilling, a wealthy, energetic, eccentric woman who wore long, dangly earrings and startlingly bright silk jackets in myriad colours, and who was still there, though she was well into her seventies. There was space and air, lots of space and air – fields, and a vegetable garden where the children grew their own fruits and vegetables, and an original Victorian swimming pool built in a beautiful original, shabby conservatory.

The fees were very steep. Maggie didn't hesitate. This, it seemed to her, this was the point of Bill's money – this was what it was for. She didn't want a seven-bedroom house on the edge of Hampstead Heath, or an Aston Martin, or five-star-villa holidays in the Maldives or Cartier necklaces. She wanted to spend the money rescuing Stan. She wanted Stan here, in this place with green and sky and room to breathe, and a new kind of normal. So much that she cried in the interview, and that was something she had never done, never allowed herself to do in the meetings at his old school, though she had often felt that unshed tears might drown her from the inside as she sat there, her fists clenched and her jaw locked. She'd never wanted anything more.

The school took him. Viola Schilling passed Maggie a box of tissues nonchalantly, as though grown women in floods of incoherent tears were commonplace in her office, and held her hand tightly, and said that she knew, she *just knew* that she could help him. Maggie exhaled for what felt like the first time in months, and then went home and told Bill. Despite their differences over Stan, she would always be grateful to him for the way he reacted. He asked all the right questions, but he never questioned her. The next day, Bill cancelled his appointments for the morning, called Viola Schilling himself and went down there to see what Maggie was talking about. An instant convert, he didn't hesitate. He'd been increasingly frustrated by what he saw happening to Stan, and to Maggie, and he admitted, if only to himself, the effect that it was all having on his own relationship with Maggie. And Ms Schilling told him all the same things she had told Maggie.

And it seemed that they had been right. Leaving him with Ms Schilling on his first day had been agonizing for Maggie. She'd dropped him herself, then driven to the car park of a nearby Sainsbury's and sat there, hands on the wheel, for so long that the guys who were washing cars for a fiver a go knocked on her window to ask if she was okay. It had to work. It had to. And it seemed it did. Stan's confidence had gradually returned. The headaches and tummy aches stopped – he wasn't looking for excuses not to be at school any more. There were friends – boys and girls – who had him to tea and came back to the house to play table football and Xbox. Academically, he was doing better than he had ever done, but what truly delighted Maggie was the return to her of her boy. God knows, she thought, I can't fix everything. God knows. But I fixed this . . .

Aly – Aly was harder, because at first glance, all was well. But scratch just a little, and Maggie was absolutely convinced that Aly had a whole different set of problems, though Bill sometimes told her she was looking too hard for something that might not be there. Aly was bright – really bright. She had always worked hard, and seemingly loved doing it, always happier with a pencil in her hand than a doll. When she was small, she was the kind of kid that wanted to watch documentaries about animals rather than manic children's television, with its hysterical presenters and obsession with fluorescent goo. She'd been a voracious reader from a young age – now, at seventeen, her favourite authors were Kazuo Ishiguro and Doris Lessing. She was an all-rounder – she'd got ten A*s in her GCSEs, and was predicted to get a clean sweep of As in her A levels this coming summer – maths, chemistry, physics and biology. She'd pretty much have her pick of medical schools for a place this coming September, according to her teachers, basking smugly in the reflected glory of a high achiever. Those same teachers didn't seem to see her vulnerability, her new fragility. Maggie wondered what it cost Aly to hide it from them. Maggie looked at her strong, able daughter – who had inherited her broad shoulders and her height, and her dad's beautiful eyes – and wondered why everyone else couldn't see the fragility she saw there.

Aly had wanted to be a doctor for as long as Maggie could remember. One of Maggie's favourite photographs of Aly was taken of her as a five- or six-year-old, in a white coat with a stethoscope and a clipboard, wearing 3D glasses she'd popped the lenses out of to lend her a studious air. For Christmas that year, Maggie had had a proper badge made for her at the local engravers – Dr Aly Barrett – and she was wearing it on the white coat in the photograph. She still had it, pinned to the noticeboard above the desk in her bedroom. She'd chosen Imperial College, London, for med school, though she had no intention of living at home, she said – just coming home to get her washing done and raid the fridge from time to time, and to see Stan. She didn't say to see Maggie. Either it was assumed, or it wasn't what she meant. Maggie veered between paranoid insecurity and hopefulness as to which it was.

Aly and Stan together reminded Maggie very much of her and Olivia as kids. Aly was fiercely protective of her younger brother, and they enjoyed each other's company far more than their respective ages, genders and interests suggested they might. She'd never really gone through the teenage stage where he aggravated her, and when Stan had first been having his problems at school, she had – of her own volition –

taken to walking to school with him every day, fixing a fearsome evil eye on the kids Stan seemed afraid of, and trying to distract him with inconsequential chatter. For his part, Stan worshipped Aly. It hurt their mother, sometimes, to see the differences between them. Everything came so easily to Aly. She didn't love sport, and yet she was capable enough of being on the A teams for netball and lacrosse, and she held the school record for long jump. She managed to be both academic and not at all nerdy. She was easily popular – the same noticeboard where she pinned her doctor badge was always full, when she was younger, of invitations to parties and scribbled notes from friends. Now that she was older, the phone was always ringing, and it was rare to find her in on a Friday or Saturday night. She was slim and pretty, with a style of her own.

You couldn't complain about a daughter like Aly. She was successful, she was someone to be proud of. She was what other mothers wanted their daughters to be. But these days, Maggie just couldn't seem to keep things on an even keel with her. The more careful she was of what she said to her, the more likely she was to say the wrong thing. For a couple of years now – and with everything that had happened – Maggie knew Aly had withdrawn herself emotionally from her mother. And, for now, it was easier not to fight it, however much it hurt. It was probably normal teenage stuff – that was what Bill said, and Liv. She didn't see much of Aly's friends' mothers any more – not like she used to – so she didn't have a peer group to make comparisons with. She knew it was normal for a girl of Aly's age to think her mother was an idiot, hell bent on destroying her fun and incapable of remembering how it felt to be a teenager. She knew it was okay for your daughter to morph into an apparent schizophrenic – never knowing which version of the little girl who had once viewed your lap as a haven was going to come out of the bedroom in the morning. But this felt like more. Maggie knew in her heart that it was connected to Jake. But she didn't know what to do about it.

Aly didn't eat breakfast in the week. It was a battle Maggie had fought for years but Aly was almost an adult now – she'd be eighteen in August – and Maggie didn't want to fight about anything, most especially not breakfast, now. Now that Stan took the bus to school, Aly sailed close to the wind time-wise – she was always rushing out of the door, it seemed, throwing a goodbye over her shoulder if Maggie was lucky. There were days when Maggie didn't even see her before she left. She remembered mornings a million years ago when all of her children would scramble into the vast bed for a dawn snuggle. It seemed ridiculous and wrong to remember that sometimes she resented that and wished they'd watch cartoons and pour giant bowls of cereal down-stairs and leave her and Bill alone. After Jake, there had been mornings that stretched into lunchtime when Stan had come into her bed, crying. There had been days she hadn't sent him, and even Aly, to school and they'd hunkered down there, not talking.

Aly adored Olivia. Amongst the many things Maggie looked forward to about her sister's impending visit was Aly being home more – she knew her daughter would hang around more to be close to her aunt. Maybe Liv would be able to get through to her – to bring them a little closer. Maggie was frightened – genuinely frightened – that if she couldn't make a breakthrough with Aly in the next few months, before the A levels, before Aly left for university, that she'd be lost to her. Not estranged – she couldn't picture that – but her chance to reclaim her child, to be close to her, properly close, would be gone, and it would be impossible, then, to fix. Liv might be a mediator. A bridge. The last time she'd felt close to Aly – properly, consciously close – they'd been with Liv. She felt more desperate for Liv to arrive every day, though she fought hard to keep that desperation out of her voice when she spoke to her.

Chapter Three

Kate Miller stopped just short of feeding the pigeons in the park – just short of being the complete cliché of the lonely, slightly scary old woman. Not that she was so old, she knew, though she probably looked it. Sometimes she liked to watch the children. She never went through the shoulder-height metal fence that encircled the climbing frames and swings and slides – she had no right, did she, when she was alone, but there was a bench just outside, and she sat there sometimes and watched them play. She liked the sound of children laughing and the sweet pain she felt when she watched the mothers gently helping toddlers climb steps that were too big for them to tackle alone. Today, a young mum had her baby in a swing, and she was running around behind him, booing and laughing, being rewarded each time by a deep, throaty laugh from her son, his small chubby fists held aloft in delight. She tried not to stare, but they were mesmerizing in their simple happiness.

A girl of two or three suddenly appeared in front of the bench, pushing an old-fashioned wooden tray on wheels with a tall handle, painted red. The tray contained, Kate could see, a small collection of objects – a dirty doll, a matchbox car, some rocks and a handful of crumpled autumn leaves. The little girl was wearing a red fleece and one of those hats with small flaps over the ears, brightly striped. Her cheeks were bright pink, and a small snail trail of snot snaked across one of them. She was staring at Kate with the still intensity only small children have, and for a moment Kate stared back. Then she broke into a smile, in spite of herself, at this little person's frank appraisal of her, and bent down a little, out towards her, thinking of something engaging to say about the objects the girl was trundling. The child carefully picked up a conker and offered it to Kate, and Kate lay her palm flat to receive it.

Whatever she had started to say was drowned out by a shrill woman's voice. 'Georgie. Georgie! Wait for Mummy . . .' 'Mummy' was a plump young woman now trotting towards them, pushing a buggy and looking alarmed. Kate looked around for a reason for the mother's anxious tone, and it took a long, dreadful moment for her to realize that it was her who was worrying. Mummy didn't want Georgie to talk *to her*. The strange old lady on the bench, watching the children. The realization was the most horrifying of Kate's life, and it hit her like a really hard punch at the base of her throat.

She opened her mouth to speak – to defend herself, she supposed – but the woman had reached her by then, and had taken the girl by the hand, pulling her arm up too high and too hard, and making her walk forward too fast. The toddler complained as her mum grabbed the handle of the wooden toy, squirming to be free, but the woman only held her more tightly, and kept walking, throwing Kate a look that was both apologetic and defiant. A look that said she was only doing what a good mother would – looking out for her child. Kate stared at them as they made their way – child squealing and mother remonstrating – down the path that led to the nearest houses. After about 30 yards, the mother gave up and stopped, hoisting the child unceremoniously into the buggy and hooking the cart on to the handle. Then she was able to stride off at her own pace, though Kate could still hear Georgie. She never looked back. Kate couldn't believe it.

Kate almost ran home, holding her skirt close against her legs, her bag clasped so tightly under her arm that the muscles ached. Inside, she went straight upstairs, to the spare room, to the top shelf in the wardrobe full of Philip's suits, the ones she knew she should have given away but hadn't. She didn't look at them now. She didn't stroke the tweed and wool, and sniff at them, hoping to catch the scent of him, as she might have done normally. She wanted to reach the box – but she couldn't. Impatiently, muttering to herself, Kate pulled over a chair from behind the door and kicked off her shoes, climbing on it. Now she could hold the big box and ease it out, a hand beneath to bear the weight, and lift it down. She sat on the bed, leaning against the headboard, and took the lid off. It was full of her past, full of photographs and letters and certificates and mementoes – the ephemera of her Technicolor life. There were the annual school photographs from her teaching days – Kate in sugared-almond-coloured linen summer dresses, surrounded by her charges, four-year-olds who were, by now, worrying about their UCAS forms and A level exams, working in shops and having babies themselves, even. She winced slightly, remembering the child and her mother in the park, and looking at her old self, clasping the hands of children who leant into her skirts. Pictures of Kate and Philip – dozens of those – in small albums, one for each year, place names written in his handwriting. Ticket stubs and unwritten postcards collected from foreign destinations. A small plastic box with a single yellow sugar rose in it – from the top of their wedding cake. A couple of its petals had pieces missing – small pieces of sugar rattled against the plastic. And Philip's letters. This was just a small bundle. Some were more notes than letters, scribbled on squares branded with the names of different drugs. But there were a few proper love letters – he'd written those at the most significant times in their life together. She'd looked desperately, in the few days after his death, for a sealed letter he might have written in anticipation of such an event, but she'd never found one, of course. He'd died suddenly, without warning, leaving a Bill Bryson open at page 34 on his bedside table, a half-finished tub of shaving cream and no letter. She hadn't read these since the weeks after his death. She'd read them, and looked at the pictures, until she could bear no more, and then she'd shoved everything roughly into this box that had once housed a pair of black knee-high boots, and levered it on to the highest shelf in the wardrobe, if not forgotten then certainly ignored until just now. She pulled a letter out of its envelope now, and gently unfolded the page, slowly smoothing its creases with the flat of her hand. She could hear his voice as she read it.

> *Kate. I'm lying on my bed, thinking about you. My Kate. That's how I think of you, you know, though I have no right to, so far as the world would see it. But I do. I know I do, because I know that I love you. Even though nothing has happened between us. I do. I love you. More than you know. More than I thought I could. And I'm not afraid to write it down. I would say it to you, if you were here. Oh, how I wish you were here next to me. I love the woman you are, but I love the woman I know you can be too – how you can be, how you could be, if you were mine. Just like I know I would be a better man if I was yours. If only. When you are. Because I have to believe that day will come. I will wait for you, my Kate. For ever.*

And she had been, hadn't she. He'd waited, like he said he would, and she had been his, and she had been different. He was right. He'd known she could be. He'd made that possible for her. It had been the greatest gift anyone had ever given her.

What would he think of her now? A vision of the dismay on his face made her shudder.

On the day of their lunch, Bill was already at the table when Maggie arrived. She'd set out from home calm, but she couldn't find anywhere to park and she'd grown frustrated and flustered. When she'd found a meter, she couldn't find change, and, fumbling around in the bottom of her capacious handbag, she'd tipped it and things had fallen on the pavement at her feet. She felt red-faced and breathless by the time she walked in, and she hated that. She worked incredibly hard at looking relaxed. Looking okay. They both loved this place. They'd eaten here, as a couple, as a family, a thousand times over the years.

They still did. They had this lunch maybe once a month – every six weeks at least. The first time, he'd asked if she wanted to choose the restaurant, and she had chosen this one. And after that, they mostly came here. Bill once joked that the waiters probably didn't know they weren't still together, but Maggie hadn't had the heart to laugh. But everything else about her world, and this arrangement, was new and strange – she could see no reason for the setting not to be the same. If he'd been surprised, he hadn't said so. It was a real neighbourhood place. A joint, almost. It was called Gianni's, although there had been no one called Gianni in residence the whole time they'd been coming. The menu was an Italian-American hybrid, and the decor was tired. There weren't quite red candles in old wine bottles wound with twine, but it was the sort of place where that was definitely possible.

Bill had already ordered wine, and it sat in an ice bucket

beside the table. A Pinot grigio. It occurred to Maggie, briefly and crossly, that she should mind him still ordering wine for her, but since Pinot grigio was what she would have chosen, and he knew that, it seemed pointless, even petty, to complain. You resented him for knowing you so well, because knowing you so well and rejecting you was a toxic combination. That's what this reduced you to, though, wasn't it? Someone looking for things – however tiny – to feel resentful about.

That was the bloody tricky bit about this situation. You knew a person as well as it was possible to know a person. You'd been intimate in every way it was possible to be intimate, physically, emotionally, practically. They were utterly familiar to you. They had been for years and years. For a larger percentage of your life than you even realized, because it crept past while you were busy living. And then they weren't. They weren't there. And they were subtly different. And they had a life that didn't involve you, and so everything you thought you knew for sure might not be true any more. They might not do everything the way they used to. Drink wine. Think. Dress. Want to live. What you knew for sure – the only damn thing you knew for sure now – was that they didn't want to do any of it with you any more.

There were no rules and there wasn't a handbook. Neither of them had a clue what they were doing.

And yet here he was. Bill. Her Bill. Still her husband. It was a new shirt, though – one of those expensive ones – plain except for the inside of the collar and the cuffs, which were vividly patterned and coloured. He'd have laughed at a shirt like that, once. They'd done nothing yet about making their split official. If he crashed his car and someone needed to switch him off, they would still call her. At thirty-nine, Bill was still a handsome man. He was tall, six foot two, and though his hair had greyed a lot, it was still thick. He was wearing it just a little longer these days, she thought, and it curled a little over his ears. It suited him. The eyes, the celadon-green eyes she saw every time she looked at Aly, were as beautiful as they had always been, and they could sparkle too, when he was laughing, or flirting, though she saw precious little of the sparkle these days, and he knew better than to flirt with her. His smile showed a wide row of even teeth and his cheeks dimpled just a little – not enough for Disneyesque cuteness, but certainly enough to be an attractive feature. It made you want to make him smile, so they would appear. As a younger man, he had always looked a little naughty, and she had always loved that about him. He had always had an easy, hearty laugh, and when he laughed, he had thrown his head back. His sexiest quality had always been his confidence. Some of that had gone, too. For years, it had felt to her, as his wife, that Bill had controlled everything. Not her, not in a bad way, at least. He'd been masterful, she supposed, and so sure of everything. He ran his business, and his life. Things had changed, though.

He stood up when he saw her, and opened his arms. She let herself be held for a moment, breathing in his familiar smell, feeling his arms around her. There was always a second, during these embraces, when she thought – when she was afraid – that she might relax and sag to the point when he would have to hold her up, all her strength and resolve gone. As a consequence, she knew she held herself taut and tight. She'd lost weight, and she was conscious of it when he hugged her, feeling her ribs against his hands, but if he noticed, he didn't say so.

'How are you?'

'Late. Sorry.'

'Doesn't matter a bit. Everything okay?'

'Couldn't park. No money.' She shrugged, then smiled. 'Story of my life . . . Shouldn't have driven, of course, but I've been to Sainsbury's. And I was running late. *Plus ça change* . . .'

Bill poured her a glass of wine and handed it to her, like he had on a thousand stressful evenings. She took a big sip and pushed her curls back from her face, making herself breathe more calmly. 'Sorry. Sorry.'

He smiled kindly at her. 'Stop apologizing.'

She smiled and took another sip.

'Better?'

She nodded meekly.

'How are you?'

'Good. You?'

'I'm okay. New shirt.'

He pulled at the paisley cuff. 'Too much?'

Maggie smirked. 'If I'd brought it home a few years ago, you'd have snorted . . .'

Bill laughed. 'That's true.'

'I like it.'

'Thanks.'

'Makes you look – edgy.'

'Edgy?!'

'That's not the look you were going for?'

'How the hell would I know the look I was going for? You were always the stylish one.'

She smiled at the compliment.

It was still surprising to her how easy it was to talk to him. Banter was an old habit for them. It helped, of course, that they had the kids to talk about – actual information needed to be exchanged. By the time Maggie had debriefed him on what had been going on at home, and he'd responded with what he'd learnt when he spent time with them, when they'd compared notes and both offered their opinions, everything else, all the nonsense, had fallen away for a while, and they were Bill and Maggie. Almost like they always had been. Almost.

Stan was pretty much the same with both of them, it seemed. He liked to play football with Bill, and he liked to lie with his head on Maggie's lap and let her stroke his hair, but emotionally, he was pretty much the same Stan with either parent. Maggie had worried, for years, that she perceived him as simpler, more straightforward emotionally than Aly somehow, because of the other issues he had. Something else to feel guilty about. But that wasn't it. Stan *was* a straightforward kid, however counterintuitive that seemed. Aly was a different case. She'd been angry with Bill when he left, Maggie knew that. Very angry. She'd closed off from him too. If anything, Bill had to work harder than Maggie to get anything out of her, and since Maggie had to work hard enough, she felt a bit sorry for him.

She talked about how much she was looking forward to Liv's visit in a couple of weeks. Bill missed Liv. They'd become close across the years of his marriage to her sister, once Liv had forgiven him for taking Maggie away from her and Australia. Liv was fun and lively and loving, and Bill loved her, Maggie knew. Liv's visits had sometimes salved irritations between them, brightening and lightening the mood at precisely the right moment in subtle, clever ways Bill didn't even think were deliberate. They'd certainly coincided with some of their happiest moments, since Liv had always flown over immediately when a baby came and often joined them on holidays.

Bill was different today, though. He was nervous. She didn't realize it straight away, but it dawned on her as they talked. He was eating pasta, and he kept dropping ribbons of tagliatelle from his fork, sauce spattering on his new shirt. He dabbed at his mouth with his napkin. It was unsettling. They'd found a rhythm, these last months, and now he was changing it.

Eventually, over cappuccino for her, an espresso for him, she asked him outright, sensing that there was something he wanted to say to her but realizing he hadn't found the moment, or the courage, during the meal.

'What's going on, Bill? Something, right? Something's going on with you.'

He took a deep breath, and for just a second he wouldn't look at her, and then he did, his green eyes wide with the moment.

'You always know, don't you?'

Maggie shrugged. True but unhelpful. 'Don't do that. You can't do that.'

'I'm sorry. I know.'

'It's okay. So – what?'

'I don't know how to say this.'

'Just say it, Bill, for God's sake.'

Still he looked at his cup.

'You're making me nervous.' Her voice sounded shrill, even to her.

He gave a small laugh. '*You're* nervous?' Took a deep breath. 'I've met someone.'

They'd been apart for a year. Twelve months since the day when, after a sleepless night where they'd rowed, again, and lay tense and far apart in the giant bed, he'd packed a holdall and left. Not in a rage but in silent, sad tears. Not for good, she'd thought that day, exhausted and relieved, but for a time, while they figured out how to fix each other and themselves and the desperate situation. A week. A month. However long it took.

When had she realized he wasn't coming back? Maybe not until now. Stupid cow. It shouldn't shock her as much as it did. She felt like she was on top of a high roller-coaster, just swooping into the first rolling fall. She was dizzy – her head felt suddenly heavy on her neck. A wave of nausea came over her, and she felt her fingernails digging insistently into her palm. What did she expect, if he wasn't coming back to her? That he'd be alone for ever? She didn't even want that. What had she been hoping for?

'Say something.' The silence was heavy.

She smiled slowly at him, though she felt like he must be able to hear or even see her heart beating in her chest.

'I'm happy for you?' It was a question. Is that what you want me to say?

'Mags,' he implored.

He laid his hand over hers where it lay on the table. It was large and warm and familiar. He'd held her hand at most of the difficult times in her life.

'I *am* happy for you. I am. Or, at the very least, I'm going to try to be.'

'I'm not looking for absolution, Maggie.'

'What are you looking for then, Bill?' She felt very tired, suddenly. She could have laid her head on the tablecloth and closed her eyes.

'I just need you to know.'

'So you can tell the kids? Or am I going to be doing that?'

'No.' He sounded hurt. She kicked herself for using the kids to make him feel bad. It was a cheap shot, and she knew it. 'I need you to know so that you know. There's never been anything you don't know about me, my whole adult life.'

'I'm sorry.'

'Don't be. I'm sorry.'

'Now you really shouldn't be. You don't want to start something new feeling bad.'

'I don't think it's that simple. I'm always going to feel bad about us.'

'But you need to move on. Right?' She could hear sarcasm dripping from her voice and it sounded ugly to her.

'We both need to.'

Maggie shrugged. She hadn't. She didn't know how to begin to move on. What the hell did that even mean, anyway? Move on. She didn't want to move on.

She pulled her hand out from under Bill's and laid both her palms flat on the table, looking at the faint age spots forming across her knuckles, the short, ragged nails. When had she stopped doing her nails, she wondered. She didn't remember. She tapped a small rhythm on the cloth, and then smiled at Bill again, and this time she tried hard to make the smile reach her eyes.

'So . . . is this a good moment to tell you I want to get rid of the giant bed?'

He held her gaze for a while, relieved to see a glint of mischief there, and then they both laughed. Spontaneously, then, he reached for her, and she let him hold her, awkwardly angled, at the table. Her arms were instantly tight around his neck, and he squeezed back, feeling her ribs beneath her sweater. She was still very thin, he thought, and her slenderness made him sad, though he'd never say so.

He wasn't brave, these days, in telling her what he thought about her. He knew she was depressed. He'd known for a long time. She was always exhausted. She looked defeated by life. She didn't care about her appearance the way she had once been fastidious about it – she still looked good, but he could see the tiny differences. He'd tried so many times to help her. To get her to go to the GP, to get some pills, to talk to someone. She'd never wanted to do what he asked. And now he was afraid to raise it.

They ordered more coffee – neither really wanted to leave the other. Maggie looked at her watch. She still had an hour or so before Stan's school bus dropped him off at the end of their road.

'Do you want to tell me about her?'

'Do you want to know?'

'I do and I don't. I mean – is it weird that I'm interested?'

'I don't think there are any rules about this. Haven't done it before.'

'I think I'm supposed to hate her. But I don't hate anyone, so that'd be a reach for me.'

'Don't reach. It isn't her fault.'

'Hate you then.'

Bill smiled. 'That's definitely allowed.'

'But I don't.' I love you. I still love you. I have always loved you. I'm going to die, loving you. The words charged through her brain like a mantra. Despite everything.

'I'm glad.'

'Do you love her? That's my one question. I'm not going to ask about her hair colour, or what size she is or where you met her. I'm just going to ask that, for now.'

Bill had inhaled sharply, and now he let the breath out slowly, from puffed cheeks. Maggie didn't think she was breathing.

'If you're only asking one, make it a doozy, hey? I don't know. It's, it's too soon, I think, for me to say that.'

'Are you just saying that? Because it's me asking?'

He shook his head. 'No. It's a big word. It's too soon. But it is serious. I know that. We're . . . we're together. I think . . . I think I could love her. You know?'

Maggie's sad smile cut him to the quick. She nodded, and

sniffed quickly, and then it was her turn to lay a hand across his, patting it reassuringly.

It wasn't until Bill had paid the bill, and they'd left the restaurant and he was walking her towards her car that she turned to him.

'Okay. I lied. I do have another question.'

Bill shuffled, staring at his shoes. 'Go on . . .'

'How did you meet her?'

'Maggie . . .' His eyes implored her.

'It's okay, Bill. I just want to know. I need to know.'

'We met at counselling.' Maggie realized she'd known that, somehow. Why else would she ask that question?

'Is she the counsellor, or something?'

'She's a part of my group.'

She'd almost known that's what he would say, and she even saw the sense in it, though Maggie wished he'd said 'on the bus', or 'at the gym' or 'she's a client'.

Maggie had never been to Bill's group, or to any other group, though some people – lots of people – Bill included, had thought she should. Olivia never had. She'd always shuddered and said she couldn't bear it, if it were her. Sitting around in a circle of strangers, in a room full of suffering, trying to articulate what was unsayable, trying to fix what was unfixable.

A roomful of strangers who had also had someone they loved die on them. A problem shared might be a problem halved, but grief couldn't be diminished in that way – Maggie was more sure of that, in the beginning, than she was sure of anything. The best, the very best you could hope for was that time would pass, while you put one foot in front of the other, and folded laundry and lay awake at night. That eventually enough time would pass and it wouldn't hurt quite so much. And then you might see the point in carrying on.

She didn't want to talk about Jake with strangers. She could barely say his name in front of Bill, his father. Or Aly and Stan, his sister and brother. She could hardly whisper it to herself.

Bill had needed it, he said. He said that might make him weaker than her, or stronger, or maybe, most likely, just different. If it didn't help, he said, his face wet with tears, at least it couldn't hurt. It wouldn't make it worse, because nothing could. This was already as bad as it could ever be. And he'd started going, once a week. A year after their elder son had died.

Chapter Four

Jake had been on his gap year between A levels and university – at the crossroads. Not a boy any more, but somehow not quite a man. He had a place at Durham to read engineering. The little boy who had always wanted to understand how things worked, endlessly taking things apart and putting them back together again – was off to find out. He'd gained three As in his A levels that summer. Not quite effortlessly, but he was a clever boy, he always had been, and although they had all been delighted, they couldn't quite claim to be surprised with the result. For three months after he left school, he worked at the leisure centre, lifeguarding at the pool, spending his evenings in the beer gardens of the pubs in the neighbourhood, drinking with his friends and planning. He'd been daydreaming about this big trip since the lower sixth, planning with his two closest school friends – Matt and Ryan – who were going with him. Saving for it. Bill and Maggie had given him his round-the-world flight for his eighteenth birthday. It had been that or a car, Bill had said, although Maggie, and maybe even Jake, had smiled – he'd probably spring for a car the following September before uni started. Bill had given Jake £1,000 when he got his A level results. And he'd saved a decent amount on his own from what he'd earnt at the swimming baths.

Jake had pinned a vast world map to the wall of his bedroom and plotted routes and destinations on it with pins and lengths of ribbon. He and Ryan and Matt sat at the kitchen table evening after evening, Googling, scribbling notes in a small notebook and debating routes and places to stay. Maggie could remember Jake shaking his head, rubbing his hair and smiling ruefully. 'There's such a lot of world to see.' Remembered Bill breaking into the lyrics of 'Moon River', leaning over her and singing into her hair, 'Three drifters off to see the world . . .'

Bill loved it. Jake was doing what he'd done. That was how he and Maggie had met, he reminded Jake, on his own trip nearly twenty years ago. 'Don't let a wild-haired minx trap you on the Gold Coast,' he joked. 'I never did get to Vietnam . . .'

They'd settled on a route, eventually. They'd fly to Hong Kong, where a wealthy business colleague of Bill's had offered to put them up for a few days in an amazing-looking house on the Peak, with staff and a driver, even though Maggie said that was so not the way they should be travelling and that it would ruin them for the rest of the trip, making the cockroach-infested hostels seem even worse. A sortie into China, and then back to Hong Kong for a day or two. From there, New Guinea, and then New Zealand – land of the *Lord of the Rings*. Jake's Uncle Tom reckoned he could get them some work fruit picking on the South Island if they wanted it. Then Australia. It was obvious he'd spend time there. Jake hadn't seen much of the country of his mother's birth, and Maggie was pleased that now he would. They'd fly to Perth, work for a while, maybe, then buy a cheap car or, better still, an old VW camper van, and drive across the middle. Work their way down the Gold Coast of Queensland, see Canberra, Melbourne. End up in Sydney, staying with Olivia or Grandad. From Sydney, straight to Thailand, to bum around some islands, like extras from that Leonardo DiCaprio film *The*

Beach, getting tanned and stoned, they said, only half joking. Then back home via Vietnam and, finally, India, for a dose of spirituality and dysentery, Ryan said.

They'd be gone from the end of September to maybe mid February, early March. Perhaps a bit longer – it depended on what money they were able to make along the way and how long the money they had lasted. To Maggie, beneath the banter and behind the smiles, it seemed like an unbearable absence. She would miss him, more than he knew. She would worry, she knew. Not quite realize, between phone calls, how she was living to hear his voice, exhaling with relief when she did and lying in bed wondering when she didn't. She didn't say so, not to Jake or to Bill. Bill seemed disproportionately excited on Jake's behalf. She felt it a little like a reproach. He was only joking when he went on and on about the things he'd never seen, but he was only just only joking. She hoped, at least, that the three boys would spend Christmas and New Year with her family. There was some talk of refilling the coffers, maybe heading off again in the summer – America, maybe. Some scheme about driving someone else's car across the middle – apparently you could do that.

The night before they left, Maggie and Bill had hosted a barbecue for Matt and Ryan's families. It had been a loud, jolly night, warm for the time of year, and the boys' anticipation had been contagious. Things had been much more subdued at the airport the next day. It was suddenly very real. It was harder than Maggie had thought it would be to physically release Jake – take her arms from around his neck and step back from him so that he could go. She didn't want to. In the end, the boys almost backed away into the passport line, nodding with tolerance as their respective mothers shouted tearful last-minute warnings and advice to them, oblivious to the stares of the other passengers.

They had patently been having a ball. As well as the phone calls, Jake sent postcards with funny messages on them – sometimes just a line and sometimes crammed with writing so small it was hard to read. Occasionally there would be small parcels wrapped in brown paper, with exotic stamps on them. Jake would send home souvenirs he'd picked up along the way – ticket stubs, boarding passes, matchboxes from bars and sometimes even a chocolate bar or a beer bottle with an unusual label or colourful packaging. Occasionally there would be a gift for Aly or for Maggie – once he sent them both a woven silk bracelet, fuchsia for Aly and orange for Maggie. She'd worn hers until it rotted and broke, and she kept it still. Maggie kept everything for him. He was just like her. A pack rat with limited baggage space, spending money to send stuff home – stuff that Bill might consider junk, but that Maggie understood was significant. They would be memory triggers for him for years to come. She envied him, in some ways. She'd never done anything like this. She could see that Bill did too, probably more. That's what he *had* been doing, of course, when he'd met her. And she'd stopped him in his tracks. The tracks Jake was finding now. They followed him on the map that was still on his bedroom wall – a new line of pins marking his progress.

But in the end they didn't stay in Australia for Christmas. They'd had a good time, but they were ready for a change – of pace, of scene. 'We want to be somewhere where we don't speak the language, Mum,' Jake had offered, over a crackling phone line, as an explanation for the change in plan. Oz was too comfortable and they were hungry for more adventure. They flew to Bangkok. From there they hopped on an internal flight to Phuket and took a local bus from Phuket down the coast to Phang Nga province. They found a place to stay in Khao Lak, a place recommended to them by a couple they'd picked apples with on New Zealand's South Island, travelling in the opposite direction. It was cheap, with what he described ruefully as sketchy plumbing, but clean enough, and in the most amazing setting. Beautiful, he said – a collection of simple shacks built just a few feet back from the beach, with outdoor showers behind woven fences on the back. Kids from all over the place in the other shacks. A few places to eat and drink, and great street curries. Paradise. Jake had said so, when he'd called on Christmas Day. They'd stay a few days at least, vegging out. He'd sounded so happy and relaxed – high, almost, like he was at the best party of his life.

And then Boxing Day 2004 had dawned. Hundreds of miles off the coast, a huge and violent earthquake had happened on the seabed, big enough to knock the planet off its axis, catastrophic enough to push oceans at land, and it had all changed, quite literally, in a single moment that had nothing to do with them and at the same time everything.

Matt and Ryan survived. They were just battered and bruised. Matt required ten stitches on a nasty cut just above his left eye and cracked two ribs. Ryan broke his arm and needed stitches on a gash on his ankle. And their spirits were crushed. They would never, ever be the same, of course, but they were still here. They might be better, maybe, than they would have been otherwise. Different. For ever altered. But they had survived and they were alive when the waters receded.

But Jake, her beautiful, smiling, smart baby, their first beloved child, had died.

It made no sense. He was a stronger swimmer than either of them: he'd been the lifeguard. He was smarter, too, though a mother might never say that out loud. He had more common sense. He was the natural leader in the threesome. It made no sense, any more than any of it did. That wasn't how chaos worked. But that was what happened.

And Maggie's life had instantly cleaved itself in two. Life before Boxing Day 2004. And life afterwards. If that's what it was. Everything that had happened since, everything that would ever happen to her again, would happen in the shadow of that event.

Documentaries about the tsunami – the endless international post-mortem of news and charity appeals and interviews with survivors – showed how the giant wave had circled out from the epicentre of the quake, along the coasts of Malaysia, Thailand, Sri Lanka, across the Indian Ocean to the Maldives and the Seychelles. And Maggie thought that it was like that for her. It was an easy comparison – a painfully obvious metaphor. Jake's death was the epicentre of the quake in her life, only its waves kept hitting her. They always would. She might never get up. Jake had died. Her marriage had ended. Bill's grief had led him to this woman. She couldn't reach Aly. She couldn't reach parts of herself any more. It was not going to end.

Chapter Five

So Bill had met this person, this woman, at counselling. In a nasty internal monologue that vaguely shocked her even as it announced itself, Maggie wondered which one of the Kübler-Ross stages of grief this represented. Bill had gone on about it for long enough – once he'd discovered what she'd dismissively called 'the recipe' – that she knew them by heart: denial, anger, bargaining, depression and acceptance, but she didn't remember shagging your way out of it as the sixth stage. Maggie's eyes had filled with sudden tears when he'd answered the question, and Bill wanted to cry too. She couldn't look at him. She kissed him briefly, dry-lipped and on the cheek, and got into the car without meeting his eye again. Bill was parked three cars behind. He wanted to talk more, but he knew his wife well enough to know that the timing was wrong. And that it was selfish anyway. He wanted to talk to his best friend, who was still her, and he knew how unfair that was. She needed time to get her head around what he'd told her. And she might never do that. He'd lost her in a hundred different ways in the last two years, and now he'd just lost her again . . .

Bill watched Maggie drive off, sitting still at the wheel of his own car. She didn't indicate, and she was driving a touch too fast, a little recklessly, as she pulled out into the road. For a moment, he truly wished he hadn't said anything – that he'd kept it to himself a while longer. The hurt on her face when he'd said the words had stung him too. But he'd been seeing Carrie through four of these lunches with Maggie. He'd tried. He'd started sentences, and then abruptly stopped, turning the conversation on a tangent. He'd practised in the mirror, but he couldn't find a way of saying it that wasn't trite. And he knew that to let it go on any longer, to run the risk of her finding out some other way was more cruel than to say it directly. It was unfair to Carrie and to Maggie and to the children, who would one day know that he'd been lying to them, albeit by omission, and who would resent him for it more the longer the deceit went on. He wondered if it was cowardly or kind to have timed it knowing that Olivia was about to arrive. For years he had known, had had to accept that although for him, Maggie was the sun, the moon *and* the stars, for her, he'd always shared the firmament with Olivia. And now, perhaps more than ever before, he was glad that was true.

His phone vibrated with a received text message. It was Carrie. He stared at the screen for a moment, thinking, and then pressed the 'ignore' button. He couldn't answer her right now – he couldn't cope with his two lives overlapping just at this moment, he needed air between these two women. His heart and his mind were still full of Maggie. He laid his forehead on the steering wheel, then banged it gently against the leather, before he put the key into the steering column and turned the engine on.

It should be easier – a new love. A new start. The 'moving forward' everyone talks about all the time. But none of this was easy. It was a long time since anything in his life had been easy.

Chapter Six

The post came between ten and eleven each morning, during *Homes Under the Hammer* on BBC 1, which Kate half watched while she waited.

The postman was called Roger, and he had been the postman on this street for about five years, since the last time the Post Office had reorganized all the routes. Roger was about fifty years old, she thought, with one pierced ear and an arm covered in tattoos that all ran into each other – a 'full sleeve' he'd told her it was called. Roger was married to Margy. They had two sons. Gary, who drove school coaches, had married the mother of his unborn child earlier this year. Steve had lost his job in administration the year before and moved back in with his mother and father, where he watched a lot of Jeremy Kyle and played too many computer games, according to his father. Margy had gone back to doing all his washing and cooking, and Roger was convinced that now Steve was never going to leave again. When he wasn't delivering post, Roger played bass guitar in a band called The Paranormals (the drummer and the lead singer had served in the Paras during the eighties and nineties), who played in local pubs and clubs. Roger had said they were quite good and Kate should come and see them sometime, though they both knew that this was unlikely.

All this Kate had gleaned from brief doorstep chats. She looked forward to them. Most days, Roger was the first human being she interacted with. Some days, he was the only one.

It didn't have to be that way, although undoubtedly the phone rang less than it once had. She'd had the man from Virgin round to show her how to install caller ID on the handset, so that the identity of the caller flashed up a warning to her. And mostly it wasn't someone she wanted to talk to. Talking on the phone would lead to lunch or bridge or a Wednesday afternoon matinée in the West End, and she usually didn't want to go. Didn't want to pretend it was all jolly and fun.

Roger was a much safer companion. She need never invite him in for a cup of tea after he'd delivered the mail. He would never have her round to dinner to meet Margy. Three or four minutes a day. Talking about his life, mostly, and not hers. A brief whinge about the weather, or a post-mortem on a news item. That was fine.

There were five things in this morning's post. Two of them were in white envelopes. She glanced at the first three items as she slid them straight into the recycling bin she kept by the back door – double glazing, a new Thai restaurant opening in town and a clothing catalogue that was sent religiously six times a year though she had ordered from them only once, years ago. The first white envelope contained a stiff card – an invitation to a friend's daughter's wedding a couple of months hence. She put it down on the work surface without really looking at the date or the venue, and impatiently opened the second letter. She deliberately didn't turn it over, wanting the promise of a reply to her ad to last longer. It was from her solicitor. He hoped she was well. He had a couple of things for her to sign and wondered if she might have time to pop in to the office in the next couple of weeks. Perhaps, he wrote, if she made it around lunchtime, they could have a bite together. Jocelyn, he said, joined him in sending her best.

Kate put the letter on top of the invitation and sat down, defeated. You're a silly woman, Kate Miller, she told herself. Silly to expect a reply. To pin your hopes on a hare-brained scheme. To hide here making small talk with Roger. Silly.

Liv and Scott had spent some of her last day home at the beach; it was a scorcher. Scott had found the energy to join an impromptu game of volleyball, and Liv had sat watching from beneath a wide-brimmed hat, hugging her knees, admiring his six pack and congratulating herself on her boyfriend's physique and prowess. They'd floated in the sea, catching the waves, for ages after that – it was the coolest place to be. Scott had held her close as they bobbed, his arms tight around her waist and resting on her hips. For the longest time, they didn't talk, just felt each other close, aware of each other's breath and skin and muscles moving to keep balance in the water. It was sexy as hell, though the presence of dozens of other swimmers meant they had to keep a check on themselves in that regard at least, but it was precious too. Liv felt their stillness in the melee. They might have stayed that way, wrinkling up like prunes, until the last moment, if a stray Frisbee hadn't landed on Scott's shoulder blade, piercing the moment. He'd laughed, pulling away from Liv and tossing the plastic disc back towards the young boy who'd thrown it. He looked at his watch.

'Wanna head back?'

'What time is it?'

One long arm hooked her back towards him so that her boobs smushed against his chest.

'Time I made love to you once more before you go.'

She smiled. 'You said that this morning.'

'Lied.'

'Come to think of it, you said that last night, too . . .'

'Again, lying . . . It's got to last me ages. You can't deny me . . .'

'I'm not trying.' She kissed his bottom lip lasciviously, sucking it into her mouth. 'Get the towels . . .'

Later, in the flat, naked in the bright light shining from the window, she'd rolled on to her stomach, resting her face on his chest.

'Will that do you, do you think, because if you're going to demand an encore, I might just miss my plane.'

Scott ran his hand slowly down her back and across her bum, groaning.

'I suppose so . . .'

She stood up, enjoying his gaze following her from one side of the room to the other, enjoying her lack of self-consciousness in front of him.

Scott pulled on his boxers. 'I'll get us a drink. Do you need me to do anything to help?'

'I'm right. All packed. Just got to shower the beach and the Scott off of me.'

'I could help with that . . .'

'Back off . . .' She giggled. 'Is that all I am to you? Huh? A sex object? A plaything. . . ?'

She wasn't serious, but suddenly he was. He took her face in his hands.

'Nope. You're everything to me. Everything, Livvy.'

Liv's heart flipped.

He drove her to the airport. 'Passport?'

She held up the blue document.

'Boarding card?'

'Yep. Printed. I'm good at this. Who's going to make sure you have all your stuff together – that's the question.'

'Won't let anything interfere with my getting on the plane, will I? I'll be on my way to you . . .'

'And I'm going to miss you every day until you get there.'

'Are you going to be okay?'

Liv shrugged.

'It isn't about me. It's about Maggie, and Aly and Stan.'

'But I'm worried about you.'

'Why worried?'

'You know why, Liv. You take too much on yourself. You worry too much.'

'I think I worry just about enough.'

'Maybe, but it takes a toll on you. I see that.'

Scott hadn't met Maggie, or the kids, though he felt as if he had. He was glad he was going to – he needed to. But he was clear, very very clear, on where his priorities lay. Liv had been coping with this alone for most of the last two years. And she wasn't alone any more.

He'd known almost from the start how important this was to Liv. How much of Liv was invested in the broken, tragic family 12,000 miles away. She'd told him not long after they'd started going out. It had spilt out of her one evening early on. They'd been exchanging the usual kind of information you shared at the start of a relationship – education, family, hobbies – and her eyes had filled with tears as she'd told him about her nephew Jake, and her sister. It had sounded right away like Maggie was a bloody mess and that helping her, caring for her, even at this distance, was Liv's reason for living.

Scott remembered being surprised to realize that – while up until that moment he had thought of Liv primarily with lust and desire – now he felt an unfamiliar rush of protectiveness; he'd had a reasonable number of girlfriends through his teenage years and his twenties, but he could not remember ever wanting to take care of anyone the way he wanted to take care of Liv that night, and every night since, for that matter.

The flights from Australia always arrived in the early morning, and the arrivals hall was inevitably crowded with eager friends and family when they did. This was particularly true in December, when families reunited for the holidays. Today was no exception – there were dozens of people already waiting for the flight when Maggie arrived. Some had posters, a few carried balloons – everyone was wide-eyed with anticipation and excitement, despite the freezing, grey day and the early start. Maggie and Stan were at the barrier at Heathrow's Terminal Four a few minutes before the plane landed. While they waited for the flight monitor to show 'baggage in hall', Maggie had bought them hot drinks from the coffee concession – tea for her and a hot chocolate for Stan – and they had staked out a great spot from which, if Stan craned his neck, which he did, he could see the automatic double doors each time they swung open and released weary travellers and their pantechnicons of luggage from the customs hall. The moment he recognized his aunt he bolted under the metal fence and ran at her, jumping into the arms she'd opened wide the second she'd spotted him. Maggie watched her sister hold her son tight and her heart swelled. Setting him down again at last, Liv's eyes searched for her sister, and Maggie waved excitedly. At the barrier, Liv and Maggie held each other for a long moment, and Maggie felt the familiar feeling of joy she had always felt when they were reunited. That hadn't diminished in two decades of living across the world from each other. It was just like the first time, all those years ago, when Liv came through holding the hand of a Qantas staffer and screamed with delight as

Maggie held a tiny bundle of Jake aloft for her to see. He'd been two weeks old.

'How the hell are you, sis?' They always kept it light at this point. There would be time for all the rest.

'Smelly, knackered and starving. But all the better for seeing you.' They pulled away, laughed with pleasure, and fell back into the hug.

'Me too. Not the smelly part, obviously.' Liv stroked her back. Stan was standing beaming at them both.

'Can we go now, please . . . ?' The momentousness was lost on him, as usual. Liv giggled and ruffled his hair affectionately.

''Course we can, Stan. Enough gooey stuff for now, right?'

'Exactly . . .' He strode off, struggling manfully with the heavy trolley, brandishing the parking ticket in his hand – Maggie had promised him he could feed the change into the machine.

Maggie linked arms with her sister, and pulled her after him in pursuit.

'Come on. Let's get out of here. Good flight?'

Liv pulled a face. 'No! There's nothing good about that flight, as you well know, except when you finally get to get off . . .'

Maggie laughed. She was right. There was nothing good about being in a plane for twenty-three hours, although it was shorter, at least, than it used to be now that they only made one stop to refuel on most journeys. For the last few years, Bill had insisted that when he did it, he did it with a flatbed, in business class. That helped a bit. But only a bit, frankly . . .

'Exhausted?'

'Exhausted, smelly, sweaty, and badly in need of a coffee . . .'

Maggie handed her the cup she'd been drinking from, and

Liv took a big drink of the hot liquid before handing it back, grimacing. 'That's tea, you bloody Pom!'

A blast of cold air hit them as they pushed Liv's luggage through the automatic doors that led to the car park.

'God almighty!' Liv wrapped her arms around herself. 'How cold is that?! Do you know it was forty degrees at home yesterday, or the day before – I'm so confused. I could be lying by the pool, working on the tan. What the hell am I doing here?'

'You're saving my life.' Maggie put a protective arm around her sister's shoulders, pulling her coat to cover them both, and led her towards the car.

Stan's excitement about his aunt's arrival didn't extend to wanting to chat in the car on the way home. He put the head-phones on, and restarted the DVD he'd been watching on the small screen in the back of the headrest of the car. *Harry Potter and the Goblet of Fire*. Again. He'd seen all of them a hundred times – knew them by heart. They were like his technological comfort blanket.

The sisters didn't talk while Maggie negotiated the airport exit and turned on to the M4 East. Once she had, Liv looked back at her nephew.

'Stan looks great.'

Maggie smiled and smacked the steering wheel victoriously. 'Stan *is* great. Things are really good for him. He's doing well.'

'Thank goodness for that.' Maggie nodded. Like Maggie, she'd held her breath when he'd started at the new school, not exhaling, on the other side of the world, until Maggie rang to say so far, so good . . . And like Maggie, she'd waited for a bounce . . . that hadn't come. It sometimes seemed to her that she felt almost everything Maggie ever felt, a little weaker, like echoes in a cave or ripples on a pond. In some ways she lived a vicarious life, through Maggie. Thank God for Scott. Liv knew she needed him. She badly needed a life of her own. To put Maggie back where she needed to be, where she should be, in her own head.

'He loves it. He's on a couple of the sports teams. He's got a bunch of friends. He's doing well academically . . . He's a different kid from before he went.'

'That's so great, Maggie.'

'It is. Not having to worry about him every day – it's unbelievable. He goes off every morning happy as a clam. What more could I ask?'

'And how's my gorgeous Aly?'

She shrugged. 'She's fine. Situation normal. All good on the surface. You know Aly. The marks are great, she's busy all the time.'

'But . . .'

'But she doesn't talk to me at all.'

'Open warfare?'

'God, no – that might be easier. She's not above talking to me in a tone that would have made Mum give us a slap on the cheek. Occasional skirmishes, for sure, but nothing so – so vital as open warfare! She talks – we talk about all kinds of stuff. We just don't talk talk – you know?'

'Okay.'

'Your mission, should you choose to accept it . . .'

'Get her to open up?'

Maggie nodded.

'Are you sure, sis – that she needs that?'

'What do you mean?'

'You're always talking about her like . . . well, like she's this emotional boil that needs lancing. That she's full of stuff she isn't expressing.' That was Liv. No preamble. She always

71

said what she meant. It was an incredibly refreshing quality, Maggie thought. So few people did that.

'Yes.'

'But maybe she isn't. Maybe that's more you than her. Maybe she's still dealing with it all differently.'

Maggie acknowledged what Liv said. 'Maybe. I just don't think so.' Liv smiled at her sister's stubbornness. The streak was a mile wide, and she'd always had it . . .

'What does Bill say . . . ?'

Maggie made a strange, choked noise. Olivia looked at her sharply.

'What?'

'Bill's met someone.' Maggie heard the sarcastic tone in her own voice.

'You're joking.' Olivia saw her sister's hands tightening on the steering wheel.

'I'm so not.'

'Christ, Maggie. You didn't say.'

'I only just found out, really. I thought I'd wait and deliver the news in person.'

What a shit, Liv thought to herself, though she knew that wasn't true. It was instinctive and protective, not fair. What a pig. Out loud, she asked, 'How do you feel?'

Maggie didn't look up from the road.

'Sorry. Stupid question.' Maggie shook her head.

'I'm shocked that I'm shocked, if you know what I mean. I mean . . . what did I expect?'

'You expected he'd come back.'

'Is that what you expected?'

Liv was watching her sister closely. 'I didn't expect him to find someone else. I know you two were apart for a reason, but, yeah, I suppose if I'd been trying to predict the future, I'd have guessed he'd come back. I mean you're Bill and

Maggie, for God's sake. Now he's going to be Bill and some-one else . . . ? Crazy. What's her name?'

'I don't know. I didn't ask.' Liv would have asked. And quite possibly, Liv would have screamed and cursed and slapped his face in the restaurant. Maybe Maggie would have done too, once.

'Who is she? Where did he meet her? How long has it been going on?'

'Any other questions . . . ?!' Maggie gave a hollow laugh.

'You don't have questions?' Liv sounded incredulous.

'I don't know. Hurts too much, I suppose. The more I know, I think, the more it'll hurt. She'll get very, very real, once I know stuff about her.'

'Oh Mags. I'm sorry. Christ.' Not for the first time, Liv wondered how much more her sister could take. It had been an unbelievable couple of years. Anyone sane knew that luck wasn't doled out fairly – that some people's was all good, while others had misfortune heaped on them. But Maggie had had a bellyful. First Jake, then all the trouble with Stan, the split with Bill. Now this. It was too much. Too damn much for one person. She felt a rush of pure rage towards Bill, even as she knew he didn't really deserve it.

Maggie tried to shrug it off. 'I know where he met her.'

'Where?'

'At counselling. Which would be ironic and funny, if I was less . . . less . . . broken.'

Liv reached across and put her hand on Maggie's shoulder.

'You are not broken.'

'Aren't I?'

'No. You're not. I won't let you be. You're bruised and you're battered. You are not broken.'

'I'm so glad you're here, sis.' Maggie's voice was full of tears now, and the strain of trying not to cry.

Liv glanced at Stan in the back of the car. He was engrossed in whatever he was watching. 'Do the kids know?'

'No. I'm not telling them, either. Bill can bloody well do that.' Maggie sniffed hard and rubbed her hand across her nose.

'Too right.'

'Anyway, you can ask him about it yourself.'

'I can?'

Maggie nodded. 'You know I told you the other day that Stan had his heart set on us cutting down our own tree? I was trying to wriggle out of it, to tell the truth. I put him off and put him off. He'd been asking since the first. I hated doing that – but I couldn't face it. So he applied kid logic. He asked Bill.'

'You're kidding?'

'Proves we've done a good job protecting the kids, I suppose. Stan, at least. He's buying into the bullshit we're feeding him. He thinks we're civilized enough to go and cut down a Christmas tree together.' They would have been, she realized as she said it, if he hadn't told her about this woman.

'God bless Stan. And you've agreed to this?'

'What could I do? What could Bill do, for that matter?'

'He said yes?' Liv wasn't feeling charitable towards her brother-in-law. Why would he agree to put them all through something like that, knowing what state Maggie was in? Surely he could have thought of something . . .

'He said yes. We're going tomorrow. Up for a game of Happy Families, Liv?'

I'm up for something, Liv, thought, but I'm not sure that's what you'd call it . . .

*

Stan's film finished and he pulled off his headphones, commandeering his aunt for the rest of the journey home from the airport.

'Did you bring our presents?'

'What do you reckon?'

Stan beamed. 'I reckon you did. What d'you get me?'

'Like I'm going to tell you . . . *Patience, mon ami*.'

'I'm doing really well in French, aren't I, Mum?'

Maggie nodded.

'*Aah, félicitations. Je suis très fière de toi* . . .' Liv spoke in her best Inspector Clouseau accent.

Stan pushed his head as far forward into the gap between the two front seats as it would go. 'What?' The women laughed.

'Good on ya, mate.'

'Is Scott going to bring presents too? Does he know what we like? Can he play football? Where's Scott sleeping, Mum? In with Auntie Liv, or does he want to share with me?'

Twenty minutes later Maggie parallel parked the car on the street outside the house. Aly, listening for the car in the big bay window, opened the front door before Maggie had switched the engine off and fell on Liv with the same enthusiasm her brother had. 'Auntie Liv!! Yeah!! So glad you're here!!'

She was still in pyjamas, drawstring trousers sitting perilously low on her hips, with the random addition of a woolly scarf, her hair fuzzed wildly into the back of her head, her feet pushed into ubiquitous Ugg boots. Liv held her tight.

'Christ, Aly. Taller, skinnier, more gorgeous.'

'Nah.'

'Yes, look at you, girl. You're stunning. And you're . . .' Liv stood shoulder to shoulder with her niece. 'Yep. You're taller than me, you bugger . . . You must have grown three inches since I saw you last!'

Aly put her arm through Liv's and pulled her up the stairs to the front door. At the car, Stan struggled to pull out Liv's bags and Maggie hovered in case he gave up and needed her to do it. She looked at her sister with her daughter and smiled. Yes, she was jealous. Mums could be jealous. But she was glad too.

Inside the house, Liv was looking around. Not much had changed, except that everything was immaculate where in previous years she'd been used to the odd dusty ledge or high cobweb. She loved Maggie's taste – and she loved the familiarity of the things she'd had for years. The house had a very wide, gracious hallway, and the first stairway faced the front door. There was a console table with a mirror above it, on which was a vast arrangement of red poinsettias, and a big pottery bowl that Jake, Aly and Stan had put their handprints and signatures on years ago as a Mother's Day gift. It was the first piece of Jake that hit you when you entered the house. The rest of the wall of the hallway, up the stairs and along both the landings upstairs, held Maggie's collection of shadow boxes – a gallery of her history.

She'd been making them for ever. Mostly black or white frames, three or four inches deep, each one telling a story. The first ones featured Maggie's life before she met Bill. Swimming medals, a swim cap and a pair of goggles pinned into a photograph of her wearing them, punching the air in victory beneath a clock showing her time. That was from 1980. She'd made one of Australiana, collected just before she left with Bill – a Vegemite label, an empty Tim Tams wrapper, a miniature boomerang and a tube of pink zinc cream. Their wedding – an eight-by-ten photo of her and Bill kissing, with confetti, the room-service bill from the hotel where they'd spent their first night, the cheap nylon garter she'd worn on her leg and a single sugar flower from their wedding cake. Each of her children's births had its own box – hospital bracelets, snaps of the midwives who delivered them, going-home outfits, the traditional *Times* announcements Bill's parents had insisted on placing, though Bill and Maggie said no one they knew would ever read them. First shoes, not brassed over but with all their scuffs and wear on display, each scratch a stumble. Pictures of them as toddlers, painting, with the finished results, an actual paintbrush and unwashed palette. Aly, adorable in a pink tutu and studied pose, aged about three, with her certificate and an impossibly tiny pair of ballet slippers, elastics sewn in by Maggie. Tennis balls. A photo of Jake the day he got his GCSE results, pictured with Maggie and Bill, all of them holding up champagne flutes and laughing, with the cork and wire from the bottle they'd drunk.

Everyone loved the shadow boxes. First-time visitors always wanted to spend ages meandering up the stairs, looking at them. People went away asking if they could steal the idea. A magazine-editor client of Bill's who'd come to the house ten years ago had been enchanted by them, and had even run a piece on her in the magazine featuring some, with a photograph of Maggie seated at a trestle table set up in the kitchen, working on one. The article had become a shadow box too, of course, with a photo of the photographer the magazine sent, an empty tube of glue and the magazine's masthead. There were at least thirty, probably more, winding their way neatly up the stairs.

But they stopped after Jake. So far as Liv knew, Maggie hadn't made one since he'd died. Up at the top of the house, it was as though the family's history screeched to a stop, the curator mysteriously disappeared. Maggie still kept everything, like she always had, in big cardboard boxes at the back of a cupboard in her bedroom – one that had once held Bill's clothes. Photographs and mementoes and piles of the things that anyone else might consider rubbish, but that Maggie's artistic eye might imagine in a shadow box. But she never looked at them. Liv knew that Maggie's desertion of her creative impulse was part of her depression, just like the fact that her sporty, strong sister no longer ran, or swam or exercised. She spent the time she used to spend doing those things cleaning – a boring, repetitive, unfulfilling job she did not for satisfaction but just for the act of moving. She'd packed her trainers and her gym kit, and she was damn well going to make Maggie run with her, though Liv loathed running. One thing at a time. One small step for Maggie . . .

Stan insisted on bringing in all the luggage from the car, up the steep flight of steps to the front door, though the next set of stairs to the guest room defeated him and he left the bags haphazardly by the hall table. Downstairs, in the kitchen, Liv stood theatrically warming herself by the Aga, as big a convert to the unique English stove as her sister. The kettle was already on the hotplate to boil. Aly was laughing at something Liv was saying about her travelling companion on the flight and Stan, following behind Maggie, went to forage for biscuits. Maggie exhaled slowly. For a while, at least, the house felt fuller. And things were going to be all right, for the next few weeks at least. She could get through Christmas again, the second without Jake, if Liv was here.

Chapter Seven

In the master bedroom of his flat, dark but for the lines of light the slatted wooden blinds allowed into the space, Bill lay with his hands behind his head and watched Carrie's naked shape as she walked to the door, her hips swaying, knowing his eyes were on her in the half light. God. This girl. His chest felt tight while he gazed at her.

She was so different from Maggie. He still thought that small, disloyal thought often, when he had the opportunity – as he did now – to observe her. It started with the physical, and then it just carried on. Carrie was tiny – barely five foot three, and slender, almost boyish, and so pale-skinned she was almost translucent. Her long, straight blonde hair swung down almost to the small of her back when it was released from its daytime ponytail. Nothing about her seemed strong. Her legs and arms were slim and fine. Her face, which he couldn't see now but already knew by heart, was fine-featured – she had enormous pale-blue eyes in a small face, and a sprinkling of freckles across her cheeks. A little, rose-bud mouth with pale lips. Her fragility was entrancing to him – deeply erotic and entirely captivating. When he put his arms around her, she felt so small and fragile. And he felt so strong. Which was absolutely how he needed to feel.

Maggie had always been strong. Maggie had been his equal. Maggie had created awe in him. She still could. The very physicality of the two relationships was in stark contrast.

Maggie was almost his height – she'd always been able to square up to him, look him in the eye. In bed, when things had been good between them, she had been an instigator, a predator, selfish and giving in equal measure.

It was so different with Carrie. Bill wasn't a stupid man. He understood what was going on. No degree in psychology required. Carrie needed to be looked after. She wanted to be taken care of. She wanted to be led, protected. And that's what he needed to do – look after someone. Maggie hadn't let him. It had never really been part of their marriage, and after Jake, that was just . . . magnified. But Carrie positively required it as an unspoken but entirely clear condition of her being with him.

He wasn't so lost in her that he didn't realize he might not have been so attracted to her if he had met her at any other time in his life. She wasn't his type. Maggie had been his type. But she'd come at the exact right moment, and she was just what he needed.

Being here with her was still surreal to him. His life had changed almost beyond recognition in the last couple of months. The flat was in a building he'd bought and developed in Roehampton – he'd converted an old schoolhouse into four luxury flats – this one had still been available a year earlier when he and Maggie had decided, if decision was the right thing to call it, to be apart, and so he'd taken it off the market and moved in. It was temporary. But wasn't it all bloody temporary now? There were three bedrooms, a large master for him and a smaller one each for Aly and Stan. After so many years in the Chiswick house he and Maggie had shared with the kids, it had taken a lot of getting used to – being alone in what was effectively a shell when he moved in and had remained that way for quite a time. Tricked out with a state-of-the-art kitchen – all glossy counters and dark wood – and fashionable 'wetroom' bathrooms with oversized showerheads, it felt, at first, like he was sleeping in a designer showroom. It had been too quiet without the kids and the constant hum of the washing machine, the ever-ringing phone, five people's divergent music tastes clashing cacophonously on the landings. He'd bought a Bose sound system and played the radio too loud all day. It wasn't him, though he'd chosen and paid for it all, and Maggie might think it was. He'd been designing for his 'customer', not himself. He'd even rented furniture – it seemed too soon, too final, too much to buy new stuff, but he needed a bed, a table, a sofa to sit on. Furniture for the kids. A year later, it still screamed showroom – there were no paintings or objects that might make it more homely, except in the kids' rooms. Aly had hung posters, and a couple of her own pieces of artwork from GCSE, and Stan had carefully (and, for Bill and Maggie, poignantly) subdivided his Lego and Transformers and brought exactly half to his dad's new place, in bright plastic boxes, though they'd barely been in the boxes since, since he seemed to prefer them strewn all over the floor. Bill daren't move them, and had asked the cleaner not to either – what looked random to him would doubtless have order for Stan, and you messed with it at your peril.

There was nothing homely about the communal parts of the flat. But Carrie being here had made it feel more that way. Carrie cooked for him in the smart Poggenpohl kitchen he'd barely used – delicate, exotic little meals with ingredients he didn't always recognize. Ingredients began to colonize the counter. She sat curled into him on the vast sectional sofa, both of them nursing a glass of red wine and listening to music. They almost never watched television. In his previous life, with Maggie and the kids, it was rarely switched off. He couldn't believe how tranquil it was without the ever-present background drone of the TV.

And Carrie lay beneath him in the bed, her big eyes never leaving his, as he made gentle, tender love to her, her tiny hands tucked under his arms to grip his shoulders and hold him close to her. For him, right now, she was home, and that had happened faster than he could have imagined.

She was, here and now, his freedom – from want, from fear, from need. Outside of this flat, he was often gripped with doubt and full of recrimination: what was he doing? To Maggie, to the kids, to himself, to Carrie? What did he expect from this? Where could this possibly go? He didn't feel that when he was here with her. He slept. He slept for seven, eight, nine hours at a time when she was there, and he hadn't done that since Jake died. Easy, deep sleep, with her moulded to his side, warm and fragrant. Maggie had never liked that. She liked to sleep untouched – she got too hot, she said, too stuffy. Carrie liked to be held, and he liked to hold her.

She was back now, sashaying across the wooden floor, with two glasses of water. She handed one to him, smiling sexily. He might have guessed – a while ago – that she'd be shy, bashful. Maybe even insecure about herself, though there was no need – she was a very pretty girl. But she wasn't any of those things. The first night he'd brought her back here, both of them knowing what was coming, she'd stood in front of him and stripped herself naked, slowly, deliberately and unselfconsciously in the light of the lamps in the room. She had a lovely body – smooth and young and soft. Small, high breasts, and a taut, concave stomach, and he saw that she wanted to show it off to him. She'd touched him first. She'd given him the unspoken permission to touch her right back.

And she loved sex. While Maggie had never been one of those women who went off it once they'd had kids, there was no doubt their sex life had settled into something more like a habit than a hobby. He hadn't questioned it. When it happened, it was good and it gave them both what they needed, and everything else about their life together was so completely intimate and close that he didn't often miss what they might have once had. There were still weekends without the kids, the odd holiday, when they 'swung from the chandeliers and jumped off the wardrobe' as Maggie might have described it – though he never remembered chandeliers or wardrobes being involved. It was certainly many years since he'd had as much sex as he and Carrie had – and it was exciting. He might wake in the early morning with her mouth on him under the covers, or hear her come into the bathroom when he was showering, to slip in with him. They made love in rooms other than the bedroom – kids had made that impossible, or at best rare and risky, in his life with Maggie – and it almost amused him to realize how erotic it could be just to change location. Carrie had told him once that she missed having regular sex almost as much as she missed anything about her married life. It wasn't what you were supposed to say, she said, but it was true. This was young man's sex. Chest-beating, me Tarzan, you Jane sex. Standing up against the kitchen counter, over the bath, in broad daylight, before they ate dinner sex. He'd had young man's sex with Maggie, of course – it was just that he'd been a young man when he had it. Now he was a middle-aged man. To be having it again was intoxicating.

It seemed he would be having it again right about now. Finishing her glass, a few drops running unchecked down her chin on to her belly, Carrie took his glass from him and put it down on the bedside table. Bill wondered whether he could do it again. But only for a moment. Pulling the sheet off him, Carrie straddled him in one easy fluid movement and began to plant small kisses on his ear. He ran his hands up and down her smooth back, feeling her push gently but insistently against him, and knew that yes, he could do it again . . .

Afterwards, as he looked at her sleeping, he knew it was more than sex. Getting to be much more. Sex had become a wondrous release for him again. In the time since Jake had gone, sex with Maggie had been all but ruined. At first, it had been almost animalistic – as though rutting and fucking could somehow help obliterate the unimaginable pain they were both in. Quickly, though, it had become so sad – they would both cry, not finish and end up clinging to each other, his hard-on withering inside her. And then it had almost stopped entirely. There was no energy. No heat. Dead on the vine. So yes, sex with Carrie was good. He was alive again. He couldn't quite bring himself to apologize for that.

But it was more. More even, maybe, than the undeniable fact that she needed him.

Bill hadn't lied to Maggie when he'd said he didn't know whether it might be 'love' and he didn't know if he wanted it to be. He'd only been in love once in his life before and that was with Maggie, and when that had happened it had happened hard and fast and with passion and desperation. He couldn't have lived without her – as simple as that. That was what he believed. Now he knew different. He knew you could live even when you didn't want to. Because after Jake, he didn't think he wanted to. And yet he did. He lived. He wasn't the same person he'd been all those years ago when he'd fallen in love with Maggie, and so it stood to reason that he couldn't fall in love the same way. So he didn't know if he was in love with Carrie. His idea of what that might be had changed so much.

And they didn't talk about it. They both accepted what was and didn't question it, at least not out loud to each other. Carrie had her own stuff to deal with.

Carrie had been married for just three years when her husband Jason had died. He'd dropped dead playing an impromptu game of rugby in the park one Sunday afternoon – one of those fit, strong young men who do drop dead with no warning. Carrie had been watching from the sideline with her girlfriends, sipping beer from paper cups and gossiping. She hadn't seen him go down. They'd been together since A levels, a teenage romance that had survived each of them being away at different universities for three years. After graduation, they'd started living together almost straight away, part of a big jolly set of young people in North London, always in the pub or at each other's little terraced houses. Carrie and Jason were amongst the first to get married, setting off a rash of weddings, one every few months or so for a year or two. They were talking about starting a family in a couple of years, once Carrie got a little more established in her career as an assistant editor at a glossy food and wine magazine, and they'd saved a bit more money. She'd watched her dreams and her future and everything she'd known her entire adult life be carried off a rugby pitch marked out with beer cans, on a stretcher, and she had her own stuff to deal with.

Jason had been dead almost nine months when Carrie started coming to the group the previous May. The big jolly set of friends didn't fit any more. When she addressed the group for the first time, a couple of weeks after she started attending, she said that at first her friends had suffocated her in their determination to look after her. There were 400 people at his funeral, she said. Her freezer was always full of casseroles she'd never defrost and eat, and she had to feign illness to get out of cinema trips, pub lunches and endless tea-and-sympathy suppers. Within weeks – she said it was frightening, really, how fast it happened – the friends had distilled themselves down to a hardcore few. And though she loved them for it, she also couldn't stand them, because they still had everything that she had lost. She called them the shiny happy people. She said she thought she'd developed an allergy to them. Not her fault or theirs. The group smiled in recognition of what she described and heads were nodded in agreement.

'Whatever they say, I know they don't want me to talk about him any more,' she said. 'And the trouble is that I sometimes think I don't want to talk about anything else.' Then she shrugged her shoulders and sat down, her explanation complete.

He'd thought she was pretty, and vulnerable, and interesting. But there was still a sense with her – the same as there was with everyone else – that even though they were in a group, and they were 'sharing', they were each in their own sadness bubble. Sealed. Closed off.

Still – the following week, she wasn't there when he arrived and he almost missed her. When she walked in a few minutes late, slipping apologetically into a chair, he felt a flutter of pleasure that she was, after all, there.

A few weeks later, Carrie's car didn't start at the end of the evening, and Bill, seeing her leaning against her bonnet talking into her mobile phone, asked if he could help, and when, with his rudimentary grasp of motor mechanics, he couldn't, he sat in her passenger seat beside her while they waited for the AA. She played an Elvis Costello CD and they sat, mostly in silence, listening to his strained, sad voice. It was the most comfortable Bill had been alone with another human being for months. This was the end of June. He'd been by himself for six months or so, and he was used to it. He'd forgotten that this simple thing could feel good.

The first time the two of them went out independently of the group – Bill's invitation, though his internal monologue was screaming at him as he issued it – was such a bizarre twist on the usual date conversation they both had to laugh. They fired questions at each other – all the usual things – but they were talking about Jake and Jason, not about themselves; an hour in, they knew more about their respective dead family members than they did about each other. After that first time, they didn't talk about them again. They talked about everything but them.

Everything in his brain had screamed at him to stay away from her. Grief counselling was the last place a person like him – or anyone else, for that matter – should be looking for a girlfriend, Bill knew that. Too much baggage. It may have seemed simple, back when they were sitting in her car, but it was, of course, anything but . . .

But he hadn't stayed away from her, and she hadn't asked him to. Now he thought he couldn't if he tried. She was here now, and she was part of what was happening. Looking at her, he couldn't be sorry that she was. That was all he knew.

Chapter Eight

Liv was unpacking her suitcases in the pretty, bright guest room. Maggie had decorated it with a vivid turquoise floral wallpaper on one wall, and soft, toning shades of blue and white on the others, with a bright orange rug and pillows on the bed, and it felt warm and sunny – welcoming, even in this wintery watery light. She must have had Australian visitors in mind.

Aly was helping. If helping meant poring over every other item in the suitcase. She had already slipped a beaded jacket on over her pyjamas and danced around in front of the cheval mirror in the corner, and now she held up a couple of dresses to herself, hips thrust forward.

'Oi! Hands off, niece.' Liv didn't mind. Aly had been doing this since she was tiny. She'd always slightly hero-worshipped her mum's little sister, and that had become more apparent the older she got. It was a part of the ritual of the two of them and it always helped them to reconnect after a long period apart. It usually cost her an outfit, these days, but it was still worth it.

'Come on! I've got this really smart Christmas party next week . . . and this one would be perfect on me.'

The dress in question was a slim, silk shift dress in a milky sea-foam green, and it was pretty new – Liv had only worn it a couple of times. But Aly was right – it would be perfect on her, with those eyes. Aly was still sashaying

– batting her eyelashes and pouting in a deliberately over-the-top way.

Liv smiled benevolently and Aly knew she'd won. She unzipped a nylon bag that contained her jewellery and pulled out a long string of beads – tiny aquamarine-coloured spheres woven with several strands of dove-grey leather and a green-coloured ribbon. She hooked it over the hanger Aly had put the dress on.

'There. This goes with it. And yes, you can borrow it. Of course you can . . . How can I refuse!'

Aly threw her arms exuberantly around Liv. 'Thanks so much, Auntie Liv. You're a complete star.' Liv held her briefly.

'Welcome. Damn you. Bet you look better in it than I do.'

'Got any shoes to go with it? A nude heel, perhaps, or a beaded flat . . .'

Liv laughed. Aly sounded like a *Vogue* article. She looked cynically at her niece's feet. 'What size are you these days?'

'Six and a flipping half. I'm like a giant. Too big.'

Liv gestured towards her own feet. 'A UK five. Sorry. You're on your own with the shoes . . .'

'Bummer. I haven't got anything nearly nice enough . . . or high enough, come to that.'

'We could always go to the West End . . . see what's about . . .'

'God! Could we? Haven't had a big shop for ages. I'd love that . . . When?'

'Better be before the smart party, I suppose. Sometime this week. I don't know what else your mum has planned. We'll ask her if she wants to come with us.'

Aly's face fell. 'Is that a problem?'

'No.' Aly wouldn't look at her. 'It's just . . .'

Liv waited while Aly floundered around for a reason.

'It's just that she has such a different style. You and me are much more similar – we like the same things and the same shops. Mum's all drapy and droopy and stuff . . .'

'Charming. Drapy and droopy?! I think your mum dresses beautifully.' She did, actually. Maggie had a different style, certainly, but she always looked more effortlessly elegant than Liv often felt.

'Yeah. All right – that was harsh. But . . . she's got Stan . . . and . . .'

Liv rescued her. 'And you want to go just us two?'

'Exactly. I hardly ever get to see you . . . and you and Mum'll get lots of time, and Stan too. I just want a bit of time on our own – when I don't have to share you . . .'

'Okay. I'll tell you what. Let me clear that with Maggie. I'm sure she won't mind.'

'Cool.'

Aly flung herself down on the part of the bed that wasn't covered with clothes waiting to be put away, and Liv carried on putting clothes away, deliberately not looking directly at Aly. Aly might find it easier to talk to her that way.

'How's school?'

'Okay. Good. It's all a bit full on, to be honest. Mocks start straight after the Christmas holidays. Exams start for real in March for most of us. Don't finish until May. The pressure is on, and some people are starting to freak out a bit . . .'

'But not you?'

'I have my moments. But I'm not really the freaking-out type.'

'Glad to hear it. Doesn't help. Your mum says you need three As for Imperial.'

'Yep. Just the three!'

She was quiet for a moment. And when she spoke, it was little more than a whisper.

'Jake got three As.'

'I remember.' Liv vividly recalled the phone call – the pride and delight in Maggie's voice as she listed the results.

'Funny to feel like you're competing with your dead brother, huh?'

'Is that how you feel?'

'I think – more and more, actually – that it's how I felt the whole time he was alive. Don't see why it should be any different because he's dead.' Aly's voice was still quiet, almost as though she was talking to herself as much as to her aunt, and she was staring out of the window.

Liv pushed some of her stuff out of the way and lay down across the bed at an angle so that their heads were almost touching. She took Aly's hand, but she couldn't see her face any more. Maybe Maggie was right – that there was a lot more going on than Aly would want you to know. Than you'd ever see with the naked eye. This – this hadn't been very far below the surface. How long had she been through the door – an hour or two at the most?

Coming here, though she loved everyone in this house very desperately, was like knowingly stepping into quicksand. The sadness in the house sucked you in before you even knew what was happening. The velvet drapes of it closed around you quickly.

Lying down, she instantly felt heavy and tired. She took a deep breath. In at the deep end. She supposed she shouldn't be surprised. Aly was like her.

'That's all in your head, Aly. You know that, right?'

'Do I?'

'No one else ever saw it that way.' She hadn't ever lived full time with Maggie and Bill and the kids for long. But she felt like she'd been a constant presence. They hadn't set their children in competition with each other – she was certain of that. There was no denying that Jake was a golden boy. Lucky.

Loved. Bill's pride in everything he achieved, this boy for whom he'd given up all the things he had thought he might achieve himself, Maggie's delight in him – all true. But they'd been that way with Aly too. Okay – Aly wasn't their first child. Aly wasn't Bill's son. But she was Aly. Clever, pretty, successful Aly. She was making this up. It was all in her head. It wasn't jealousy, but it was a weird kind of wallowing, none-theless, and Liv sensed that it was dangerous. Far more straightforward to be envious of Stan, with all his special needs, demanding an unequal share of his parents' attention. But Aly loved Stan. Though she had loved Jake too.

'But he was perfect.'

Liv shook her head. 'No. He wasn't. He was wonderful. But not perfect, any more than you are or I am. No one is perfect, Aly.'

Aly laughed, but it was a small, bitter-sounding laugh. 'Jake was. He was pretty much perfect while he was alive, and you'd be surprised if you knew how much more perfect he's got since he died . . .'

'What are you talking about?' Liv knew she sounded a bit exasperated, but she really didn't understand what Aly was talking about.

When Aly turned to her, she saw that her eyes were full of sudden tears. The sheer speed of her mood swing was almost frightening.

'I'm sorry. That was a crappy thing to say.'

'Oh, sweetheart.' Liv pulled Aly to her and held her tightly. Aly's shoulders and then her whole body shook with sobs that seemed to have come from nowhere. For long minutes there was nothing to do but hold her, and stroke her hair. Eventually, the crying subsided and Aly was calm.

Liv got up and went to the en suite, coming back with a box of tissues that she handed to her niece. Aly blew her nose hard and dabbed at her eyes. The mascara she hadn't washed off the night before was smeared across her face.

'No. I see exactly what you mean. Not the freak-out type at all,' Liv gently joked with her.

Aly laughed through the last of her tears. 'Sorry. It's you.'

'Thanks a lot.'

'You know what I mean. I don't do this in front of Mum and Dad and Stan. Ever. So when I see you . . . I guess it all sort of catches up with me.'

Liv knelt on the bed again. Aly was licking the tissue and rubbing at her eyes. She peered into the cheval mirror. 'Christ – I look a fright now.'

'Why don't you do this with your mum, Aly?'

'I can't, can I?'

'Why not?'

'I was just his sister. She was his mum.'

Chapter Nine

When Maggie swung the car into the crowded car park, Bill was already there, leaning against his Mercedes, hands thrust into his pockets. Stan banged against the closed car window. 'There's Dad. There's Dad. Park next to Dad, Mum. There's a space – right here . . .' In his impatience, he yanked hard on the handle, though the door would not open while the car was in drive.

Liv turned to Maggie. '*Courage, mon brave . . .*'

Maggie smiled. 'I'm okay. How about you? Are you going to be all right – jet lag and biting cold? All this wintery nature . . .'

'I'll live. It's all a bit bloody surreal. But I'm working hard on my Christmas spirit. Feels entirely wrong though. Christmas is for barbies and bikinis.'

Maggie laughed at her. 'The northern hemisphere begs to differ. Don't recall any carols on that theme either, come to think of it . . .'

'Hello . . . Bethlehem? Hardly a winter wonderland, is it? Jesus might not have survived his first night, shoved in a barn in six foot of snow. Let alone the damn camels . . .'

'All right, Ebenezer. Give it a rest.'

'And don't even get me started on the weirdness, the unfestiveness, if that's even a word, of us meeting your estranged husband here to get a tree for the Christmas he isn't going to be a part of . . .'

'I didn't. You started that on your own. I've told you how this happened.'

Liv spoke in a rough facsimile of the old black-and-white film star. 'That's another fine mess you've gotten us into, Stanley . . .'

Stan had jumped out before Maggie had turned off the engine and run to Bill, so he didn't hear.

'Just shut up and get out!'

'I'm saying nothin' . . .'

'That'll be the day!'

Maggie and Liv pulled on their hats and gloves, grimaced quickly to each other and got out.

Bill went to Maggie first. She let him kiss her cheek and briefly hug her, but only because Stan was watching. She wanted to hit him, a sharp fist in his gut, and that surprised her a bit. It had been a long, long time since she'd had the energy to be really angry.

Then he turned to her sister, displaying, she thought, those damn dimples.

'Hey Liv. It's been a long time. How are you?'

In spite of the anger of the previous day, Liv put her arms around Bill.

'Good, Bill. I'm good. Bit knackered, you know . . .'

'When did you get in?'

'Yesterday.' He nodded, shifting from foot to foot.

'No Aly?' He peered into the car.

'She's studying. In the warm. Sensible girl, that one . . .'

Aly had been the only honest one at breakfast. She'd waited until Stan had gone upstairs at his mother's bidding to brush his teeth, then she'd hissed across the table to Liv, knowing Maggie would also hear, 'That's a bit fucked up, isn't it? Going with Dad?'

'Aly. Don't swear.'

Aly had rolled her eyes, standing up from the table. 'Yeah, Mum. *That's* the problem. My language . . .' and gone out and up the stairs before anyone could say anything else.

Maggie had opened her mouth to call out to her. Liv had stood up, in front of her, close to. 'Sssh. Let her go.' Maggie had. Aly was in the shower when they left, deliberately, it seemed to her mother, so that she didn't have to say goodbye.

'Did you bring the axe, Dad, like I said?' Stan asked.

'Of course I did – were you planning to cut it down with a penknife?'

Stan laughed delightedly. ''Course not. Can I hold it? Can I do the first chop?'

Bill opened the boot and took out the axe. 'You can hold it, if you're careful. As to chopping, why don't we wait and see what we choose first, hey? I promise I'll let you help, son.'

'Come on then. This way. Come on. I saw some good ones while we were driving in . . .'

Stan pulled at his father's hand. Bill looked quizzically at Maggie.

'Go ahead. I think we have to register or something – tell them we're here. Then we bring it back when we've chosen, and they charge according to the height. That's right, right? I don't remember . . .'

Bill shrugged. 'How high do you want it?'

Maggie shrugged. 'What do we usually have?'

Aly was right, Liv thought, watching them have this domestic conversation. It was a bit fucked up. If Maggie hadn't told her yesterday – that Bill had someone new – she might have been flushed with optimism. But she had told her. This obviously wasn't the beginnings of a made-for-TV-

96

movie Christmassy reunion. This girl, whoever she was, better be made of stern stuff, because none of this was cut and dried. These were two people who didn't know how to be apart any more than they'd known how to be together, at the end.

Bill shrugged back. 'Seven feet or so. Are you putting it in the same place?'

'I hadn't thought. Yes. Yes, I guess so.' Maggie looked bent down, almost, and Liv felt for her. She'd told her sister that she wasn't broken, just battered and bruised. She hoped she was right.

Bill turned to follow Stan and the axe.

Liv turned to Maggie. 'Good job I promised not to say anything, because otherwise I might be saying . . . "strangerer and strangerer . . ."'

Maggie grabbed her sister's sleeve and pulled her towards the Portakabin with the signage.

An over-excited Stan and the logistics of selecting and harvesting a tree mercifully ate up the rest of the hour. Bill was patient with Stan. He made a big performance of letting Stan deliver the final, felling blow to the trunk of the tree. Bill tied the tree to the top of Maggie's car with ropes he took from the back of his car.

'I'd never have thought of that.' Maggie smiled weakly. 'Thanks.'

'You're very welcome, Maggie. You know I'm glad to help. I could come to the house . . . help you put it up, if you wanted . . .'

'You don't need to do that.'

'It's no trouble . . . I don't need to be anywhere.'

You need not to be in my house, Maggie thought. 'I don't want you to do that.'

Bill looked at his feet.

97

'I'm sorry. That sounded sharper than I meant it to.'

'It's fine, Maggie. I shouldn't have pushed . . .'

No, Maggie thought. You shouldn't. You shouldn't be so keen to make yourself available to us, when I know you're not any more, not really . . . Maggie took Stan round the side of the Portakabin to get hot apple cider from the catering truck parked there, leaving Bill and Liv standing together by the cars.

'She's told you, I suppose?' Liv had been on the ground more than an hour. Of course Maggie had told her. They probably hadn't navigated airport parking before she'd told her. He'd long understood that there were no secrets between these two . . .

Liv nodded her head slowly.

'Bloody hell, Bill.'

'I know.'

'I don't know what to say to you. I honestly don't.'

He didn't respond. A wave of something that felt like shame rolled over him under Liv's hard stare.

'I mean . . . I thought . . . I always thought this was temporary. I thought you'd be back. Didn't you think that?'

'For a long time I did.'

'Not now?'

'I don't know.' He wasn't sure that was true. He wasn't sure about much.

'You don't have much to say about it, do you, Bill?'

His response sounded angrier than he felt. 'What do you want me to say, Liv? Do I feel shitty about it – yes, I do. Of course I do. I knew it would hurt her, and I didn't want to hurt her and I have. And I feel like a creep. Okay?'

'But you're doing it anyway?'

'Yes. I'm doing it anyway, Liv. Because I have to do something. I have to move forward. I wanted to do that with

Maggie. Christ – you know better than most people how hard I tried to do that. But she wouldn't.'

'Couldn't, Bill.'

'Couldn't. Wouldn't. She asked me to leave, Liv. She did. And I went, because she asked me to. First I lost Jake, then I lost her and Aly and Stan too – at least lost them a little. But I did what she asked me to do. And I lived my life. I had to. And do you know what, Liv. I'm a little bit happy. Tiny bit.' He held up his finger and his thumb a few centimetres apart. 'I don't know what this thing I have with Carrie is. Where it's going. I just know that when I wake up in the morning, I don't feel like just rolling over, putting the pillow over my head and denying the day any more. I want to get out of bed. For the first time in a bloody long time. Should I have to feel like crap for saying that, or for feeling it? Should I really?'

His eyes were imploring her.

Maggie came back before she could answer him.

That night, Liv couldn't sleep – her body clock was all over the place, and it took her a few days after the flight to sleep all the way through. She crept downstairs to warm a glass of milk in the microwave. The house seemed quiet and Maggie's door was ajar so she could see the light wasn't on. Downstairs, she drank the milk leaning against the counter, watching the digital display on the radio flick over the minutes. A few moments later, creeping as quietly as she could up the stairs, she was stopped in her tracks by the sound of her sister crying. She held on to the banister and sank on to the carpeted stair, drawing her knees up to her chest, hugging herself and listening to the awful sound.

A few evenings later, Maggie and Liv were settling in

with a bottle of wine, a Marks and Spencer ready meal and individual sherry trifles, a favourite of Liv's, and Maggie's well-worn copy of *It's a Wonderful Life*. Stan had gone to Stamford Bridge to watch the football with Bill. He hadn't come in when he'd picked Stan up, just honked once and waited in the car. Maggie had been glad not to have to speak to him, although she'd waved at him from the front door and he had waved back through the car's open window, smiling deliberately at her, though she could see the strain on his face. Liv had suggested that they get dressed up and go out themselves – Aly had plans and Stan was staying the night with his father after the match – but Maggie had demurred. Too much seasonal jollity, she'd argued. Liv had acquiesced, just as happy to stay home. Companionable silence, in front of the telly, she reasoned, had its role to play.

But she kept thinking about Scott. He was going to a party in a bar on the harbour tonight – a party they'd both been invited to. With champagne and fairy lights and oysters and prawns. With happy people who didn't hate this time of year, who would be laughing and dancing and drinking too much. Liv had felt a real pang, for Scott and a warm, close night, and the happy people. He'd texted her earlier. 'Won't be the same without you.' She sort of hoped it wasn't. It was okay for him to miss her. She was sure as hell missing him. She was counting the days . . .

Aly had been upstairs for ages, getting ready for this party she was going to. She and Liv had bought shoes, as promised, earlier that day, alone in town. Maggie had affected not to mind, claiming she had plenty of baking and wrapping to do and that she'd be glad of the peace, but she'd watched them wistfully as they walked arm in arm down the road towards the station. Aly had hardly looked at her since Liv arrived. Hardly addressed a remark to her. Any chance she got to follow Liv off upstairs and closet herself in the guest room with her – she took it. Liv hadn't said that much about Aly when they got back, Aly clutching an L.K.Bennett bag, just that Aly had been fun to hang out with. Maggie hoped she might say more once Aly had gone.

'How are you getting there?' Maggie had asked, trying not to sound annoying, though she knew she irritated Aly almost every time she opened her mouth.

'I called the cab firm.' It was the one they always used; Maggie knew it was safe.

'Are you picking anyone else up on the way? And on the way where – by the way . . .?'

Aly pulled a face, and Maggie knew she'd gone too far. 'Maybe. Not sure yet. I will if someone needs a ride. And I told you, Mum – it's a twenty-first. Of the brother of a friend of mine . . . a girl from school. You don't know her, but she hangs out in the same group as I do. It's in a restaurant in the West End . . . And you know I'm going to be late back, right? Like late enough that you two shouldn't wait up for me.'

Maggie had been about to insist on more details when Liv threw her a silencing glance from the other side of the kitchen. When Aly had left the room – if Maggie had been describing it, she might have said 'flounced out' – Liv scolded her gently.

'You were riding her a bit hard, weren't you?'

'I hardly said a word.'

'It's not that. It's the sort of simmering that's going on with this . . .' Liv gestured with a sweeping finger that took in Maggie's face and body language. 'It's the way you were squaring up for aggro. If I can see it, sis, then you know she can too.'

'Did she say something, while you were out? About me giving her a hard time?'

'No. Not at all. Thought of that all on my own . . .'

'It's called parenting, Liv.' She caught herself sounding patronizing, and tried to tone it down in the next sentence. 'She's not an adult yet. I ought to know where she's going . . .'

'She's seventeen, Maggie. She practically is. Do you need me to remind you where you were when you were her age?' Liv had archly lifted an eyebrow. 'In a few months, she'll be gone altogether at uni and you'll have to get used to not having a clue what she's up to from day to day. You've got to let her loose some time. She's a sensible kid – she isn't going to do anything daft.'

'You know that, do you?' Maggie was irked, a little. One afternoon in the shops and Liv was an expert on her daughter. Again. Then the quick shot of guilt – how could she be critical of Liv, when Liv was here taking care of her?

'I don't know, no. But I'm pretty sure.'

'I worry.'

'I know.' Christ knows I'd be worried, Liv thought. I'd be so scared I couldn't breathe, the moment one of my kids was out of my sight. But it's wrong and it's not fair and she can't do it. 'I know all the reasons why you worry, too. But you need to try. Try not to. You're pushing. Clinging.'

Maggie smiled ruefully. 'How can I push *and* cling?'

'You know what I mean . . .'

'Maybe. Smart-arse.'

'Pass the corkscrew and put Jimmy Stewart in the machine right now, will you. If you're reduced to name-calling, I know I've won . . .'

Aly looked older than seventeen when she finally came into the living room a while later to say goodbye. Liv pressed the pause button on the remote control. George Bailey had just saved his little brother from the icy pond. Aly looked like a woman, a lovely young woman. Maggie's breath caught in her throat, and she bit hard on her lip to stop a sudden wave of emotion she knew would be distasteful to Aly. The cab was already waiting. Liv had waved at the driver from the bay window when she'd heard him pull up, and called up the stairs to Aly.

'Blimey, Aly – you look flipping gorgeous!'

She did. She'd done her hair in fashionable loose waves. Liv had bought her some new make-up, too, though they hadn't told Maggie. The girl at the counter had shown her how to put it on, and Aly had done a good job of reproducing the look – her eyes were smoky, her skin was smooth, her lips glossy. She had been right about the damn dress too, Liv thought ruefully – Aly looked amazing in it.

'Give me a minute – I'm going to get the camera . . .' Liv went to the hall, where she knew her camera was in her handbag.

Maggie hadn't said anything yet. Aly turned to where her mother was sitting in an armchair and opened her arms as if to say, 'So?'

'You're beautiful, darling. You're beautiful and I'm 105 years old.' She smiled a broad and genuine smile at her daughter, who actually seemed to glow beneath the make-up at the compliment.

The cab sounded his horn, impatient now for his passenger. 'Come on, Auntie Liv. He's getting pissed off . . . I've got to go . . .'

'One second . . . flash . . . Strike a pose, baby!' The flash exploded, even if Aly's pose was rather self-conscious. Liv held the camera monitor out at Maggie. 'Look at that!'

'I'm out of here . . .'

'Have a good time. Be safe. Call me if you need . . .' And then the door slammed.

It wasn't just teen spirit that made Aly elusive with details for her mother. She didn't really want her to know where she was going or, more importantly, who she was going with. The disconnect between them had never been bigger, she realized. Not even in the early days after Jake died. Sometimes she looked at her mum and saw a stranger she neither understood nor cared to. Sometimes, she swore her mum looked back at her the same way. She hadn't told Liv either, though she had wanted to earlier, while they were shopping. She didn't trust her aunt not to tell Maggie, and she didn't want to deal with that. Not now.

She *was* going to a twenty-first birthday. That much was true. Also true was that it was being held in a restaurant in the West End. But she had no idea whose birthday it was – certainly someone she had never met before. She wasn't going with a schoolfriend. That was what she had most wanted Maggie not to know. She was going with Ryan. Jake's friend Ryan. The friend who, along with Matt, the third boy, had survived the tsunami. And she honestly didn't know how her mum would react to that. Besides – she didn't want to share it. She didn't even really know what it was, and probably couldn't have put it into words, but she knew that it was hers and hers alone . . .

Ryan had been Jake's best friend for ever. They'd virtually lived in each other's houses: there'd been four kids at breakfast most Sunday mornings that Aly could remember from her childhood. Matt had only moved into the neighbourhood and started at the school Jake and Ryan went to when they were about fourteen. Ryan and Jake had been a twosome since pre-school. One dark and one blonde.

Equally tall and sporty. Both bright, and good-looking. When she was eleven and they were around fourteen or fifteen, Aly had developed a huge crush on him, almost as big as the one she had on Johnny Depp, whose posters plastered the walls of her bedroom, but in some ways more intense, since the object of her affection was in her house most days, in the flesh, not on paper with staple holes in it. It had been pretty obvious, and Jake had tortured her mercilessly about it. Ryan never had, though he had stopped well short of offering her any encouragement. He only had a big brother, and wasn't as relaxed as Jake was about teasing and ridiculing Aly. For that, as a tender-hearted pre-teen, she declared, via her diary, unending love and devotion. It had worn off a little, over the years, as Aly grew up and started to meet 'real' boys, her own age, to dance with them at school dances and eventually to kiss them in the dark corners of the auditoriums. But still, right up until the time the guys left on their trip, if Ryan was in the house, she felt a bit butterfly-tummied.

She remembered, vividly, a moment that passed between them the night before the boys left on their trip. Late on in the evening, when the parents had drunk a few bottles of wine, someone had turned the music up and they'd all danced in the garden. Maggie had strung coloured paper lanterns along the dividing walls between theirs and the adjacent gardens, and Bill had lit the outdoor fire pit. Mostly it was the parents dancing, the teenagers watching. Jake had led his mates back into the house in search of more beer, and, when he'd slipped past her, for just a moment, Ryan had put both hands on her waist, where the skin was bare beneath a short top. It hadn't been necessary. As he touched her, he'd looked right at her, beer and firelight and maybe something else making his eyes sparkle. It had been for maybe four or five seconds, that was all, but she'd thought about it every night for weeks afterwards.

That had stopped, of course, after Jake died. Aly remembered exactly the moment when the front doorbell had rung that January afternoon and Ryan had been on the doorstep. Maggie had answered, and she had stood frozen for a few moments. Ryan's chest had risen and fallen visibly; he seemed out of breath, though he had walked calmly up the front steps. He had known Maggie for as long as he could remember, but she'd never looked like this – hollow-eyed and ashen, haunted. When she didn't speak, he took a step forward.

'Mrs B. I'm so, so sorry . . .' His voice had broken.

She'd put her arms around him then, and held him in a long embrace.

Aly had watched the whole thing from the top of the stairs. No one had noticed her there. Jake had been dead about three weeks. No one had noticed her much at all then. Everyone was moving around like unseeing zombies. No one could carry anyone else. They couldn't help each other. They'd been the loneliest weeks of her life.

Maggie had taken Ryan down to the basement and made him a cup of coffee. They'd sat at the kitchen table and spoken softly to each other for ages – Aly had sat on the step outside the kitchen door and tried to hear, but most of what the two of them said was muffled and quiet. She knew her mum was asking questions – lots of questions. Ryan was answering. They were both crying.

Aly remembered being angry. Angry and frustrated. She wanted to know the answer to those questions too. She had questions of her own about her brother and what had happened to him over there. Questions no one but Ryan might know the answers to. She didn't know whether her mother had shut her out deliberately or simply forgotten that she was in the house. She knew only that she hadn't consciously included her. There'd been a lot of closed doors in those dreadful, slow weeks. Lots of conversations that didn't include her. She was fifteen years old.

She hadn't seen Ryan much after that. He hadn't come to the house again, and without Jake there was no real reason for their paths to cross. Another one of the imperceptible shifts in her new life without her big brother. Ryan went off to university that September, just like Jake would have done. He'd gone to Edinburgh, and she'd all but forgotten about him.

Until late August last summer, when she'd run into him randomly. She'd been at a cricket match in Richmond with a big group of girlfriends from school – all pleased to see each other after the long break that had scattered them to the four winds with their own families. Someone's big brother was playing for one of the teams, and it was a good excuse to get out on a beautiful day – hot and sunny, with a cerulean-blue sky. Ryan was there, meant, through some other connection, to be playing for the other team but invalided out of the action by a sporting leg injury that made him limp a little.

He'd spotted her first; she'd been more absorbed by her friends and the picnic they were consuming than by the action of the match or the small crowd around them. He'd come up to her as she was sitting with her mates, cross-legged on the grass, spreading Branston Pickle on a pork pie with her finger, since no one had remembered to bring cutlery.

'Aly Barrett?' He was bent over at the waist, peering at her, with his face sideways, but she knew him instantly, of course.

'Ryan?!'

'I thought it was you. How the hell are you?' His voice was too loud, too full of faux bonhomie. Aly could see his self-consciousness.

She'd stood up, and taken a couple of steps forward, off the picnic rug. They were face to face. 'I'm fine. Wow. I'm so surprised to see you . . .' She was nervous too – aware that she kept twirling the long lengths of her hair, pushing strands ineffectually behind her ears.

'Me too. You got tall . . .'

He gave her a quick brotherly hug, his hands on her shoulders, pulling her briefly towards him, only slightly awkward.

Aly was aware of the naked curiosity on the faces of her friends. They didn't know who he was. They were just interested in the hot, clearly older guy who'd come and picked out Aly from the crowd. It had been pretty brave of him, she reflected, to run the gauntlet of tanned, hair-tossing teenage girls to come and talk to her.

And he *was* hot, she realized, wondering if her cheeks were flushing at the thought. He'd always been cute, but he was definitely cuter now – he had a short, spiky haircut – trendier than he'd been before – and he was stubbly all over, rather than just above his lip, as she remembered. He'd filled out a bit too – beneath the thin T-shirt he was wearing were muscles she was pretty sure hadn't been there before. He looked really nice.

'Do you want to get a drink?' Ryan gestured at the beer tent. 'Chat for a bit?'

'Um. Sure. Why not?' Her friends were beaming at her now, throwing each other knowing glances. Her face turned away from Ryan, she scowled at them briefly and grabbed her bag.

'I'll be back, you guys. In a bit . . .'

In fact, she hadn't – they'd talked all afternoon, and her

friends had been forced to come in search of her when they were ready to leave. Ryan grabbed two plastic glasses of beer from the tent while she waited outside, perhaps never more aware of being only seventeen, and then he'd directed her to a clear patch of grass on the boundary, away from most of the throng. He'd sat down, his legs crossed in front of him, and leant back on his elbows, facing the match but watching her. Every time bat hit ball, he glanced at the pitch, but his eyes would come straight back to her once the outcome became clear. She could see the scar on his ankle, from the cut he'd got in the tsunami, when his trouser legs rode up – about three inches long, it snaked neatly around the swell of the bone beneath the skin. She wanted to reach out and touch it.

Neither of them, it seemed, wanted to talk about Jake or Maggie and Bill. Aly was relieved. She couldn't just have a casual conversation about her brother. She'd never done it yet. To talk about him would be to let the dark clouds roll in across this beautiful day, and to let it be ruined. There'd be tears and snot, and everything would be ruined. A day never recovered completely. So she was glad when Ryan didn't ask, and she understood. They talked about Edinburgh, and his degree course. About her A levels and her UCAS application – her choice of Imperial. He asked lots of questions – the right ones. They discussed music and bands and television. Food. Stuff. All kinds of stuff. It was weird, because he'd been in her life for such a long time, but she'd always been on the periphery of his – she was his mate's little sister. This was easily the longest conversation the two of them had ever had, without any awkward pauses or silences at all. And the easiest. Actually it might be the easiest conversation she'd ever had with any boy . . .

Aly hadn't had a lot of boyfriends. Not really. She'd 'gone

out' with a few, but only in the way her friends had. She remembered Auntie Liv killing herself laughing once, when Liv had asked how you could tell, when you looked at a gang of teenagers, which ones were going out with each other. 'Easy,' Aly had answered, right off. 'The ones walking the furthest apart and not talking to each other – they're the couples . . .' There had been a few of those. Things had progressed a little, of course, but not much. She'd had a few slow dances, and a few snogs and a few Valentine's cards, and crushes. Nothing like the crush on Ryan, and nothing that made her lie in bed at night hugging herself and dreaming . . . The last couple of years, of course, she'd been concentrating on her exams. That and surviving the loss of Jake and the gradual disintegration of her family. Sports were her outlet, and her friends were her world. Not much room for boys. And boys were exactly what they seemed to her – her male contemporaries didn't seem to have a lot to offer.

But Ryan was different, of course. He was much more grown up. When her friends had rounded her up, ready to leave, it felt like it was too soon. He'd kissed her on both cheeks before she left. She could smell him. When he looked into her eyes, she was transported back to the moment two years earlier, when he'd put his hands on her skin. He had the same smile in his eyes. 'It's been good to see you, Aly. Really good.'

'You too.' For a moment they just looked at each other.

'Aly!' Her friend was calling, and the group were trailing away in the direction of the car park. 'Aly. C'mon . . .'

'I better go.' Reluctantly, she began to walk away, backwards. She didn't want to go.

'Are you on Facebook?' he called casually after her, almost as an afterthought.

She'd nodded. 'Yes. Aly Barrett.' She blushed. 'Obviously.'

'Obviously. I might friend you . . .' It was a little bit sexy, the way he said it, his smile . . .

And he had. Not the next day, but within the week. When she saw his friend request, she admitted to herself how much she'd been waiting for it – how much she'd hoped he'd look for her . . .

At home that night, she'd pulled an old lidded box from the top shelf of her built-in wardrobe. It had her old diaries in it – the ones she had kept religiously up until the time Jake died, when she didn't want to write any more. One a year since she was eight – there had always been one in her Christmas stocking, and nothing had seemed more exciting to her than the clean blank page on 1 January each year, with all its possibilities. She picked up 2003 and flicked through it, looking for mentions of Ryan. It didn't take long to find them: his name seemed to be on every other page, occasionally in the body of the text, but more often encircled in a heart on the top corner of a page, as though thoughts of him had permeated all other thoughts. The prose was entirely cringeworthy – flowery and over the top, full of declarations, sure in their permanence and references to eternity. What a difference three years made. She almost felt as if she was blushing, alone in her room, and within a couple of minutes, she'd snapped the diary shut, rolling her eyes at her younger self, and shoved the box back on to its high perch. Still, though, the bits she had read had reawakened something long forgotten, and Ryan crowded her thoughts as she lay in bed that night, much as they had done when she was fourteen years old.

From Facebook, she learnt, with a frisson of pleasure, that he was single, and, with a little disappointment, back in Edinburgh now. He had 456 friends – 457 with her name added. She scrolled down the list, scanning it for names she knew. He'd posted on her wall a couple of times, and she'd answered, trying not to seem embarrassingly keen. Within a few more days, they were writing to each other privately, and in a couple of weeks, they'd abandoned Facebook and were writing long emails to each other every couple of days.

It was on the emails that he first raised Jake.

Hi Aly. I've been thinking about you. And I've been thinking about Jake today. The Kaiser Chiefs were on the radio when my alarm went off this morning. 'I Predict a Riot'. Jake was singing that pretty much every day while we were away. He used to sing it before we went out at night. I was wondering what he'd have to say about you and me talking (?!) like this. He'd take the piss, I expect. I hope it's all right to write about him. I think about Jake at some point almost every day, to be honest. I didn't want you to think I don't. I didn't bring him up when I saw you at the cricket because it's too big a thing to start talking about on a sunny day at a cricket match with loads of people around. I hope you understood that – I felt like you did. I always thought that about you, actually. I always liked talking to you. I just couldn't do it much! I think about your mum and dad too. And Stan. I hear bits from my parents, though I don't think my mum sees too much of yours these days. Too hard, for both of them, I suppose. Mum says Maggie and Bill have split up. I'm really sorry. I don't want to stick my nose in, it's none of my business, but I guess it must have something to do with Jake. I remember when your dad went back to Thailand. It seemed weird to me at the time. But I think I get it now. I've been back too. Not to Thailand. I don't think I could go back to that exact place. I went to Sri Lanka for six weeks in the summer – before I saw you in August. I'd only been back a while. I don't know why I didn't say so. I volunteered with this group that were rebuilding an orphanage in an area that had been flattened by the wave. It was pretty intense. But it helped. I understood why your dad went. But maybe your mum didn't. Anyway. Like I said, it's none of my business. I'm just sorry. I still miss Jake. I don't know that I'll ever have a friend like him again. We just clicked, you know. Of course you know. You were always around. I wish I'd stayed in touch more afterwards. It was crap of me. It was too hard. Your mum's face, that time I came round – it killed me. How are you, Aly? How are you really, I mean? I know that school and stuff – exams – that's all going brilliantly. You were always really clever. I remember that. But how are you? You don't have to tell me. Maybe you have lots of people you talk to about Jake. But I don't. No one here even knows what happened. Not exactly a classic Freshers' Week conversation. It doesn't feel right to talk about him. And I don't like to talk about the day. But I suppose what I'm saying – if it doesn't make me seem entirely weird and creepy – is that you can talk to me . . . if you want to.

God – just read this back, and I sound like a creep. I'm not. Honest. Okay. Pressing send now . . .

Ryan x

Hi Ryan. Glad you pressed send. You don't sound like a creep. I don't talk about him much. Not to my friends either. They don't mean it, but they make a drama out of it and then they're all weird with me, once they know, so it's easier not to go there. I talk to my Auntie Liv sometimes, you probably remember her, but she still lives in Australia. I never talk to my parents about it. I know that drives my mum crazy. Dad too. They did split up – just after Christmas last year. Dad lives in Roehampton now. Stan and me see him quite a lot. I don't know if they'll get back together. Dad seems to be in better shape than Mum, to be honest. She asked him to leave, I think, and I think you're right – I think him going to Thailand was maybe the beginning of the end for them. Dad got into all this self-help stuff too. He read all these books about grief and he started going to counselling after he came back from

Thailand the second time. And Mum couldn't handle all of that. So Dad was happy to talk about it all the time, and Mum never wanted to. Stan was Stan – he got sad, but then he was fine, more or less. He didn't exactly forget about Jake, but maybe you know what I mean. He picks up on other people's emotions and takes his cue from them. He was having a really hard time at school, when it happened, but Mum moved him to a new place – he sort of has these special needs and he's somewhere that's better at dealing with them. And much, much happier, with loads of friends and everything. I sometimes wonder how much he'll remember Jake. I don't mean remember – he was eight when Jake died, so of course he'll remember – but he never really knew him, you know? And me? Sometimes I think I'm a bit of a mess. Sorry to admit that. I feel like I never got to properly grieve for Jake. I was too busy trying to be strong for my mum. And I think I did too good of a job. It was like I was invisible. Like my sadness wasn't as important as theirs. Because he was just my brother and he was their son. I got a bit lost. I hope that doesn't make me sound selfish. I never say that.

Aly x

It doesn't make you sound selfish at all. I get it. I completely get it. It's like there is this hierarchy of grief. Other people have more right to be sad than you. I remember at Jake's funeral, making these fists so tight so I could try not to cry. Your parents weren't crying, so I felt like I had no right. Didn't work, though, did it? I cried like a girl. It's not true, though, what you say. You felt what you felt. I'm sorry no one was listening. I'm listening now.

Ryan x

I was doing the same thing. I thought I was the only one. Mum cried all the time before and for ages and ages afterwards. I'll never know how she held it together at the funeral. I've never

tried to explain that to someone before. And the fact that
you understood it means a lot to me, Ryan. Thank you.
Thank you. ☺

Aly x

And that had been it. A dam burst. They had written to
each other every day since then. It wasn't always deep – not
always about Jake. They wrote about everything. Even if it
was just a line or two. It felt really grown up to Aly. Like
they were really getting to know each other. She checked
his Facebook page all the time. Sometimes there were pictures of him – in pubs and stuff. There were lots of girls in
the photos, and she stared hard to see signs of . . . she
didn't even really know what. Of something. But she didn't.
At the beginning of December, he'd written that he
wouldn't be home for a couple more weeks – he was working at some language school for a while, teaching English
to Japanese students, who came away with Scottish accents
– he was broke, he said, and desperate for the money. But
he'd definitely be home for Christmas. Then he'd invited
her to the twenty-first. It was a boy she didn't know, he said,
but he had a plus-one invite, and he wanted to take her.
Ryan hadn't asked her whether Maggie knew about their
correspondence and he didn't offer to pick her up before
the party. Not that she'd have let him.

The night had grown more and more significant in her
mind. When she'd seen the dress in Liv's suitcase, she'd
instantly wanted to wear it. She wanted to look sophisticated
and grown up, like the girls from Edinburgh in the Facebook
photos. Not like a naive sixth-former. She wanted him to see
her differently.

By the time the cab pulled up in front of the restaurant,
and she'd handed over the fare, Aly was bona fide nervous.

Ryan was waiting out front for her like he'd promised, looking improbably handsome in a suit and tie. It was only the third time she'd seen him in two years. It didn't feel that way after all the emails. But standing in front of him now, it did.

He squeezed her tighter. 'Of course you would, you sweet girl.'

They hadn't decorated his flat for Christmas at all. Stan had been outraged by the absence of a tree on a visit the previous week. Bill had play-pummelled him in the stomach and said he'd had no energy for his own decorations after the struggle with the tree for Maggie's house. There'd been no evidence of Carrie, either – Carrie returned to her own place when Bill's kids were due, taking everything with her except a few bottles and a woman's razor in the shower in Bill's room, where the kids never went. There were no Christmas baking smells and no King's College Choir singing carols. No cards, either. Bill didn't know if he could ever do it again – Christmas. It was too much wrapped up in his memories of losing Jake. The first year – the last time he'd been with Maggie at Christmas – she'd insisted on going through the motions. For Stan, she said, and for Aly. Even at the time, it had felt to Bill as though she was just clinging desperately to normality, but he went along with her, of course – part of the eggshell dance between the two of them. There was a tree with the usual painted macaroni decorations, and cards pinned on wide red ribbons around the picture rail and bunting strung above the Aga. Poinsettias in the hallway and Christmas-scented candles. A wooden nativity, bought at a Christmas market in Cologne years ago, on the hearth, where Stan took his turn to rearrange it, as his brother and sister had done before him. As it had always been. She'd done it with a dogged, single-minded determination he had given up trying to understand. There'd been a full-on Christmas dinner with bread sauce and chipolatas wrapped in bacon and two kinds of stuffing and none of them had eaten a mouthful of it. He remembered Maggie standing with her hands, white-knuckled, on the sink, her shoulders hunched, her back turned from him, desperate sadness in every sinew. Around 4 p.m., Bill had called a local shelter, and he and Stan had driven down there with the whole meal wrapped in tin foil and clingfilm. When they got back, Maggie had gone to bed, and she hadn't said another word for about eighteen hours, or let him hold her. She was blank – that was the only word he could attach to it. Blank.

Carrie came round on Christmas morning, after Bill had dropped Aly and Stan back with Maggie and Liv. Neither of them had gifts for the other. It seemed unnecessary. She was there when he got back, nursing a mug of coffee. Without words, Bill took the coffee from her, and led her into the bedroom. They stayed in bed for the rest of the day, holding back the tides with sex and too many glasses of wine.

In the morning, he made her scrambled eggs for breakfast, and waved her off, issuing a fatherly warning that she be careful on the icy roads and asking her to text him when she arrived safely.

'You sound like my dad.'

'Not your dad. Just a dad.' A Maggie memory flashed before his eyes. Whenever he had driven off with Jake, Aly and Stan, leaving her for some reason, she had said, 'You drive carefully. You've got my world in that car.'

Carrie pulled him back into the present. 'Absolutely not my dad.' She took his face in her hands and kissed him deeply, using the kiss to say what she knew he didn't want to hear out loud. Once he'd watched her drive away, he thought he might sleep again, but he couldn't. He put his trainers on and ran – four, five, six miles – too fast, so that his lungs screamed at him and he couldn't catch his breath. The roads were quiet and there were few people on the pavements. Back in the apartment, he stood under the shower until the hot water ran out. He ate a sandwich. At three o'clock he poured a glass of neat vodka and, once he'd hovered a little by the drawer, tried and failed to resist, he slipped a DVD he took from it into the player in the bedroom – and watched his son Jake come back to life on the screen. Jake in a paddling pool, big bellied, pouring water from one plastic cup into another, oblivious to Maggie's voice entreating him to look up and smile for the camera. Jake kicking a football. Jake running full pelt at the camera and shoving his face right up into the lens, backing away laughing. Jake caught unawares, gelling his hair in the bathroom mirror, kicking the door closed angrily. His boy. His beautiful boy. Tears streamed down his face and he couldn't stop them, noisy sobs piercing the silence.

An hour later, he was on Maggie's doorstep. Maggie must have heard his car. Maybe she was waiting to hear it. Before he'd rung the doorbell, she flung the door open, her eyes red rimmed and swollen, her hair wild around her head. Bill was only vaguely aware of Liv coaxing Aly and Stan back into the living room and softly closing the door on them before the two of them fell into each other's arms, sobbing quietly.

They stayed that way, clutching each other in the hallway, for a long time. Eventually, they stepped back from each other and looked at one another's stricken faces. Bill wiped a tear from Maggie's cheek, and she caught his hand with hers, pulling his fingers down to her mouth to kiss them with dry, chapped lips.

'I'm glad you came.'

'It's okay? I wasn't sure.'

'Of course it's okay. This is still your home, Bill. This is where you should be, today.'

There was no defiance in the statement. No anger and no question.

He looked at the poinsettias and the cards. 'It's Santa's fucking Grotto in here again, I see.'

Maggie half laughed, half sobbed. 'I don't even know why I do it.'

'Because you're you. How are the kids doing?'

Maggie shrugged and sighed deeply. 'We're all having a crappy day. Yesterday was okay – thanks to Liv. She worked herself to death – cooked the whole dinner. We did the whole . . . Christmas thing. But we all went to bed dreading today. And it's been . . . well, it's been as you might expect. It's horrible, Bill.'

'I watched the DVD,' he confessed. She knew, of course, which DVD he meant – they had one for each of the older kids, a montage of footage of their early years. There was much more footage of Jake than of the other two. There'd been more time. More focus. Two of them and one child . . . Bill had had them made for their thirteenth birthdays, laid over with sentimental songs about fathers and daughters or fathers and sons. Cat Stevens featured heavily on Jake's. Maggie found her copies excruciating to watch – of both of them, since each featured in the other's. They were from before, when everything now seemed golden. Watching Jake alive was a terrible trick to play on her brain.

Maggie smiled through pursed lips. 'I didn't. Crazy man. Three hundred and sixty-four better days in any year to watch that.' But her hand was on his arm.

'I miss him, Maggie.'

'I miss him too.'

'I miss everything about our life before he left us.'

'I do too.'

Bill leant against the wall and exhaled. 'And there's nothing else to say, is there?'

Maggie shook her head. 'Not today.'

Stan opened the door suddenly and ran at his parents. Liv and Aly were behind him. Bill hugged Stan to him with one arm and held the other out to Aly, who dissolved into tears and came to stand against him. Maggie threw her arms around all three of them.

Watching her beloved, broken family from the door, Liv hugged herself and silently thanked God that Scott was arriving tomorrow. This was hard. Too hard to do alone. She needed him here.

Chapter Eleven

Back at Terminal Four the next morning, Liv waited anxiously for announcements about Scott's flight, held in a circling pattern at a busy time and already twenty minutes late landing, stifling a yawn. Last night, Bill had stayed to have some supper with them and then hadn't left until ten or so. Liv had called him a taxi, because the three of them had drunk two bottles of wine, and Maggie and Bill had started with stiff drinks she'd poured for them and made them swallow. For an awkward moment, with Stan and Aly asleep together on the sofa in the TV room in front of *Die Hard*, she had been afraid Maggie might ask him to stay and that he might have agreed, so she'd bossily taken charge and called the cab. That wouldn't do either of them any good, and it wasn't going to happen on her watch. Lonely heartbroken people make bad decisions, she reasoned, and need to be protected from themselves. She knew Maggie had paced around downstairs most of the night because this morning the kitchen looked like Nigella Lawson was about to arrive with a film crew and start cooking, but when she'd opened the bedroom door a crack just before she left, Maggie was asleep in the middle of that ridiculous bed – with a postcode of its own – with her face deep in the pillow. Aly was too. Stan, of course, was raring to go – wide awake, fully dressed. Airports enchanted him, with their luggage trolleys, their parking machines and the ever-present potential for hot chocolate with marshmallows. Whereas it was Scott who enchanted her. Here he was, suddenly in front of her. Even after the long flight, he was beautiful to her – like an angel walking through the doors.

Scanning the crowd for her face, Scott broke into a wide smile when he saw her and walked fast towards her. Reaching her, he first smiled warmly at Stan and patted his shoulder, offering a hand to shake, at which Stan beamed and shook back vigorously. He was a good-looking guy, tall and broad and tanned, pushing back a shock of dark blond hair that flopped across his forehead. He was carrying two black sports bags – wildly unsatisfactory to Stan, who rushed off to procure a trolley he could load and push, which he then took charge of, skidding it towards the exit, alarmingly close to groups of people doing the same thing. With Stan distracted, Scott pulled his girlfriend into his arms and kissed her deeply, his hands moving to her face. 'Hello my darling girl. My God, how I have missed you. Was it really only ten days? I missed you so, so much.' He kissed her with each 'so'.

'It was twelve days. Me too. Felt like for ever.'

He kissed her again, a long, lingering kiss, and held her close to him, rocking slightly for a moment. When Liv pulled back at last, Stan, some distance away now, stopped by the lifts, was looking at them with disgust. Scott laughed.

'Okay then. Not a spectator sport, hey, mate? Got it.'

Back at the house, Maggie was up and dressed. She looked hollow-eyed with tiredness and too much crying, but she smiled warmly at him, taking his two hands in her own. 'Scott. At last. Welcome. We are so happy you're here.' Scott put his arms around her in a brief easy embrace.

'Glad to be here. And so pleased to meet you, Maggie. Should have happened a long time back.'

She acknowledged that with another smile. 'You're here now. Long enough flight for you?'

'Long boyfriend,' Liv answered. 'Far too long to be folded into one of those tiny seats for twenty-four hours. You should have seen him at the airport, trying to stretch himself back into the normal shape.'

Scott was arching his back ruefully, rubbing his coccyx. 'You're not wrong. There's a lot to be said for business class, I say.'

'You wish.' Liv stroked his shoulder affectionately.

Aly was up. Made-up and coiffed and dressed, to Liv's great surprise. That was a first for this time in the morning, during the holidays. She was beginning to do the tasks in the kitchen that her mother had asked of her – which was equally shocking. She was filling the coffee maker and putting jams and spreads from the refrigerator on the table without being nagged. She'd been okay, in general, Liv thought – these last few difficult days. She'd been more cheerful than usual, in fact, at least up until Christmas Eve. Liv had a sneaking suspicion her mood was somehow connected to the party she'd been to in her green dress before Christmas. She'd been a bit 'floaty' the morning afterwards – like Audrey Hepburn, coming back from the ball in *My Fair Lady*. She was waiting for Aly to tell her herself, but it bore the unmistakable hallmarks of boy-induced joy. It had been tragic to see it wither across Christmas, as they'd all pulled the great blanket of sadness over their heads for a while and blocked out the light. She'd been worried about Scott coming so close to 'the day', but now she could see that it was perfect. Stan was excited. Maggie would pull herself together to be a decent hostess, which would be distractingly helpful, and Aly . . . well, Aly was quite a revelation.

Aly felt a teenage girl's awkwardness in the face of this hunky boyfriend of her aunt's. He was really fit. He kept touching Liv – holding her hand or putting an arm around her shoulder as they leant against the kitchen counters, and once he spun her around into his arms and kissed her lightly on the lips. Aly felt a rush of something – jealousy, delight at the romance of it, something indefinable and hard to explain. That was what she wanted. Someone to spin her into his arms and kiss her, who wanted to be touching her whenever she was within reach. She thought of Ryan and last week's party, and warmth suffused her. It was odd – being able to think of someone and feel that way. She wondered if he'd call today . . . they hadn't spoken yesterday, and she'd like to talk to him . . .

'Alone at last!' Scott leant against the closed door of the guest room and pulled Olivia to his chest, landing kisses all over her face and neck. It started lightly, but grew instantly more serious as they touched each other after so long apart . . .

'Mmmm. Mmmm. You smell fantastic.'

Liv ran her fingers through his hair and kissed him back. He ran his hands down her back and cupped her bum, then ran them around the front, to her waist, and up under her shirt to stroke her breasts. Liv felt her knees go weak, but she made a slight attempt to push him away.

'Maggie's making lunch for us all.'

'Making. Not made. It'll be ages yet. She thinks we're unpacking. I'm more interested in undressing . . .'

'Scott! Come on . . .' He was still stroking her, insistent and soft, and Liv's resolve was weakening.

'I won't take long, I promise.'

'What about a shower?'

'I'm up for that. Whatever you like, as long as I can have you . . . now.'

Liv giggled, and ran her own hand down the front of his jeans, where he was hard and ready. 'I can see that . . .'

'Come on, Livvy. I've missed you . . .'

Reaching behind him, Olivia turned the lock on the bedroom door. She'd missed him too.

True to his word, Scott was quickly sated. He backed her over to the bed, the two of them pulling their clothes off as they went, and he was inside her almost before they lay down.

Liv marvelled at how his touch drove the sadness, the heaviness of the last few days, far away. For a few minutes, this was all she thought about. Him and her. How much she loved him. How good he felt. It occurred to her that he was her home now.

Afterwards, she lay in the crook of his arm waiting for her breathing to slow down, as he stroked her hair gently.

'God, I needed that. You feel bloody fantastic. I love you.'

'I love you too, Liv. How has it been?'

Liv shrugged. 'Like I said in the emails . . . some good, some bad . . .'

'How was yesterday?' He knew how she'd been dreading this anniversary of Jake's death. He'd hated that he'd been in the air almost all day – unable to speak to her. He'd tried – on his mobile, from Singapore – but his phone had been playing up and he hadn't been able to get through – not that it would have helped much, shouting down the line to her from a crowded terminal still pretty much on the other side of the world. He hadn't been able to get here fast enough, and now that he was here he wanted to look after her – to help. He felt like he knew all of these people. They loomed so large in Liv's life.

'Ghastly. Maggie pretty much cried all day. Aly spent a lot of time shut in her room. Stan didn't know what to do with himself . . . I cooked. We watched a lot of telly. At least – we sat in the room with the telly on. For hours. And Bill showed up in the late afternoon . . .'

'He did? I thought he'd be with . . . what's her name?'

'Carrie. Apparently not. It makes sense, I suppose, that he'd want to be here.'

'Was it okay?'

'He stayed and ate with us. I think the kids were pleased, in a way, that he was here.'

'And Maggie?'

'Maggie would have let him stay, I think.'

'Did he want to?'

'I don't know. I couldn't tell. I sent him home. They were both a bit drunk, by the end of the evening . . . not a good idea.'

'How do things seem between them?'

'I can't tell. Maggie's definitely gutted about this new person.'

'But you think it's serious.'

'Don't know that either. I talked to him, a bit, before . . . I think he's wary of me. Wary of upsetting anyone. Maggie especially.'

'Poor sod. I feel sorry for him.'

'And I don't?'

'I didn't say that.'

'I feel sorry for him. But he's not my sister. I can't worry about Bill. I've got enough on my plate with Maggie . . .'

'Hey. I know. I'm just saying. He's alone, isn't he? He's had the same loss as Maggie, but she's still here. She's got you. She's got the kids. What's he got?'

'He's got a Carrie.' She didn't mean to sound so sarcastic. Exactly like Maggie. It must be contagious.

'Maybe that's what he needs.'

Liv sat up. She didn't want to talk about it any more. 'And I need a Scott.'

'And you've got one. Special delivery.' Scott sniffed his armpit. 'Stinky. But here.'

Liv giggled and tried to roll him off the bed.

'I love him however he comes, but I'd prefer a more fragrant version, if that's okay. Bathroom's through there . . .'

Scott groaned. 'Can't I go to sleep . . . just for a while?'

'Absolutely not. That's the kiss of death for jet lag, my friend. Change your watch and get over it . . . I'm going to keep you up all day.' He ran a big hand across her hips, into the curve of her belly – it made her shiver.

'You are, are you? Up all day.'

She wriggled away. 'Not that kind of up. Awake. You can go to bed early. Sleep as late in the morning as you like.'

'No nap now though?' He pouted like a child.

'Absolutely not. Get up.' She nudged him towards the edge of the bed.

Conceding defeat, Scott stood up, and she gazed at him a moment before she started pulling her own clothes back on. He was a bronzed, beautiful god, so far as she was concerned. The cuddle, the chat, the sex, the orgasm – the very presence of him – made her more relaxed than she'd been since . . . since the last time she'd been with him. The sureness of her feelings for him, and her faith in his reciprocation, was like a cloak around her.

He picked up a towel from where it had fallen off the bed

on to the carpet and grabbed his washbag from the top of his open bag.

'Talk to me while I shave?'

'And I'll unpack you. I want to hear all about the outback Christmas . . .'

Chapter Twelve

'All the times I've been to London, I've never been here!' Liv was gazing at her surroundings, her face a study of distaste, her nose wrinkled.

'I've lived in London for twenty years and *I've* never been here either!' Maggie was laughing.

'So you've been lucky so far, then?!' Liv giggled.

'I came on a school trip once, I think,' Aly offered. 'But it seems pretty different . . .'

The London Dungeon was the second place on Scott's private whistle-stop tour of 'all things London Liv and Maggie could happily have gone the rest of their lives without seeing'.

They'd started the day a few hours earlier at Madame Tussauds. Utterly pointless, so far as Maggie and Liv could see, but Scott, Stan and Aly had seemed to enjoy it, posing for pictures with the inanimate statues, Stan flexing his muscles next to a waxy Sylvester Stallone as Rambo, and filing dutifully through each room, the sisters trailing behind them, whingeing gently to each other at how little resemblance most of the statues bore to their subjects.

This was infinitely worse. Waxworks were pointless but they weren't disgusting, and almost everything in this place was. They'd already been subjected to the Great Fire of London and Jack the Ripper. They'd broken into a trot to escape the 'real smells' the museum sprayed into their plague tableau, and covered their eyes in the macabre operating theatre as the 'surgeon' amputated a hand, fake blood squirting theatrically into the air.

Liv turned away, her hand across her mouth, laughing in spite of herself. 'That's absolutely disgusting. Completely gross.'

'Stop being such killjoys, you two,' Aly reprimanded them. 'You're like a pair of grumpy old ladies.'

Maggie and Liv made faces at each other. 'We *are* a couple of grumpy old ladies.' Aly was laughing and pointing at the boys.

'And look at those two – they're having a ball . . .'

At this point, Scott and Stan were sitting in Sweeney Todd's barber's chairs, waiting to be flung backwards as Todd's hapless victims would have been when their throats were cut. Stan had already done this twice, but each time he'd let out a high-pitched squeal of delight, and now he'd persuaded Scott to join him. The museum wasn't busy, and there was nothing to stop him, it seemed, from doing it repeatedly. They could be there until closing time.

Liv giggled. 'Oh, I've got to get a picture of that. Look at his face!' She leant forward, calling Scott's name to attract his attention as he hammed it up for Stan's amusement.

Maybe Scott knew what he was doing, Maggie reflected. She hadn't seen Stan this animated all week.

At lunch, which they'd eaten at Wagamama in Covent Garden, Stan – who had even been persuaded to try a noodle dish, though Maggie suspected that Stan's hero worship of Scott meant he would have eaten dog food if Scott had suggested he should – had exclaimed that he'd never known Central London could be this much fun.

'We come into town all the time, Stan!' his mother had reproached him. Not so much lately, maybe, but she'd always made regular trips with the kids – it was so easy.

'Yeah. And we go to boring old museums. Not these really cool places . . .'

Maggie didn't bother to launch into a defence of the Natural History Museum or the Science Museum . . . she knew she couldn't compete with Scott's selections.

Earlier in the week, unable to entice any of the three women in the house along, Scott had taken Stan off to the Tower of London, and the Imperial War Museum. After that, they'd ridden the top deck of a tour bus, even though it was freezing cold and intermittently hailing and they'd had the whole thing to themselves, bar a couple of disgruntled staff in yellow raincoats. Stan had declared it the best day EVER, with all the emphatic enthusiasm a ten-year-old boy could muster, and a sneezing fit.

At home there had been Xbox and carpet wrestling and football in the back garden. Scott had laughed heartily at Stan's childish jokes, appallingly delivered and often entirely devoid of a punch line at all, and watched the whole *Lord of the Rings* trilogy with him. Scott's passing knowledge of the Harry Potter films cemented his place as cultural legend, so far as Stan was concerned, and having a willing companion for a Tolkien marathon was the icing on the cake.

He'd pretty much saved them . . . all of them. And in so doing, attained something akin to godlike status in the house. Their very own Queensland knight in shining armour. Scott had arrived the morning after the blackest of days. He'd swept in like a breath of fresh air. It wasn't just Liv who'd needed him, Maggie realized. He knew their history, but he wasn't a part of it. He was Liv's future – that much was obvious to Maggie before she met him, but it became clearer and clearer with each passing day. Liv lit up like a firework when he was in the room. It touched Maggie immeasurably. The two of them had to be always holding each other – they sat knotted together on the sofa, his hand was always on her arm, at the table they sat so close their thighs touched. Scott kissed her all the time when he thought no one was looking. The kisses were often sweet and innocent, but sometimes full of lust and longing. It made Maggie envious. How long had it been, since she'd been this much in love, this happy? How long since her life had been as uncomplicated as theirs seemed to be now?

But he was doing them all good. He wasn't tainted. He arrived with fun on his agenda, and he was forcing them to have it with him. And it felt really, really good.

At night, after a dinner that always seemed now to be a collective effort – Stan peeling carrots, Aly laying the table – he would open a second bottle of wine, and once the table was cleared, they would all play a game. There was a long wide shelf in the family room of long-forgotten board games that would have been covered in Miss Haversham quantities of dust if it weren't for Maggie's avid night-time dusting sessions. But they hadn't been played in a long time.

Now they were playing two or three different games each night. Stan would go off and come back staggering under a pile of boxes of games he'd forgotten the rules to. He always insisted on reading the instructions himself and then translating them for the group, which often resulted in impenetrable directions, hilarity usually ensuing. Even Aly, who had been in the habit of late of sloping off to her room as soon as she could after dinner, was sticking around to help load the dishwasher and then, even more miraculously, to play with them. Monopoly, Operation, Jenga . . . Stan was like a dog with two tails.

There was music, too. Scott had plugged his own iPod

into the sound dock on his first night, and filled the ground floor with sound. He had an eclectic selection, with a heavy Australian bias – loads of Crowded House, INXS and Midnight Oil – and putting the device on shuffle was an interesting and unpredictable romp through the music of the last four decades. And from time to time, there was even just a little bit of dancing. One evening, he'd pulled Maggie up from the chair where she'd been watching him twirl Liv to dance to Boney M, and another, Stan tried to teach him to dance Stan's interpretation of a few hip hop moves to an old Run DMC number, with hilarious results.

It was lovely to have him there. So far as Maggie was concerned, and certainly so far as Stan was, he could have stayed for ever, shining light on the dark corners of their house and their lives . . . She didn't let herself think about it much, but when she did, she dreaded the New Year, when first one and then the other of them would leave.

Maybe Scott could have stayed for ever. But once at the London Dungeon was definitely enough. It was long dark when they finally emerged, and colder than it had been in the wintery afternoon sun.

'Are we really staying for the fireworks? It's not for hours . . .'

'We so are! We've still got to eat dinner. And the Eye first.' He'd booked fast-track tickets ages ago, as soon as he'd known he was coming.

Stan, in his excitement, could barely stand still. 'The Aquarium? That's right by the London Eye, right, Mum? . . . We might have time to do that too. Do you like aquariums, Scott? Can we, Mum? D'you think it'll still be open?'

'Great!' Liv frowned and wrinkled her nose. 'Another smelly attraction . . .' Scott put his arm around her and grinned at Stan.

Chapter Thirteen

Across town, Carrie had cooked supper for her and Bill in the Roehampton kitchen, and they'd eaten it from shallow bowls, cross-legged in front of the wood burner in the living room. In a garden or a park nearby, people had been setting off fireworks since it got dark much earlier in the evening, and now that midnight was approaching, it was getting noisier outside – snatches of music and loud, drunken laughter occasionally drifted up from the stairwell outside the flat.

'Are you sure you don't want to go out?' Bill worried, sometimes, that they didn't have enough fun. That their relationship might be too unhealthily private. They preferred to be in than out. They preferred to be alone than in company. There was a quietness about their relationship, a singularity that he was sometimes afraid might not be sustainable. It had been necessary, at first – when Maggie didn't know. But that wasn't true any more. They couldn't hide in here for ever. 'We're not too late – for the pub, or maybe we could drive to the river, watch the fireworks at midnight.'

'If you like.'

'What do *you* like?' He'd leant forward, gently banging fists on her knees.

'I'm happy here. With you.'

'Sure?'

'Totally sure. I'm exactly where I want to be. With who I want to be with.' Her expression threw him a challenge. 'Or whom. I never know which . . .'

By way of an answer, Bill kissed her. Gently at first, but then she'd groaned slightly and opened her mouth wider, her hands on the back of his head.

Bill pulled back, breaking off the kiss. And now Carrie's face was worried, her tone tinged with alarm.

'Is something wrong, Bill?'

'Not wrong, no.'

'What then?'

'I don't want to do . . . that. I mean, I do.' He stroked the length of her thigh. 'Of course I do. But first, Carrie, I want to . . . I want to talk. Is that okay?'

'Of course.'

'We haven't talked enough, I don't think.'

'Enough? You make a lot of rules; do you know that, Bill?'

'I just mean . . . I want to know you. I want you to know me.'

'That's what I want too.'

Now he felt foolish. She watched him for a minute, her head on one side. Carrie smiled a gentle, crooked smile.

'Okay . . . so . . . let's talk. Politics, religion, Beatles versus Stones . . . ?'

He laughed a small laugh. 'I'd like to talk about Jake, I think.'

They'd talked before about Jake's life – mostly on that first date. But he hadn't ever told her much about Jake's death. At group, he'd told the story, briefly and falteringly, but that was before she'd joined. It wasn't the point, anyway. How people died. It wasn't what they talked about mostly – though he knew that Margaret's daughter had taken an accidental overdose of crack six months before her twenty-second birthday, that Nicole's little boy had had meningitis that went undiagnosed for far too long by an exhausted junior doctor, that David's mother had battled emphysema in the bedroom next to his for six years and he'd gone to work each day for the last six months of it wondering if she'd be alive when he got home. It wasn't how people died that they were supposed to talk about, really. At least, that wasn't the main focus – the story of how you had ended up at group. It was about how people grieved. How they survived.

Carrie didn't speak. She refilled their glasses, then uncrossed her legs and curled into the corner of the sofa, her foot just behind Bill as he leant back. And then she waited. She couldn't see his face as he started speaking, directing his words into the fire.

When he began to speak, it was almost as though he was in the middle of a thought he'd already expressed. 'After it happened, Maggie's sister, Liv, flew in from Sydney and I flew out to Bangkok. We'd agreed, or at least I think we did, that someone had to go. I caught a plane with Ryan's dad – we knew each other a little, through school, Saturday mornings on the touchline, that kind of thing. Ryan was one of his friends, his best friend, but there'd been three of them – Matt, Ryan and Jake. They were all good mates. The two of them – Matt and Ryan – they were hurt but not badly. I think Ryan had a broken arm. They both had some cuts and bruises. I can't really remember. But nothing serious, you know? It was Matt who called first. We'd woken up on Boxing Day and we'd seen it all on the news, of course, like everyone else had and we'd been calling Jake's mobile phone like every five minutes. It was hopeless – you couldn't get through. I suppose everyone else was doing the same thing. I was using my own mobile phone because we didn't want to tie up the landline, in case he was trying to get through to us. Maggie was using hers too. I was trying, trying really hard, not to imagine the worst. The numbers were big, that much was already painfully clear, but still, you told yourself – I told myself – the odds were still good. That our boy was fine. He'd be helping out, if he'd been anywhere near – that's what I told myself. That's the kind of guy he was. People always say that, don't they, about dead people? But he was. He really was. Liv rang – it hadn't taken her long to realize Jake might have been caught up in it all. Matt and Ryan's parents – everyone was frantic to know what was going on.

'I don't think I believed, at that point, that he might not be okay. I mean, it was huge – you could see that. But it wasn't the whole country – it wasn't everywhere. And even if it had been, I figured he might not have been on the beach. We kept listening, on the news, for the name of the place he'd said he was. But, you know, plans changed – they were footloose and fancy free – they could have met people, headed somewhere else. They could have been anywhere. He could have been miles away. Even if . . . even if he'd been there – he was such a fast runner. Such a strong swimmer. Such a clever boy. He'd have figured it out. He'd have outrun it. He'd have climbed something. I just didn't let my head go there . . . you know . . . refused to think the worst. He'd be busy helping – that was all.

'Maggie was hardly speaking at that point. It was like she was frozen. A friend from down the road took Stan. Someone else – someone who knew, I suppose, that Jake was there – brought food in Tupperware. Not that we ate it. Made tea. Aly stayed with us. She was on the computer the whole time, trying to find out things that might not be on TV. It was a state of limbo. Hours and hours.

'Matt called his parents, of course – not us. He and Ryan were together. They'd lost Jake. They'd all three been together, we thought, when the wave hit, but they hadn't found him yet.

'Oddly, with hindsight, when Matt's father called me, I felt relief. Matt and Ryan were okay. Jake must be too. He'd have been separated from them, that was all. You could see it was chaos on the TV. Maggie couldn't switch the damn thing off. She was sitting glued to it. I think she was thinking she might see his face. But there was nothing else to do.

'Matt told his dad that he and Ryan would look for Jake. They'd go to the hospitals. The consulate or whatever . . . That they'd call when they found him. If he knew then – if he knew Jake was dead – he didn't tell his dad. Or his dad didn't tell us. I don't know. And I don't think I'd blame him. How would a kid – how the hell would a kid know how to even start to say that to me – to tell us that?

'Liv had booked a flight the moment we told her we'd heard from Matt. I think, at that remove, she'd always seen it a bit more clearly – less hope, more realism. They were starting to talk numbers by then. There were Europeans all over the news. They represented a tiny percentage of the dead but a huge proportion of the news coverage, of course. It's always like that, isn't it? As soon as I knew she was coming, that there'd be someone here with Maggie and the kids, I knew I had to go. It was killing me, not to be doing anything. Killing me. I literally thought I was going to explode or something, with the impotence. I never felt anything like that before. Ryan's father wanted to come too. Bring his boy back.'

Carrie went to the wood burner and opened the door to put in a couple more logs from the pile. Bill took a long drink of his wine. When she turned back, she smiled at him encouragingly.

'Maggie wanted me to go. She wanted me to find him. That's what she said, when I left. She looked at me and said, "Find our boy," like it was an order. I took the first flight I could, with just a passport and duffel bag of clothes. Aly made a poster with a picture of Jake on it and numbers to call. We made a hundred copies of it. I remember that we couldn't find any drawing pins, and Aly was really bothered by that. She said if I didn't have drawing pins, I wouldn't be able to hang up the posters. Tape wouldn't stick. She went to the copy shop up the road to buy drawing pins.

'I had no idea what I was going to find. Seemed like most people on the plane were going for the same reason, or maybe it just felt that way. I don't know what happened to all the holidaymakers who should have been on the flight, but they weren't. Or if they were, they weren't exactly in the holiday mood. I don't know. But it felt like we were all parents. Volunteers. It was a surreal flight. No one was watching in-flight films. No one was drinking wine with their meal. Eerily quiet. I remember the pilot coming on, saying he was sorry he couldn't fly us there any faster.

'We didn't need the posters, as it turned out. We were there – a plane, another plane, a long drive – within about sixty hours, I think. I'd lost track of time. I must have been knackered – I hadn't slept at all – but I was running on something superhuman. Once I was there, it felt sort of ridiculous. Why would I have thought I could find him? What possible good would I be able to do? I was just going to get in the way. How the hell could anybody have ever been found, in all that muck and sludge and debris? It was as hot as hell and it stank everywhere. Stank so you wanted to retch. Your eyes were seeing stuff, but your brain couldn't process it, you know? The landscape made no sense. It wasn't all the stuff everyone saw on the news – the fishing boats a mile inland and cars in trees kind of stuff. All that was there. It was more the sheer scale of it – stretching in every direction, as far as you could see. That didn't come across – not really – on the TV – not like it really was. By the time we got there, Ryan and Matt had been looking every minute since they'd left the hospital. And they had already found him.'

Bill's voice broke, and for a few moments he couldn't speak at all. His hands were fists on his knees. Carrie's heart ached for him.

He shook his head and his shoulders before he resumed speaking. 'It took me a long time to think of that as good luck, though I do now. I don't know how I'd have coped with what some people had to do – spending days and days peering under cloths to look at bodies that were already decomposing in the heat. Looking at thousands of bodies before I found Jake. They'd done that for me. God knows what it had done to them. And there were so many bodies, so many, that they never found. Those relatives never knew. You know what they say – that whenever there's a disaster, like the Twin Towers or something, that there are people who survive, and then they walk away . . . ? That would kill me. Not knowing. Couldn't do that.

'This was hard enough. There's nothing harder.'

Bill was crying now, softly, as he spoke. In the firelight, sitting beside him, Carrie could see tears shining on his cheeks. She hugged her knees. She wanted to hold him but she stayed where she was because she didn't want to stop him from speaking. To break the spell of what he was saying. He wasn't finished, she knew. There would be time to hold him, when he was done.

'They'd been bringing bodies to these tents. I don't know how the tents got there – who put them up. There were too many bodies, of course – they couldn't keep up. They were all under these white sheet things. They were so white; it seemed incredible in all that muck. They'd been trying to put the bodies in some kind of order. Tourists and locals. The boys took us to Jake, and he was under a white sheet too. He was too tall – his feet were sticking out as we walked up to him. I recognized his feet. Strange, isn't it? I didn't know I knew them that well. He was dirty, his hair was all matted. Huge cut on his head. Big bump. As far as anyone could tell, he'd banged his head on something and it had knocked him out and that's why he'd drowned. That's why he hadn't swum, or run, or climbed. It was as random and apparently as instantaneous as that. If what had hit him had hit him anywhere else, he might still be here. They were fine. That morning, all three of them, I suppose, had been sitting all in a line looking at the sea. The other two walked away just before it happened. To get something to eat. And my beautiful boy stayed, and because of that, he died.'

Words failed him now, and Carrie moved to sit behind him, one leg on either side of his arms. He relaxed and she felt his whole weight on her. She stroked his hair softly, his head lying in her lap. After a few minutes, he sniffed, like a child, and spoke again.

'Being busy helped, ridiculous as that sounds. I had things to do. I'm surprised I could put one foot in front of the other, but I could. I called the house. Liv answered the phone. I told her I'd found him. I'd done what Maggie had asked me to do. Maggie couldn't talk, so we didn't speak that first day. When she did come to the phone, the next day, it was weird, horrible. It was her voice I was hearing, but it wasn't Maggie. We talked about arrangements. I had to get him out of there. Get his body home. I don't even remember much of it, to tell you the truth. I think I was an automaton. I didn't cry once, the whole time I was there. Not even when I saw him.

'One hundred and fifty British nationals died in the tsunami. Something like that. One hundred and thirty-one of them died in Thailand. One hundred and thirty-one out of more than three hundred thousand people. You say that number, but you can't imagine it – not really. Three hundred thousand people. Almost all of the English that died were on holiday. A lot of them were young people, like Jake, but there were babies and children and old people too. Members of families. All kinds. It was incredibly complicated, dealing with Jake's body. It shouldn't be, should it? We just wanted them home. People were angry. Most people didn't go to claim a body – they had to wait in England, for the consulate and the British Red Cross to sort things out. It was the end of January before bodies started to come home. Kids who'd lost their parents, husbands whose wives had died, friends whose mates had been swept away. They all had to go back without them. A month. It was a bloody mess. It was extraordinary to keep having these moments, in the middle of it all, of thinking you were lucky. I was lucky I could get there. I was lucky there was a body. I was lucky I saw him before they put him in a coffin, because then they sealed the coffins. I suppose they had to. Maggie never saw him. And he was one of the first to come home. I fought for what I could. I did what I could.

'After I got back, it was still all busy. We'd had so many letters and cards. An overwhelming number. I did all of that – answering them. Maggie didn't want to. At last we had a funeral to arrange. We'd never gone to church, so we just found one. The biggest one we could find – we knew there'd be a huge crowd. There were hundreds of people there. Kids. Loads of kids. Girls crying. Boys too. Virtually his whole school, it felt like. It was a day without end, that one.'

Carrie smiled wryly. 'I wanted everyone at Jason's funeral to go away. We had sandwiches and tea afterwards, in the hall of the church, and I just didn't want to be there.'

'Me neither. It's supposed to be comforting, I think. But it wasn't. He wasn't their boy, all those people. I know they loved him, or at least they liked him. I know everyone was there to pay their respects, to say they were sorry. But he wasn't theirs. He was mine.'

Carrie nodded her understanding. 'I remember the vicar saying we were there to celebrate Jason's life, but I wasn't ready. I wasn't celebrating anything, I was mourning. It seemed like an outrage to me, him saying that.'

Bill nodded his understanding. 'Jake hadn't had a life. Barely. Jason neither. How could you celebrate what hadn't happened? He'd hardly started.'

'It was the end of the beginning, though. For me, anyhow.'

Bill shook his head. 'It was all one for me. It wasn't the end or the beginning. I couldn't reach Maggie. Right from the start, she shut me out. The night I came back from Thailand, I wanted – I needed – to talk about what I'd seen, but she wouldn't let me. I ended up sitting in the kitchen for hours with Liv and a bottle of Dewar's. She was the one who listened. When I went up to bed, Maggie wasn't there. She was curled up on Jake's bed. I knew she wasn't asleep but when she heard me at the door, she turned her back on me. "I can't, Bill." That was all she said. I don't even know if she knows she did, or if she knew, then I don't think she knew why. It wasn't deliberate, I know that. But if she'd been different, I wouldn't have gone back.'

'But you did go back, didn't you?'

'I couldn't stop thinking about it, once I got home. I kept ringing the Red Cross and giving them more money – you remember the news at that time, the stories. It was crushing. Heartbreaking. But I couldn't sleep. I'd been there – I'd seen some of it, smelt it, watched it, felt it. What we'd been able to do, as Westerners – it seemed obscene compared with the people who actually lived there. The numbers of people who were homeless. No schools. Hospitals washed away. Orphans with no one to take care of them. It was never-ending for them – just the start of years of hardship on a scale it is almost impossible to imagine. I couldn't get it out of my head.

'Still. I'd have stayed here. I'm not blaming Maggie, but if I'd been able to do something to help here, I wouldn't have needed to go back there to do it. Going back to Thailand was what saved me, I think, those first months.

'I took a sabbatical from work. I had good people working for me – people who could keep it all ticking over. That was all it needed to do. And I went out there and volunteered. I stayed four months. Sometimes I think my marriage was over by the time I got back, and the rest was just us limping on in denial. Ending things would have just seemed like heaping hurt upon hurt. We didn't go there. But Maggie couldn't forgive me. Aly couldn't even look at me. Even Stan.

'I only saw how incredibly selfish it was after the event. It wasn't like I thought I was doing some fantastic selfless thing at the time. I just didn't feel like I had any option. I've never worked so physically hard in my life. I worked my nuts off – all day. Shelters, schools, hospitals – wherever they needed help. I ate when I was hungry and I slept when I dropped. For four months.'

'Do you still think of that as selfish?'

'I don't know.'

'Does Maggie?'

'Don't know that either.'

'How was she when you came back?'

'Distant. Remote. Everything I did seemed to move us further apart. I started reading books about losing someone – anything I could get my hands on. I'd been a stranger to the self-help section in the bookshop before then. I don't even remember what got me started. I was just desperate, I suppose. I started trying to understand my grief. To work with it. That made it worse. We were definitely in our "chronic dysfunction" phase. From outside it must have looked like we'd found a new normal. Aly was still doing well at school, though that always spooked me a bit – it seemed so controlled. Maggie had thrown herself into the rescuing of Stan, I was back at work . . . but my home was full of dark, deep depression. It was like a maze neither of us could find our way out of.' He shrugged, the gesture full of the hope-lessness he was expressing.

'In the end . . . we turned in different directions. She asked me to leave, in the end. And I wanted to go, in lots of ways.'

'But stay, in others?'

Bill looked directly at her. For the last twenty minutes, half an hour, he'd been talking at the fire. He'd almost forgotten that she was there, and he certainly hadn't been thinking about how she would feel about what he was saying. She'd been crying too, he saw, though he hadn't been aware of it while he spoke.

'Stay, in others. Yes.'

'And go back? Do you think about going back?'

'I did. For a long time.'

Carrie held her breath. When Bill spoke again, his tone was one of surprise, as though it was the first time the thought had occurred to him.

'I don't now.'

Chapter Fourteen

The day before he returned to Australia, Scott asked Maggie if she'd go for a walk with him. Stan was with Bill, having gone as prearranged though slightly unwillingly, since it meant leaving Scott, and Liv had promised Aly a few hours on Oxford Street with her Christmas money. Shopping was shopping whichever hemisphere you did it in, he declared, and he hadn't gone with them.

Maggie drove them to Richmond Park, and the two of them, well bundled up, tramped through the frosty grass at a trot to ward off the biting cold, their hands buried deep in their pockets and their heads down out of the wind. They didn't talk much at first, both almost out of breath at their pace.

After about 15 painful minutes, Scott turned to her.

'Bugger this. Amnesty International would recognize this as actual torture of an Australian citizen. We're not made for these temperatures. Is there a pub around here? I could use a drink . . .'

'I thought you'd never ask,' Maggie retorted. 'I don't know what the hell we're doing out here in the first place. It's absolutely bloody freezing. Follow me . . .'

A few minutes later, the two of them were huddled in the booth of a pub she hadn't been inside before, vigorously rubbing feeling back into their fingers and nursing whisky macs. There was a roaring fire, but it was already well surrounded, and they'd taken the only free booth, too far from its warmth to feel much benefit. Maggie's scarf was still around her neck.

'I asked you to come for a walk because I wanted to ask you something, Maggie.'

'And you couldn't have done that in front of the fire at home?!' But she was smiling at him, already aware he may have had an ulterior motive for separating her from the herd, as it were.

He acknowledged her with a nod. 'I was nervous. I *am* nervous.'

'Don't be. I don't bite. Much.'

Scott laughed, but he ran his finger around his collar nervously. 'Okay. So. I want to ask Olivia to marry me. I suppose I want . . . well, if not your permission, then your blessing.'

Maggie's eyes had filled with instant tears, though she had known this was coming. 'Scott – you can have both. Of course! I'm thrilled for you both. I really am. Really . . .' The tears spilt down her cheeks, and Scott pulled a handkerchief out of his jeans pocket. 'Oh God. Waterworks. Sorry. I'm like a rheumy old man these days – they're never far away . . .'

'Here.' She blew her nose hard and dried her eyes.

'Don't mind me.' She took his hand and squeezed it warmly. 'Happy tears.'

'Really?'

She put her hand on his cheek. 'Only happy tears, I promise. She loves you, Scott. Such a lot. I know how much she wants this. And I can see that you love her. It's perfectly obvious.'

'More than I knew I could.' His voice was choked with emotion too.

We all can, she thought. We can all love more than we

thought we could. More than we thought was possible. It's what makes us so happy and it's what makes us so vulnerable.

'You think she'll say yes?'

'Hell, yes. You'll be lucky if she lets you get to the end of the question. She'll chew your arm off. You must know that.'

'I think so. I don't want to be cocky.'

'You haven't got a cocky bone in your body, Scott. I haven't known you long, but I know that much about you. You're a great guy.' She mock-punched him in the arm.

'I so want you to think so.'

'And I do. Don't think Stan's quite made his mind up about you . . . but I have.' She laughed. 'Did you talk to our dad?'

'I will. Of course. But you first. I had to ask you first. You're Liv's world, really. I know that she cares more what you think than anybody else alive. Cares more about you than anyone, too.'

'But I'm going to have to share top billing now, right?' She cocked her head at him and smiled.

'I'd never want to come between you two.'

'I'm *kidding*.'

'But I know she's torn. She's been torn the whole time I've known her.'

'Torn?'

'Between Australia and here.'

'Liv made her decision years ago. She's an Aussie, through and through. She doesn't want to live here.'

'She wants to be near you. Since Jake, especially. She worries about you so much, you know.'

'I know. I don't want her to. I want her to live her life.'

'I do too. Marrying me means that she'll be living it in Australia.'

'And that's the right thing, Scott.'

'Will you tell her that?'

'I don't need to. She knows.'

Scott looked at his glass. He wasn't sure if Maggie really understood how invested Liv was in her happiness. Or if Maggie knew how much she leant on her sister. How Liv was bent and bowed with it. It wasn't a conversation for now. He knew that. But he'd seen it. Firsthand now – instead of a feeling garnered from listening to half of a thousand phone conversations – he'd seen it. Maggie leant and Liv held her up. And he held Liv up. And he didn't mind doing it. His love wasn't conditional and his feelings were real. This was the woman he loved, and this was her family, her life. But he wished it were less . . .

'Have you asked her yet?'

'No!! That would make a mockery of this whole tradition thing, wouldn't it?'

'Bought a ring?'

Scott reached into his jacket pocket and pulled out a small black box, which he handed to Maggie. She closed her hand around it.

'I bought it when I was in town on my own for a few hours the other day. When you were at that chick flick. I found the Burlington Arcade – that's where I wanted to go. I'd read about it online.'

'I don't want to see it before she does. That's not right.'

'You have to! I need to know if you think she'll like it! I could change it . . .'

Maggie smiled at his doubts. 'If you chose it, she'll like it.' But Scott was already opening the lid. Inside was a ring she guessed to be antique – Edwardian, she thought – a sizeable diamond in an unusual ornate platinum setting.

'It's beautiful! Gorgeous. I think it is exactly the kind of thing she'd have chosen.'

'Really?' He looked like an eager schoolboy.

'Really. She'll love it. When are you going to ask her?'

'At home, I figured. Once she gets back.'

Maggie squeezed his hand.

'Listen to me, Scott. I know Liv worries about me. I know she loves me and the kids. God knows, I love her too. But she needs this. You and her – you'll be a family now. A family of her own. We'll always visit, and she'll always be my sister. But she needs to do this, for herself. You're her future. I see that, and I'm so glad you've been here and I've had the chance to see that for myself. I don't need to ask you if you're going to take care of her and love her and not hurt her, because I've met you and come to know you a little bit and I know the answers already. I am so happy for her.'

He kissed her cheek.

'Thank you, Maggie.'

When he went to the bar to get another drink, she sniffed hard, and bit down on her lip. She meant every word she had said to him, but now her chest hurt so much she felt it was crushing her heart and lungs. And she didn't even quite understand why.

Chapter Fifteen

New Year's Eve 1984

Bill Barrett met Maggie Walker in the bar of a sailing club on Sydney Harbour. He was almost nineteen, and she had turned seventeen the summer before.

Bill was six months into a round-the-world trip between school and university. He'd been left a few thousand pounds by an unmarried elderly great-uncle he'd barely known, and encouraged by his parents, or by his father at least, he was using some of it to travel before he went to college to study chemistry the following autumn. His dad had done National Service and was definitely of the type who mourned the fact that Bill's generation wouldn't. His mother hadn't left the country until a Round Table/Ladies' Circle cultural exchange weekend to Amsterdam when Bill had been seven. He always had the feeling she felt she'd seen enough then. She certainly hadn't been in any rush to go abroad again, preferring windswept English beaches and the Lake District to more exotic climes. It was part of what had split them up, Bill figured – her resolutely unadventurous nature. His parents had divorced when he was eight. He was their only child, and he'd stayed with his mum, of course – to have done anything else at that time would have been strange. He and his mum stayed in the home he'd been born in, while his dad got a place nearby. He'd rather have been with his dad, and spent whatever weekends and holidays that he could with him. Bill's dad had a building firm – a pretty successful one – and

Bill worked with his father from a young age, learning the various trades. He loved that – being outdoors most of the time, doing something practical with his hands, making things – the camaraderie of the work gangs, eating lunch, smoking fags and drinking tea in their breaks, looking at the girls. It was at his mother's insistence that he was going to university. He'd have preferred to go straight to work for his dad, and he wasn't always sure that his dad didn't feel that way too, though he was a little too frightened of Bill's mother to say so. The windfall was a blessing – it bought him a little time and a little freedom.

Bill was having more fun than he'd ever imagined possible. He already barely remembered the boy he'd been when he set out from his landlocked, provincial hometown the previous July. He'd started out with a friend, but they'd parted ways, amicably enough, in the US, a couple of months earlier – his mate Charlie had gone north, to Canada, and he had headed far south, landing first in Perth and travelling east, via Adelaide and Melbourne, across to Sydney. He'd been in Sydney for a few weeks, sleeping on the sofa of friend of a friend in a large ramshackle Victorian house in Paddington, a southern suburb of the city. He loved it here. He loved the weather, and the water and the people. The house he was staying in played host to an ever-changing cast of travellers and visitors, and there was always someone to go out for a beer with, or catch a cheap dinner at one of the extraordinary Thai cafes that lined the streets. Everyone was broke, or at least on a tight budget, and everyone was out to have fun – the irresponsible kind that was the preserve of transient youth. He'd scored a job in the restaurant at a sailing club just across the Harbour Bridge – washing dishes in the hot kitchen at first, but then, after a few weeks, when he'd proven he was reliable and once he was liked and known by the other staff, he was promoted to serving at tables. It was always busy – full of laidback, easy-going Australians making the most of their leisure time – never wanting to be far from the water that seemed to define this beautiful city.

Bill was surprised to discover that he felt at home here. England, his parents, and his precious place at university seemed a million miles away, and he often wondered, late at night, as he headed home after a shift, whether he'd be able to leave when the time came. He was supposed, in January or February, to head north to the Barrier Reef. He wanted to learn to scuba dive. He had some people to ring, one in Townsville and a couple of names of people who might know of jobs on some of the reef resort islands. From there he would hit Malaysia, he reasoned, Thailand, Sri Lanka . . . India, if he'd time and enough money. Be home sometime in August, then get back to life as it was going to be. But now he wasn't sure . . . wasn't sure it would be enough. His life here was so gloriously Technicolor – a world all light, and bright, all turquoise sea, cobalt sky and yellow sunshine. With a soundtrack of laughter and music. Full of freedom and possibility and fun. When he fast-forwarded his imagination, the sun went behind a cloud and life looked grey and mono-chromatic. He wasn't sure any more . . .

And then he met Maggie.

She was part of a large table of diners – a family group, he thought – who arrived to eat late on in the evening. He hadn't seen her here before – he knew he would have remembered the dark curls and the deep dimples, the white, even teeth. She was tanned a deep golden colour and slender and – he thought – quite extraordinarily attractive. Bill wasn't bad-looking himself – he'd never had to work particularly hard to attract female attention, but he realized he felt an unfamiliar shakiness as he took her order and brought her and her companions iced water. His heart was beating fast. She was wearing a small halter-top in a shimmery fabric and she had the most beautiful back. Her shoulders were broad and muscular and tanned, and the smooth glossy curls were cut in a short, almost old-fashioned bob, high on her long neck. A soft whorl of hair curled down the vertebrae on her neck to the top of her back, and a perfect Orion's belt of tiny freckles lay across her left shoulder. He badly wanted to stroke it – maybe even kiss it. It was fantastically disconcerting. He spilt a little water as he refilled her glass. She laid her still folded linen napkin across the spill quickly and quietly and smiled conspiratorially at him. Back at the bar, he knew he was staring at her while he waited for Jed, the barman, to fill the bar order. He was surprised.

She looked directly at him again when she ordered – mussels to start, and lamb. The diners at the sailing club were not unfriendly, but he had become accustomed to a certain servile invisibility. This girl looked into his eyes. She smiled broadly, and her eyes twinkled. While he was serving at other tables, he could feel her eyes on him, and each time he caught her gaze, she smiled again.

He concentrated on not making any more mistakes all evening. But his heart rate didn't slow much. At one point, she went to the loo, and he realized that she was tall – almost as tall as he was, with endless slim legs. If this girl wasn't a swimmer, she ought to be – she had the perfect body for it.

Midnight burst into a cacophony of poppers, erupting streamers, champagne corks and colour as everyone moved to the terrace to watch the spectacular fireworks across the harbour, in front of the Opera House. He looked for her, but couldn't spot her head amongst the crowd. He felt an absurd surge of disappointment. Suddenly, though, she was beside him, almost exactly his height, her big eyes shining and her mouth slightly open.

'Happy New Year.' She grinned at him broadly, speaking as though they were friends, not strangers.

'You too.' He nodded and smiled shyly. At that moment, to his profound mortification, he couldn't think of anything cool to add and his own silence amidst the din made him want to squirm.

She giggled. 'You always this chatty?'

Bill shrugged. 'I think you make me nervous.'

'Good. I like the sound of that.' She looked almost smug. She reached out her hand. 'I'm Maggie.'

He took it, soft and slender, in his own. 'Bill.'

'Bill.' She repeated it speculatively.

From the direction of the water, someone called Maggie's name. He was still holding her hand; she pulled his arm so that he moved forward, leant in and kissed him briefly on the cheek. She smelt powdery and sweet, the smell strangely, intoxicatingly at odds with the simple strength of the way she looked. While her mouth was close to his ear, she half whispered, 'Are you here every day, Bill?'

He nodded. 'Apart from my day off.' Then, hearing something like desperation in his voice, he continued, 'We don't know our days off until a week ahead . . .'

God. Shut up. Shut. Up.

'I'll have to take my chances, I s'pose, then.' Was she laughing at him? If she was, it didn't feel mean. It felt warm, and somehow, stupidly, familiar and fond.

And then she was gone . . .

But she didn't keep him waiting for long. Three days later, she showed up in the bar in the late afternoon, while Bill, who had worked the lunch shift, was polishing wine glasses ahead of the evening service and watching the clock.

The shyness and awkwardness he had felt on New Year's Eve evaporated when he saw her, because this time he knew she'd come for him. He poured her a glass of sparkling water and she waited for him to be finished, watching as he held the goblets up to the orange glow of afternoon sunshine, checking their shine. The smile was as warm and as ready as he remembered it. He hadn't heard the laughter clearly before – Maggie's laugh was deep and throaty, a classic dirty laugh, ribald and fruity.

She was Australian, of course. She'd been born in Newcastle – a town about 100 miles north of Sydney, she told him, though she had moved to the city with her parents, and her brother and sister, about six years earlier. They lived in Wollstonecraft, a northern suburb. Her dad was an accountant who worked for David Jones, the big department store chain, and her mum was a nurse at the Sydney Children's Hospital.

She was in her last year of high school, due to finish that summer, though she claimed school didn't interest her and she'd no idea what she wanted to be. He had been right in his assessment that first night – she was a swimmer. That was her thing, she said. As she talked, it became apparent that their daughter's swimming career had had more than a little to do with her parents' decision to relocate the family. She'd been competing for Newcastle and New South Wales even as a seven-year-old.

'How good are you, exactly?' he asked.

Maggie blushed and looked down for a moment. 'Quite good.'

'Be a little more specific! Do you still swim for New South Wales?'

She nodded and held his gaze.

'What – there's more?'

She nodded again, slowly.

'You swim for Australia?'

'I'm trying . . . I mean, I have . . . But I mean, the main goal – that's got to be Seoul, in '88.'

'My God! Really? You're good enough to swim in the Olympics?' He was incredulous. 'You're not winding me up?'

Maggie laughed. 'No, I'm not "winding you up". I hope so. It's all I've wanted, ever, really. I live and breathe swimming. It's pretty much all I think about.'

Bill shook his head. He hoped that wasn't quite true. Since for the last few days *she* had been pretty much all he'd thought about.

'That's amazing.' He was suddenly painfully aware that he'd never been particularly dedicated to anything much. 'What stroke?'

'I do most of them, but butterfly is my thing. Two hundred metres, specifically.'

'I can't swim two metres butterfly.'

'Everyone says that, until they've been taught. Not as hard as it looks.'

'False modesty?'

'No. I'm saying anyone can do it. I never said anyone can do it as fast as I can . . .'

'And how fast is that?'

'I'm around 2:20 at the moment. Need to shave a few seconds off that.'

'To win?'

'To qualify.'

Bill whistled.

'Gold medal this summer went to a 2:06:90.'

'And that was an Aussie?'

She shook her head. 'We got silver. 2:10:56.'

'You just have all these numbers in your head, do you?'

'Olympic geek. Sorry. Best to cop to it straight off. Can't exactly hide my obsession.'

'So you're practising what, how many times a week?'

'Every day.'

'Blimey. Every day.'

She nodded. 'Five thirty a.m. Every day. For two hours.'

Bill shook his head. 'And that's just the swimming . . .'

'There's more?'

'Weights. Running . . .'

He was gazing at her now. 'You are so out of my league, Maggie.'

Within a week or so, out of his league or not, he was setting his alarm for 6 a.m. and meeting her at the pool. He liked to get there early so he could watch her from the viewing gallery. Not just so he could admire the way she looked, although that was a part of it. Even in her distinctly unsexy racer-back navy-blue regulation swimsuit and a rubber swim cap, her face obscured by goggles, she was gorgeous. There was no question that she was incredibly fit, but her musculature failed to entirely dominate her feminine form, and small round breasts swelled beneath the suit. And she had a great arse. There was no apparent end to the tan, and he began entertaining daily fantasies about the white bits. But it was her attitude that fascinated him most. He thought he could watch her all day. She just kept going. She'd swim, rest, looking at her times, then swim again. Up and down. Utterly focused.

Well – not quite. Bill being there was distracting, and being distracted was new for Maggie. She was surprised how quickly she'd fallen for Bill. The whole thing was vaguely surprising to her, actually. The wanton way she'd sidled up to him that first night, at the club . . . that was so not her style.

She was much shyer than that, usually. If she was bothered at all, which she usually wasn't. It was something about the night and the boy . . . and it had felt sort of good, flirting like that. She'd been a bundle of nerves when she'd shown up a few days later – it had killed her not to show it.

And now he was practically stalking her. And she liked it. She liked it very much indeed.

Chapter Sixteen

January 2007

Liv had come armed with sneakers and Lycra. She'd forced Maggie to run with her every morning, except the morning Scott arrived. It had been like pulling teeth the first couple of times, but they'd found a rhythm surprisingly quickly. Maggie had the residual fitness of a young athlete – never far away.

Early starts and late nights: Liv's recipe for deep sleep. It was working pretty well so far, especially if she medicated with Pinot noir as well. Maggie looked better. Felt better too, most of the time. Liv allowed herself a tiny measure of pride.

But it was 11 a.m., three days after Scott had left, and Olivia and Maggie were still ensconced in the giant bed. Sometime around 3 a.m., Maggie had woken, damp and breathless, from the end of a horribly familiar nightmare and to the beginnings of a relatively unfamiliar hangover, the result of an ill-advised second bottle of wine at dinner the night before – a really rotten combination. She'd come round crying, and Olivia, sleeping in the guest room at the top of the house, had evidently heard her padding to the bathroom, still heaving with a sob she couldn't help. Five minutes later, as Maggie sat wide-eyed in bed, with the duvet pinned to her sides by stiff arms, trying to convince herself that the palpitations she was experiencing were the result of too much alcohol and not the precursors of a heart attack, Liv had come in with mugs of tea and two paracetamol. She'd shaken her head in mock shame. 'Look at the state of you. Thank God the children aren't here to see this . . .' Aly had slept at a friend's house after a party, and Stan was with Bill. Which was, of course, the only reason she'd let Liv talk her into the second bottle in the first place. It was their fault. Hangover logic.

Maggie had groaned. 'Don't make fun of me. I think I'm actually dying.'

Olivia harrumphed. 'Dying swan, maybe. You're not dying. You're hung over. Hell, I look like you most Saturday mornings. Well, maybe not quite that bad . . . But not good.'

Maggie put her head in her hands.

'Hurts.'

'Take these, lightweight.' Liv tipped the pills from her palm to Maggie's proffered hand and watched while her sister took them with a scalding mouthful of tea. She pushed Maggie's hair back behind her ears and ran two thumbs under each eye, drying the last tears. Maggie sniffed.

'Thanks.'

'Move over. I'm coming aboard. Good job Scott's gone. I'd have to get him in here too, and that could be hard to explain. And a bit weird.'

They'd always done this. Once upon a time, it had been the two of them in one or the other's narrow single bed. Different bed – same comfort. Liv had talked, Maggie listening with her head back against the headboard and her eyes closed, and eventually the pounding had eased and she talked back, and then they'd laughed about nothing in particular – silly stories they told each other about when they were kids, back in Oz. It was such a safe territory – that time. The memories were good, bathed in the soft sepia glow of distance and nostalgia.

Sometime around dawn, Liv put a DVD in the machine – *Mr Blandings Builds His Dream House* – but they were both asleep before their favourite scene, the one where Mrs Blandings is trying hard to describe the perfect yellow to the more prosaic house painter – and they didn't stir again until after ten, when Maggie playfully kicked Olivia under the duvet and whispered, 'More tea, vicar . . .'

Now the two of them were sat propped on too many pillows, with the Sunday papers spread around them in a crumpled, newsprinty mess that would have driven her husband crazy. Bill had always – for ever – had the *Sunday Times*, the *Sunday Telegraph* and the *Mail on Sunday* delivered, and she had never changed the order, though there were many sections she didn't read until much later in the week and many not at all. Not since Jake died. Her capacity to read bad news had disappeared. When she read things that previously would have made her sad, they now threatened to engulf her entirely. She could find herself in floods of tears over the plight of strangers. Jake had made her that vulnerable. Losing Jake. There had been a brief tussle over the magazines and the style section, but now they were both concentrating. Liv had brought tea in a teapot this time, and it was between them on the mattress, on a tray with a carton of milk and a plate of chocolate HobNobs. Maggie was wearing her reading glasses on the end of her nose, and a very old grey cardigan of Bill's. Olivia was far more glamorous, still golden from her Australian springtime, still pert and bouncy under a strappy satin nightie. Radio 4 was on in the background. At some point, Liv giggled at something she read but didn't look up. Maggie looked over at her sister and realized that here, now, this moment with Liv was the happiest she'd been in as long as she could remember. Maybe happy wasn't the word. The most at peace. She felt really calm and still.

'It's all better when you're here, you know?' Her voice

broke at the end of the sentence, though she had tried hard not to let it.

Liv reached over and squeezed her hand. 'I know.'

'It's been fun.'

Liv nodded. 'It has.'

Maggie didn't return to her newspaper. She gazed at the window. For a moment, she tried not to express what she felt, thinking about what Scott had said, but she couldn't help herself.

'I'm lonely, Liv.'

'I know that too.'

'I've been such a stupid cow.'

'How so?'

'I don't mean about Bill. Everything else. I've shut myself away. Closed myself off. I've isolated myself. I thought it was what I needed. I thought it was what I could manage. But now I'm lonely.'

'Your friends are all still there, I bet. Work could still be there, if you wanted . . .' Work wasn't something Maggie needed to do for financial reasons – Bill had made it clear from the start that he would continue to fund all their lives as he always had done – but maybe, maybe it was something she needed for other reasons . . . 'You could . . . I don't know . . . get back on the horse, Maggie. Re-activate. Couldn't you?'

Maggie shrugged. 'I don't know.'

'You could, sis.'

Maggie didn't answer. She sifted through the bits still unread and picked up the home section of the *Sunday Times*.

Liv was reading the classifieds. She'd always loved that section of English newspapers – there was nothing quite like it in the *Sydney Morning Herald*. She pored over it now – the Court Circular, with its innumerable small engagements, each one an hour or two of a royal's precious time but a year in the planning for the organizers. The births – posh kids with a string of daft names being born at the Portland Hospital. Especially the deaths – written proof that everyone had a story, and, apparently, everyone battled long diseases courageously and not, as she suspected she might, self-pityingly, angrily and with floods of tears. She didn't understand the *in memoriam*s. Why might you need to share with the masses that you still missed Frank every day, though he'd been dead for fifteen years?

This morning one advert in particular caught her eye.

Mature, healthy, solvent lady with own house seeks room in busy family home, in exchange for cooking, light housekeeping, company and, hopefully, some childcare.

The ad gave no names or other details, just a PO box number for written replies.

Later, hunger drove them down to the kitchen for bacon sandwiches. Maggie went downstairs to get them started. Liv took the section of the paper with the ad and put it on her bedside table. The beginnings of a random, bizarre idea were sprouting in her brain.

Chapter Seventeen

Bill knew he had to tell the kids about Carrie. He was tempted to start with Stan, who would no doubt be easier to tell. But that wasn't fair, and it wasn't brave. He had to tell Aly first.

Their relationship had been the most difficult since he left. Since he went to Thailand, in the first year after Jake. She'd been angry with him – he knew that. But she'd never blown up at him and never let him make her talk about it. The thaw had been gradual and, since then, sometimes he still felt her anger. He tried to remember that along with everything else that played into their relationship, Aly was a teenage girl. It gave him some comfort to know that Maggie struggled with her too. Living apart didn't help. With Stan, he'd a long list of shared interests that were no different from before – they still went to Stamford Bridge, and to Twickenham. He'd put more energy than before into playing games with Stan, too. Stan was a mainline reminder of Jake. The guilt he'd first felt when Stan's dyspraxia was diagnosed had been partly assuaged by hour upon hour on the tennis courts and in parks, tossing tennis balls and kicking footballs together. He'd found patience he hadn't known he possessed. Maggie sent difficult school projects or homework to Bill's house these days – Bill found he could manage to spend real time helping Stan with number problems or science assignments. They were reading *The Hobbit* now, too. They took turns to read to each other, at Bill's insistence. It was taking them for ever, but they were both dogged and determined to stick with it. They had their shtick, and it seemed to work for Stan. He'd felt a bit displaced, jealous even, when Liv's boyfriend had been over – Stan had almost turned him down, he knew, and he almost wished he had, since Stan had spent the whole day in a chorus of 'Scott says' and 'Scott and me . . .' But mainly, he thought Stan thought of him the same way as he had before. Maggie had agreed, at all their lunches. If Stan was suffering, traumatized by his parents' split, he was hiding it so well it was undetectable even to his mother, and, knowing Stan and his penchant for external processing, that seemed unlikely . . .

Stan wasn't Jake. They were alike to look at, but the similarities pretty much stopped there, and Bill hadn't seen it clearly enough soon enough, and he blamed himself for that. He'd put a lot of energy into making up for it.

Aly was different. As her father, if he was totally honest, he felt he'd always been slightly on the periphery of her life, by virtue of gender and expectation. Aly hadn't needed things from him, when she was young. She'd very much been Maggie's. She'd been a surprise to him. He'd been expecting another son. He'd had his 'my boy Bill' moment with her when she'd been born, and he was fiercely protective of her, but he'd always been something a little like frightened of her delicacy. Maggie had had to get cross with him, he remembered, to get him to change Aly's nappy, though he had always happily changed Jake's without even thinking of it. He couldn't have explained why, it was just something in him that felt different. Her loveliness as a little girl, perfectly pretty in the old-fashioned smock dresses – more English than the damn English, he used to say – that Maggie dressed her in, with her baby curls pinned up, had filled his heart with joy and pride, but almost as an abstract thing. He didn't take her to ballet lessons, or teach her to cook or help her tame her hair as a self-conscious teenager. Once she hit puberty, Aly was even more of a mystery to him than she had been before – a whirlwind of hormones and mood swings.

So living apart had presented very real challenges for their relationship. Maggie was a filter, a translator, a facilitator, and Maggie wasn't there. It sometimes seemed to him, when the three of them were alone in Roehampton, that Aly was like a substitute mother to Stan, and that perhaps she concentrated on that role in part because it meant she didn't have to address her role as his daughter. She had accepted the split with very little comment. They had never, to his shame and regret, had a real, in-depth discussion about it. He knew from Maggie that she was sometimes difficult at home. Sometimes remote.

She was less often difficult with him these days. But always a little remote. And all this before he'd told her about Carrie. He was terrified, he realized, of what might be unleashed by his revelation.

He chose a public place. Cowardly, definitely. A pattern. He'd done the same thing with Maggie, although with his wife options were limited. He could have told Aly in the Roehampton flat, but this seemed safer. Pizza Express. Stan was at a friend's birthday party – 'and there's a sleepover too, Dad, and I have to take a sleeping bag' – and Carrie was with her parents. She'd gone to give him the space to do it.

And now he was sitting here with his *giardiniera* pizza untouched in front of him, feeling like a shifty schoolboy, unsure at all of where to begin his confession. It was an odd feeling. Aly was wearing her hair up in a casual, scruffy bun, and she had eyeliner on, he noticed.

'Pretty earrings,' he noted lamely. Pizza Express was always full of divorce dads on a Saturday, saying lame things like that to their kids. He hated being a cliché.

'Thanks.' She felt her earlobes, obviously not sure which pair she was wearing. She shrugged. The small silver hoops were obviously not a big deal to her. 'I'm thinking of getting a second piercing in the summer.'

He raised an eyebrow. 'Really? What does Mum say about that?'

'Haven't said anything to her. Auntie Liv has a second piercing. Here.' She touched the top of her ear. There was defiance in her tone.

Bill winced. 'That always looks like it has to hurt. And I remember your mum telling Liv she thought she was a moron when she wanted it . . .'

She shrugged again – the special choreography of the teenager. 'And she did it anyway . . .'

Now he chuckled. 'Yes, she did . . . You're right. So it'll be tattooing next, will it? Now your eighteenth is looming and we can't stop you?'

Aly smiled in a way he realized was coquettish. 'And how do you know I haven't already got one?'

'Now I'm shocked. Is this my daughter before me, or some clone?'

Aly laughed, and it was a lovely sound – one he didn't hear often enough. 'Busted. I'm far too scared. And too sensible, of course – you're right . . .'

She picked up a dough ball and trawled it through the garlic butter on the dish, then pushed it whole into her mouth. It was a childish thing to do – that was the whole thing with this age. She was this part-girl, part-woman creature – hard to understand, harder to predict.

'So, Aly . . .'

'So, Dad . . .' It was almost as though she was mocking

him. He was a little shocked by this dinnertime persona. There was a new confidence about her, something a little 'screw you' in her demeanour that he hadn't noticed before. Maybe he'd blame Liv's recent visit – some of the spunkiness had rubbed off, perhaps. Teenage Liv had been a little like this. Maybe she was just growing up. He had that familiar feeling of uncertainty he often had with his daughter, which he'd never had with her brothers. He was on shifting sands with her.

'I've brought you here because I want to tell you something.'

Another dough ball. She had fixed him with a hard, unblinking stare, though, which didn't waver as she chewed and swallowed. One eyebrow was raised in a question that was pure Maggie.

He'd practised some different preambles, but it seemed better now, sitting in front of her, to just come out with it. He forced himself to meet her stare.

'I've been seeing someone.'

Aly nodded once, twice, three times, slowly, her expression unchanged.

'A woman.' Obviously, you idiot, he thought. Now he rambled, which seemed the more palatable alternative to silence. He was dizzy with how fast the familial tables had turned – parent to child, child to parent . . .

'Her name is Carrie. Your mum knows about her. I told her before Christmas. I've been waiting for the right time to tell you. Stan doesn't know – I wanted to tell you first. We've been . . . seeing each other for a few months now. We met last summer. And got together a few months after that, I suppose.' He realized he was answering questions Aly hadn't posed, but he kept going. 'She works for a gourmet food magazine – she's an assistant editor there.' At last, he stopped. And waited.

'I knew you were, Dad.' Matter-of-fact, calm.

That stopped him in his tracks. 'You knew? How?' Had Maggie done it after all? She'd seemed so adamant she wouldn't. Perhaps she hadn't trusted him to do it properly – however that might be.

'It wasn't Mum.'

'How then?' Not Liv. That wouldn't be fair. It wasn't up to her.

'You've been different lately. A bit more cheerful. Lighter, you know.'

Bill nodded. Lighter was right.

Aly smiled.

'And then there were the clues . . .'

'What clues?'

Without missing a beat, Aly began counting things off on her fingers. 'Miso paste and pastel-coloured macaroons in *your* fridge. Clean sheets on the beds more than once every couple of months. Detangling conditioner in your shower. For all the tangles in your half-an-inch-long hair? Oh, and the biggie . . . ? That would have to be the condom wrapper I found down the side of the sofa the last time I was at your flat.'

Bill felt himself colouring up. Fuck. He'd been completely out-manoeuvred, and Aly was now completely in control of the conversation.

'Elementary, my dear Watson. You'd either gone gay or you'd got a girlfriend, Dad. Frankly, this option is easier to deal with than the first one. Although the condom wrapper was pretty gross, if I'm honest. You're lucky it was me, not Stan, who found that.'

'God.' He grimaced. 'I'm sorry.'

She shrugged nonchalance.

'I can't believe you, Aly. I can't believe it. How long have you known?'

'Suspected? A couple of months. Known – since the condom debacle.'

'And you haven't said anything?'

'I figured you'd tell me when you were ready.'

'And you're not upset with me.'

'I'm not upset, Dad.'

'Liv said she thought, said she was waiting for me and your mum to get back together . . . Weren't you?'

Aly shrugged.

'I thought that might be what you wanted.'

'That's because you don't really know me, Dad. I'm not sure you ever did. Not really. Not since I grew up, anyway. And I did grow up. You weren't around, remember?'

She sounded resigned, not angry, and the tone, so adult, made his chest hurt.

'I'm sorry, Aly.' He laid his hand over hers on the table.

'You don't get it, do you, Dad?' She didn't pull her hand away. 'Enough with the sorry. I don't think you need to be sorry. You did what you did.'

'I never meant you to be hurt by what I did.'

'I know that.'

'But you've been hurt, haven't you?'

'Yeah. Okay. I have. Every kid wants their parents to be together all their lives. But then every girl wants her big brother to come back from his gap year too. And her little brother not to get bullied at school for stuff that's not his fault. And her life to be all easy and sunny. Only it isn't. Not just my life. Everyone's life. It's like it starts off all perfect, but it doesn't stay that way. Not just mine. No one's. There are loads of kids at school whose parents have split up, who have complicated families. It's not that big a deal these days. My mates have stepmothers and stepfathers and stepbrothers and stepsisters, and half-brothers and half-sisters. There's no normal any more, is there?'

'But there was your normal. Our normal.'

'Yep. And that ended, the day Jake died. Two years ago, Dad.'

It hurt him, hearing her say the words. Aly had picked up her spoon and she was rubbing the bowl of it between her fingers, shining it, looking down as she spoke.

'I let you down, Aly.'

She shook her head, but she didn't deny it.

He wanted to apologize again, but she'd said she didn't want that.

Bill pushed his pizza to one side. Out of the corner of his eye, he saw their waiter hovering and he waved him away.

'What do you want now, Aly? From me?'

Her eyes snapped up and met his. The question had surprised her.

'What I want now has become pretty simple. Mostly it's about me and not about you, and if that makes me sound selfish, then I'm sorry. But I've had quite a lot of time on my own to figure it out. I want to be happy. I want to be a doctor, and save lives and make people better. All that hackneyed stuff. I want someone to love me and to love them back. I want to live my life. For me. For Jake. He didn't get to live his. What's the point in me telling you that you let me down? That you left when I needed you? Because it all happened already, and you can't come back.

'I don't want to be all twisted about it any more. I just want to go past it. I've been angry with Jake, I've been jealous of him. I've hated you – really hated both of you. And I've been so, so sad, for so long. I don't want to feel like that any more. Sometimes I don't want to hear Jake's name, and I don't want to think about him all the time.'

God knows, Bill could understand that. She smiled a small, speculative smile at him. 'And I want you and Mum to be happy too. If that means someone else, for you, Dad, and not Mum, not Mum any more . . . then that's okay. You don't need my permission.'

Aly excused herself to go to the loo, and Bill watched her walk away. It was odd how, though 20 seconds ago she'd been sitting beside him, he could still register shock, watching her, at how grown up she was. His little girl, almost a woman. He wasn't sure he was buying all of what she was saying. Some of it rang true and some of it sounded rehearsed – for him or for her, he wasn't sure which. Bill agreed with Maggie that there was something, still, quite brittle and vulnerable about their Aly. Something she didn't want anyone to see.

And in the toilets, Aly sat with both hands clamped across her mouth, overwhelmed by a flood of sudden, hot tears she didn't entirely understand.

Chapter Eighteen

Five days after she'd sat in bed and read the classified ad, Olivia sat stirring sugar into a small vat of cappuccino in the far corner of the coffee bar around the corner, waiting for a total stranger who would answer to the name Kate Miller and wondering what the hell she was doing here. Her laptop was in front of her, still secure in its neoprene slipcover. She'd told Maggie she had a caffeine craving, needed to do some work emails and that she'd be back in an hour or so. She was nervous. The plan that had seemed to make perfect sense when she first conceived it, lying in bed beside Maggie, and when she'd written a brief note and sent it to the PO box number, and even when, within two days, this Kate Miller person had called her mobile phone and left a voicemail message, seemed dippy at best now, as she sat here. Destructive and dangerous at worst.

She'd arrived ten minutes ahead of 11 a.m., the appointed time. Kate Miller, it turned out, lived in Sevenoaks, she said, in Kent, and would need to take a train to Charing Cross and then an underground to get to their meeting. The door had opened twice since Liv had been sitting there. First, a young mother pushing a stroller containing a disgruntled baby with a hacking cough. And then, evidently a friend of hers, five minutes later, who had fallen on the baby joyously and was holding her, cooing and gurning inches from the infant's bemused face, while the mother, who, Liv could see, had dark circles under her eyes and limp, unwashed hair, lay her head against the wall beside her and watched with a watery, tired smile.

Kate Miller had sounded quite posh on the telephone. A little bit World Service, as Maggie might say. Middle-aged, perhaps a bit older – that was quite hard to tell just from her voice. They hadn't talked much. Liv had said, in the note, that she was acting on behalf of her sister, and that there were no guarantees. Kate Miller said she was happy to meet, and that she didn't expect any. She sounded quite anxious that they meet, actually. Olivia had the feeling she hadn't been inundated with responses to her ad. She hadn't asked, of course. The obvious question. How the hell did you get here, Kate Miller? How did you end up mature, healthy and solvent, with your own house, but no one to care for? She'd been imagining scenarios ever since. Had Kate Miller had her own tragedy? Was she an innocent victim too, like Maggie? Or was it of her own making? Had she had someone, and lost them, or had she always been alone? She didn't know what might work best, and that's when it began to occur to her that there was no reason why Kate Miller might be alone that would help Maggie, who was also alone, for reasons Olivia was entirely familiar with.

When she'd been a teenager, Maggie had joined a fledgling Green Movement in an adolescent flood of civic responsibility and environmental conscience. There'd been a line in the literature she left lying around (with supercilious attitude) that Liv had never forgotten. Something about how being a member of the Green Party, and supporting all things green, would make you 'a part of the cure and not a part of the problem'. She'd always remembered that line. It seemed to her a very sane way of describing behaviour, and it was a question, all these years later, she still often asked herself. That and 'What would George Bailey do?' She'd been asking herself that since the first time she'd seen *It's a Wonderful Life* – at Maggie's bidding, of course, the first Christmas she'd spent in London with Maggie and Bill. George Bailey, in the film, always, always did the right thing, the decent and honourable thing, whatever it cost him. She sometimes found herself muttering under her breath, 'What would George Bailey do?' Scott had heard her say it, a few months ago, and not understood. She'd pulled out the DVD and made him watch it that night, despite its seasonal unsuitability, so that he could understand, and although he had laughed at her fondly, he'd said it made perfect sense – the religion of Capra, he called it. A few weeks later he'd said it himself, in the car, when someone had cut him up on the inside lane, and Liv, sitting beside him, had almost cried with joy.

Kate Miller could go either way. She could be a part of the problem or a part of the cure. It would be impossible to know, unless they all tried, which one she might be. George Bailey? George Bailey might see what she was trying to do . . .

She had almost lost her nerve, and was standing up to go when the door opened again, and a woman walked in.

Kate Miller, for this was surely she, was . . . a pretty normal-looking woman. Average height, average weight. Liv judged her to be in her mid fifties, maybe a little younger than she had expected. Her hair was silver but still thick, a shoulder-length curtain of straight, smooth hair. She was well dressed – in a long black wool coat, belted at the waist, with a colourful silk scarf tied at her neck, and flat-heeled suede boots. She was wearing leather gloves, which she was pulling off as she came inside, and there was a good leather handbag on her arm, expensive, Liv judged, but not flashy. She was quite attractive, just the sensible side of glamorous. She looked like she might be your friend. It made Liv feel a bit calmer that she looked so ordinary. She didn't look like a crazy person or what Aly might describe as a 'hot mess'. She looked . . . nice.

Anyway, it was too late now. She was here, and Liv had to talk to her, even if she had lost her nerve slightly about the scheme.

'Olivia? Olivia Walker?'

'Kate Miller?' Liv stood up and extended the woman her hand.

'Nice to meet you.'

'You too.' Kate Miller nodded, and smiled and took the offered hand, shaking it warmly.

She had a good smile – easy and open. Up close now, Liv could see that she was wearing make-up – the carefully applied, stylish kind that wasn't obvious from a distance.

'Have a seat.' Liv gestured to the table, and Kate took off her coat, laying it neatly across the empty chair at the table before she sat down.

For a few minutes, they filled the awkward silence, busying themselves ordering coffee and talking about the trains and Kate Miller's journey. English people's favourite safe subject – the cold snap. Versus the hot Australian summer. Kate had never been to Australia, though she'd love to see it one day, she said. It was easy enough, while they waited for the coffee, to make this small talk. They might have been strangers introduced at a party, or shoppers passing the time in a long line. The weirdness receded just a little.

But when the waitress had put Kate's coffee down in front

of her and gone back behind the counter, Liv cleared her throat, and Kate sat up a little straighter in her chair, as though she were ready to begin . . . Liv, for a second, felt like she was interviewing for a new assistant at work.

Liv smiled. 'I don't really know how to do this.'

'No. I know what you mean.' They smiled at each other. Both keen to show good intent, even if they weren't sure how to proceed. Kate Miller nodded a small, encouraging nod.

'So, Kate . . . I guess maybe we should talk about you a little, first . . .'

'Of course.'

Liv smiled. 'I'm just not . . . I suppose I'm just not quite sure what I should be asking.'

'What would you like to know? You can ask me anything.'

'Well . . . could you tell me a little about yourself? That's probably a good start.'

Kate nodded and took a deep breath.

'Sure. I can do that. I'm Kate Miller, but you know that. I live in Sevenoaks, but you know that too.' She laughed, a little, at herself. 'I've lived there, or near there, for most of my life. I'm sixty-three years old.' That was quite a bit older than she looked, Liv thought. She'd worn well.

If Kate saw that reflection pass across Olivia's face, she didn't react.

'I was a teacher, as a career. Primary school. I taught the littlies, you know, for years – the reception class. And I loved it. I was married. My husband was a GP. But I'm widowed now. My husband died almost three years ago.'

'I'm sorry to hear that.'

'Thank you.' It was an oddly formal response, Olivia thought, but then it was an almost impossible remark to react to. She looked at Kate's left hand. She still wore a yellow gold wedding band, and an engagement ring – a round emerald, encircled with tiny diamonds.

'And you've no children of your own?'

Kate shook her head and looked down at the table.

'And you've hit the nail on the head, Olivia. That's more or less what all this is about. It's pretty simple. I don't have a family. It was just my husband and me.' She smiled. 'We were enough for each other, it seemed. We were very, very happy. But he's gone. And he's been gone a long time. And I find myself alone.'

She shook her head and pulled a handkerchief out of her sleeve. For a horrible moment, Olivia thought Kate was going to cry, but she didn't.

'I'm sorry. It feels a little strange to be saying all this to someone I don't know at all.'

'I'm sure it does.'

'But I have to tell you, to make sense of the ad; so you know I'm not a crazy person.' Liv almost blushed at how accurately Kate Miller had read her.

'I am healthy. My husband left me well taken care of. I own the home we lived in together, and there's no mortgage on it. We have, I mean we had, I have . . . no debts. I have friends, of course, but our lives are so different. Some have moved away – they've raised their families and retired to other places. Some are still around, but they're all mothers and grandmothers. Enjoying their husbands' retirements with them. There's a lot of golf, and bridge. It's amazing how your face stops fitting when your circumstances change. Or maybe it's you that changes, I can't be sure. A bit of both, maybe. But you can feel bloody lonely in a crowd of people like that, when you're by yourself.

'Besides, I don't play golf. Dull, dull game.' And here she smiled sideways, and her eyes twinkled.

'And I want to feel useful, Olivia. I've thought for a long time about all the different ways I could do that. Volunteering, in a home, or a hospital or a soup kitchen. A job.' She shrugged. 'Maybe going back into school in some capacity. I've thought about it a lot.

'But I want to be a part of something. That's what I need. I want to be a part of a family. I want to care for people who I come to know. I want to be needed.'

She looked imploringly at Olivia and, for her part, Olivia believed entirely what Kate was saying. She was disarmed by this elegant stranger.

'Have you had many conversations like this – many interviews, I suppose I mean?'

Kate shook her head. 'None. I don't know if I should admit this, but you're the only person who has responded to the ad.'

'Did you just place it?'

'It was the second time. I had put it in a few weeks before. And heard nothing. I was going to try *The Lady* next. Someone told me that was the right place . . .'

'I'd never have found you in *The Lady*.'

Kate smiled and shook her head a little.

'I think you're very brave.'

'I don't know about that.'

'I do.'

'Thank you.'

And I like you, Liv wanted to say. I've only known you for a few minutes but I like you. Maybe you're even a part of the cure . . .

A silence that wasn't quite awkward but wasn't exactly comfortable either had descended on the table as the two women looked at each other and assessed each other's intentions and auras.

'Perhaps you'd tell me a bit more . . . about your sister . . .'

Olivia's letter to Kate hadn't said much about the circumstances. It had mentioned Maggie's separation from Bill and that there were children in the house, but nothing else.

It was Liv's turn to take a deep breath.

'Maggie's my big sister. We grew up in Australia, but you already know that . . .' They smiled broadly at each other.

'She's eight years older than me. But we were really, really close when we were kids, despite that age gap. I love her more than anyone on the earth.' Olivia felt emotion rise in her throat and she swallowed it hard.

'Maggie moved to England when she was still pretty young to be with Bill — that's her husband. They've been separated quite a while now. They had three kids — Jake, Aly and Stan. But Jake died. In 2004.'

She heard Kate's sharp intake of breath.

'I'm so sorry.'

Liv nodded. 'It's been . . . it's been really, really hard for Maggie, since then.' Kate's eyes were full of empathy.

'Jake was her baby, you know. He was six foot two and eighteen years old but he was still her baby. He was travelling with friends . . . a gap year, you know. And he was killed in the tsunami in Asia.'

She had to stop talking for a second. It never got easier to say that out loud. And when she did say it, when she heard her voice say it, she always heard Maggie's voice immediately afterwards, the inhuman, unrecognizable voice Maggie had had on the telephone when she'd called to tell her Jake was missing. It was like an echo.

When she looked up, Kate's eyes were damp.

'I can't imagine . . .'

'Unimaginable is a good word for it. That's exactly what it is . . .'

'How is she now?'

Olivia shrugged. 'I called you.'

Kate nodded. It was as eloquent an answer as any.

'She doesn't know I've called you. I don't know what she'll say. But I have to do something.'

Kate just nodded again. She was a good listener, Liv would say that for her. Part of the cure?

'So . . . how is she? That's a hard one to answer. She doesn't sleep. Hardly at all. She's scarily in control when she's awake – I mean the house is spotless, the kids are immaculate. She even looks pretty great, which is weird, because she ought to look like death warmed over. But Bill's gone. Sometimes she and Aly can barely talk without rowing, which is pretty common, I suppose. Stan's a doll, but he's had his own issues, bless him. He's ten. He's a baby. Aly – Aly's hurting, like her mum. But they hurt apart, not together. It's a mess. It's a clean, tidy, orderly mess. If that makes sense.'

'It makes complete sense. Poor people.'

'And I have to go home. My life is at home. I have a job, and a boyfriend. Our dad is still there. Our mum died. Eight years ago. I have to go.'

'And she doesn't understand that?' Kate looked puzzled.

'No, no. No. That's not Maggie. She doesn't think that way. She was always the one that took care of me. It's me. I can't leave her without helping her. I have to help her. I have to make it better for her.'

'And that's why you contacted me?'

'Pretty much.'

For the first time, it occurred to Olivia that Maggie might

be too much for Kate. That maybe Kate herself was looking for a cure and not a problem, and that Maggie was a problem.

Why would someone volunteer for what she'd just described? A mourning mother, a troubled teenager, a struggling little boy. Who would walk into that world?

'Does she . . . does she talk to anyone?'

'Like a shrink, do you mean?'

Kate smiled. 'A shrink, or a good friend . . . does she talk about it?'

'She talks to me. She never talked to Bill. She always refused to see a professional. That was part, I think, of what drove Bill away in the end. That's a huge part of what went wrong. They grieved differently, you know. He went to counselling. He went to Thailand, when it first happened. They coped differently and they both survived – they just realized they couldn't do it together. Really sad.' Liv wondered if she was being disloyal. Maggie was pretty private about all of this. Not for the first time she wondered how Maggie was going to react to this and felt slightly afraid. The worst thing she could ever, ever do to Maggie was betray her, and a tiny part of her feared that was exactly what Maggie might call this.

'It happens to people.'

'I know. The loss of a child is the biggest threat a marriage can face. I've read all the books – all the books Maggie wouldn't.' Liv smiled.

'She's lucky to have you.'

Liv shrugged. 'But I have to go home.'

'What do you think I could do to help?' It seemed to be understood between them then, that Kate would try to help.

'I think you could take care of them. I think you could

talk, and listen and broker peace between Maggie and Aly. Get Aly to show her soft underbelly. Play with Stan. Make the three of them all sit down together to eat dinner. Make them smile. Keep them going.'

'That's quite a shopping list.'

'I know. You probably want to run screaming for the hills.'

'I don't. Not at all.'

'Really?'

'Does that make me sound crazy?'

'Maybe. You'll think about it? Really?'

'I'd like a bit of time, to think about it.'

'Of course.'

'And you'd need to think about it too. Think about whether you think I'm a good fit.'

Liv nodded. But she didn't have to. She trusted this woman. And that wasn't like her.

'And, of course, you'd need to get it past Maggie.'

Olivia bit her lip.

'And I think we both know that might not be easy.' Liv knew she was right.

Olivia looked at her watch. The hour she had promised had passed. She couldn't believe she and Kate had been chatting for so long.

'I should go. Maggie's waiting for me.'

Kate looked out of the window at the street.

'And she lives around here, I presume?'

'God, we didn't talk about that, did we?' Kate smiled.

'It doesn't matter, especially. Anywhere but Sevenoaks is good for me at this point.'

Liv laughed. 'Chiswick isn't Sevenoaks, that's for sure. Maggie lives around the corner. About a five-minute walk from here.'

Kate nodded.

'Aly walks usually – she's at school nearby. Stan takes a bus. He goes to a special school, a few miles away.'

'Maggie works?'

Liv shook her head. 'No. Not for years. Not since Stan was born. And not at anything serious before that. She should. I mean, I think she should. I think it would help. But she says she's not ready . . . But maybe, maybe she could . . .'

If she had you. That's what she had been about to say. But she didn't want to scare Kate any more than she might already have done. She felt suddenly and certainly that Kate had to come. She had to. And so now she didn't want to put pressure on her.

'I have to go,' she said again.

'Of course. You go.'

'You'll call me?'

'I'll call.'

'I go back to Sydney – at the end of the week.'

'I'll call tomorrow.'

Olivia finished buttoning her coat and looped her wool scarf around her neck.

'If you've got any more questions. Anything you think of. Anything at all.'

She held out her hand, and Kate took it and put her other hand on the back of Olivia's.

'She's lucky to have you, Olivia.'

'You don't think I'm insane to be asking, then?'

'Do you think I'd be insane to say yes?'

Liv laughed. 'Probably.'

Halfway home, she stifled a giggle, excitement bubbling inside her. 'I've found her a real live Mrs Doubtfire.' She felt strangely elated. Relieved. And, above all, she felt hopeful. Some of the weight she'd been shouldering for the last two years was already starting to lift. After one coffee and a chat. Perhaps she was the crazy person . . .

Chapter Nineteen

She practised saying it out loud on Scott, on the telephone, that afternoon while Maggie was out with Stan.

'Mrs Doubtfire?! Are you sure?'

'I wasn't. I nearly ran away while I was waiting for her. And now I am. Completely sure. It was weird. You had to meet her, Scott. It must have been all those years of dealing with pre-schoolers or something. Or having a loss of her own. She understood. She was calm and warm and she was a great listener, and I know – I just know – this is what Maggie needs.'

'Are you sure it's what Maggie needs? A roommate? Or is it maybe just a bit what you need?'

'Not a roommate. Like an au pair, but older and more helpful, and emotionally supportive. What do you mean, what I need?' She tried but failed, she knew, not to sound outraged. 'This isn't about me.'

'Don't get bent out of shape. Let me explain . . . It's the only manly quality you have, gorgeous girl. The need to fix things. Especially where Maggie is concerned.'

'Manly?'

'You know what I mean. You bring me a problem, I want to fix it. I can't for the life of me see the point in talking about it if you don't want me to come up with a solution. Most women aren't like that. You are. It's one of the things I love most about you, actually. But it makes me wonder if this isn't more than just a little bit about you wanting to fix Maggie.'

'How do you know so much about the female psyche, Dr Freud?'

'Sisters. Aunts. And you lot aren't quite as mysterious as you like to think you are, actually . . .'

'Is that right?'

'In my experience.' She loved the sexy chuckle in his voice. It was profoundly distracting.

'Of course I want to help. There's nothing wrong with that.'

'I never said there was. I know you hate leaving her. And you're coming home to me. And a part of you hates that, I know. And feels guilty about that.'

'If you think I've come up with this plan just to assuage my own guilt 'cos I'm not here all the time, you're climbing up the wrong bark tree, mate.'

'Not just that, Liv. But you've got to admit you'll be just a little bit happier, you'll find it just a little bit easier to walk away from her at the weekend, if you've fixed this thing, right?'

He was right. He often was. Mostly she loved that. Now it made her feel grumpy.

'I'll take your unusual silence as acquiescence, shall I?' She could hear the smile in his voice, which made the patronizing remark vaguely okay.

'Look, Liv. I think you might be on to something. Maybe this person – this Mrs Doubtfire you've found – maybe she can help. I see what you're doing. And why. I'm just saying that you should be prepared for your sister to think you're off your head.'

Liv was prepared for that.

Chapter Twenty

Sitting on the 13.55 from Charing Cross to Sevenoaks, her hands folded neatly in her lap, and a copy of the newspaper neatly folded and unread tucked into her handbag, Kate was going over the conversation she'd had with Olivia.

She'd lied. A small lie, with a shake of her head, not with words. It might not even matter to Olivia. She hadn't noticed.

She wanted to help them. She was a little bit frightened. But this was what she'd been waiting for. This was what she needed.

Loneliness had started as a predicament and become a habit, from there a way of life. Being without Philip, her beloved Philip, was only a part of it. She'd isolated herself from everyone. It was as though without the company of the one she had loved best, enjoyed the most, everyone else's company had become unpalatable to her too. Instead of seeking comfort with them, she'd set herself apart and tried to comfort herself. She didn't even understand why, and Kate was a woman who, over the years, had been better than most at trying to understand why she did what she did. A random line from Shakespeare – *Hamlet*, she thought, though she wasn't sure, as Philip would have been – kept popping into her head. Something about all the uses of the world seeming weary and stale and flat and unprofitable. She sometimes said the words over and over to herself. Weary, stale, flat and unprofitable.

People wanted to help. She knew that. But it didn't. It just didn't. Platitudes about Philip irritated her. Anyone who wanted to share an anecdote, or a fond story or talk about a quality he had possessed just made her think to herself that they didn't begin to know him the way she did. She could trump any story. She was fonder than anyone. She'd known those qualities more than any other person could begin to know. And she'd lost more than anyone else had, too.

It was nasty. And it showed, she feared, however hard she tried to greet each utterance with a smile and an understanding nod of her head. Truthfully, she didn't want to hear them. There was a selfishness about her grief that she almost cherished.

And so eventually she had reaped what she had sown. The friends who had tried so hard to 'be there', and to include her in gatherings and conversations and their lives, receded – beaten back by her indifference to their efforts.

She hadn't meant it, but then it was too late. She saw her own brittleness, and she hated it. She had never been like this. Bereavement had altered her beyond recognition, even of herself.

But how to fix it?

Her life had become a dull routine, punctuated by television programmes. She watched far too much boring television, but their showing times and their theme tunes were the clock of her day. *Homes Under the Hammer*, *Escape to the Country*, *Come Dine With Me* and then *Coronation Street*. She hadn't read a novel for as long as she could remember – the stories of fictional people just weren't interesting to her any more. Over the months, a stack of cookery books had migrated from the shelf in the kitchen, where they were no longer needed because she no longer cooked for anybody, to her bedside table, where she flicked through them before she slept – reliving recipes and the life she and Philip had had when they were eating those meals. All the beautiful clothes he'd bought her and loved her to wear hung in the wardrobe while she rotated three or four outfits – no scarves, necklaces or high heels – the wardrobe of a woman who has given up.

The ad in the paper had been a middle-of-the-night decision – she'd sat in her nightdress in the slipper chair in her bedroom, watching the moon and listening to the owl that nested somewhere just west of the house, and written it on her knee. Thinking, as she sometimes did, of how disappointed Philip would be in her. Not angry. Disappointed. He'd poured so much love and confidence into her in the time they'd had together that he couldn't help but despair at how easily it had seeped out of her without him. She wondered if she was starting to hate herself. She'd acknowledged that she was depressed but couldn't face going to the GP's surgery for pills. She couldn't face them all knowing. She could still fake it, for a while, when she was out – she thought no one knew how bad it had got, how far she'd sunk. That night, though, there had been a sudden revelation. Kate had sat up in bed with a start, instantly wide awake, fear making her heart pound, as though an intruder had smashed a window downstairs. This could not go on – she sensed she was teetering on the brink of a point from which there might be no return. Something had to change. This was no life. How her mind had leapt to the ad, she'd never understood or remembered. It was proactivity. That was all. She didn't question it. She'd never placed a classified ad and the wording took several attempts. It was near 5 a.m. when she went back to bed, though not to sleep. Possibilities wove themselves around her brain, and she felt, for the first time in a long time, the tiniest frisson of excitement.

In the morning, though, that had largely passed. She ought to have thrown it away, the way a disgruntled employee writes an aggressive email at the end of a bad day but doesn't press the send button before the cold light of day illuminates the screen and the mistake that pushing send would be. But she didn't. Something made her look in the morning paper, pushed through her letterbox just after 7 a.m., to see where a classified ad needed to be sent. To address the envelope and affix a stamp. To shower and carefully dry her hair. To choose a long-forgotten outfit to wear, as though respondents to the ad would already be lined up to interview her at the postbox. To walk the mile or so to the small parade of shops, with its anachronistic greengrocer's and butcher shop, and its tall, round, red postbox.

The moment she'd dropped the letter in the post, she'd regretted it, looking around her furtively to see who had witnessed her act of bizarre daftness – as though someone would know the contents of the small Basildon Bond envelope. She'd contemplated waiting at the postbox to try and reclaim the envelope from the postman when he came to empty it, but she thought this wouldn't be allowed. Sipping a cappuccino in a café across the road from the postbox, she watched the red van pull up and the postman funnel letters into his brown sack, hurl it in the back of the van and drive off.

When she didn't hear anything at first, she was almost relieved. Of course there'd been no response. What sort of crazy person would respond to an ad like that? She must sound like a nutter, an identify thief, a headache . . .

But then Olivia had written. And the excited feeling was back. She'd still been acting, though, dressing carefully, taking the train and walking into the coffee shop where Olivia had asked to meet her. Pretending to be confident and laid-back and not crazy. She hoped that by pretending, she could recapture it – she *had* been that person, before Philip died, and she wanted to be that person again. She wanted Olivia to believe she already was. Because she wanted to do this . . .

The story of Maggie and her children had been the only story – real or imagined – that had interested her in three years. She ached for this bereaved mother. She wanted to help this grieving teenager, this vulnerable son. She wanted to make things better. And make herself better at the same time.

There were things closer to home that she could fix – that maybe she should be trying to fix. And maybe she would – after she had done this.

Chapter Twenty-One

'Why on earth would you do a thing like that?' Maggie's tone was part incredulity, part irritation and part curiosity. She was half laughing at Liv – a nervous, almost embarrassed laughter, sitting at the kitchen table, three nights before Liv was due to leave. Liv had waited until Aly had disappeared and Stan had been tucked in and fallen asleep. She'd checked on him before she came down. She'd made two cups of tea, and then she'd sat down opposite her sister and outlined what she had in mind. That Kate come on a trial basis for a couple of weeks, to help out with the house and the kids and to act as a kind of adult companion for Maggie in the evenings and at the weekends, when the kids were with Bill or their friends. She thought it sounded okay. Maggie's expression indicated that she didn't know whether Liv was joking or serious.

'Let's clarify what you're suggesting, shall we? You want me to let a complete stranger, who knows next to nothing about us and who I've never met, come and live with us. Be a part of the family. Just like that.'

'That's not what I said.'

'It pretty much *was* what you said, Liv.'

'I want you to just stay calm a minute and think about it.'

'I don't need to think about it, you loon.'

'I think you do. I think you should.'

'An ad in the paper? You answered an ad in the paper. What sort of person puts an ad like that in the damn paper?'

'She's nice. Maggie – she's lovely.'

'Based on what – half an hour in the coffee shop? Do you know how wacky that makes you sound, Liv? And don't even get me started on you telling some stranger all about me, all about us. 'Cos that might make me angry. And I don't want to be angry with you when you're about to go home. I really don't.'

'That's not what I want either, God knows.'

She'd been afraid this would happen. Maggie wasn't listening.

Maggie stood up and went to the kitchen door. 'Good. So we're agreed. Enough of this nonsense. If you've told this fruitcake she can come, you better call her and tell her she bloody can't. I'm going to go upstairs and take a shower, and when I come down, we'll watch something on TV and pretend this conversation didn't happen, okay?'

Bill saw his old home number flash up on the phone mid morning the following day. He was inspecting a site with a few members of his crew. 'I'm going to take this, guys. Excuse me. Back in a minute.' He pulled off his hard hat and moved away from the group, into a quieter spot.

'Maggie?'

'It's not Maggie, Bill. It's me, Liv.'

'Everything okay at home, Liv?' His first thought. Always. Since.

'Everything's fine. And everyone. I need your help, Bill. I need to talk to you about something. Can you meet me this morning? Somewhere near the house?'

Bill look at his watch. He had back-to-back meetings. 'Of course I can. Forty minutes?'

'Fine. Starbucks on the High Road?'

'I'll see you there . . .'

She desperately needed Bill *not* to react the way Maggie

had. She was already sitting at a table when he came in. She watched him order with the barista, peering into the food cabinet and pointing at something. He smiled at her while he waited for the drink and the hot sandwich, then joined her where she was sitting, sliding into the seat across from her. Without much preamble, she outlined her proposal to him, and he sat and listened, as she'd made him promise to do, taking occasional bites from his egg and sausage muffin. By the time she'd finished her explanation, he'd finished the sandwich, and, wiping his mouth with a paper napkin, he sat back and folded his arms on his chest.

'So? What do you think?'

He smiled at her kindly. 'I see what you're trying to do, Liv.'

'You do?'

'Absolutely. And it's sweet.' The word made Liv's hackles rise. He'd always had a tendency to do this – it was the way a big sister's boyfriend talked to the kid sister and he'd perfected the tone twenty years ago – but she was 30 years old now – no one's baby sister – and she didn't want to hear 'sweet'.

'I'm not trying to be sweet. I'm trying to help Maggie.' She hoped the missing end of her sentence – 'because you're not helping her' – hung eloquently in the air.

If it did, he gave no sign of it. 'How is it that you think this would help, though? I'm not sure I get it.'

Liv was frustrated. She so wanted to make him see what she meant – what she intended.

'And what exactly do you know about this woman, Liv?'

'Oh my God, Bill. Not you too. What is it with this family and the lack of trust? Not everyone is a serial killer, you know . . .'

'I know that. But you're being incredibly naive, don't you

think? I'm not saying she's a serial killer. But she could so easily be a con man. Con woman. Whatever. You've got to admit it's an odd thing to do. Advertise in the paper that way. I mean, did she give references? Did she offer them when you met?'

'It wasn't that kind of a meeting. And you wouldn't say that if you'd met her. I honestly think you'd get it, if you were to meet her. You'd see that if she was there with Maggie, she really might help. I'm not talking about adopting her, for goodness sake. I'm talking about something temporary.'

'Well, maybe I should meet her.'

'You don't need to meet her. I'm not trying to find support for *you*. You seem to have taken care of that on your own. It's Maggie I'm thinking about.'

Bill winced.

'Sorry. I didn't mean that. Uncalled for.' She held her hands up in a gesture of slightly grudging surrender. 'But you know what I mean. It's Maggie who needs to meet her. Not you. I honestly think if she did that, she'd see that she's a really nice woman.'

'I don't know, Livvy. It still sounds weird to me. It's what they used to do in the old days, isn't it? Pay a companion for a lady . . . didn't they?'

'No one is talking about paying Kate. She wants the same thing. Company. Someone to look after.'

'And why is that? Why does someone find themselves in that position at her age? Hey? That's what I'm getting at.'

'I don't know, Bill.' Liv's tone was exasperated now – a little angry. 'How do we all end up where we are? Isn't it that life happens? Things change . . .'

The two of them sat for a while without speaking.

'Even if I agreed with you, Liv . . . what do you think I could do about it? I'm hardly the first person Maggie consults these days when she makes a decision, am I?'

'I want to be able to tell her you think it's a good idea.'

'So *I'm* a reference now, am I? For this complete stranger I haven't ever set eyes on? The one you insist repeatedly, by the way, that I don't need to meet . . .'

'Yes. You are. And I want you to help me get the kids on side. Both of them. That's what'll swing it really. If the kids are into it. Yes. That's what I want you to do for me, Bill. That's what I'm asking. And I want you to do it because I'm asking that of you and because you trust me. You know I'd never do anything that would hurt Maggie. You trust me.'

Bill remembered the night he'd sat up for hours and hours, just him, Liv and a bottle of Dewar's. She'd listened to every awful word he'd said – about finding Jake, about what he'd seen. She'd listened when Maggie wouldn't – Maggie's kid sister, who'd sulked when he took Maggie away and then grown up behind his back. She'd cried with him, and for him, and she'd held him while he cried. It was a night seared in his memory and it had forged a bond of trust and a debt of gratitude he would never forget. He did trust her.

In the end, Liv was right. It was Stan who was the one who nailed it most simplistically and straightforwardly in his own verbose, meandering style.

'I get it. She's like an au pair, right? A few of my friends have those. James has one called Anna and she's from Poland. She's very pretty and super skinny. And James's mum says you can't beat a Pole for hard work. Ned has one called Manon, but she has to teach him French twice a week as well as pick him up from school and stuff. Ned says she wears too much gloopy mascara and her skirt is so short you can some- times see her pants. And Alex had one, I can't remember her name. But Alex said his mum sent her back to Romania because she'd started looking at Alex's dad funny. No idea what that means. You mean someone like that, right, Auntie

Liv? Except she's old? Like a granny, kind of. So we'll never have to see her pants. And Mum won't get cross because Dad is looking at her too much, even though Dad doesn't live with us any more, so he won't even know her . . .'

Stan had never had a granny. He'd been a baby when Bill's mother died suddenly of a heart attack and just a toddler when Maggie and Liv's mum had died too.

'Exactly, Stan. That's exactly what I mean. Good idea, hey?'

'Yeah, I reckon. When is she coming? Can I have a biscuit? I know it's dinner soon, but I'm really hungry . . .'

Without waiting for an answer, Stan delved into the biscuit barrel, inspected the chocolate HobNob he extracted, bit into it and ran up the stairs. Liv held her arms in the air in Maggie and Aly's direction.

'Okay. So. Stan's up for it, a rent-a-granny . . . What about you two?'

Liv's flight was leaving late in the evening, so Maggie took everyone to Gianni's for an early supper before she drove her to Heathrow. Aly was quiet, Stan his normal ebullient self.

'I suppose you're excited to get back to Scott?' Aly made it sound like a reproach.

'Yeah. Course I am. But that doesn't mean I'm not sad to leave you lot.'

Aly didn't answer, and the two sisters exchanged glances. Maggie rolled her eyes and Liv narrowed hers reproachfully. She wished Maggie wouldn't be so easily riled.

'When are we going to see Scott again, Auntie Liv?'

'So it's Scott you're missing now, is it, sport?!'

'You too, obviously. But, well . . . you know, Auntie Liv . . . Scott's a bloke and I'm a bloke . . . and . . .'

'I know,' she smiled. 'Don't worry, Stan. I get it . . . I don't know. Any ideas, Mags?'

Maggie felt tearful, as she had done all day. She was genuinely terrified of Liv's departure. The last day was always the worst, because it loomed. She'd go to bed and cry and wake up tomorrow and it would already have happened and she'd get on with things again . . . But today, the thought of Liv walking through to security at the airport had placed a large enough lump in her throat that she was surprised she could still speak.

'I don't know. We'll have to have a think about that . . .'

'I know Dad'd love to see you all. Scott too, of course . . .'

Planning ahead wasn't her thing these days, but Maggie smiled at Stan. 'We'll fix something, hey, mate? We've just got to let Aly get these wretched A levels out of the way first, haven't we?'

Aly seemed to slump down a little further in her chair.

Maggie had asked Aly to look after Stan while she drove Liv to the airport. She'd agreed reluctantly, and Stan had been persuaded it would be boring and that he should stay at home, with the TV and the PlayStation. Maggie wanted these last few minutes with her sister.

But she found herself without much to say. She was happy for Liv – she knew, but couldn't say, that Liv was going home to the beginning of a new life. A proposal from Scott, a wedding . . . a family of her own, hopefully. And she was happy for her. But again, that feeling of Liv's life throwing her own into sharp relief was always there. And more than anything else, she knew she was going to miss her . . . so much. Liv made everything better. She'd drive back now, in the dark, let herself in to the house, and she'd be alone. As lonely as she'd ever been in her life.

'You all right?'

She shook herself out of the reverie. 'I'm . . .'

'Don't you dare . . .'

Maggie searched for a new word. 'I'm good. I'm good. I'm good.'

'I've got a good feeling about this Kate Miller . . .'

Maggie curled her lip.

'Right . . .'

'Promise me you'll give it a go.'

'Okay.'

'Promise.' Just like when they were kids.

Maggie laughed. 'Promise. Okay. I promise. You promise me something?'

'Anything . . .'

'Promise you'll stop worrying about me.'

'Can't do that . . .'

'Oi! Not fair. I've promised and you have to. I want you and Scott to be stupid happy together, not worrying about me all the time . . .'

'How about I promise to try to worry less . . . That's the best I can do.'

'Okay. Give me a hug.'

The sisters stood, folded in each other's arms, for a good minute.

'I love you, Olivia.'

'And I love you, Margaret.' No one ever called her Margaret, because she hated it. Liv had used it when she was little, to torture her. The name sliced through the emotion and made it possible for Maggie to let her go.

She was fumbling in her handbag for the short-stay parking ticket and her purse when her mobile phone rang. It wasn't a number she knew and she meant to press the ignore button to send the call to voicemail, but her fingers, busy with the detritus of her bag, inadvertently pressed the wrong key. She heard a man's voice saying her name.

'Maggie. Maggie. Can you hear me?'

She didn't recognize him. Tutting in irritation, she put the phone between her ear and her shoulder and carried on pulling things that weren't the parking ticket out from the depths.

'Hello. This is she . . .'

'Maggie. Charlie Nelson.'

'Sorry? Who?'

'Charlie Nelson. Imogen's father.'

'I'm sorry. Do I know you?'

The voice sounded a little tremulous now.

'Our daughters – they're friends. Same class . . .'

'Charlie. Sorry. Yes, of course . . .'

Even as she said it, Maggie was mentally flicking through class dads, wondering which one this was . . .

'I've caught you at a bad time . . .'

She'd been in England long enough to learn that you never admitted such a thing. Maggie sighed and put the handbag down on the concrete floor. Standing up straight, she took the phone out of its now painful resting place in the crook of her neck and held it to her ear.

'No. I'm just . . . I'm at the airport. I just dropped off my sister for the Sydney flight. Sorry.'

'Don't apologize . . .'

Why was he ringing her? She vaguely remembered him now.

'I'll get to the point, then. Don't want to hold you up. I don't know if you know, but I'm class rep . . .' Did they still have those – for seventeen-year-olds? Maggie had no idea. She'd done the whole thing, when Jake and Aly had been little – the Christmas fairs and summer barbecues and fund-raisers for minibuses and band tours to obscure Austrian towns. But she'd kept school and all things committee at arm's length for years now.

'No. Sorry. I didn't . . .' She wished Charlie Nelson would get to the point. She looked at her watch. She'd just missed the thirty-minute charge and now she'd be paying the full hour, and Stan would not, she guessed, be putting on his pyjamas and brushing his teeth . . .

'Well, I am – last term and all that – and we're organizing a curry night. It's next week. Sort of a get-together where we can all compare notes on this crazy revision schedule the kids have been given . . . you know. There was an email . . .'

There may well have been. Maggie gave those the most cursory of glances. If they were pertinent – curriculum nights or parents' evenings – she made a note in her diary. If they were social, she hit delete. Since Jake died, she hadn't had the heart for it. In the months after the tsunami, if she had to drop Aly off, she'd hide in the car behind dark glasses or intently gaze at a book or her phone, not catching anyone's eye.

'Right.'

'I just wondered . . . I just wondered if you were going to be coming?'

'I hadn't thought . . .'

'It's just that we . . . I mean, that I haven't seen you, for a long time . . . And I thought it would be nice . . .'

'I'm not sure I can make it, Charlie. What night is it again?'

She made it sound like she was writing it down as he spelt out the name of the restaurant, the street, day and time . . . She should just tell him she had no intention at all of going, but he sounded sincere and she didn't want to hurt his feelings.

'So we might see you there?'

'I'll do my best . . .' Non-committal.

'I'd love that, Maggie.' He put emphasis on the 'love'. But Maggie wasn't really listening any more.

'I'd better go, Charlie . . .'

'Of course. Sorry to keep you . . .'

'Not at all.'

'And I'll look forward to it . . .'

'Goodnight, Charlie.'

If Maggie had thought about it at all, she might have wondered whether the entire class was getting a personal phone call to remind them of the event or whether Charlie was reaching out to her specifically. And if so, then why he might . . . But she didn't. The ticket miraculously came out with the next handful of stuff, and she paid the exorbitant fee and drove home thinking of Liv . . .

Chapter Twenty-Two

Of all the things Maggie had done for Liv in the last thirty years, this thing that she was doing today seemed to her to be easily the most bizarre. It was early afternoon. She was at the very top of the house, finishing clearing out the wardrobe in the house's sixth bedroom. She hoped this Kate had good knees and hips. She could have offered her the official guest room, on the floor below, where Liv had been sleeping, but this seemed a better idea. Even if it was a bit maid-like, in an *Upstairs, Downstairs* kind of way, to put Kate Miller up here. It wasn't huge but it was a pretty space, this room in the eaves. One large sash window overlooking the garden at the back of the house let in plenty of light. There was no room in here for a king-size bed, but there was a small double, with a distressed white iron frame and a fashionably faded floral quilt. China-blue walls and a pair of long, filmy voile curtains completed the look. There was a small, white-tiled shower room through the door in the corner. The room had never had a long-term occupant, though Maggie had decorated it this way many years ago, when Bill had been keen that she get an au pair or a live-in to help her with the children and the house. He could afford it, he had said, and she should have more free time to do what she wanted. She told him she was doing what she wanted – she'd never felt the need to have time off from her children when they were small. She always thought, afterwards, that it was when she was happiest. She'd agreed, when he wouldn't let it drop, to have a cleaner twice a week to dust, vacuum and do the ironing, but she'd drawn the line emphatically at someone living in. It wasn't her style, she'd insisted. And she'd won, of course, though Bill had been exasperated.

Truthfully, he'd probably imagined that he might have a little more of her, if she had more help at home – he might have imagined more nights at the theatre, more dinners in smart restaurants. Bill had enjoyed making some money – it had seemed an improbable state of affairs to him when he and Maggie had started out. He wanted to spend some. But Maggie wasn't into that. The money was a cushion to her more than it was a pleasure – it represented security more than anything else, and she'd never spent conspicuously. There'd been no live-in, no nanny.

The wardrobe had been stuffed with out-of-season, out-of-style clothes in plastic dry-cleaning bags, but Maggie and Liv had tackled most of it yesterday, making a few cathartic trips to the charity shop in the afternoon. Now there was about three feet of hanging space, and there was a dresser too, with a little mirror hung above it. It was clean, and pretty . . .

And Maggie didn't know why she was worrying. She wasn't at all sure about this and she'd committed to almost none of it. She'd bowed under pressure, that was all. She remembered what Scott had said, when he'd taken her to the pub. About Liv feeling so responsible for her. Worrying so much at that great distance. She didn't want that. She really didn't. She'd lain in bed, the night after she and Liv had fought about Kate, and thought about her sister's trip. It was shameful, she realized, how little she and Liv had talked about Liv. She was on the threshold of a new life – all that excitement and discovery and wonder – and instead of celebrating it with her,

Maggie had leant on her sister. It wasn't fair. It hadn't been exactly a threat or a warning that Scott had given her that day in the pub when he'd asked Maggie's permission to marry Liv. It was more a plea. And it had weighed heavily on her – that *cri de coeur*. That was why – in the end – she'd said yes to this. That and Stan and Aly. Bill and Liv had obviously done a number on Aly. Which was clever. Sly but clever. Maybe living alone with her was far worse than she imagined, even in her darkest moments, she realized. How bad must it have to be, for her teenage daughter to welcome a middle-aged stranger with open arms?

She couldn't see it lasting. She'd give it a couple of weeks. She'd made Liv promise that if it didn't work, if she wanted Kate to go, that Liv would do it. Maggie wasn't good at that kind of thing. She'd never fired a cleaner, let alone a . . . well, what should she call her? Not companion – the word Liv had used. That was too Jane Austen. That implied a level of social inadequacy Maggie couldn't admit to, even if it was true. Not an au pair – that was ridiculous. Maybe she'd call her a friend, if she needed to call her anything at all. Who would know she was here? She'd cut herself off so well that the casual acquaintances she sometimes had lunch or coffee with were unlikely to ask, or even to discover her existence, if Maggie didn't allude to her. People didn't come back to the house much these days. Kids did, friends of Aly and Stan. But it was up to Aly what she told her friends, if she wanted to tell them anything at all. Stan had clearly got it all sorted already. Rent-a-granny. Maybe that was as good as anything else. Kate would be their rent-a-granny. For a week or two. And then she'd call Liv and say it wasn't working and get Liv to get her to leave.

For now, though, Kate would sleep up here in the shabby-chic second guest room. If her knees and hips were up to the stairs.

When she arrived, though, Kate was nothing at all like the person Maggie was expecting. She arrived by town car, for a start. Not on foot or in a black cab. By something you might almost call a limo, although the driver wasn't wearing a cap. He jumped out, nonetheless, to retrieve two smart black rolling suitcases from the boot and to open the passenger door for Kate to climb out. She was smart – almost glamorous. Maggie hadn't been expecting that. Liv hadn't said. She hadn't asked Liv what this woman looked like – and so she'd imagined someone more . . . more like a granny. Like Robin Williams in *Mrs Doubtfire*. She loved this person's silver bob, and her raincoat and her bag. A brief image of Mary Poppins and her capacious carpet bag danced through her mind. Might this lady be able to do magic too?

As Kate smiled at her and climbed the flight of stairs to the front door, Maggie felt her curiosity piqued to the degree that, much to her surprise, her anxiety had abated considerably. Her smile wasn't nervous or hesitant. If she felt those things, she was hiding it well.

'Maggie?'

She nodded and felt herself smiling back at the woman. Kate offered her hand. 'I'm Kate. Kate Miller.'

'Where would you like these cases?' Behind her on the steps, the driver was waiting for an instruction.

'Oh, just here. Thanks. We can move them later . . .' Maggie stood back from the door to let him through.

Once Kate had thanked him and he'd left, she closed the door and the two women stood together a little awkwardly in the hallway.

Maggie recovered herself. 'I'm sorry. Let me take your coat.'

'Thanks.' Kate took off the mac and handed it to Maggie. Beneath it, she wore a slate-grey wool tunic over wide-legged

trousers, and a long silver chain with a big stone pendant –
moonstone or labradorite. The overall effect was of someone
well put together and stylish. Someone she would be friends
with.

'I love your necklace.'

'Thank you.' Kate fingered the heavy chain for a moment,
then lifted the stone so Maggie could see it more closely. 'It
was gift from my late husband. It goes with everything – he
was clever that way . . .'

Maggie didn't know what to say. It was too soon for that.
She wasn't ready to swap heartbreak with this woman. But
she didn't wish her anywhere but here either.

Kate gestured around her. 'Show me round? I love this
kind of house. My absolute favourite. High ceilings and big
windows. Fabulous. We don't have many of these in Sevenoaks. We're a bit Arts and Crafts down there. But this is
gorgeous . . .'

It was a clever ploy. It could have seemed pushy, but
somehow it didn't strike Maggie that way. Maggie loved the
house, and it was a long time since anyone new had seen
inside it. She took her through the ground floor and down
to the basement. Kate complimented her colours and made
all the right noises about the original features – she knew
about architecture and design, clearly. She glanced at the
shadow boxes as they passed them but didn't linger. It
was an odd sensation to know that this stranger already
knew . . . about Bill, and about Jake. About her. Maggie was
amazed to find that it was almost a relief to know the point
would not come . . . the point where she had to say it. 'My
husband and I are separated.' Or, 'My eldest child died.'
The point when the face of a new acquaintance would
change, registering shock, the features reassembling themselves into an expression of pity or sorrow or sympathy.

Sometimes blind panic. Kate already knew. And she was still here.

At the entrance to the kitchen, Kate exclaimed. 'An Aga!'

'Do you have one?'

'I did. Once. Two-oven, cream. Not in the house I have now – that's a much more modern kitchen. But I still miss it. I always think that once you've had one, you always miss it.'

'I'm Australian. I'd never heard of them, before I got here. My . . .' She hesitated, unsure what to call Bill for the purposes of this conversation, then remembered that Kate knew this too. 'My husband – his mother had one. I was so damn cold, my first winter here, with this damp, bone-splitting cold you have here, I spent the whole time huddled in front of it. If the warming oven had been big enough, I might have spent time actually in it. Thus began a love affair that never really ended.'

Kate laughed. 'Exactly. It's a love thing. Can't say that about any other kitchen appliance. I can't, at least, though I'll confess to a fondness for a dishwasher. Certainly can't snuggle up to a Miele double oven, can you?'

'Doesn't iron the sheets either.'

'Does not. Love that. Fold them up, pop them on the top – two hours later, perfectly pressed sheets.' She made a gesture like waving a magic wand.

'And I used to put the kids' coats on the top when they were younger. On cold mornings. Send them off toasty warm.'

Kate nodded emphatically. 'And you could have put a tiny lamb in the warming oven too, if you lived on a farm.'

'Only lamb that Aga's ever seen was a leg of, when we were roasting it.'

They both laughed, lightly enough, and it was easy and natural.

Later, on the phone, during the promised debrief, Maggie

told Liv they'd bonded over a love of Georgian architecture and Aga ovens. 'Joanna Trollope would have been proud of you,' Liv had joked. 'Your very own Aga saga.'

After that, Maggie had made tea. Milk and half a sugar for Kate. And the two of them had sat at the kitchen table until Stan came home, chatting.

'I wondered how you saw this working,' Kate said eventually.

Maggie had no immediate answer. 'I haven't the slightest clue.' She'd shrugged.

'Well . . . me neither. I suppose we're in the same boat in that regard. I want to help. But I don't want to be in the way. Muscle in. I love to cook. Bake. Garden, a bit. I was a teacher . . . I don't know if your sister told you?' Maggie nodded. 'So I might be handy for some homework. If, that is, you think Stan might . . .'

'Stan has some special needs. Did Liv . . . ?'

'She told me some, although of course I'd love to hear about it from you. Mothers are the experts. I've had some experience of that sort of thing. Not a lot. I don't have any qualifications or anything like that, but I have bucketloads of patience. And I like it.'

'That sounds great.' It did. There were afternoons when giving Stan her undivided attention for as long as he needed it was a daunting proposition.

'And Aly must be mid mocks, I suppose?'

'She's about to be, poor kid. But Aly's an academic kid. Bright, you know? She's going to medical school in the autumn.'

'Golly. Clever girl. My late husband was a GP.'

'Really?'

Maggie heard Stan's key in the lock at 4.30 p.m., startled to see how long the two of them had been sitting talking. She hadn't had a conversation that long or that easy with anyone but Liv for the longest time.

The suitcases in the hall must have reminded Stan of the arrival of rent-a-granny – he bounded down the stairs two at a time without taking his coat off, then came to a halt, suddenly shy, in the doorway.

'You have to be Stan.' Kate went straight over to him and held out her hand, which Stan took. 'I'm pleased to meet you.'

'I'm pleased to meet you too,' he parroted back. Then he looked at her hard, appraisingly, the way only a child can do. 'I like your hair. What colour do you call that?'

'Stan!' Maggie remonstrated.

'That's perfectly all right.' Kate smiled warmly at him. 'Well, I can't bear to say grey, Stan – it makes me feel old, and I'm too vain for that. So I might go with silver. Or maybe platinum.'

Stan nodded. 'It's pretty hair.'

'Thank you.'

'What am I going to call you?' he asked. 'Mum called you "rent-a-granny" but she said I couldn't call you that.'

Kate started to answer, a smile playing around her lips.

'Mrs Miller,' Maggie interjected sternly, her cheeks instantly flushed.

'There's no need for that, Maggie,' Kate protested.

'I call all my teachers Mr or Mrs or Miss,' Stan said. 'Mrs Miller is fine.'

Maggie nodded and Kate conceded with a small shrug. 'Mrs Miller it is then.'

Stan drank a glass of milk, leaning against the fridge, ate a biscuit and sat down at the kitchen table, pulling homework from his bag, chattering the whole time. The exercise books all had bent and torn corners, and the loose papers were in no particular order and looked like they'd lined a dog basket somewhere between school and home. Maggie lurked against the work surface and watched Kate watch Stan as he explained some science experiment the teacher had shown them that day – his arms waved exuberantly and he talked so fast it was hard to catch every word. She nodded and listened, interjecting every so often to let him know that she understood. It was as though Maggie didn't exist. She wasn't acting for her benefit – of that Maggie was sure. Kate's eyes were bright. She wants people, Maggie thought. She wants people.

Aly was a couple of hours behind Stan – she often stayed to study in the library after school. She let herself in just after six o'clock, dropping her rucksack in the hall and going straight up to her room. Maggie waited a couple of minutes, then knocked quietly on the door. Aly gave her usual monosyllabic response, which Maggie interpreted as 'enter', and did . . .

'How was your day?'

'Fine, thanks.' It could have meant anything.

'Kate is here. I thought you might come down and meet her . . .'

'Can I come down in a minute? I just want to do something . . .' She had her back to Maggie and her computer was already switched on and glowing.

'Sure.' Maggie closed the door behind her.

It was more like half an hour. Maggie had made dinner and the three of them were already sitting at the table when Aly eventually responded to first Maggie's and then Stan's cries up the stairs. Maggie was irritated. It mattered to her that Kate knew Aly and Stan were good kids – well brought up. So far, only Stan was conveying that.

When she sauntered in and slid into her chair, Aly had

Chapter Twenty-Three

It was Friday night. Liv had been back in Sydney for a week and back at work for five days. She'd just about caught up on the emails, meetings and minutes that she'd missed, working long hours and falling asleep in her salad bowl most evenings. It was blissful to be back in the hot sun – she'd felt her body unfolding and relaxing over the last few days. Maggie had called a couple of times and they'd chatted, but she couldn't figure out how it was going with Kate, except that it seemed, on the surface, to be going well. Kate was still there . . . Better than she might have dared hope, actually, but she hadn't had that much time to talk. She'd promised Maggie and herself that she'd call at the weekend, when she had time, and they'd have a long talk. But this evening was for Scott. He'd picked her up from the airport last week and they'd had Sunday together, but they'd been the proverbial ships passing all week. She'd suggested he meet her after work and they'd go for a drink in the Rocks and maybe have some dinner by the harbour. Reclaim the city.

Scott, it seemed, had had other ideas. 'Come home,' he'd said. 'I want to cook . . .'

It was still a little strange to think of his place as her home. Things had moved so fast and been punctuated by her long trip to see Maggie and the kids. She'd given up her own apartment just before she'd gone to England and moved in with him the week before, so it didn't feel entirely like her place yet. It hadn't taken much thinking to choose his over hers. Scott owned, she rented. She'd felt no real attachment to her place. Magnolia walls, paper blinds at the windows and not enough cupboard space. Five minutes too far from the bus. And with some particularly noisy Greek neighbours, who were lovely and warm but kept late hours. Scott's apartment was in a cooler area – just off Darling Street in Balmain. It wasn't huge, but it had two bedrooms and a balcony off the largish living room, which had the kitchen along one wall. She wouldn't mind repainting the place – it was bachelor off-white throughout and a splash of colour, she thought, would do wonders for it. She'd brought her well-upholstered sofa with her and made him promise to get rid of his own stained two-seater, which had seen much, much better days. New bed linen had brightened up the bedroom, and while she was away, he'd set up a study area for her in the second bedroom, with a flat-pack Ikea desk and her computer. He'd unpacked her books and stacked them on the shelves alphabetically, and that touched her immeasurably. There were just a few more cardboard boxes to unpack and then she would be home.

It was sweet that he wanted to cook for her – he was, it seemed, as keen to play house as she was. She stopped at the hip delicatessen on Darling Street and picked up a bunch of gladioli and a bottle of white wine from the chiller cabinet.

He'd already thought of both. He handed her a glass of champagne as she walked through the front door. He'd changed into shorts and a T-shirt, but they were smarter than his normal weekend garb. He'd got her kitsch fifties apron on over the top of them, and she winked at him, smiling. Some kind of meat was marinating in a bowl on the work surface and the barbecue was fired up on the balcony. Two different salads were on the table, where a single red rose was in a bud vase.

'Wow.' She sniffed the marinade, her nose deep in the bowl. 'You've really gone to town. Marinating. Fancy.'

'I've gone to the deli, you mean!'

'Wherever you've gone, it smells delicious. And I'm not making it, so you'll hear only praise and compliments. You may be establishing a precedent, I should warn you. Thank you, roomie. Cheers!' He clinked glasses with her and kissed her lightly on the lips.

'Cheers. Happy Friday. Happy weekend!'

Liv stepped out of her heels, with relief. 'Have I got time to change?'

'Sure. Barbecue's not even hot yet.'

She wandered into the bedroom and put her glass down on the dresser while she unzipped her work dress and stepped out of it. Reaching into the overstuffed closet – thinking that they really would need to do something about that – she pulled out a pink cotton sundress. She unhooked her bra, feeling the instant relief of not being encased in nylon and wire, and pulled the dress on over her head.

'That's much better.' She wandered back into the lounge and then out on to the balcony, where Scott was laying lamb on the hot grill. He put the lid down and turned to her.

'How's it been, then?'

'What?'

'This. The first proper week of living here with me. In sin.'

'The sin's been a bit thin on the ground.'

'I thought we might start rectifying that tonight . . .' He nuzzled her neck.

'Sounds like a plan.' Liv ran her hand slowly down his back on to his bum in a possessive gesture.

'But the rest?'

'You fishing for compliments, Scott? The rest is great. Wonderful. I love being here with you.'

'You sure? Not missing Maggie and the kids too much?'

She sighed. 'I always miss Maggie. That's just how it is. If I'm missing Maggie, though – there's nowhere else I'd rather be doing it and no one else I'd rather be doing it with . . .'

His arms snaked around her waist. 'Good. Because I'm nuts about you.'

'I know. Thank God.'

Then he stood back.

'And I've got something to ask you . . .'

He pulled a small box out of the apron pocket. And Liv immediately knew what was coming.

'I've thought a lot about how to do this . . .'

Her hands flew to her mouth. Funny how you could be so surprised, even when you pretty much knew something was settled. Even when you'd been half expecting it.

'And in the end, I decided I wanted it to be just us. Just us doing our normal stuff. Because this is what I want to do – with you – for the next however many years. For the rest of my life . . .'

'Scott!'

'And I knew I wanted to do it properly . . .' He got down on one knee. 'And I just couldn't imagine doing that in front of a whole bunch of people in a restaurant.'

'Scott . . .'

'Sssh . . . Let me do this, will you?'

She put a finger up to her lips in a gesture of silence.

'Olivia – will you marry me?'

Liv got down on her own knees so that they were on a level and took his face – his beloved face – in her hands, planting kisses all over it.

'Yes. Yes. Yes. Of course. Of course I'll marry you . . . God, Scott . . . Yes!'

'Soon. I want to do it soon.' They'd finished the champagne, and some wine, and the lamb and salad. The sun was setting and they were lying, both on one sunlounger, wrapped in each other. Liv was wearing her ring and kept waving at no one so the fading light caught it and made it sparkle.

'You don't think people will think we're rushing it all?' Scott said. 'I mean . . . a year ago, we had just met. We're living together. Now we're engaged.'

'Don't care what people think. The people who know us know it's right. We know it's right. What's the point of waiting?'

'I agree. I don't want to be engaged for ever. I want to be married. To you.'

'Where shall we do it?'

'You want to tell my parents we're not doing it at their place?' He was laughing.

'A country wedding?!'

'Why not? It'd be nice.'

'It would.' Liv hadn't thought of it, but now that she did, she could visualize it. She wasn't into flashy, not really. A country wedding would be picturesque and intimate and very family. Perfect. 'Not too big, though, right . . .?'

'That's one way to keep it small, for sure. There's a limit to the number of people who are going to want to go all the way out there. A destination wedding is going to sort the wheat from the chaff.'

Liv leant on one elbow, her ring hand on Scott's chest. Her eyes were sparkling and her cheeks were pink. He'd never seen her look lovelier and he was proud to be the reason.

'So. Did you ask Maggie, while you were over?'

'Of course I did. Your dad too. But Maggie was the clincher.'

'What did she say?'

'All the right things, Livvy.' He squeezed her shoulder. 'She wants you to be happy. She wants you to have your own family. She really does.'

'I know. I'm going to call her.'

'Call her tomorrow, Liv.' He tightened his grip on her. 'Tomorrow you can call whoever you want. Tonight, you're mine. I'm not letting go . . . They've all got to wait.' His voice had a stern edge and she knew he was serious, and she knew why, too.

Liv sat up and straddled him. 'That's how it's going to be, is it? Got the ring on my finger and now it's okay to start issuing the orders . . .'

Scott slapped her arse. 'Damn straight, woman.'

The next day, Maggie was the first person she called.

'He asked me, Maggie. He proposed. You don't have to sound surprised. I know he told you he was going to do it . . . You just have to sound deliriously happy for me.'

Maggie squealed. 'I am, Liv! That's fantastic!'

'I know! I'm so happy, Mags. It was perfect . . .'

'So, come on. The kettle's on. I'm alone in the house.'

'Alone in the house? Is that a good or a bad thing?'

Maggie laughed. 'Good. Weird, but good. Stan is out with his latest crush, Kate.'

'He likes her?'

'He loves her.'

'That's fantastic. I mean, it is, isn't it?'

'It's nice, yes. It's nice to see.'

'I'm so glad. Where are they?'

'They've gone to the London Dungeon!' Maggie giggled, and the girlish sound made Liv glad.

'Again! He didn't get enough of that crap the last time?'

'Guess not. Kate had never been . . .'

'Poor woman. She'll send him home in a cab and you'll never see her again.'

'I don't think so . . . But enough. Enough about us. I want to talk about you for a bloody change. I want to hear all about it . . . Leave no detail out.'

'I will. First, though . . . We're going to do it at Easter. Here. Say you'll come . . .'

'How could you even ask? Of course. We'll all be there.'

Chapter Twenty-Four

'Kate?'

'Olivia?' Kate recognized Liv's voice on the phone, though it wasn't a great line.

'Yes. It's me. How are you doing?'

'I'm well, thank you.'

'Good. Is Maggie there?'

'I'm sorry, Olivia, she isn't.'

'No.' Liv's voice sounded relieved. 'I'm glad. It was you I wanted to speak to . . .'

'Is something wrong?'

'No. No. Everything's fine here. I just wanted to know how it was all going, at your end . . .'

'Has Maggie said something?'

'No, Kate. Relax. Maggie says you're great.'

'Really?'

'Really. I want to know how you're . . . how you're finding them all . . . You know – how you think they all are. I talk to Maggie all the time, but I just . . . I just . . .'

'Want to know how they *really* are?'

'Exactly. Sometimes I think Maggie tells me what she thinks I want to hear.'

'And you wonder if it's completely true?'

'Yeah. I'm not asking you to spy . . .'

'I understand, Olivia.' She did. There was always how you said you were feeling and how you were really feeling.

'I thought you would.' Liv's voice was instantly more relaxed. 'So, do you have a minute to chat . . . ?'

'Of course.' Kate sat down, and pulled the mug of tea she'd just made for herself over towards her.

'Is she sleeping?'

Kate shook her head, though Liv couldn't see it, of course. 'Not brilliantly, I don't think. I hear her, most nights. She goes to bed, sometimes early, but the light is always on when I go past and then I hear her creeping down – 3 or 4 a.m. most nights. Sometimes she's dozed off on the sofa when I get up to make Stan's breakfast.'

'Ah . . .' Liv sounded disappointed. Kate carried on. 'But she has kept up that running you and she were doing when you left. She's running quite a bit, actually.'

'I thought that would help with the sleep.'

'It will. It will, I'm sure. It takes time . . .' Kate didn't mention Maggie's red-rimmed, baggy eyes, the eyes she appeared with three or four mornings a week, the eyes Aly and Stan, she knew, recognized, and understood, and ignored. She didn't want to lie to Olivia but she didn't want to burden her either, living her own life so far away. Wasn't that why Liv had called her in the first place? It couldn't be wrong to emphasize the positive. 'She loves it – I can tell.'

'She always did. You knew she was a swimmer, right?'

'I gathered . . .'

'She doesn't swim any more.'

'No.'

There was a long-distance pause. 'Aly?'

Kate took a deep breath. Aly was a complex girl. She hadn't exactly cracked the hard-boiled exterior, but she just knew – she was sure – there was someone soft and vulnerable and sad just below it. It was in the quiet, quick glances she gave her mother when Maggie didn't know she was looking.

It was in the way she ruffled Stan's hair and kissed the top of his head whenever she walked past him. But mostly Aly and Maggie circled each other, cautious and careful, and the tension between them was palpable. That brittle atmosphere had to be affecting Stan, though on the surface he seemed oblivious to it. It was more than just normal teenage angst. They weren't seeing each other. Not really. Kate thought it had probably been years since they had. Two years, to be precise, she supposed . . . It was heartbreaking to see. Kate imagined Aly's inner voice crying out, unheard – I'm still here, Mum. Jake's gone but I'm still here.

'Aly's complicated, I think.'

Liv laughed. 'D'you think?'

Kate smiled. 'But aren't we all?'

'But you're happy there, Kate? You want to stay, for now, at least . . .?'

It was a long time since anyone had asked Kate if she was happy. Probably longer still since she'd have been able to say yes.

'I'm really happy here, Olivia. I'm loving looking after them.'

'I'm glad. I'm relieved, and I'm glad . . .'

'Tell me about when you were married, Kate . . .'

Kate was cooking. Aly was in the kitchen with her. She'd taken to coming down for dinner early, when her head had taken all the physics and chemistry it could – Kate was usually making something from scratch and Aly liked to watch her work, and to chat. Kate was good to chat to. Easy and interesting. By virtually unspoken agreement, Kate made dinner during the week and at the weekends the kitchen became Maggie's domain again.

Mum had started running again on her own since Liv had

left – she ran three or four miles while Kate made dinner. Sometimes more. She hadn't run this way since Jake was born, she'd told Kate. She'd forgotten how much she loved it. How good it felt. The runs were doing her good – they could all see that. Not just physically. She seemed brighter, lighter. She was sleeping for longer, waking less, dreaming less . . .

Aly had had marriage on the brain since Liv's announcement. Revising was dull and tiring, and her brain appreciated the escape into the fantasy of her aunt's wedding – and everyone else's for that matter. She'd stared at the shadow box of her mum and dad's wedding – utterly familiar but strangely mysterious. It had hung on the wall up the stairs for ever, but she'd hardly ever really looked at it. They looked so young, and so happy, Dad's hand across the slight swell of Mum's belly. It seemed so strange – that she'd been pregnant when they got married. That they were that kind of couple.

'What do you want to know?'

'Tell me how he proposed . . . the mushy stuff.'

Kate laughed and tucked her hair behind her ears. 'It wasn't all that mushy. And it wasn't all that exciting – at least I don't suppose you'd think so. I'm afraid you might be disappointed.'

'Tell me anyway . . . I don't even know his name.'

Kate was rolling pastry. She floured the rolling pin and went to work on the dough, turning the plastic board she was using every couple of rolls to create a perfect circle.

'His name was Philip.'

'Okay – so you and Phil. Dish.' Aly had her face in her hands, her elbows on the table, ready to listen.

'Philip. He was never a Phil.' She made a mock stern face at Aly, then smiled. 'Okay – I'll tell you, since you insist. Well. It was at dinner. We were in London. We'd been to a matinée show – *Miss Saigon* – and we'd gone to a restaurant nearby afterwards for an early dinner . . .'

'Hold on – were you living together at this point?'

'No. We certainly weren't . . . We each had our own house. They were close by, though.'

'But you'd been . . . you know . . . You two were together . . . ?'

'Yes, Aly – we were a couple!' Kate made the face Aly had come to recognize – a combination of faux primness and mischievousness. It meant that was all she was going to say on that particular subject.

'Okay, okay. So . . . was it summer, winter, what?'

'It was a balmy August night, as I remember. The rare kind when you don't need a cardigan in the evening . . .'

'Right. Scene set. What were you wearing . . . since we know it wasn't a cardigan?'

Now Kate laughed. 'I have absolutely no idea, you crazy girl!'

'Just asking! I think I'd remember. What happened?'

'He asked me, at dinner. I said yes . . .'

'Was there a bended knee? Do you remember what he said – the exact words?'

'No bended knee. And yes, I remember.'

'And . . . ?'

Kate smiled. 'He asked me if I would do him the honour of becoming his wife.'

'Aah . . . !'

'You're so funny, Aly. There are only so many ways a man can ask, you know . . .'

'But that's a good one. "The honour." I like that . . . Old school. Traditional. I like it.'

Kate laughed. 'The proposal doesn't really matter, Aly. Any more than the actual wedding does. It's the marriage that matters.'

'I know that. But I like weddings. What kind was yours?'

'Very small.'

'How small?'

'Just us and two friends. We didn't tell them what was happening until the day – they thought they were just coming for lunch. We went to the Register Office, got married in ten minutes flat and then the four of us had a posh lunch. That was it.'

'Honeymoon?'

'Not straight away, no. We were moving house. "Old school" – not living together before marriage, I know.'

'Gotta try before you buy, you know, Kate.'

Kate frowned at the vulgarity but Aly had her eyebrow raised, the way her mother did, and she didn't really mind the gentle teasing.

'We went to Africa on a safari a few weeks later, once things were settled.'

'Safari. Very intrepid.' Kate flicked the flour from her fingers in Aly's direction.

'It was wonderful.'

'I'm being serious. I'd love to go on a safari. Dad used to talk about taking us . . .' Her voice trailed off, and Kate knew what she meant. She'd learnt that – since she'd been here. There were two lives in this house: the one lived before Jake died, with its promises of safaris and skydiving and all manner of other things, and there was life after Jake. The colour had gone, and the energy.

Aly shook it off. 'I want a huge wedding.'

'Then I daresay you'll have one. How big is your Auntie Liv's going to be, do you think?'

'Not sure. If they only have Scott's family, there'll be a hundred. He's practically from a clan; there's loads of them.'

'Are you the only bridesmaid?' Liv had called a couple of

weeks previously and asked Aly if she would do it. No naff dress, she'd promised. She'd give Aly the colours and let her choose her own. She'd pay. Maggie said it was okay so long as she promised it wouldn't interfere with her concentrating on the exams that would follow hard on the heels of the trip.

'Yep. I think she quite wanted Mum to be a matron of honour, but she said she'd hate it. Refused to go, I believe, until Auntie Liv said she didn't have to do it. I'm going to love it though.'

'It's a rite of passage, they say, for young girls. Nice to get to do it. You haven't been one before?'

'Nope. Never. Were you?'

'Twice.' Kate nodded. 'Now you're really going back . . . Don't even remember who for – one was my mother's brother, I think . . . No clue who the other one was. I just remember the dresses. One was stiff, scratchy pink, and I hated it. One was pastel green and I felt like Elizabeth Taylor in *National Velvet* when I was wearing it!' Kate laughed to herself at the vivid childhood memory.

Aly sauntered to the counter and pulled out the envelope Liv had sent with the colours in it – they were paint swatches on cardboard from a paint shop – but she said they were a good match for the flowers and the tablecloths – cornflower blue and a soft primrose yellow. It would still be pretty warm, though it was definitely autumn for them. The shops here were starting to fill up with summery stuff and weddingy-type outfits, and she'd seen a couple of possibles at the weekend in town. One gorgeous silky clingy dress – floor length, with spaghetti straps – in exactly the right blue – had particularly caught her eye. She wasn't sure she could get away with it so far as her mum was concerned – it was definitely a sexy dress. Liv had made her promise to take a photograph on the phone of whatever she was thinking of buying. Maybe she'd take Kate on Saturday and see what she thought her mum would think of it, use her as a filter . . .

'How long were you married?' she absently asked Kate now.

Kate hesitated for just a moment before she spoke. 'Ten years.'

Aly was surprised – she looked at her sharply and thought that Kate wouldn't catch her eye. She'd have thought it would have been much longer than that.

Kate had finished rolling out the pastry and her pie was ready for the oven, so her back was turned.

Aly was about to ask her more, but Stan came haring in from football practice, smelling, sweating and shrieking, and the moment passed.

Chapter Twenty-Five

Kate had to bite her lip sharply to stop hot tears springing into her eyes, grateful that Aly and Stan had sloped away to another part of the house to watch TV or chat on the phone. Tears that sprang, three years on, quite often when she thought of Philip. She still missed him every day – she always would. Aly was right about one thing. It hadn't been long enough. Ten years with him hadn't been anywhere near enough. A lifetime wouldn't have been, either.

Philip had been the best man she had ever known. The best man anyone could know. It wasn't lucky to have lost him, but she was lucky to have had him. She'd always assumed she'd die first. He had been, after all, ten years younger than her. The natural order would mean it was Philip, and not her, left alone.

It had been a heart attack that killed him. An ordinary, unforeseen, sudden massive coronary. No opportunity to take care of him, no chance to nurse him. She hadn't even seen him until she'd arrived at the hospital, and he was already dead, laid out in the room they reserved for that specific, ghastly moment when a loved one sees a body for the first time. He'd died on the floor of his office, after morning surgery, his fellow GPs at the practice helpless in the face of the attack's severity, for all the equipment that surrounded them. That morning had been like all the others. He'd always risen earlier than her – he liked to make a pot of coffee and read the paper, potter in the garden. Kate liked to stay in bed. He showered and dressed quickly and quietly, and made her a cup of tea. She would invariably open her eyes as he stood at her side of the bed, the clink of a porcelain cup being put on the nightstand her wake-up call. He'd smile at her, kiss her gently and then go to work. Sometimes that was their only connection in the morning – often they said no words to each other. She'd never been able to remember, afterwards, whether he'd said anything. Whether she'd replied. Not that it mattered. They both knew. It was understood.

It had sometimes seemed to Kate that she'd lived her life the wrong way round. She'd been a giddy, deliriously happy newly-wed in her early fifties. He'd been forty years old when they'd married – she'd been almost fifty-one. They'd married in the Register Office in Tunbridge Wells on a sunny, cold February morning, his sister Steph and her husband, Bryan, the only witnesses. She'd worn a smart cream suit. Steph, despite their protestations that everything was to be very low key, had arrived with a beautiful orchid corsage for Kate, and buttonholes for Bryan and Philip. They'd had lunch afterwards at a fireside table in the restaurant at the Hotel du Vin – Steph had ordered champagne and they'd toasted quietly their future. Hands down, the happiest day of her life.

He'd brought her to life. She saw something in this family. The lights had gone out when Jake died. Everything was dimmer and duller and darker. The opposite was true with her and Phillip. The lights had come on and everything had glowed. She might have wished that she'd found him when she was younger, but something about having lived so much of her life without having the feeling of being loved and appreciated and just . . . seen made it more precious. She was grateful, every day, for him, and she wondered whether young brides felt that in quite the same way.

He wasn't particularly handsome, though he was lovely to her. Average height, a little overweight, truthfully. Receding hair and round glasses. He'd loved Alexander McCall Smith novels and opera and Mornington Crescent on *I'm Sorry I Haven't a Clue*, roses and his lovingly restored Austin Healey Sprite. He'd been a GP, in the same practice for fifteen years, a partner for ten, and he'd never tired of his work, devoted, it seemed, to the patients he'd known and cared for for so long. You might have called him a pillar of the community, if you used that kind of expression. She'd been incredibly proud of that. And he'd loved her.

They'd bought a house together, both having sold the homes they'd had before they were a couple. It was a fairly modest three-bedroom detached house in the Riverhead part of town, close to where Philip worked, but it was very pretty, with a large, established and much-loved garden, and they'd filled it with antiques and artwork they bought together, trawling furniture shops and galleries at the weekends.

They'd only had ten years. But what a time they'd had. She didn't regret a moment of it. They'd travelled whenever they could – the Kenyan safari was an extraordinary honeymoon, cruises in the Norwegian fjords, and to the Italian Riviera. Walking in the Scottish highlands and weeks visiting vineyards in Bordeaux and the Dordogne. At home, they'd had a small circle of good friends – mostly his – and there were dinner parties and concerts and theatre trips. Philip had loved to take her shopping for clothes. He had great taste and a good eye, and he loved to see her in stylish outfits. He was a great gift-giver – he found beautiful pieces of jewellery – and he gave her presents often, and for no reason, except that it pleased him. They had been the greatest of friends – confidants. They'd been lovers – she missed that side of their life together almost as much as anything else, that sense of physical well-being that came from being physically loved well. It had been everything and more than she'd ever wanted and ever imagined marriage could be.

Sometimes, since he died, she'd wondered if she had deified him. Could anyone have been as perfect as he sounded? As good a husband? She tried to remember fights, but there'd been so few cross words – anyway, who cared? Who had the right, or even the need to tell her that *wasn't* how her marriage to Philip had been? Let her have it; that was all she had left, after all – a memory. A memory of a man who she knew loved her deeply for exactly who she was. And a marriage that had crammed a lifetime of happiness into a decade. There would never be another husband. She didn't want one.

At his funeral, from the pulpit, in a church full to bursting with his patients and their friends, she'd read – amazed at the strength and the power and the steadiness of her own voice – from the Tennyson poem *In Memoriam A.H.H.*, about it being better to have loved and lost than never to have loved at all. It expressed exactly how she felt. His will, which left her more than comfortable for the rest of her life, was lodged with his solicitor, along with a love letter that she now kept inside a volume of Tennyson's poetry, on the page of the poem. She didn't need to read it any more – not the Tennyson, or the letter. She knew both by heart.

There was just one regret. One thing marriage to Philip hadn't left her with, because it had been too late, when she met him, to start: a family. That was why she'd placed the ad. That was why she was here. That was what she wanted. She hoped it was understood that it didn't come from a need to be cared for. It was a need to care for someone else.

And already she felt she might be helping, just a little. It was always easier to diagnose other people than yourself.

She'd been in the house less than a week before she felt like she understood some of what was wrong, apart from the bald, obvious fact that this family had disintegrated in the aftermath of a tragedy. Aly was a gorgeous girl – funny, kind, smart. But she'd had her heart broken – badly – when her brother died. A brother she'd loved, looked up to, emulated and still, Kate suspected, almost competed with two years after his death. She'd half-killed herself trying to hide how much she was hurting – deferring to her parents' more obvious, more recognized pain. But it was still there and maybe it wasn't dealt with yet. Several times Aly had started to talk about Jake to her, and Kate had been conscious of her holding herself back. If she did that with her, Kate suspected she did it even more with her own mother. Maggie saw some of it – Kate knew that. But Maggie didn't know how to reach her daughter. And she didn't grasp, Kate thought, how this slight girl had buckled under the self-imposed weight of trying to carry her whole family – her dead brother, her beleaguered brother, her shattered mother, her alienated father. It was too much. Kate's heart ached for her. Beneath the self-assured exterior of an almost-adult, Kate was sure Aly was just a little girl who needed to feel loved and looked after, because she'd done too much of that for herself and for other people. Stan was a little boy who needed bags of attention, infinite quantities of patience. Maggie had thrown herself into caring for him after Jake, into fixing a more concrete problem; Aly had fallen between the cracks. Kate wished she had met Bill – he was a missing piece in the puzzle she was trying to piece together. She wanted to look at him and figure out why he'd had to go. Whether he might come back. What recalibrations would need to be made for that to happen . . .

She hadn't pushed Maggie to talk about anything at first.

The two of them had chatted a lot, but not deeply at all. But a couple of days earlier, she'd been going upstairs when the two of them were alone in the house and Maggie had been stood, frozen, halfway up a flight of stairs, staring at one of her shadow boxes. It contained, Kate knew, because she'd looked one day while everyone was out, a bright-orange water wing, a blue rubber admission wristband and a tiny pair of goggles pinned on to an eight-by-ten photograph of a baby – maybe six months old – that she knew must be Jake, held aloft in Maggie's arms. Water droplets sprayed from him, her hair was slicked back. Her tanned skin was in sharp contrast to his baby whiteness. It was a terrific photograph – you could almost hear the giggle that must be emitting from Jake's delighted, excited face as his mother held him high above the water, her mouth wide open in a mirroring face, eyes open wide. Their eye contact was unbroken – their connection immediately obvious. It was a photo of a mother and child that had made Kate's heart contract with envy when she'd first noticed it. Maggie's hand was gripping the banister as she stood there, and she didn't seem to have heard Kate coming up behind her.

'Is that Jake?' Kate asked, knowing full well that it was.

Maggie nodded but didn't look at her.

'Will you tell me about him?'

Something like a groan came from Maggie then, and she sank down on to the stair. Kate sat beside her, and waited. She was shocked when Maggie laid her head on her shoulder briefly. They had had no physical contact at all since their first handshake. She sat still, and waited again.

When she raised her head, Maggie started to speak.

'Oh, he was a gorgeous baby. I gave birth in water. I'd grown up in water, and when I was pregnant and I read about it, about water birth, it made so much sense to me. It was where I felt happiest – in the water. And this was 1986. It wasn't that unusual – though from the way Bill's mum went off you'd have thought I was planning to give birth on the top of a double-decker on Oxford Street.' Maggie laughed at the recollection. 'We had this birthing pool thing. It was more like a high-sided paddling pool. Bill blew it up weeks too early and there it was, in the living room of our first flat – which was tiny, so there was basically no floor left. We were walking around it for days. His mum wouldn't come round after the first time she'd seen it – so it wasn't all bad. Said it made her feel queasy. Daft woman. It made me feel calmer, weirdly enough. Bill said I was like a mermaid in a fairy tale – only at peace when I was in warm water. You couldn't get me out of the bath, my first few months here. It was the warmest place, except in front of his mum's Aga, but in the bath I didn't have to listen to her going on! That woman wasn't happy unless she was moaning about something.'

'And you got to have him in the water.' Kate knew it didn't always work out.

Maggie nodded, smiling, deep in the memory. 'Yes, I think I was lucky – it was a straightforward labour, I guess. Eight hours. I was only in the pool for the last three or four hours. Bill had to keep refilling it with hot water. One big push at the end and I was able to pull him out with my own two hands. I have this incredibly clear memory of the first time I saw him – coming up towards me like a water baby with his eyes wide open.'

She fell silent.

'Did he love the water too, after that start?' Kate gently encouraged her. It was good to hear her talk about him like this.

'He had no choice. I had him down at the pool the minute he'd finished the first lot of vaccinations and we were signed off to be there. Every other day. Sometimes more. He learnt to swim really young . . .

'But he was always a fast learner. The kind of kid things come to easily, you know? He saw something, he went for it . . . He was always moving, always on the go . . . He'd chase another kid's ball across the park, or follow someone's puppy, you know?' Kate nodded. 'And happy – he was always such a happy boy. He used to sing, in his pushchair. I couldn't get round Sainsbury's when he was small – old people used to love him, they'd come up and cluck over him, and he'd just sit there and chortle away – loving all the attention. He sang himself to sleep too. We'd put him in his cot and creep out, and sometimes just sit outside his room listening to him singing to himself . . .'

She choked back a sob that instantaneously replaced the smile in her voice.

Then looked right at Kate.

'Do you know what makes me really sad? He was going to be such a man . . . such a nice, good man. He was going to have a great life. You could just tell, you know?'

'I know.' Kate lightly stroked her arm. 'I know.'

'And he didn't get the chance. It just seems so . . . wrong . . .'

That night, Bill poured a glass of wine for Carrie and for himself. She'd changed into one of his sweatshirts and a pair of the yoga pants he found almost irresistible, but this evening he was preoccupied.

'Dinner and cinema?'

'Cinema and dinner? That way round?'

'No way. Dinner first.'

'You sure? Maybe we could go ice skating or something?'

'Skydiving?'

'Now you're making fun of me . . .'

'I'm not, I promise.'

'I just want it to go well.'

'And it will, Bill – unless you get too uptight about it. This isn't like you . . .' Bill was sitting on the sofa with his feet up on the coffee table and his laptop open in front of him, clearly Googling furiously.

Carrie perched on the arm of the sofa behind him and gently ruffled his hair. He leant back against her and she kissed the top of his head.

'I'm sorry.'

'Don't be. I understand.'

He had Aly and Stan on Friday night. And he was going to introduce them to Carrie for the first time. It was time. He felt the need, now, to connect these two vital halves of his life.

He'd asked Carrie first. And then Maggie. The order was significant, he realized – a subtle shifting . . . Carrie had smiled her crooked rosebud smile and nodded, her pleasure evident on her face. Maggie had been less enthusiastic, although since he had telephoned her, not gone round, he couldn't completely gauge her reaction. He thought he understood every nuance of her voice, but maybe he didn't any more.

She'd been quiet for a moment and then asked, 'Are you asking me or telling me?'

Bill had no ready answer. 'Bit of both.'

He was smiling when he spoke, but there was less warmth in her response. He heard a deep sigh.

'No point keeping them apart, Bill. You don't need me to tell you that I don't think it's a good idea – especially for Stan – to introduce them to a parade of different girls . . .'

'There are no different girls!' He knew he sounded indignant. But she was out of line.

'You didn't let me finish . . .' He'd hated that tone of voice when they'd lived together. The way she sometimes talked to him like he was one of the children. But he let her finish.

'I know she isn't just some girl. I know she means something.'

His turn to pause. Then, 'Thank you, Maggie.' Though he couldn't see her, he imagined the small, resigned shrug, so unlike his Maggie, old Maggie, and he felt sad.

Aly was torn, once her dad had called to arrange the evening. He'd said Mum knew, and she was fine with it, but how could she be? Aly figured it had to feel really weird and probably horrible. But she didn't want to raise it with her mum – they weren't in 'that place' right now – Liv had helped and Kate was helping, definitely, but still . . . She talked to Kate instead – while her mum was out on one of her pre-dinner runs. Stan was glued to the Disney Channel upstairs and Kate was cooking in the basement. Kate handed her a colander of sugar snap peas and a small knife. Kate was really good at making spaces to talk into. Aly couldn't figure out how or why her mum's silences seemed so different, but they did. Kate turned down the news so that the newsreader was mute and carried on rubbing a crumble mix in a bowl while Aly began to top and tail the peas.

'Did Mum tell you me and Stan are going to meet Dad's new girlfriend on Friday?'

'She did,' Kate nodded, slowly.

'Is she okay with it, like Dad says?'

Kate looked up from the crumble. 'Did you ask her?'

'I'd rather ask you. I know she talks to you.'

'She'd like to talk to you . . .'

''Cos I won't go, if it's freaking her out.'

Aly determinedly pressed ahead, side-stepping Kate's gentle nag.

'I'm sure she'd be touched to hear that. And equally sure she'd tell you to go. Aren't you curious to meet her?'

Aly shrugged. 'It's a bit strange.'

'Bound to be.'

'I don't know what she's supposed to be to me. I don't even know if I want her to be anything.'

'I wouldn't plan it. There's no hurry. She's just a person.'

'A person who is bonking my father.'

Kate stifled a smile. It made Aly giggle.

'I mean, I'm seventeen, for God's sake. I'm supposed to find that disgusting, right?'

Kate, her fingers all crumbly, raised one arm to rub her nose with her forearm.

'I think that's probably pretty normal, yeah.'

'Must be that times a hundred for Mum.'

'Your mum is okay, Aly. Go. Meet her. Keep an open mind. It's not a disloyal thing to do, truly it isn't.'

Aly slid the colander along the work surface towards Kate and her bowl. When she was right next to her, Aly put her head on Kate's shoulder.

'I'm glad you're here, Kate.'

Me too, Kate thought, as she briefly laid her own head against Aly's soft, sweet-smelling hair. Me too.

Thank God for Stan. At some point that Friday night, Carrie, Bill and Aly all thought it. Thank God for Stan and his boisterous, bouncy noisiness, his incessant, inconsequential chatter. He filled an awkward silence like no one else.

Aly had thought she was pretty chilled before she'd walked in, but Carrie's age and her ethereal, tiny prettiness had thrown her. Carrie wasn't what she'd pictured.

Stan had rushed up to Carrie and shaken her hand, brandishing his pack of UNO cards and asking her if she played. Aly had hung back while Carrie talked to him. After a few minutes, Bill took Stan to the bar with him and left Carrie and Aly together. Carrie gestured to the table and Aly slid into a chair opposite the one on which Carrie had already draped her jacket and handbag. A really nice handbag actually, Aly registered.

'Your dad tells me you're up to your eyeballs in your A levels.' The tone was bright and friendly, but it wasn't a question so Aly didn't answer.

'That must be hard work,' Carrie persevered.

Aly shrugged. 'Yep.'

Carrie lined up her knife and fork, straightening and restraightening them. Aly felt a twinge of guilt.

'What do you do again?' She remembered well enough, but what the hell.

'I work for a foodie magazine.' Aly thought it was a really cool job, but she was buggered if she was going to let on.

'You want to be a doctor, right?'

'Yes, I do.'

'That's very cool.'

Aly just nodded.

Bill and Stan were still at the bar. Suddenly Aly couldn't stand it any more. She stood up.

''Scuse me, I need the loo.' And she fled.

Carrie exhaled sharply and took a gulp of her white wine. Bill turned and raised his hands in a question. Carrie shrugged and bit her bottom lip, her eyebrows raised. Bill winked at her and smiled reassuringly.

When he got back to the table, while Stan shuffled the UNO cards and read the menu, he reached across the table and picked up Carrie's hand, bringing it to his mouth to kiss it. Across the room, Aly, who had sat on a toilet seat for as long as she dared, saw the gesture, saw her dad's expression as he looked at Carrie, saw Carrie gaze back at him, realizing in an instant that these two people loved each other, and tried to decide how she felt about it.

Later, Bill drove her and Stan home. They'd pretended, or at least Aly thought they'd pretended, that Carrie was heading home to her own place. Stan had fallen asleep almost immediately. Aly stared out of the window.

Bill looked over at her profile. 'How was it for you?'

Aly shrugged.

'I do hate the shrug, Aly. It is no substitute for words.'

'She's very pretty. She's very young. She's very nice.'

'So why the edge of nastiness to your voice?'

'Give me a break, Dad. What did you expect?'

'I expected that you'd be mature enough to give her a chance.'

'I came, didn't I?'

'You almost needn't have done.'

He was surprised by himself. He'd expected he'd walk on eggshells – skirt around Aly's feelings. But she'd pissed him off. Carrie hadn't deserved the frosty reception she'd received. Aly had been sullen and uncommunicative at best, rude at worst.

He was spoiling for the fight he figured Aly wanted too.

But when she'd turned to him, as he stopped at traffic lights, he thought he saw a tear on her cheek.

'You love her, don't you?'

Bill didn't answer straight away.

'You love her and she loves you. I could see it.'

It brought Bill up sharply, that she'd seen it.

And then the transformation was complete: the snarling teenager was the little girl. One, two more tears – rolling unchecked down her cheeks.

Bill pulled over into a lay-by outside a kebab shop.

'Are you going to stop loving us?'

And then he was holding her. The gearstick poked uncomfortably in his ribs but he didn't care – he held her tightly, rocking her back and forth, murmuring into her hair that he would never, ever, ever stop loving all of them, his own voice choked with emotion and his own eyes filled with tears.

They stayed that way for a few minutes, until Aly calmed down and Stan stirred. Aly sniffed and snorted and rubbed mercilessly at her face and by the end of the journey was almost restored. Outside Maggie's house, Bill couldn't say much because Stan was listening.

'Call me. Any time. I mean it, Aly. Whatever you want, whatever you need – I'm here. I'm always here. I'm going nowhere . . .'

'Well, I am. I'm going in. I'm desperate for a pee . . .' Stan broke the mood and opened the door.

Chapter Twenty-Six

Stan, Kate discovered, could talk about Jake totally incidentally – as though he were someone he knew once, even as though he might still be alive, somewhere – without real emotion and sometimes with just passing interest, although often his remarks were tinged with pride. Jake supported Chelsea too, and had played in goal for the school team. Jake was really good at maths. Jake had been brilliant at Lego. Stan mentioned him regularly.

Aly hardly ever did. She had a knack, Kate realized, of heading off any conversation that might lead to a discussion involving Jake – she would make a remark that abruptly about-faced the whole moment. So it surprised her one evening, in the kitchen, when Aly, who was talking about a classmate's plans to InterRail through Europe after exams, said, 'I don't know if they'd let me go, even if I wanted to . . .'

Kate was ironing a school shirt for Stan. 'Why wouldn't they?'

Aly looked at her sharply. 'Duh. Jake. Went off for his gap year – never came home . . .' Her mouth pursed, and Kate could see her biting down on her top lip.

'I know that.' Kate's tone was gentle. 'Did you want to go? On a gap year?'

Aly shook her head. 'I'm not scared, or anything like that . . .'

'It would be understandable if you were, sweetheart.'

'I'm not though. It sounds weird. I want to get past him.'

Kate didn't understand. 'I want to get beyond the point he was at . . .' Aly sounded exasperated by her own inability to explain herself. 'He never got to uni, did he? I mean, he had the grades and everything – we knew he was going, and where and what he was studying . . . all that . . . but he never actually got there.'

Now Kate knew what she meant, but she wasn't quite sure why it mattered. Aly was quiet for a couple of minutes and Kate thought she had closed the subject. She carried on ironing – now a pair of Maggie's jeans – and waited to see what might happen.

'He was extraordinary.' It was a strange word for a sister to use. 'Everyone said so. I think it was the adjective I heard most, when I was a kid, when it was about Jake. He was extraordinary.' Kate nodded. 'I always thought that meant I was just . . . ordinary. No extra.'

'I'm sure that wasn't true, Aly.'

'I know it makes me sound mean and jealous and twisted. But that was how it felt. Do you know, only one person ever really made me feel extraordinary, when I was young. And only sometimes . . . Jake.'

Kate felt at once the burden Aly carried. The loss of the brother she had loved and worshipped, alongside all the envy and the competitiveness and the feelings of inadequacy – a cocktail of sadness and regret and guilt.

'You loved him, but you were jealous of him.'

'That's right.'

'That's normal.'

'It doesn't feel normal. I want to be older than my brother was when he died so I can outdo him, and he's not even here any more. And I know if he were, I'd never outdo him. What's normal about that?'

'All of it, I think . . .'

When she dared look up from the ironing, Aly was look-ing right at her.

'I sometimes feel so twisted up . . .'

Kate wanted to hug her but she sensed it wasn't what Aly wanted. What Aly wanted was to be listened to. So she kept ironing, and Aly kept talking about Jake, about moments in their childhood when she'd loved him so much she thought she'd burst and when she'd almost hated him. About moments when she hadn't really understood how she'd felt about losing him. About the loneliness she'd felt for so long after he'd died, and how it had felt sometimes like her whole family had perished that day, not just him. She didn't cry, though sometimes, just from her voice, Kate could tell that tears weren't far away. And Kate didn't touch her until right at the end, when she sensed she'd talked enough and exhausted herself with it, and then she'd just held her hand for a while, there in the kitchen, and they'd sat that way until Maggie came home and Kate had known that Aly wanted to act normal, and so she'd got up and boiled the kettle for tea and chatted inconsequentially to Maggie about *The Archers* and the fish she'd got for dinner and the window cleaner who'd called earlier, so that Aly could slip away.

She hoped it had helped, saying some of that out loud. She hoped it would happen again, when Aly needed it to.

It was the end of February before Aly saw Ryan again. He was teaching English to foreign students in Edinburgh to earn extra money, and the job had taken him back there straight after Christmas. She hadn't seen him since the magi-cal night of the green dress. 'Wow.' He'd said it twice. 'Wow.' Aly thought his speechlessness, his head shaking, was the nicest compliment she had ever been paid. All he'd done was kiss her. At the end of a gilded evening, where they'd talked and held hands and danced closely together, her head on his shoulder. He'd introduced her to a load of his mates and there'd been some small talk, but mostly he hadn't seemed any more interested in them than she was. He wanted to be with her, Aly was sure of it, and the feeling was more intoxicating than the vodka Red Bulls inside her. Like Cinderella, she had seen the time and almost fled. The return cab had been pre-booked (you had to, if you wanted to be sure they'd be able to come and get you) and she knew, despite her telling her mum and Auntie Liv to go to bed, that they probably hadn't. And even if they'd gone up, one or the other or more likely both of them would still be awake. Mum thought Aly didn't know about her nocturnal life, but she did. Ryan had taken her out, the cold air hitting them both hard after the warmth of the dance floor. The kiss had been sweet, and gentle, and over too soon, before it got too passionate but not before she knew it absolutely could be the most passionate kissing of her young life. People were spilling out of the door, hailing taxis or smoking.

'Thank you. I've had the best time.'

'Me too. I'm glad you came.'

'I don't want to go.'

'Not as much as I don't want you to go . . .' And there'd been one last, lingering kiss.

She'd turned around in the cab and watched him watch her drive away, then she'd fallen back into the seat, hugging herself, her shoulders hunched in delight.

January had seemed long, though they had still written almost every day. Aly was primarily a science and mathematics student, but she was a prolific reader, too. She loved the idea that she and Ryan had a relationship through letters – or at least through the twenty-first-century version of letters – it seemed incredibly romantic to her. As did the secrecy. She hadn't told a soul – not even Liv, before she left. They wrote more than they talked, though he rang her mobile several times a week.

But now he was coming back – he had a reading week, and he was coming south for it. And she was going to his house on Saturday night. His mum and dad were away and he'd agreed to look after the dog. Aly wasn't worried about the implications of that, about what it might mean. She was excited.

She didn't like lying to her mum, but it was easier, some-how, to lie to Dad, and she was supposed to be with him on Saturday night. She took a calculated risk in telling Dad she would spend the day with him on Saturday, but not the night – that she was sleeping over with a friend, hoping he would not tell Mum.

One of the reasons she was keeping this all to herself was that she didn't know what this was. All the fluttery feelings she had ever had about Ryan when he'd been Jake's best friend and a permanent fixture in her house had come flood-ing back. She often wondered what Jake would make of the fledgling relationship. She tried to imagine a scenario where he discovered them, kissing, in her bedroom – how he'd react, how Jake would deal with it. He'd certainly take the piss out of them – she could hear his incredulous response, imagine the jokes he'd make. But maybe he'd have been all right with it, once he'd had a chance to get used to the idea. It could be great – the three of them. A new way to win Jake's approval. What better choice of man could Aly make than the one man Jake was closest to – the one who'd already had Jake's whole-hearted endorsement? She wanted to ask Ryan what he thought Jake would think about them, but she didn't.

She'd dressed incredibly carefully, aware that she was

choosing underwear that someone else might see. All of hers seemed childish, but she hadn't time to shop for new stuff and besides, she didn't know what men – what Ryan – might like. She hoped white cotton wasn't a deal breaker. Because she thought that if he wanted to see it – see her – she might like to show him. It was thrilling and scary all at once.

He'd bought supper from the supermarket – he pulled two or three aluminium containers out of the oven and served the contents on to plates. She'd never been to his house. He had always been at theirs. His was much smarter and more formal. His parents had sculptures and art books and expensive-looking rugs, but the whole thing felt a bit more like a hotel lobby than a home. No wonder he'd always been at their house.

Ryan looked gorgeous. She thought for the trillionth time that it was extraordinary how someone so damn cute could fancy her.

'I'm not much of a cook. I do a mean spaghetti bolognese but that's about it, unless you count fried-egg sandwiches and beans on toast.'

'I like spaghetti bolognese.'

'Next time.' The phrase was easily uttered but laden with meaning. 'I hope you like . . .' he picked up the cardboard sleeves that still lay on the kitchen counter, 'chicken in black bean sauce with red and yellow peppers and white rice.'

'Sounds delicious. Positively gourmet. Smells good too . . .'

'Wine or beer? We have both . . .'

She hesitated. She'd drunk alcohol before, obviously. She'd even been drunk once or twice. But it was weird to be offered alcohol in this civilized, grown-up setting. Dad some-times poured her half a glass with Sunday lunch. Ryan, she realized, was treating her like an adult. She liked it. 'Or coke? Diet coke? I'm not trying to get you drunk, I promise . . .'

She laughed. 'Beer. A beer would be great. I never thought you were. Trying to get me drunk, I mean. I suppose I just feel a bit odd, in your mum and dad's house . . .'

'They don't have a nanny-cam, you know.'

'I know that . . . Sorry – I'm being daft.'

'Doesn't Maggie let you drink?'

'Yes, of course. A glass of wine with dinner . . . sometimes.'

'There you go then. You're doing nothing wrong.'

He popped the tops on two bottles of beer and handed her one, clinking the neck of his bottle against the body of hers. She took a long drink. It was good.

She took a bite of her chicken. It was searingly hot, so she followed it with another gulp of the beer. Ryan was watching her, his eyes on her mouth, in a way that made her feel really self-conscious in a really good way. Maybe this was how sexy felt.

'I'm really glad you're here, Aly.' He held out his hand, demanding hers, and she reached across and took it.

'Me too.'

The kissing had started while they were clearing up after dinner. Aly was loading the plates into the dishwasher when Ryan put his arms around her waist as she bent over and pushed her hair to one side, kissing the side of her neck gently.

'Leave that. It can wait . . .'

Walking backwards, his eyes never leaving her face, he'd pulled her by the hand through into the sitting room and down on to the sofa, pushing her gently back on to the cushions, leaning over her, kissing her mouth now. Aly felt herself start to respond to him, and almost immediately she was in uncharted territory. His hands were in her hair, his thumbs stroking her ears, his mouth hard against her lips. Everything felt extraordinarily good. His breath was coming hard and it was sexy to think she was making it do that. She was lying along the length of the sofa now, and he was on top of her. She stroked his back, above his shirt at first, and then, as he kept on kissing her, under it, feeling his warm soft skin for the first time. He was thrusting at her rhythmically, gently but insistently, and she could feel him, hard against her pelvis, through his jeans. This was new, very new, but she knew how she felt, and she wasn't scared and she knew she wanted it not to stop. One of his hands was on her breast now, squeezing and stroking it through her thin sweater. It felt unbelievable.

Ryan stopped abruptly. His stubble grazed her cheek. He pulled away from her, then put both arms underneath her and pulled her into a sitting position, their legs scissored together, so that she was almost sitting in his lap.

'Whoa.'

'What?' She hadn't done anything like this before. It alarmed her that he'd stopped. 'Did I do something?'

'God, no.' He ran his hand through his hair. 'You're lovely.'

'What then?'

'I just want to make sure that you're sure. You know . . . before either one of us gets carried away. Because I don't know about you, but I'm about this far' – he held two fingers about an inch apart in the air – 'from carried away . . . and I don't want to do anything you'll be sorry about . . . afterwards.'

His eyes were searching her face.

'I mean – I know we haven't talked, or written, about this specifically, but I'm kind of assuming you haven't done this before . . .'

'No.' Aly blushed.

'I have.'

'I figured.'

'Not a lot. I don't want to give you the wrong impression.'

'Ryan . . .'

'But it isn't my first time and it would be yours, so you need to be sure . . .'

'I think I'm sure.'

Ryan laughed. 'That's an oxymoron. Or something. You can't think you're sure.'

'Okay. I'm sure.' She leant forward and kissed the hollow at the base of his throat.

'Sure you're sure?'

Without moving her lips, she reached up and undid the top button of his shirt.

'I think so. Sure.'

That was all Ryan needed. He was just a guy, not a saint.

They weren't in his room – he still had a single bed and a Gisele Bündchen poster in there. Nor in his parents', which would be awful. There was a guest room – he'd put her bag there ostentatiously, when she'd first arrived, anxious to let her know from the start that he had no expectations. He had hopes, that was all. There was a small glass of ranunculus on the bedside table and a fluffy white towel was folded and laid neatly on the counterpane. He must have done all that, and she was touched.

Now, upstairs in the guest bedroom, lit by the landing light through the door he left ajar, she tried to hold her breathing steady. This was a feeling more like panic than she'd expected. She thought she'd be lost in the moment or something – what did they say, swept away, carried away . . . implying abandonment, almost involuntariness . . . but that had stopped, when he'd made her sit up on the sofa so he could talk to her. They hadn't been carried away when they'd walked up the stairs, though he'd taken her hand. It was all a bit . . .

deliberate, conscious. She wasn't carried away. She was a bit frightened.

She didn't know whether she should take her own clothes off or whether he was expecting to undress her. She sort of hoped he would take the lead: he was the one who knew what he was doing, after all. She wasn't sure she knew how to undress in this context. She couldn't see herself in the role of seductress. Ryan was looking at her intently, his eyes dark and piercing. Was it lust, she wondered? The feeling of being out of her depth was alien and unsettling. The beginnings of queasiness bubbled in her stomach, and the garlicky sauce of the chicken supper made her mouth taste metallic. But she couldn't think of a love story where the heroine slipped into the bathroom just before the crucial moment and came back minty fresh to pick up where she'd left off . . .

It wasn't lust in Ryan's eyes. Abruptly, he spun around and sat down on the edge of the bed, his hand covering his mouth. For a second, it looked horribly like he was going to be sick.

'What is it, Ryan?'

'I can't do this. I'm really sorry, but I don't think I can do this, Aly.'

The bizarre coagulation of rejection and relief made her sit down too. She kept her back to him for a moment so he couldn't see her face.

'Did I . . . did I do something?'

'God, no. Please don't think that.'

'What then?' Shame was creeping up on her.

'I just looked at you, just then. And I saw Jake. I saw Jake.'

His voice was small and it shook slightly. It was haunted. God knows, Aly recognized the tone.

She did not know what to say. He knew who she was. He'd known all along. He'd known her since she was a pre-schooler. He'd known that day at the cricket match last summer. And he'd known every time he pressed send on an email. AlyBarrett4@aol.com. Barrett. She'd always been Jake's sister. He knew that.

'I'm so sorry, Aly. I didn't think it mattered.'

'Does it matter?'

'It was just . . .'

She turned slightly – his hunched shoulders were shaking too now.

Aly scooted across the bed and sat beside him. 'Are you crying, Ryan?'

'God. Fuck. Fuck! I haven't done this in a long time. You just brought him back. Completely.'

By just being herself. By just looking like him, Aly thought.

Aly had seen a lot of tears in the last few years. She still thought men crying was the most moving sight . . . She couldn't feel ashamed or rejected – not now. Aly was well used to putting her own feelings away to help other people deal with theirs. She didn't even know she was doing it any more. It was subconscious, instinctive.

'I don't ever talk about the last time I saw him. Alive, I mean. I never have. Not even to Matt – and he was there too. I pretty much thought I'd buried it. I had to. Even though that felt disloyal. But I'm used to that – feeling disloyal. It felt disloyal to stay alive, you know? Doesn't that sound fucked up?'

It might, to anyone else, but it made perfect sense to Aly.

'They call it survivor's guilt, don't they?' She had her arm through his.

'Well, whatever it is,' he shrugged, 'it's a shitty feeling.'

'You know it wasn't your fault. You know there was nothing you could have done. Right? You've known that this whole time?'

'It isn't that simple. Yes, I know that. I understand it. Isn't the same as feeling it or believing it. Not the same at all.'

'What do you mean?'

'I've played that scene out in my own head a million times since it happened.'

'Do you want to tell me what happened?'

'I can't. I can't talk about it, Aly.' Aly remembered the time he came and talked to her mum and she'd sat at the top of the stairs and listened to the muffled sounds of his words and his sobs.

'I think you have to.'

'But not to you. Surely not to you?'

'Why not?'

'We were hung over. Way hung over. We'd been totally drunk the day before. Gone to bed drunk, woken up drunk. We'd been in a dirt-cheap bar up the beach. Shots for – I don't know – God, pennies, really. And we'd done a lot of shots. A lot. Jake wanted to stop. He was always more sensible. He went outside at one point and he was sick. Really sick. He wanted to stop. I told him he could keep going because he'd been sick. I remember he looked at me – you know that face, that face he had – and said okay. So he had a few more. I thought we'd sleep until lunchtime. Later, maybe. Didn't matter. We had nowhere to be, right? This was what it was all about. But I heard him getting up – he had palpitations and stuff, he was in a really bad state. I was pissed off because he'd woken me up. But I wasn't as badly off as he was. I had a pounding headache and a mouth like an arse, but I wasn't like him. He was really brown by that point – you know how brown you guys get – but that morning he was pale under the tan. I sat with him for a while, but then Matt got up too – the pair of us were starving, hung-over hungry, you know? There was a place where they did a fair approximation of a fry-up. About a quarter of a mile from the hut we'd got on the beach. We'd been there pretty much every day. Matt suggested breakfast – I agreed. Jake said he'd come and find us. He couldn't get up off the chair yet, he said. Ten more minutes. We laughed at him. Called him a lightweight. Matt threw him a bottle of water. And we went.'

'For breakfast.'

Ryan nodded. 'We went inland to the café and we left him on the verandah of the beach hut.'

'And he didn't come and find you?'

'No. I suppose he might have fallen asleep. Maybe he was on his way. I don't know, do I? No one does.'

'So you think . . . because you made him drink shots and left him while you went for breakfast . . . you think you're somehow responsible?'

He looked at her, wide-eyed.

'For the tectonic plates on the ocean floor? The nine-point-something earthquake? The absence of a warning system? The universal ignorance about what a tsunami looked like? The umpteen-metres-high waves that pushed inland for miles and miles? You're responsible for all that, are you?'

Ryan didn't answer her. Tears or snot or both were running down his nose, a drip forming at the end of it. He was utterly transformed from the guy he'd been a few minutes earlier – an object of blind lust.

'Like my parents are responsible because they raised a son who wanted an adventure. And like Jake is responsible because he wanted to bum around like Leonardo DiCaprio in *The Beach* and left Australia early?'

'Stop it, Aly.'

'Don't you see how ridiculous you sound, Ryan? Don't you see how little sense that makes?'

'We had a head start. We were inland. We were in a stupid little straw café, but it was next to a four-storey concrete hotel. We had time and we had somewhere to go. We heard the screaming and the shouting and we saw – not the wave but first the mist. Heard the noise. You've no idea how loud rushing water sounds when it's rushing where it's not supposed to be, Aly. We had time – to run into the hotel, to run upstairs. To stand on a bloody balcony next to a rack of drying bikinis and watch it all happening in front of our eyes.'

'And thank God you did. Otherwise you and Matt would be dead too. And that would be worse. Three of you dead, instead of one.'

'How can you say that? He was your brother.'

'And more than a quarter of a million other people who died that day weren't my brother. They weren't anything to me. I never met them and I never would have done. But they died too. You didn't. You lived, Ryan. You have to live.'

'I have to live with the fact that when I saw what was happening, instead of running back to the beach, instead of going after Jake, I ran upstairs to safety . . .'

'You did the only thing you could have done, Ryan. You did what I would have done, what any of us would have done. That's instinctive. Human nature. You're going to hate yourself for that? You can't.'

She pulled him around to face her, and kissed him. She wanted to stop him from talking now. She wanted Jake out of their brains, out of this room. She wanted to feel better and for Ryan to feel better. She wanted to feel lost. Lost in him. For it to just be about the two of them, here, now. The kiss was open-mouthed and passionate, her hands on his head, her torso cleaving to him. She could taste the salt of his tears and the garlic of the chicken on her own tongue, and she kept kissing him.

And then something changed in him, and he kissed her back. His own hand found the back of her head, his fingers twisting strands of her hair, pulling them, and he pushed himself at her and they fell backwards on the bed, rolling, and all the awkwardness of earlier was gone. She wrapped her legs around his back and he pushed his hands up under her clothes. She tugged at the belt loops on his jeans, not knowing exactly what she wanted but knowing it was him who could give it to her. They were naked then, skin to skin, hands moving over each other. Something took over and Aly knew that she knew what to do. She wasn't afraid any more.

And then Jake wasn't in the room with them any more.

Chapter Twenty-Seven

Bill had never fainted or passed out. Not even in the oppressive heat of Thailand. But he felt the room moving around him now, here in Roehampton, in his kitchen, and figured this might be how it felt if you did. He put down the pan he was holding and perched on the edge of a bar stool, waiting for everything else to stop moving too.

'You're what?!' Bill's heart was beating like a hammer in his chest.

'I'm pregnant.'

It was the third time Carrie had said it and he had heard the word each time, but he couldn't make sense of what she was saying. He could feel his mouth opening and closing, and he could see Carrie's lovely face watching his intently, but he was entirely lost for words. He felt like he was standing stock still in a maelstrom. A hurricane of different feelings blowing from all directions. He couldn't order them, couldn't articulate them.

'How?' It wasn't what he meant, of course, but it was all he could manage to choke out. Even as he said it he knew it was wrong.

She almost winced at his question. 'I didn't mean it to happen, Bill.'

'But it happened? It's happened?'

She nodded. Now he saw that she looked frightened. He saw that he needed to put his arms around her and hold her.

As he took two steps towards her, she held her hands up to stop him.

'I didn't, Bill. You have to believe that. I didn't do this on purpose. I didn't plan it. I'd never . . . I'd never try and trick you, trap you . . . whatever. The point is I wouldn't. I didn't.'

'Sssh. Sssh, Carrie. I never thought you would. I'm sorry. I'm sorry.' She put her hands down and let him draw her into an embrace. He knew that he'd let her down. That's what I do, isn't it, he thought, to the women I love? Maggie and Aly. I let them down. The hug let them both hide their faces. He wasn't sure he believed her, and she wasn't sure she was telling the truth. Not about the trapping him part. About the getting pregnant part.

Because Carrie wasn't sorry she was pregnant. That was the truth. She hadn't engineered it but she was glad. She'd known for sure for two days. Maybe longer, if she was honest. She'd missed periods before – after Jason died, she'd lost twenty lbs in a few weeks and everything had gone haywire physically – but she'd never had boobs that hurt so much it woke her up in the night when she rolled over. Or this tiredness – she sometimes felt she'd been tired all the time since Jason died, but this tiredness was physical not mental. There was a heaviness, a dragging sensation in her belly she hadn't ever had before as well. She hadn't been sick, but she'd definitely felt queasy in the mornings for the last few weeks or so. Nevertheless, she'd felt like a fraud buying the pregnancy test at Boots in her lunch hour. She'd been on the pill when she'd been married to Jason. She and Bill used condoms. Every time. It had been every time, hadn't it? They'd played some dangerous games, she supposed. Got carried away a few times . . . But almost every time, certainly. She'd felt embarrassed about the condoms, the first time. He was a man in his forties. He'd been married . . . for ever – he probably hadn't needed to use a condom for years. He might have expected her to be on the pill, or have a coil or something. He'd been really nice about it, though, that first time, and always afterwards. It hadn't been an issue. She'd supposed, once they started sleeping together, that she might start taking the pill again, but she hadn't done anything about it. And now it was too late.

She couldn't believe the positive result. She took the second test in the box. Same two pink lines.

Sitting in an office toilet cubicle, the momentousness of it had swirled around her. It was what she'd always wanted. She was *that* kind of girl – the kind that had always seen babies in her future. Family. She and Jason had both wanted that.

But this baby wasn't Jason's. And there was no family. Her family had died that day on the green grass of the park. And Bill's family lived a few miles down the road in a tall white house. Two shattered families.

She hadn't had to see Bill in the two days since she'd found out. He'd had his kids on one night and she'd had a work function the other – she'd been covering a showcase of bright new chefs in the capital for the magazine – though she knew she'd only gone through the motions of the event. Afterwards, she couldn't remember a thing she'd eaten or a single conversation she'd had. She was glad of the space . . .

Waking up the first morning, she'd slid her hands down her flat belly and left them there, cool against the skin beneath her pyjamas. And knew that she was pleased. She was delighted. She was so happy that immediate hot tears ran down the sides of her face on to the pillow. There was a person – her person – in there beneath her fingers.

She knew Bill might feel very differently. In the next twenty-four hours, on the underground, at the party, washing her face in the sink and smiling at herself in the mirror, she made herself see this from all the angles he might.

But she couldn't see this tiny human as a complication. He or she might make life more complicated. But he or she was a good thing. A blessing. A new beginning. A family. Not the family Carrie might have dreamt of. Not the family Bill might want, maybe. But the family she'd been given.

However she tried to protect herself from the fantasy, she knew she was struggling to imagine Bill being absent.

But now she didn't know. His face had looked thunderous, when she'd said the words.

Chapter Twenty-Eight

Alone in the Roehampton flat, Bill poured a large glass of whisky and sat in the dark, staring at the wall. He hadn't asked Carrie to leave after they'd talked, but he hadn't wanted her to stay either. He needed to be alone. She'd mumbled something about needing to be somewhere early in the morning for work and giving him some space, but he'd been hearing everything from far away, his brain racing to process the news she'd delivered. He couldn't think about where she needed to be. He couldn't even try, yet, to see it from her point of view. Just his. It was only the second time in his life that a woman had told him, out of the blue, that she was pregnant. With Aly, and then with Stan, he and Maggie had been consciously trying to get her pregnant, although he had undoubtedly been less willing with Stan. Her menstrual cycle and the taking or not taking of pregnancy tests had been the subject of whispered conversations and exciting moments of sexy domesticity. Not body blows. Jake had been a shock. Probably, no, definitely the greatest shock of his life. Maggie had fallen pregnant with Jake a few months after she and Bill had met. His plans for university had imploded the second she told him, all the cogs and wheels of his schemes scattered, landing completely rearranged with a speed that made him dizzy. Sitting in the dark now, he tried to remember exactly how that had felt. Had he been horrified?

He'd loved Maggie. He'd known that for a while. Maybe, if you believed that stuff, from the first night. He couldn't imagine a life without her, and that pressing thought had intruded, as it had to. He'd been supposed to be somewhere else – to have moved on from Sydney weeks, months before. But he couldn't leave. She'd been a magnet, pulling him in.

They'd only been sleeping together for a while. It must have happened really quickly. They'd lost their virginity to each other on the beach one chilly night in June. They'd spent a sunny day with a bunch of his mates riding the roller coasters and carousels at Luna Park, but she'd peeled him away from the group in the late afternoon and they'd gone, with a bottle of cheap fizz and a couple of blankets, to Nielsen Park, settling themselves amongst the shelter of some bluffs in a small, secluded bay to watch the sunset. Huddled together in coats, scarves and hats under the blankets, they'd watched quietly until all the light was gone, replaced by a canopy of bright stars they'd wished on, unselfconscious and high on their romance. He'd told her, that night, that he couldn't leave. That he loved her. That not one of the things on the agenda he carried in his head – and had done for so long – for the next weeks or months or years seemed as interesting or as appealing to him as simply being close to where she was. He hadn't meant it as a seduction speech, but he wasn't about to turn her down when she'd turned herself into his lap and started kissing him in earnest, or when she slowly began unbuttoning their clothes so that their warm flesh was touching inside their thick coats. It had been cold, he remembered, but it had been perfect.

Jake had died a virgin. At least, he was pretty sure he had. They'd had this great conversation, a few months before he'd left, sitting in a pub, drinking a pint together. It had seemed to Bill, then, a perfect moment of fatherhood – sharing a drink with his son on a warm, late spring night, talking about the stuff that really matters. Jake had asked him about his own experiences, and he'd told him, light on the details, heavy on the sentiment, about that night with his mother all those years ago. He'd said he didn't want to sound corny but that he knew it had made all the difference feeling that he was in love with Maggie. Jake had agreed. And there'd been no reason for him to pretend. And there'd been no one special that summer before they left – at least no one Jake had brought home. So Bill supposed he'd died a virgin, and it was one of the things that made him ache with sadness for Jake, knowing that he'd missed that feeling he'd had that night . . .

It hadn't been easy for the two of them to be alone. Maggie was still living at home with her parents, her brother and her omnipresent, adoring younger sister. They liked Bill, but there was no doubt that he was confined to the public spaces and under their watchful eye. There was always a crowd of people at his house, and it wasn't always possible to barter for a bedroom where the two of them could have some privacy. A couple of times, Bill paid for a hotel room, and those nights were expensive but utterly magical – long, deep baths full of bubbles, no one banging on the door for their turn, and big beds with clean white sheets. All the promise of a do not disturb sign. Maggie gloriously naked. There was the back seat of his car, parked in secluded spots. And there were beaches. Lots of beaches. Sex that got better and better each time they did it, until it became, for a while, the only thing he thought about – his need for her and hers for him.

And then she'd told him. She'd taken a test but she hadn't been to the doctor. He was a family friend – she'd known him all her life, she said. She was ashamed and afraid. It had been surprisingly easy to take her in his arms and comfort her, to tell her she wasn't alone. He never once remembered wanting to bolt. This was all happening in the wrong order – he could see that much. But it was all that he wanted. He realized that within maybe ten minutes of her saying the words.

It had been different for Maggie. Her long-cherished childhood dreams for her future had evaporated in a moment. Swimming for Australia in the Olympics had been what she'd dreamt of and wanted for so long. She said it had only been a dream, that there'd been no guarantees, no promises. But she'd been so close.

There was never any question of an abortion. Not for either of them. And not for Maggie's parents. Her mum and dad would hate that too, all their sacrifices notwithstanding, and so would she. She loved Bill. She was, already, as sure of that as she was of anything. And this was their baby. Hers and Bill's. Even if she and Bill could recover from an abortion, even if they stayed together, eventually had more children – this would always be their past. How could she love another baby, knowing she'd killed their brother or sister? That was very much how it felt to her. The timing was their fault, not the baby's, and she knew an abortion would haunt her for ever.

He'd tearfully said, almost straight away, that he would understand, though he knew she'd sensed no real commitment in his words.

'I'd get it. If you couldn't have it. I know how much the swimming means to you . . .'

'It doesn't mean more to me than you do.'

'That's easy to say now. If you give it up, if you walk away from this, because of me, you're always going to resent me. You'll always remember that it was my fault you didn't get your dream. I don't know if we can survive that. I don't know if anyone could.'

'Our fault, Bill. I was in it too.'

He brushed that off. 'Can you honestly say that if you go ahead and have this baby, you're not going to think about it every day – what you've given up?' His face implored her.

So she made a new dream. She used all the willpower and determination she'd been developing and working on strengthening for the last ten years to walk away from that old dream and to focus on another one. A dream of Bill and of their baby, and of a life that stretched beyond two weeks in the summer of 1988 in Seoul in Korea.

The gold medal in the 200-metre butterfly in Seoul was won by an East German swimmer on 25 September 1988. In 2:09:51. No Australian woman made it to the A or B final, and the fastest Aussie girl in the heats swam 2:18:17. That day, thousands of miles away in London, Maggie took Jake, aged about two and a half, to the local swimming baths and spent an hour watching him bob in the shallows in giant orange armbands, giggling and blowing bubbles in the water. She swam around him in circles, watching her own arms moving through the water. Each time she got back to his front, Jake shrieked with delight, and as she disappeared again, he flailed around, trying to follow her. It was a game he could have played for hours. Bill brought flowers home with supper and afterwards made gentle love to her on big cushions in the back garden while Jake slept upstairs. Much later, Bill fell asleep in their bed and she wandered the house for a while, working on a shadow box, sticking her head around both respective bedroom doors to gaze at her boys, and reflected that, though this was still her dream, she might always, always wonder . . . Any resentment Maggie might have felt beneath the surface she kept hidden from everyone, including, most of the time, from herself. Both of them had wondered, since they split up, whether it was one of the fault lines that had weakened the foundations of their marriage, but neither, honestly, knew for sure.

And Bill had made it work. Truth to tell, his father didn't mind that much, his not going to university. He immediately agreed to take Bill on in the business. He wanted to give him a good grounding in every aspect – an apprenticeship of sorts – and then, he promised, he'd help him start up on his own. Bill's father might even have been secretly relieved. He'd been a bit afraid of Bill the graduate, Bill the business-man. Afraid that a son who spoke a different language and lived in a different world would become remote and distant. Relieved that now they would have this in common. Bill's mother had been furious with him, then disappointed in him, which was far worse and more wretched, and then, at last, grudgingly accepting. Her greatest fear had been that Bill would stay in Australia, on the other side of the world. But in the end he'd provided her with the best reason of her life for complaining, and she'd settled, in the end, into that.

The decision to make a life in England was harder than the decision to keep the baby, in lots of ways. Bill loved Aus-tralia, but he had no prospects there. Back home, he had something that would mean he could support Maggie and the child from the start. They could live alone, the three of them, not rely on their families – not start their life together beholden. It didn't have to be for ever, he told Maggie. Just while he got himself started. They could always come back. He'd believed it, too, when he'd said it.

Leaving Olivia behind in Sydney had been the worst for Maggie. Worse than leaving her parents or her brother. She'd been so young. So distraught. He knew how much it had hurt them both to be separated. He felt so responsible, barely nineteen years old, for Maggie's happiness and well-being, for the baby's. He grew up overnight.

They'd had a tiny wedding. His parents didn't come. His dad cited work, but Bill always knew his mother wouldn't stamp her approval on his marriage by showing up. Her parents had made the best of it. There had been a single-tiered cake, and confetti, and a posh lunch for the family. Her father had made a speech in which he just managed to keep his resentment out of his tone, although he talked more than he should have done about Maggie's swimming career and how proud that had made him – the clear implication, if you were listening for it, being that he was so much less proud of this. Not all of Maggie's mother's tears seemed happy ones. Liv had an approximation of a bridesmaid's dress, but by now she knew Maggie was leaving, and her childish joy at being an aunt at the age of eleven had been entirely eclipsed by that thought. Someone had taken photographs and they'd had a night in a hotel as a present. They'd flown to England instead of having a honeymoon and Jake had been born five months later.

Aly was born in the summer of 1989, when Jake was three and a half, conceived deliberately and welcomed ecstatically. She was only just one when Jake started school, solemn in an oversize grey blazer and shiny shoes. He adored his sister from the second he laid eyes on her, appointing himself chief assistant to Maggie and filling the nursery with clouds of talcum powder each time Maggie changed Aly's nappy.

Jake and Aly were ten and seven respectively, both at primary school, when Stan came along in 1996. Bill had needed encouragement to agree to a third pregnancy. He had been rather enjoying this stage of life, he said, free from the paraphernalia of babies and toddlers. They'd had the worst row of their marriage over it. For the first time in ten years she threw their past back at him.

'After all I've given up for you.' Her tone had been dark and thunderous. 'My home, my family, my career . . . After all of that, you want to tell me that *you* don't want another baby. And you expect that to be more important than what I want.' She laughed ironically. 'Well, why would you? Everything's always gone your way. Everything. Why not this too?' The unfairness of this had hit Bill like a sledge-hammer, but he hadn't pointed it out. He should have pointed it out.

So Stan was born, and, of course, within moments neither would have had it any other way. He was a beautiful baby, born fast, compact and sleepy, with smooth skin and long eyelashes.

And now there was another baby. Carrie's baby. Sitting in the dark, Bill felt very old and very tired, and very, very sad.

The next evening, after a day at work where he felt he'd just been on autopilot, he called Carrie from the car on his way to Maggie's. She sounded breathless, as though she'd run for the phone.

'Are you okay?'

'I'm relieved to hear from you.'

'You've remembered it's parents' evening?' It was Aly's last ever parents' evening, in point of fact. An evening with Maggie. Lousy timing.

'Yes. You said, the other evening.'

'Can I come round, Carrie, afterwards – to see you?'

'Of course you can. I'm here.'

'I want to talk. We need to talk about this, right? I'm sorry I was so crap, so inadequate, last night.'

'You were shocked. I understand that.'

She shouldn't let him off the hook. 'Which is no excuse. I didn't handle it well. At all. And I'm sorry for that.'

'Just come later, Bill.' Her words were carried on a sigh.

And that cut Bill. Maggie's sigh had replaced Maggie's deep throaty laugh as the sound he most associated with her; it was the sound he most dreaded hearing. Now Carrie was sighing.

Chapter Twenty-Nine

He picked Maggie up from the house, as he'd agreed. She wasn't ready when he got there. Punctuality had never been her strong suit. A silver-haired, handsome woman answered the door, and even though he knew she would be there, for a second, Bill was shaken to see Kate. This had been his home for so long. Now he didn't even know all the inhabitants. It was weird, however plausible Liv had made it sound.

'You have to be Kate?'

'Bill.' She extended a hand and a warm smile. He wondered what she knew about him and almost squirmed, like a boy caught doing something naughty, but her tone gave nothing away. 'Good to meet you. Come in and wait for Maggie. She's been running – she said she was just going to jump in a shower. I'm sure she'll be down in a minute.'

He stood in the hall, strangely awkward in his old home, in the company of this stranger who was living with his family. Bill put his hands in his pockets.

'She's running again?'

Kate nodded. 'Almost every day.'

'That's good. That's really good.'

'Yes.'

'How's it all going?'

She smiled her understanding of his embarrassment – an empathetic smile. 'Good. Good, I think. At least, I'm enjoying being here. Your kids are great, Bill.' He acknowledged the compliment. 'Stan's a complete character. Lots of fun. All boy. And Aly is a very lovely young woman. Beautiful and very smart. With a sweet way about her.' She stopped, as though she thought she was gushing suddenly. 'But then you know that. They're yours.'

'But it is good to hear it from someone else.' Kate smiled and gave the smallest nod of her head in acknowledgement.

'Dad!' Stan bounded down the stairs in full Chelsea kit. 'Have you come for supper?' He jumped at his father, and Bill staggered backwards a little under the sudden weight of his boy. They hugged for a moment, and then Bill set him back on his feet. Kate watched how Bill closed his eyes and buried his nose in Stan's neck for a second; the gesture spoke volumes about how he felt about his son, and she felt almost invasive for observing it and feeling its poignancy.

'No, buddy. Not tonight. It's parents' evening at your sister's school. I've come to get your mother so we can go together.'

'Too bad.' Stan shrugged. 'Kate makes the best dumplings.' 'Mrs Miller' had been abandoned after about three days. It didn't feel right, Kate had protested to Maggie. She wanted to be just Kate.

'I'm sure she does.' Bill winked at Kate. 'Some other time.'

'Least it's not parents' evening at my school.'

Bill tousled his son's hair. 'That'd be bad because . . . ?'

'Bad?' Stan affected to look innocent. '*Moi?!*'

'Course not. Why the kit? You played this afternoon?'

Stan shrugged again. 'Nah. I just like it.' He spun around, revealing his name emblazoned on the back of the shirt.

'Is Aly about?' he asked Kate now.

Kate nodded. 'She's in her room. Revising. Poor kid. Seems to be a way of life, just at the moment.'

'Do you mind if I go on up, just to say hi?' Why was he

even asking? This was his home, for God's sake, and these were his kids. There was just something so . . . damn matriarchal about Kate and her knowing face.

She didn't answer him, just smiled enigmatically – almost as though she was thinking exactly the same thing that he was – and stood back to let him pass.

On the first landing, Bill knocked and, when Aly answered with a single teenage noise, he opened the door. She was lying on the rug in the middle of her floor, on her back, her head on a fleecy pillow bearing a neon-pink peace sign, with a textbook held on her chest. Chemistry, it looked like, though Bill was certainly no expert.

'How's it going, kiddo?'

She groaned melodramatically. 'My brain hurts. It is actually throbbing. Can a brain actually get full? 'Cos mine definitely feels like it is . . .'

'Not overdoing it, are you?'

'You'll hear it yourself, tonight . . . they're really sitting on us. Even if you did well in your mocks – maybe especially if you did. The ones who screwed up are too scared to let up. Those of us who did okay – well, they don't want us to get complacent. God forbid we should stuff up and mess with their league table . . .'

'So young, yet so cynical.'

'Cynical. Bored. Stir crazy. I swear to God, Dad – I've got cabin fever.'

'Is it that bad?'

'Worse! I'm painting a good picture . . . Actually . . . glad you're here. I was thinking . . .'

'That tone of voice coupled with that sentence usually costs me money . . .'

'And this time is no exception. I was thinking we should go on holiday, when all this is done . . .'

'You're going to Australia with your mum at the end of the month, for the wedding, aren't you?'

'That's not at the end. That's in the middle. I'll be taking a rucksack full of books. I'll probably have a copy of the periodic table tucked in the order of service in the damn ceremony.'

'My poor baby . . .'

She wrinkled her nose in disgust at his patronizing tone. 'After it's all done. A holiday. You, me and Stan. You could even bring what's-her-name . . .'

'Carrie. Her name is Carrie, Aly.'

'Sorry.' She looked contrite. 'I didn't mean to be rude.' She had, of course.

The couple of times they'd met had been tense, with an atmosphere. A holiday together seemed a long way off. What he had with Carrie felt far too undefined right now. Especially now.

'When do you finish?'

'End of May. Results come out in August, so I have to be here then, or at least somewhere where there's a phone. In case I've fucked up and I have to do the whole clearing system thing.'

'Not a chance.' Bill ignored the swearing.

'Might be going to Ayia Napa with some mates, but that's more of an idea than a firm arrangement,' she said.

Might go somewhere with Ryan, she added, to herself, but that's all still a complete mystery to you, Dad, right now, and I don't know, because we haven't talked about a future. At all. Bill saw something cross her face.

Might have a baby by then, Bill was thinking, but you, my darling Aly, have no idea that unexploded bomb is lying in your future.

They'd both wandered into their own private thoughts.

'We'll see, hey?'

Aly sighed. That sounded like a no. She wasn't even all that serious. It was a test, that was all.

The sound of Maggie on the stairs behind him rescued the moment.

'Sorry, Bill. Ready . . .'

Maggie's hair was still damp, curling irresistibly at the ends, though she'd attempted to tame it with a wide band of fabric. She was wearing barely any make-up and a simple black dress, cut quite low in the front with long tight sleeves, and she looked lovely to him. She always had.

'Running, I hear . . .'

'Yes. I've been doing a bit lately. Since Kate came, really. Remember how I used to love running?'

He nodded. He remembered. 'I'm glad.'

'Mind you — I had no idea how out of shape I was. The first time I went I was on my knees after a couple of miles. Up to ten now.'

'Show off!' Aly grinned from her bedroom floor. Maggie threw her daughter an amused glance, her eyebrows raised.

'Ready to go?'

Bill bent down and kissed the top of Aly's head. 'See you, kiddo.'

In the car, he looked at Maggie's profile as she sat gazing through the windscreen. How many times had the two of them sat side by side, like this, in a car together? This was a Mercedes. They'd started in a battered old Golf. Twenty years. It was a long time. It had been a long journey. There were moments when it hit him like a battering ram — the realization that they'd reached a fork in the road and they were choosing different paths. Or maybe not choosing. Maybe the paths had been chosen for them. Maybe neither wanted to take them. They just had to. The children would mean they were never strangers to each other, but the day to day, the journey, had changed for ever. It was wrong. He didn't know how to go backwards and make the outcome different, but he knew, sitting here beside her in the darkness, that it was wrong in so many ways that they had ended up like this. It wasn't what he'd ever expected, or what he wanted.

But Carrie was in his head too. If Maggie turned to him now, her big brown eyes wide with forgiveness and with love, the right kind, and asked him to come back, he wouldn't know what to say. He truly wouldn't. It wasn't simple any more. What a mess. What a bloody mess.

'So . . . Kate. How's that working out?'

Maggie smiled. 'You think it's weird, don't you?'

'I did. At first. I wasn't buying entirely into the whole rent-a-granny thing, I admit. As hard as Liv was selling it.'

'Me neither. I agreed for Liv's sake, not my own. Truthfully, I was expecting it to be deeply odd and that we'd have sent her packing by now . . .'

'But you haven't?'

'It's nice having her there.' She answered in a faraway kind of voice and shrugged.

'Nice?'

'Nice!'

'What does she do, exactly?'

'She helps. In a very practical way. I mean, she's an amazing cook. She cooks, a lot. Hence the running – she makes dinner, I run. She has a thing for laundry – never my favourite, as you know. Practically a fetish. I take something off dirty and I get it back the next day, clean and folded into a four-inch square. She even likes ironing . . .'

'So far, so good. But I'm confused, a bit. Do you pay her for all this "help"?'

Maggie bit back the slightly arch urge to tell him it was none of his business.

'No! That's not how it works. She's here because she wants to be. She doesn't want money. She doesn't need money.'

'She looked pretty well-heeled.'

'She is, I think.' She'd noticed the smart clothes too. 'I mean, I pay the bills and stuff. Buy most of the food, though she contributes – she does the shopping sometimes . . . It's not a formal arrangement.'

They hadn't a formal arrangement, either. Money was not the problem. Bill paid housekeeping into Maggie's bank account, like he always had. He'd put the amount up quite a bit, when he'd moved out, though she hadn't asked him to and she hadn't commented about it. He'd wanted to explain why – but he'd been afraid to start a conversation and so he'd waited for her to ask, and she never had. He'd always paid the school fees and the mortgage had long been paid off. The bills all went out by direct debit, from their joint account. It didn't make any sense, he knew, maintaining this particular status quo, but neither of them had ever had the stomach to open a dialogue about divorce, or legal separation. Easier that way. It was denial, Bill had acknowledged to himself. On both their parts. He wasn't worried about the money. She'd earnt half, or whatever the court was bound to award her. It was half of quite a lot these days, and so they'd both be fine. He was worried about the finality.

'But that's not the point of her. She's good company. She's . . . good for us, I think. Stan *loves* her. Aly's different, too, since she came. A bit more relaxed. A bit more open.'

'And you?'

'I like her. She's good to talk to. Easy to have around.'

'What's her story?'

I'm not going to tell you, Maggie thought. Even if I knew

it all, I wouldn't tell you. It's Kate story, not mine to tell. And she hasn't really told it yet.

She shrugged non-committally. 'We all have a story, Bill. We don't all share them.'

They arrived at the school – forced to park a few streets away by the mass of cars already parked in the prime spots by the keen parents who'd shown up early. The children were safe ground. Here, still, they were united.

'Should we be expecting any shocks here?' he asked. They'd always done this. Maggie had always managed the school stuff – Bill was used to being briefed on the run over to an event. To be honest, they'd never had a single difficult conversation with a teacher about Aly. Nor had they with Jake. Stan was their problem child. Their beautiful, warm, funny problem.

'Not that I can think of.' Maggie shrugged. 'She's completely on track for the three As. Mocks went well. Just a question of keeping the nose to the grindstone for the next few weeks . . .'

'Do they – the school – know about the Australia trip?'

'Not from me. I don't know whether Aly has told them. Not up to them. Besides, she's on full-time study leave practically from now . . .' She sounded defensive.

'Of course not. Sounds to me like she's planning to work while she's away anyway. How long are you going for, by the way?' He made his tone light. He didn't want Maggie to think he was criticizing either.

'Still two weeks.' Her tone was short. She'd told him that already. 'The wedding is on Easter Saturday and we'll be back the middle of the following week. She'll still have a few days before school starts again.'

It felt odd to Bill that he wouldn't be at the wedding. He thought of Liv as his sister as well. He understood it, of course, but it was one of the odder things about being separated. You didn't quite understand – at least he hadn't – that you were separating from a whole group of people, not just the person you were married to. He'd barely met Scott– just a quick handshake at the door when he'd been over in January and Bill had picked Stan up. And he wouldn't be at the wedding – of a woman he'd known and loved since she was nine years old. Maggie was scratchy about his questions, he realized. Maybe that was because it was odd for her too. Whatever problems they'd had in their marriage – even during rocky patches – they'd both been softies at weddings, holding hands during the vows, gazing at each other as the bride and groom kissed for the first time, voices breaking during the singing of 'Jerusalem'.

They were a few minutes late, but it was clear that in the huge school hall things were already wildly behind schedule. Parents' evenings had always been vaguely gladiatorial at this school, he remembered. Upper-middle-class parents with professions and ranks within them were used to being kowtowed to and not accustomed to being kept waiting. He wouldn't miss them – the parents' evenings, perfunctory meetings he had always felt were vaguely pointless. Or the parents – dozens of acquaintances, very few friends.

'Might as well grab a cup of tea.'

'Always thought they'd do better with wine at these kind of things.'

'Really? You think it might go more smoothly if the parents were half-cut?' Maggie smirked.

'Maybe not,' he conceded.

'Tea it is, then. Tastes like dirty dishwater, but it's something to do while we wait. See the line for Dr Taylor?' She gestured at a man Bill thought was Aly's physics teacher, who was engrossed in conversation with two parents who were leaning forward earnestly, oblivious to the two or three couples hovering behind, throwing daggers.

'I'll get them. You wait here . . .' Bill smiled ruefully and started in the direction of the refreshments.

There was a wait at the tea table too, though. Several people were ahead of Bill, chatting while they filled their paper cups from the large thermos flasks. Bill turned to see where he'd left Maggie. She was talking to someone. A tall, slim man Bill didn't immediately recognize. Doubtless he knew him, if Maggie did. He might ask on the way home, and if he did, Maggie would say, slightly exasperated, 'Of course you know So-and-so. Their daughter Wotsit has been in the same class as Aly since they were four. You've been on quiz-night teams with him . . .' She was always irritated by his inability to connect names and faces with anecdotes – she said if he was the same in business then he'd be out of business, so why couldn't he apply the same brain he used at work to school? Funny how married people repeat and repeat the same behaviours and the same conversations year in and year out. Funny? Maybe not.

This guy, though, Bill didn't think he knew – he couldn't place him, anyway. Maggie was talking more animatedly to him than he'd seen her do in ages, and he noticed that she'd picked up the string of black beads she was wearing around her neck and was fiddling with them as she spoke. She looked positively flirtatious. And very pretty. A tiny spasm of jealousy shook its way through him, unfamiliar and strange. He'd never been possessive when they were together. Nor suspicious. To the point that she had occasionally berated him for it, seeing his trust – as he saw it – as somehow insulting. As though no one else would be interested, she might say. A stupid, cyclical argument about absolutely nothing. The kind that left him bewildered. The kind only women had the guile for and the interest in having. He had even less right and less justification now. But it was there nonetheless – the slight indignation that this man was talking to his wife like that. Making his wife twirl her beads and swing slightly on her hips and laugh a little.

'Who was that?' The man had moved on by the time he returned with the two scalding-hot teas, but not before he'd held both Maggie's shoulders in an oddly possessive gesture and kissed both her cheeks. When he'd done that, he hadn't moved his face back as far as social convention dictated, so that their noses had almost brushed between kisses. At least, that was how it had looked to Bill. He remembered kissing Carrie's cheek once, before . . . putting his mouth so close to the corner of her mouth that he could feel it.

'You know Charlie.' Here we go, he thought. Do I? 'Charlie Nelson. His daughter Imogen is in Aly's class. Has been since about halfway through seniors.'

'I expect we've been on quiz-night teams together, have we?'

She looked at him askance. 'I don't remember. Maybe.'

'Nice guy, is he?'

She didn't stop looking at him. 'I don't know him, not really. He seems nice. He's divorced. Imogen and Aly aren't really friends – not close, anyway. They don't hang out with the same crowd, as far as I know. But yes, he's nice.' She shrugged and turned to see a space opening up at Dr Taylor's table.

'Come on. Quick . . .'

Maggie had forgotten all about Charlie Nelson and the strange conversation in the airport parking garage. She hadn't gone, of course, to that damn curry night. And she'd heard nothing from him since. But he'd made a beeline for her tonight – once Bill was out of the way. There'd been something about how pleased he looked to see her that was at once flattering and slightly disconcerting. It was a look she hadn't seen on Bill's face for a long time. Or anyone else's for that matter. She really had never taken much notice of him before. But he was quite nice-looking. And he seemed . . . he seemed nice. Interested in her. Like what she said was new, not like he'd heard everything she had to say a thousand times, knew her so well he could have finished her sentences for her. He'd been eager to please her, she realized. If you'd asked her, before the event, how that would feel, she might have answered 'pathetic' – but it wasn't. It wasn't at all.

Bill wanted to stop the car and come in. He wanted to talk to Maggie. He wanted to kiss his sleeping children and smell their skin and hair. But he'd told Carrie he'd go to see her, and it was already later than he'd expected it to be. When Maggie kissed his cheek before she climbed out of the car, her mouth was a long way from the corner of his mouth and her lips were dry.

Parallel parking a few houses down from Carrie's place, Bill sat for a while, his hands still taut on the steering wheel. He didn't like being here. That was why they hardly ever spent time here. This was where Carrie had lived with Jason and the house was still full of him, in a way Roehampton was devoid of Maggie. A clean slate. When he sat on the sofa in Carrie's sitting room, he imagined Carrie and Jason lying cuddling on it, watching a DVD from the cupboard next to the TV – *The Wire* or *24* or *Six Feet Under*. Jason's choices, he supposed. They weren't Carrie. Not the Carrie he knew, at least. When he drank a glass of wine here, he knew it was from a glass they'd probably got for their wedding, in a crystal pattern they'd chosen together. It wasn't like him – to think this way. It was a form of jealousy, he knew. And it wasn't like him. He almost chuckled to himself, thinking of earlier in the evening. Maggie could have told you it wasn't like him.

The whole evening so far had unsettled and confused him. He'd felt so close to Maggie – doing something so familiar and so habitual. He'd felt envy when that bloke – what was his name, Charlie something? When he'd been with Maggie. But he'd felt irritated too. Felt somehow tired by all the old habits. Bill felt middle-aged tonight.

Carrie must have been watching. Perhaps she'd even been at the window and recognized the car, watched him drive past looking for a space to park. Knew he'd sat in the car for a while before he locked it and walked slowly towards her front door. Thinking. She opened the door before he'd rung the bell. She'd showered earlier and her hair was still a little damp, tucked behind her ears. Her face was entirely clean of make-up, scrubbed pink. She was wearing a boat-necked T-shirt, which revealed her fine collarbones, and yoga pants rolled low so that six inches of her flat, toned stomach showed, and she was barefoot. She looked all of eighteen years old. She looked like a girl Jake should be bringing home. She looked – although he knew that she was anything but – simple, open and uncomplicated, clean and fresh.

She opened her arms without saying a word, and Bill walked gratefully into them, his mouth finding hers and kissing her deeply, letting her calm and quiet suffuse him. He splayed the fingers of one hand wide and laid them across her stomach – his palm was large enough to cover it all now – and felt her own hand cover his, her little fingers squeezing his. He exhaled and relaxed.

Later, much later, the two of them lay in Carrie's bed, and he wasn't thinking at all about Jason lying there in the same sheets. For the last hour, he hadn't thought about anything except how good she felt and tasted and made him feel. He had buried himself in her and the oblivion of it was wonderful, blotting out everything else for a while. Now, they were both quiet and calm. Lying across the bed, uncovered, he had his head on her stomach and her fingers were in his hair, stroking him.

'I want us to keep it.'

'Really?' Carrie's heart beat fast. She hadn't asked – she'd been too terrified. She already knew she was keeping it. It was the 'us' part she hadn't counted on. They'd barely spoken. He'd been so strange when he'd arrived. He'd looked so lost. 'Are you sure?'

'I'm sure.' And he was. How else could he feel about this? 'I love you, Carrie.' It was the first time he'd said it out loud, though he'd felt it for a while, and she must have known. Even Aly knew.

She wanted to ask whether he thought he was sure in just this moment or in every moment going forward. She wanted to ask whether he loved her enough. She wanted to ask how it would work. How much 'us' he meant.

As if the questions hung heavy in the air, Bill shrugged his shoulders, almost violently, and rolled over, off her stomach, up on to his elbows, so he was looking her in the eyes.

'I'm all in, Carrie. I promise. We're going to do it together. All of it.' When she didn't respond, his eyes filled with tears. 'If you'll have me.'

Chapter Thirty

Charlie Nelson's phone call two days after the parents' evening at Aly's school took Maggie by surprise. When she heard his voice – he said, 'Hello Maggie,' but didn't say his own name – she couldn't immediately place him.

'It's Charlie. Charlie Nelson . . .'

'Charlie! Of course.' She blushed, although he couldn't see her, of course. 'I'm so sorry. You must think I'm a total ditz. I was in the middle of something else.'

'I'm sorry – have I called at a bad time?' It sounded like Charlie Nelson might be blushing too.

'No, no. Not at all. How are you?'

They'd chatted for a few moments and then, with a slight cough and what she swore was an audible swallow, Charlie launched into his request.

'I was actually calling, Maggie, to ask you if you'd like to, um, go out sometime. For dinner. Or lunch, if dinner . . .' He trailed off.

Maggie was utterly shocked. No one had asked her out in . . . well, maybe ever. Not like this. Not since Bill.

Her silence obviously panicked him. She felt a hit of empathy for him.

'I'm sorry. You're still, I mean you and Bill . . . you're still . . .'

'Oh, we are, Charlie. We have been for some time, in fact.'

'Oh.'

She said yes because she was embarrassed for him. Because

to say yes was infinitely easier than to say no, which was what she wanted to say. But her courage deserted her, and she felt bad and she could hear in his voice what it had cost him to ask her, and so she agreed.

He sounded gratifyingly pleased. 'Oh, that's terrific.' Terrific? Who said that? 'I'm so glad.'

Too late now, she thought, squirming as she held the receiver a few inches from her face.

'And dinner – dinner would suit?' He had a strangely old-fashioned turn of phrase. Maybe it was nerves. She didn't remember him speaking like that in person – like a black and white film. And he was nervous. She could tell. Poor man.

'Dinner sounds lovely.' She tried to sound gracious . . . and not to say terrific.

They talked a minute more, a little awkwardly, about dates and times, and types of food she might enjoy, and then he rang off.

Downstairs, Kate was doing the crossword, although the delicious smell wafting from the oven testified to the fact that she'd been baking. The woman was a real-life Mrs Kipling. She looked up when Maggie came in and saw her slightly mystified smile.

'What's up?'

'I was just asked out by a man.'

'Was that the phone call?'

Maggie nodded. 'That was a Mr Charlie Nelson. He's a dad at Aly's school – divorced. We've only spoken a few times, I'd guess. I bumped into him the other night – we chatted for a while . . . That's all we've ever done, really, chat – small talk.'

'Not that small to him by the sound of it.' Kate was smirking.

Maggie made a face at her.

'So? What did you say?'

'I said yes.'

'Because you actually want to go out with him? Or because it was easier than saying no?'

Maggie looked at her, gimlet-eyed, amazed at Kate's pinpoint-accurate perceptiveness. 'You're a wise old bird, you are.'

'No point getting older if you don't get wiser. Which was it? Easier, right?'

Maggie put her face in her hands, groaning and laughing at the same time.

'Oh, God. What an idiot. How am I going to wriggle out of it?'

'Why would you want to?'

'I *can't* go out with him.'

'And I say again, why not?'

'I don't do this.'

'You didn't do this. You were married, before.'

'I'm still married.'

'You're separated. Why shouldn't you go out and have some fun?'

'Because it wouldn't be fun. I don't know how to *have* fun any more.'

'I just think it's a long time since you tried.'

'What are you saying – good for the gander, good for the goose?'

'Not at all. Though that's true enough.' Kate laughed.

Maggie tried to imagine Bill's face. He'd never asked her, had he, if there was anyone else for her? She knew he'd be shocked. Would he be jealous? Angry? Possessive? Or just relieved, his guilt over Carrie instantly assuaged. She wondered . . .

The two women sat in companionable silence for a while.

Kate did another couple of crossword clues. She was brilliant at this – making the space to talk properly. She didn't push, she wasn't always asking questions and prodding at you. She didn't feel the need to fill silences with chatter. And so you could think, and you could process stuff. And you ended up talking more, in the end. It was one of the things Maggie was most appreciating about her being here. It was one of the things about Bill that had started to set her teeth on edge. She had dreaded him coming home at nights, sometimes, because she knew he was going to sit down – at the kitchen table, on the sofa, on the edge of their bed – and ask her how she was feeling. She remembered one day when she'd snapped, and counted off a list of her worries and sadnesses to Bill on her fingers. 'Do you want to know what's wrong? I'll tell you what's wrong . . . My baby died. Aly hasn't spoken to me, not really, truly talked to me, in two days. Stan is shrinking, getting smaller in front of my eyes. I don't want to get out of bed in the morning, not ever, ever. We aren't friends. You haven't touched me in months. I miss Liv. My baby died. He died, Bill . . .' And with that last, the tears had come and Bill had reached for her, and she had pulled away . . .

'You married quite late in life, Kate?' Kate's life was a safe thing for Maggie to talk about. If Kate minded the questions, if Maggie was sometimes Kate's Bill – mental fingernails down a chalkboard – she didn't let it show.

'I was married once before.' Kate's voice was quieter than usual as she answered.

'What?! You kept that quiet . . .'

'I don't talk about it that much.'

'I'm sorry. I shouldn't pry.' Maggie felt bad. Insanely curious now, but bad for pushing.

'No.' Kate waved away her apology with a small motion of

her hand. 'Don't worry. I mean, I could tell you about it, if you wanted . . .'

'I don't want to intrude . . .'

'I probably ought to tell you. It makes sense of me, a bit, I suppose. It's a big piece of my puzzle. I'm just not used to talking about it – for many years I haven't . . .'

'I'd like to hear.'

'My first husband was John. I married him in 1963. I was nineteen years old. He was older – twenty-four, I think, at that point. We'd grown up together, in the same village. I'd been friendly with his younger sister Irene, at school. Hadn't had much to do with him when we were at school or anything like that, but it wasn't a big village and we all sort of knew each other, just from around and about. He was a handsome fellow – quite tall, you know, dark and . . . well, handsome. Quite a hit with the girls. Sporty too – he played for the village cricket team, and the football team too. He went away for two years, on his national service, when I was still at school, and when he came back he had this sort of sophisticated air he hadn't had before he went. Made him even more popular. It sounds ridiculous to say he was exotic, but things were different then and he was, a bit. He had some stories. He'd seen some things. Most of us hadn't been further than London, and some not even that far. Butlins in Bognor Regis was a glamorous destination. And he liked me, it seemed. He could have had almost anyone else in the village. But he picked me. By then I was working in Chatham, in an office as a secretary, and I used to take the bus. He had a job in a printer's in town after the army, and he took the bus too. We used to talk, the two of us. Sometimes we caught the same bus home. Truth to tell, I could see him walking past the office window at the end of the day and I'd wait, with my hat and coat on, until I saw him, then I'd leap out and

pretend I'd bumped into him by accident. I suppose he knew.'
Maggie saw Kate smiling to herself at the recollection.

'Courting, we called it. Our social life revolved around the pub – the Fox and Hounds, it was – the village pub, but it had a room at the back and we'd sort of take it over, this gang of ours, we'd be in there every weekend. On the weekdays, we had the bus. I was in love with him, I suppose. I wanted all kinds of things – I wanted to leave my parents' home and set up my own. I wanted to be married and to have children. I sort of settled on John. Truth is, I never seriously went out with anyone else. Different times. We didn't all chop and change the way people do nowadays. God, that makes me sound old . . . But we didn't.

'And we didn't sleep together either. There was none of that before you were married. A bit of kissing and cuddling and the odd fumble if you were racy, but we all knew what was expected.'

'Sounds like a hundred years ago. Sorry. But it does . . .'

'Well – it was forty or so. A generation at least. I daresay it wasn't like that in the bigger towns and cities, but we weren't there. Christ, we were still mostly going to church on a Sunday morning. Imagine sitting in the pew behind some boy's mother if you'd been messing about with him on Saturday night!'

Maggie laughed. 'You didn't say you were religious.'

'I'm not. Never was. That's the point. We were doing what was expected of us . . .'

'I suppose.'

'We got married after we'd been courting for a year or two. And I got the house of my own I'd been wanting. Nothing very grand, and we rented – we hadn't the money to buy. All the furniture was bought on tick. And there wasn't much of it. We were happy at first. Really happy, I'd say. I learnt to cook and keep house, and he went to work every day and brought home his pay. I kept my job at first, but I had to give it up when Rebecca was born.'

'Rebecca? You had a daughter?'

'I did. Rebecca Kimberley Jane. Born August 1968.'

'You never said.'

'No, I didn't.'

'Is she . . . did she?' Maggie's heart contracted.

'She was fine. She was perfect. A lovely baby. Healthy. We'd been trying for a while. It didn't happen for a couple of years. But eventually it did, naturally. I carried her really big – I was the size of Moby Dick weeks, months really, before she was born. No ankles whatsoever. Puffed up like . . . well, like a vastly pregnant woman.'

Maggie smiled.

'So Rebecca would be . . .' Maggie knew she was prying.

Kate nodded. 'Thirty-eight years old. Yes. Your age.' Kate's gaze was unwavering.

'But you and she . . .'

Kate shook her head. 'We don't speak, no. We haven't spoken for more than ten years. Nearer fifteen, actually. We haven't seen each other since her father died, in fact. At his funeral, to be precise. Which was in 1993.'

Chapter Thirty-One

Aly was lying on her bed, ostensibly revising but in reality she was thinking about Ryan. About her and Ryan. Over the last few months, she'd allowed him a space in her exam-fuddled brain, but he was taking up more and more – in percentage terms, it was getting dangerous. She might look at the pages of her books but it was his face she could see, not the equations and formulas she was supposed to be absorbing.

She hadn't seen him since the night at his parents' house. It seemed almost like it hadn't happened. He'd gone back to Edinburgh the next day. It had lent the whole evening a dream-like quality. She remembered every minute. Of course – it had been the first time.

Not how she'd imagined it. Looking back, it seemed an almost reckless thing for her to have done. To go to his house, knowing what was most likely to happen when she did. It wasn't her. If her parents knew – either of them, and she couldn't imagine telling her mum or her dad – she knew they'd find it bizarrely out of character. Aly didn't do things like that.

She wondered if Jake had had girlfriends he had slept with. She had no idea. They didn't talk that way – at the time he went away. They might do now, if he was still here. She might be able to tell him about what had happened with Ryan.

Except that she had the slightly uncomfortable feeling that what had happened with Ryan had *only* happened because

Jake *wasn't* around now. She understood. She knew she'd used sex to comfort Ryan. He was so upset. It shouldn't have been like that, probably. Not her first time. It should have been more about her.

It had been quite fast and almost, but not quite, good – physically. Emotionally, she had felt very connected and close to Ryan while it was happening. He kept his eyes open the whole time, staring into hers. She'd almost found it disconcerting, but she knew – from years of watching rom coms and reading novels – that this was the Holy Grail of love-making, a man who would keep his eyes boring into your soul while he made love to you. It shouldn't make you feel uncomfortable – it should make you feel wonderful. It was too . . . intense. She'd been almost frightened. And it had been fantastically distracting – it was her first time and she hadn't been able to, well, to concentrate.

Maybe there was something wrong with her.

Afterwards, he'd wanted to hold her tight and fall asleep with her. She wished he'd go next door and let her sleep. If she could. Mostly, she felt a slightly panicky need to get up, get dressed and go home.

In the morning, she'd smelt their garlicky morning breath and nausea had risen in her. Ryan had tried to kiss her and she'd sat bolt upright, trying to pull the cover across her naked breasts, and asked where the bathroom was, trying to figure out how she could get out of the room without him seeing her naked. In films, women pulled a sheet out and fashioned a toga from it. But this was a duvet.

It had been too soon. It had happened on a night too emotionally charged with other things. She wasn't in control. And she needed to be. That was Aly's shtick, she reasoned. That was all. If he hadn't left almost straight away, they might have been able to talk about it. There was a chance she might have been brave enough to tell him how she felt. And maybe to try again.

He still wrote every day. He wanted her to come to Edinburgh. She felt hopeless. She couldn't go to Edinburgh. She'd have to tell Mum where she was going, and she wasn't ready to talk to anyone about it – least of all Mum. Weird, but she would probably find it easier to talk to Kate. Except Kate might feel like she had to tell Mum. She could see Maggie's disappointed face. Hear the questions she'd ask. She couldn't face that. She hadn't even told her friends. A few of them had already slept with their boyfriends and details had been shared, at late-night sleepovers. She didn't want to share details. She didn't understand what it was. The idea of Edinburgh terrified her, if she was honest. Ryan cajoled. She was in Australia for the exact two weeks he was home at Easter, so they wouldn't be able to see each other then.

Aly didn't know what to do. So she kept staring at the formulas and the equations and trying to push him out of her brain. And to stop being so angry with herself. She heard Jake's voice in her head. The two of them had been lying on the trampoline, the summer before . . . before he went away. They'd been talking. 'You're always so hard on yourself, Aly,' he'd said. 'You're always pushing yourself. Why do you do that, d'you think?' 'Keeping up with you?' 'That's bollocks, Aly.' 'Easy for you to say.' 'No, really, it is . . . No one else compares the two of us, you know. That's all you . . .'

'Rebecca isn't Jake, you know, Maggie.' Kate knew Maggie was watching her. She'd been looking at her this way for days, since the revelation. Like she couldn't understand her. Kate needed to make her understand. Not just because it was uncomfortable now, being here with her like this.

'I know she isn't.' There was an edge of belligerence in

Maggie's tone, but Kate could tell she was trying to moderate it. 'My child is dead, Kate.' Maggie stopped for a moment. Kate wondered if she always did that – stopped after she'd said it, as though her brain hit a wall each time she acknowledged out loud that Jake was gone. Softer now. 'I feel like I know you a little now. Maybe I'm wrong, and I don't, but I feel like I do. And because I do, I can't believe that you don't love your child the way I love mine. But your daughter is alive. She's out there and she's alive, and you don't know anything about her life. I don't get it. I just don't.'

'That was her choice, not mine.' Kate heard her own tone now – calm and slow.

'How can you be so passive? I don't get it.'

'No. You don't get it, Maggie. That's exactly right.' She sounded sad, not angry.

'Why not? Tell me to mind my own business if you like, Kate, but I've been thinking about it ever since you told me about her and it doesn't make any sense.'

'You don't think so?'

'Absolutely not, no. You're not that kind of person – not the kind of person to be estranged from your daughter, from your only child. That's why you're here. Make me understand.'

'You make it sound like it was my decision . . .'

'I can't believe it was. That's what I'm saying.'

'That much is true. Of course it wasn't.'

'So what happened?'

Kate looked at her hands, folded in her lap, and when she answered this time, her voice was quiet again. 'Rebecca made a choice. She didn't choose me.'

'Who did she choose? You said your husband died.'

Kate nodded. 'He did. She chose the memory of him, I suppose . . .'

'I don't understand. You're talking in riddles.'

'I don't mean to. It's just hard for me.' Her voice broke. It was the first time Maggie had heard that sound from Kate – a voice close to tears. Instinctively she put an arm around Kate. Kate grabbed the hand on her shoulder and squeezed it tightly, but she didn't relax into the embrace and so Maggie pulled away. She'd become an expert, over the years since Jake had died, in unwanted physical attention and how to repel it. People – all kinds of people – had wanted to hold her. And she had just wanted to hold Jake. And they didn't help – sometimes their touch had just made it worse.

'I'm sorry. Forget it. You don't have to talk about it any more. I'm just being nosy, and it isn't right . . . I'm sorry, Kate. Forget it . . .' Maggie didn't want to upset her.

Kate shook her head. 'No. Let me get this out. I want to, Maggie.'

Maggie sat beside Kate on the sofa. It felt to her as though Kate was about to do something she maybe never had and Maggie felt the importance of the moment for her. Kate pulled her handkerchief out from her sweater sleeve and wound the corner around her fingers as she spoke. She didn't look at Maggie while she spoke; she stared into the middle distance.

'John was an alcoholic. Not at first, not when we met or married. Not when Rebecca was born either. Everything was fine until she was . . . a toddler, I suppose. We were happy. At least I thought we were. It started later. And like these things always do, it started slowly. I didn't even know enough then to know that's what it was – alcoholism. He drank a lot. He drank more than anyone I knew, but he didn't get falling-down drunk. When you live with someone every day, you don't notice, somehow. It gets worse and worse and you don't notice.

'And when you do, you blame yourself because he blames you. You're too ashamed to tell other people so no one is telling you it isn't your fault. The bad stuff is easier to believe. John's life wasn't what he'd wanted it to be. I don't know why. He drank because he was disappointed, I think. In himself and in me. It just got worse . . .' Her face was haunted now, and she was speaking as though she was alone.

'Did he hurt you, Kate?' Maggie feared the worst.

Kate shook her head. 'He never hurt me with his fists. Not once. He never raised a hand against me in anger. I used to wish he would. Then I'd have to leave. I'd have had to take Rebecca and go. No one could stay under those circumstances, could they? But he never did.'

'But?'

'But what he did with words and deeds was much worse. What's that expression – sticks and stones may break my bones, but words can never hurt me. That's not true. He said things to me, when he was drunk, cruel, heartless things. I could never repeat them. I've spent most of the rest of my life trying to forget them. He made me feel very small. Very insignificant. Very unworthy. Very low.' She listed these last slowly, as though just to say the words was painful.

'And Rebecca?'

'Rebecca was the apple of his eye – the only good thing in his life, so far as he was concerned, I think. He never made the connection. Rebecca had to be protected. It was the only thing we agreed on, though he never put it that way. She never once saw him drunk. Never. My doing, mostly – I kept her out of harm's way. I was complicit in the drinking and I thought I was doing it for Rebecca's good. But I was helping him too. They'd call me an enabler now. Maybe if she had . . . maybe things would have been different. Around her, his drinking made him the life and soul of every party. He wanted her to think he was a god. And she pretty much did. The two of them were a real item. Me, he almost completely ignored. Jekyll and Hyde. Years went by – literally years – without a kiss or a cuddle, a kind word. Sometimes – very occasionally – there would be promises and some remorse. He'd stop, he said. He'd get better. He'd get help. He never did.'

'Why didn't you leave him, Kate?' Kate furrowed her brow before she answered. She knew how little sense it made if you didn't know, and how much if you did.

'I was afraid. And I was ashamed. I always felt it was my fault, in some way. I felt I couldn't take Rebecca away. Not that Rebecca would have wanted to go, incidentally. She'd have had to be dragged, kicking and screaming. She adored him. She'd never see that there was a reason to leave him. That was a part of it. And I had nowhere to go. No money of my own. Lots of reasons. None of them good enough, I know. But they were different times. Not at the end, maybe, but when it started.

'I found some gumption from somewhere and went to teacher-training college, once Rebecca was at school full-time. I was in my thirties by then. He didn't want me to do it, but I threatened to leave. That was the one and only time I did. Found some courage somewhere, at long last, I suppose. Not quite enough, but some. I said I would go and take Rebecca with me if he didn't agree to me having this one thing for myself. And he gave in.'

'And that was your outlet?'

Kate nodded, smiling. 'That was what made it all bearable. That and Rebecca, and the belief that staying with John was the best thing for her. I loved teaching, right from the beginning. I was good at it too. The children loved me . . .'

'I can see that from the way you are with Stan. You're a Pied Piper type. A Mr Chips!'

Kate laughed. 'It was my vocation. My escape. My therapy.'

'I still can't believe you stayed all that time.'

She shook her head. 'I was married to John for thirty years. We were happy for maybe ten. I can't believe it either, sometimes. It seems such a waste.'

'What happened to him in the end?'

'He died.' Her voice was entirely matter of fact as she said it.

'How?'

'The alcoholism killed him, pretty much. It says heart attack on his death certificate, but he drank himself to death. It wasn't fast, either. He had chronic liver disease, his kidneys packed up. He was malnourished. He was a bloody mess.'

'And you took care of him?'

'There was no one else to do it. Of course I did. Rebecca was twenty-five years old by then. She'd been to university – she was living away from home, in Oxford, at that point. I don't know where she is now . . . But then she was living in Summertown, in one of those grand houses that have been divided into flats.'

'And you were still protecting her from the truth?'

'In some ways she was very grown up, but in others still very much a child. I suppose I'd hoped that she'd work it out, that she'd see it with adult eyes, once she'd lived away from home and came back, and that the penny would drop. Maybe it did, but she never admitted it. I thought one day she'd ask me a leading question, maybe, and that would be my chance to tell her . . . But if she had any questions, she certainly wasn't looking to me for the answers.'

'You were all alone with him.' Maggie could imagine the unrelenting grimness.

'Most of the time. He had to stop work – he was in no fit

state for anything. I kept going as long as I could, but eventually I did too. Money was tight, after that. He got sicker and sicker, and still he kept drinking. However hard I looked, it seemed I could never find it all. Bottles hidden in the most obscure places. And then bottles he didn't bother to hide – left lying about like a dare.' Kate sounded almost wistful. 'We had a wonderful doctor. Incredibly understanding. Kind. He would make home visits when he really needn't – and because of him, John was able to stay at home, and he died at home in his bed.'

'With his secret intact.'

'Exactly. Just me and the doctor knew, really, how bad he'd been.'

'Never Rebecca?'

Kate shook her head, and was quiet for a moment.

'I feel humiliated, when I say it all out loud. I can't equate that person with the person I see myself as now.'

She didn't look the part of the browbeaten wife, Maggie conceded. It was hard to believe, sitting beside her now, that she could have lived unhappily for almost a quarter of a century.

'I don't understand, though . . . about Rebecca. He had died and she had never known what killed him, not really known. So what happened between the two of you?'

Kate took a deep breath and smiled, her eyes widening. 'I married the GP who treated her father.'

Maggie exhaled slowly through pursed lips. She was good at the dramatic revelations, she'd say that for Kate. She was like a gentle, live version of *The Jeremy Kyle Show*, playing right here in the kitchen.

'So what?'

'So . . . John told her – pretty much a deathbed confession if you like, though it was a confession on my behalf and untrue at that – that we'd been having an affair the whole time he'd been dying.'

'But you hadn't?'

She shook her head vigorously. 'No. No. I wish to God we had been, but we hadn't. By then I knew I'd wasted such a big part of my life. I started to believe I deserved to be happy. But we hadn't.'

'Why would he do that?'

'Thinking back on it, I think he'd been doing that to me for as long as he and Rebecca had had a relationship. Undermining me. Doing what he could to turn her against me.'

'Why would he want to do that?'

'Because he desperately wanted Rebecca to be his and not mine. He didn't want to share. He wanted her to himself. I think, in his whole sorry life, the only thing he was proud of was her. And giving me some, any, of the credit for that was something he couldn't do. So he poured poison in her ear, whenever he could. I'm certain of it now, though I didn't see it as it happened, I'm afraid. I wish I had.'

'So he just made it up? An affair?'

'Not entirely. Not one inappropriate thing ever happened between Philip and me while John was alive. Not one. But we talked. We spent time together. A lot of time. It was me he was doing it all for, it turned out. Not my husband. It started with him feeling sorry for me, I suppose, seeing what life was like for me. But it was more than that, quickly. Soul mates, I suppose you'd call us. We were . . . he was . . . he was the love of my life. The irony is that I think John saw what was going on before I did. He could see that there was something between us. It might have been his most perceptive moment.'

'But Rebecca believed him when he told her the two of you were . . . ?'

'She believed him. She told me I'd betrayed him. She came

the day he died. He must have known – that was when he told her. I saw her once more, the day of his funeral. She wouldn't sit with me. God, that was hard. She sat across from me and she wouldn't even look at me. And I haven't seen her since.' She ended quietly.

'Christ. God. That's shocking, Kate. That's the most shocking thing I've heard in . . . I don't know how long.'

'I tried. I tried, many times. I wrote, I called, I even showed up at her house once. But she didn't want to see me. She moved, not long after that, and I didn't know where to. I got the classic return-to-sender message on my letters.'

'Oh, Kate. Oh, my God. How did you . . . ?'

'How did I survive?' Maggie nodded. 'I carried on living, Maggie. You know something about that, I think. I carried on.' Her face softened. 'And I married Philip. For the first time in as long as I remembered, I felt loved and cared for. He was a wonderful, wonderful husband. I didn't forget about Rebecca – of course I didn't. It hurt me, it *has* hurt me every day of my life since it happened. I think of her *every day*. But I had to let go of my anger. And I had to let go of her. You can't hold on to someone who doesn't want to be held.'

Aly was packing for Australia. Kate had packed for Stan and his black duffel bag was already on the landing, waiting to be carried downstairs. Aly, of course, was packing for herself. Allotting roughly two-thirds of the space in her case for textbooks and revision notes and ring binders. Maggie was nagging. She wanted everything done by tonight, she said. So they wouldn't be stressed tomorrow. Stan had just said, as he agonized over what toys to take in his carry-on bag – the kind of decision that was always, had always been, inordinately complex and difficult for him – that he couldn't see the difference between being stressed today, which he assured her he was, and being stressed tomorrow. But Maggie was running around manically, talking about phone chargers and Australian dollars, and she wasn't listening. Aly had smirked sympathetically at Stan and shut the door of her bedroom against the melee. Now she was sitting with a small pile of knickers in one hand, her head against the wall and her eyes closed. Literally worried sick.

Aly had always been told she was a clever girl. By her parents and her teachers and, latterly, by her peers, in tones of grudging envy. Now she was wondering whether she'd done something far stupider than any of her mates might ever do. Something that might muck up everything . . .

Her period was four days late. And it was never four days late. Not these days. She'd been very irregular, when she'd started, but so was everyone else she knew. And then, when Jake had died, she hadn't had a period for six months, but the GP had told her and Mum that was normal too. But in the last year, she'd been like clockwork, every twenty-eight days.

Sex without birth control. Chapter One in the *Idiot's Handbook*. The one thing you should never, never, never do. How many times had she been told that? By Mum, and by every zealous, well-intentioned health teacher and school counsellor she'd ever encountered. But that was exactly what they had done.

The stupidest thing was she'd had a condom with her – in her bag. She'd had three, for God's sake. She'd taken a deep breath and bought a packet in the Boots next to the tube station on her way to Ryan's house that night, feeling unbearably self-conscious but at the same time mature and vaguely cool. She'd assumed he'd have them but she'd wanted to be sure, and to be grown up. She'd wanted to be responsible. That was who she was, wasn't it? Responsible, reliable, sensible, clever Aly.

Ha! Some joke. 'Carried away.' That's what all the other morons, the ones on *Jeremy Kyle*, said, wasn't it? We got 'carried away'. And that was exactly what had happened, though they had been carried away less by lust than by an overwhelming sadness and the need to block out the dreadful past. She couldn't remember the exact moment when she'd been so unbelievably cavalier with her own body and her own future – the whole night seemed blurry to her now. He hadn't asked; she hadn't said anything . . . She'd forgotten. Carried away . . .

It didn't matter what, or why. The only thing that mattered was that she might be, she could be pregnant. She was flying to Australia to be her aunt's bridesmaid tomorrow, she was coming home to do her A levels a few weeks after that and she was supposed to be starting a medicine degree that autumn. Not having a baby. Not telling that to Mum or Dad.

She knew she needed to tell someone. She needed to take a test and find out. But she was paralysed by the fear. And who to tell? It sure as hell wouldn't be Maggie. Not Ryan either – that was far too heavy a piece of information to lay on the flimsiness of their relationship. Not friends at school. She'd almost told Kate, last night. Kate was the obvious person, she realized, with a sudden flood of gratitude that Kate was here. She didn't judge. She listened. She was calm. She'd know what to do.

'What's the stupidest thing you've ever done, Kate?' They'd been washing up after dinner. Maggie had been with Stan, out of earshot, arguing in their habitual manner about the number of Transformers that might be necessary on a two-week holiday. Kate hadn't looked at her – she'd studied the suds in the sink and carried on slowly scrubbing the batter off the toad in the hole pan.

'Crikey. Big question. You better let me think about that

for a minute . . .' She was buying herself time. It was obvious Aly had an agenda, but Kate didn't want to frighten her out of it by asking questions back . . .

'Do you mean stupid as in "whoops, how about the time I microwaved the dog by mistake" or stupid as in "that really messed up my life"?' 'Cos, she thought to herself, if you mean the latter, you might be sorry you asked, once I start to tell you . . . Aly didn't know the half of it.

Aly shrugged and repeated, 'Stupid.'

Kate laughed. 'Well, there was that time I accidently micro-waved the dog.' But Aly didn't laugh.

Kate put the dish down on the draining rack and dried her hands with a tea towel she'd kept on her shoulder. 'We all do stupid things, Aly. Everyone. It's what makes us human.'

Aly humphed, still not meeting Kate's eyes.

'Did that sound clichéd? Yes. It did. I didn't mean it to. I'm just trying to tell you that it's okay to do stupid things. I'm pretty sure you do fewer than the average person.'

'Are you now?'

Kate stroked her arm. Maybe that was the problem. This pedestal Aly was on – whether she'd put herself on it or other people had raised her aloft. It was a lot of pressure.

'I am. Do you want to tell me about it?'

Aly looked at her now. She nodded, and Kate saw to her horror that Aly was close to tears.

Stan chose that moment, with pinpoint accuracy, to descend the stairs – the last four in one jump – and slide across the polished wooden floorboards in his socks. Maggie was five seconds behind him.

Before Kate had the chance to look back at Aly, she'd turned away, and before Maggie and Stan had even spoken, she'd gone up the way they'd come down. Maggie rolled her eyes. 'That girl . . .'

A while later, Kate had knocked gently on Aly's door, but when she'd opened it, Aly was listening to her music, staring at a book, and it was obvious the moment had passed. Kate stayed for a moment or two, giving her a chance, but Aly kept the conversation between them brief and perfunctory. 'I didn't mean anything. I was just rabbiting on . . .' she said. Kate knew she was lying, but she also knew she couldn't make her talk. Kate had to hope that whatever it was, Aly was all right. And what she hoped most was that Aly might talk to Maggie about it . . .

Chapter Thirty-Two

Maggie had forgotten the colours of Australia. Vivid, stronger, brighter – the colours and smells of her childhood flooded back the moment she stepped outside the terminal in Brisbane, twenty-two hours after they had boarded on a typically grey and damp early spring day in London. When she was little, Aly was obsessed for a time with holding buttercups under your chin to see if you liked butter. They cast that yellowy tone on the neck of almost everyone – proof of their fondness for that particular fat, according to Aly, who couldn't get enough of it one summer. That was what Australia reminded her of – it had a special light you didn't see anywhere else, and certainly not in the UK. It was good to be home. She spoke the thought to herself in her head and was shocked to hear herself say 'home'. Had she always done that?

Of course, normally they'd have flown into Sydney – they were in Brisbane because it was closer to Scott's family's farm – a two-and-a-half-hour drive almost due west from this glimmering Gold Coast. Nothing in terms of Australian distances but a vaguely daunting prospect after so long on a plane, so Maggie had booked them all into a beach hotel for the night – they could be there in twenty minutes, once they'd got their bags, maybe take a walk, eat dinner and fall into bed, giving them one night to try to adjust their body clocks before they set off. Liv was flying up from Sydney in the morning, and they'd pick up a people mover and head off together. There were two days then before the wedding.

It was strange to travel without Bill, although she had done it before, once or twice. It was hard to get used to. No one to share the responsibility with, the decision-making. It was strangely lonely.

One of their bags was the last one on the conveyor belt. Aly got progressively more edgy – it was the garment bag that contained her bridesmaid dress, the blue one that she'd first won Kate over to and then enlisted her to help persuade Maggie – while Stan got more and more bleary-eyed, sitting on a bench beside the trolley they'd already loaded with their other three bags. Aly had seemed pretty agitated in general, the last little while – snappier than normal and not as excited as Maggie had thought she would be at the impending wedding. Maggie had put it down to anxiety about the studying she should be doing, and had tried to channel Liv's tolerance and understanding. On the flight, she'd noticed Aly sitting with a chemistry textbook open on the tray table, but not looking at it at all. She'd been staring out of the window at the clouds, her head leaning against the plastic wall of the plane. No headphones, no in-flight movie. Maybe it was all too much, Maggie thought. But she – they – couldn't have missed this, could they? Maybe she should have asked Liv to consider moving the wedding until after Aly's exams. But that wouldn't have been fair either. No, she told herself – Aly was fine. This break from all the hype and the pressure would do her good. She was working so hard – too hard.

The hotel was lovely, but it hardly mattered by the time they got there – they were almost boss-eyed with exhaustion.

'I want to go swimming, Mum.' Stan was using the last vestiges of his energy, after sitting like a Labrador in the open window of the car that had brought them – the breeze blowing him temporarily awake again. 'Come, please come. Will you?' He was tugging at her hand. A quick glance at Aly, who shook her head vigorously, told Maggie she was on her own. Aly wouldn't be coming down.

Maggie hadn't swum for as long as she could remember. There was just the dream, the horrible, frightening dream of water. She hadn't had it for a while, she realized. Maybe it was the running, making her physically tired in a way she hadn't been for months before. Maybe it had something to do with Kate, talking to her about her greatest fears and horrors, conversations that had chased them out of her subconscious. With a stab of fear, she wondered for the first time if it was the passage of time. Had Jake been dead that long – that she was starting to get better? She wanted that and she didn't want that, and more than anything right now she didn't want to put a swimsuit on and go downstairs with Stan to the pool.

But Stan had opened his case and pulled a pair of trunks out. He was naked from the waist down. 'Where's yours, Mum? Come on. Hurry.' Things were seldom other than urgent with Stan. With a deep sigh, Maggie hoist her case on to the wooden stand and unzipped it. She had put a suit in at the last minute, almost subconsciously, like you might pack an adapter or a travel alarm clock, so the black Lycra one-piece was near the top. Aly had disappeared wordlessly into the adjoining room by the time Maggie came out of the bathroom, tying the hotel's white cotton robe over her swim-suit, and Stan was holding open the door into the corridor. A quick glance before she left revealed Aly lying on the twin bed nearest the window, still wearing her Ugg boots, with the ubiquitous chemistry book lying open and unread on her lap – Maggie was beginning to think Aly was using this text-book as a shield against her.

The hotel pool was a functional rectangle with wide, deep steps at the shallow end. At this time of the day there was no one else here. A bored-looking attendant had handed Maggie two blue towels as she passed him, and she sat beside them on a rubber-strapped sunlounger as Stan peeled off his fleece and, without stopping to test the temperature of the water, let alone its depth at his proposed entry site, he ran full pelt, jumping and clasping his knees to his chest in a bomb, sending shimmering arcs of water splashing over the tiles and his mother's legs. Maggie loosened the robe and lay back against the lounger, squinting against the yellowy sun and enjoying its warmth on her skin.

'No, no. You've got to come in. I want you to swim with me . . .'

Stan knew nothing about the dream, of course. He was just a boy who didn't want to swim alone. Who wanted everyone to be happy. And, right now, everyone to be wet. She smiled at him.

'Okay, Stan. You win. I'm coming in.'

But as she stood on the top step, water bubbling and lapping across the arches of her feet, she wasn't sure she could. She was suddenly cold, though the air temperature hadn't changed, and the pool was hardly chilled – it was tepid, almost. She made herself take another step and the water was at her mid calf.

An impatient Stan, treading water confidently at the deep end of the pool now, heckled her relentlessly. When that didn't immediately work, he began to swim towards her in earnest. Within splash range, he stood and began to wave the surface of the water towards her in great pushes, flinging droplets that covered her thighs and stomach and hands.

'Stop it, Stan.' She felt almost desperate. But Stan read nothing into it and kept splashing relentlessly.

A moment later, something shifted inside her, and Maggie gave up and plunged headfirst into the water off the second step, her arms together above her head. As the water closed over her, she held her breath to see how it would feel. To see if something would change because she was submerged in it. She moved her arms and legs in swimming strokes that came as naturally to her, even after all this time, as walking did.

The water wasn't churning around her and the sunlight shone bright and sure from only one direction – from above her. She stopped swimming and turned, under the water, so that she was facing upwards. She let herself float there for a moment, knowing that she was drifting inexorably towards its surface. Her body moved with the water, not against it. She felt suffused with calm. It was Stan's face, not Jake's, waiting for her above, the ripples in the water distorting the image but not transforming it. He was giggling at her, his face in a wide smile. He was ten years old. She was in the present, in the water, with her son. Stan.

She broke the surface, feeling its rivulets run off her face back into the water, and then tipped herself forward, slowly, on to her feet, pulling Stan into her arms, squeezing him so hard he squirmed and wriggled to be free. She wanted to cry, but she wasn't crying.

Stan managed to escape, leaping backwards from her in the water.

'Come on, Mum, let's race. You've got to give me a head start, though . . .'

Liv found them in the hotel's restaurant in the morning. They slept ridiculously late, and breakfast had almost finished by the time they emerged. Maggie didn't remember feeling so refreshed after a sleep – not in for ever . . . though she'd still been in deep sleep when Stan woke her by jumping on the bed, already fully dressed. Now Stan was polishing off a stack of waffles, while Aly picked at a fruit plate and Maggie sipped coffee. She jumped up from the table when she saw her sister and the two of them squealed girlishly.

'You're here! You're all here! I'm sooooo happy to see you all . . . NOW it feels like I'm getting married!'

The waiter – irritated that breakfast was to be prolonged further by this new visitor – grudgingly took a coffee order for Liv. Stan, caged now that he'd finished eating, begged to be allowed to go outside and explore the hotel's garden. Aly stopped pushing kiwi fruit around her plate and, after she'd hugged Liv and admired the ring, excused herself and went upstairs, and the sisters were alone.

'Is she okay?' Liv asked. 'That was . . . low key. I thought she was totally into it . . .'

'How the hell would I know? She's been like that for a few days . . .'

'Is it the exams, d'you think? Is the trip a bit much?'

'I honestly don't know, Liv – she's barely talking to me at all. I think the exams are a good excuse, but I don't know if that's it . . . not really. She's being very strange . . .'

Liv looked thoughtfully at Aly's retreating back.

'I got the feeling things had been better altogether, since Kate came.'

'They had. They have. She and Aly spend all this time together, and though Kate never tells me what they talk about, I do know that they talk. And things have been – easier.'

'I thought she was excited about all this . . .'

'She was. So excited. We heard little else for ages. This is new. And it's starting to piss me off . . .'

'Hey – the bride demands calm and harmony.'

Maggie motioned a zip closing across her lips. 'Zzzp.

Shan't say a word. I shall take whatever teen spirit is doled out and smile beatifically. For Liv has willed it so.'

'And I have. Bridezilla. That's what Scott's mother called me the other day – last weekend, when we were up there finalizing stuff. She wasn't talking to me, of course – she was talking *about* me, to her sister. I overheard.'

'What did you do to earn that sobriquet?'

Liv held her hands up in a gesture of surrender. 'Not a damn thing!' she said, her eyes wide and innocent.

'Liv . . . ?'

'Had an opinion about my own wedding? Expressed a preference? Breathed too loudly? Breathed at all . . .? Could be any of those things.'

'Is it that bad, Liv?'

Liv laughed a light peal. 'Not really. No. They're very sweet. They just have a different view on things, I suppose. Not the big stuff. Just the details. And the details – they seem huge, and there's a million of them. How could they not love me?!'

Maggie nodded sympathetically. Liv's coffee and her refill were delivered and Liv slowly stirred a sugar cube into hers.

'And I've just felt – a bit outnumbered, I suppose. There's so many of them, and just me.'

'Scott isn't automatically on your side?'

'Scott doesn't want to take sides. Or Scottie, as he seems to be known here. Scott couldn't give a toss about the details, and I think he isn't quite sure why I don't just completely cave in to his mother, like I think he's probably been doing for the last thirty years – just for a quiet life.'

'Sounds like a plan.' Maggie's own wedding had been so small, and so free of details. 'Let them have the wedding, you have the marriage, eh?'

'And that, sis, is exactly the kind of priceless little pearl of wisdom I have needed you to be here to say. That and the fact that you swell the numbers on my team. Once Dad gets here tomorrow, it's a more even playing field. More Walkers. Thank God.'

She stroked Maggie's arm and then laid her head briefly and lightly on Maggie's shoulder.

'Excited?'

'So very excited. I can't wait.' It was a calm and faraway voice.

'Happy?'

'So, so happy, sis. I didn't know what a big deal it would be. I loved him, he loved me. We've been living together. Officially not for long, maybe, but in reality for ages. I didn't expect that this would feel so . . . so important. So auspicious. Does that make sense? All those people who say they don't need the piece of paper . . . I think they're so wrong.'

'Absolutely.'

'And what about you? Are you happy to be here?'

Maggie nodded. 'I really am.'

'You look good.' It wasn't a throwaway remark. Liv was peering at her closely – the way only a family member could without it being weird.

Maggie nodded, smiling. 'I feel good.'

'Well, it shows . . .'

Maggie wanted to tell her about the swim. She wanted to tell her she wasn't having the dream so much any more – that maybe the dream had even stopped altogether. But she'd made a promise to herself, somewhere over Singapore. This fortnight belonged to Liv and to Scott. Nothing was going to spoil it. It was Liv's turn. And this was happy news. This would be a happy day. For too long, Maggie had been the leaner and Liv had let her lean. But not now.

*

319

Aly was quiet and even sullen on the long drive inland to Scott's family's hometown. Maggie and Aly were to stay in a hotel in town, a few miles from the farm. It was pretty basic, by city hotel standards, Liv said, but she thought it was clean and comfortable, and they'd get a bit of peace there, for Aly to study. 'I might need a bolt hole, too,' she'd joked, 'once everyone else hits town . . .' Liv would go out and stay at the farm to oversee preparations and be on hand to hear her future mother-in-law's thoughts on all details, though on the night before the ceremony she would bunk up with her sister and niece. Stan had successfully petitioned to stay on the farm – Scott had a trillion young cousins and nephews who were all to be housed in the old sheep-shearers' barracks that still stood in the acreage of the farmhouse, so he would go with his aunt, who had thrilled him by producing an outback hat for him when they got in the car.

'Are you here for the wedding, Stan, or the farming?' she asked him, her eyes sparkling. A rabbit in the headlights, Stan recognized a tricky question when he heard one, and he opened and closed his mouth wordlessly until Liv took pity on him, patted his head on top of the hat and said, 'You're all right, sport!'

Several times, Liv tried to talk with Aly, who was sitting in the back seat with Stan, but Aly's responses were brief – she would answer, then fall silent again, staring out of the window. The sisters stole a glance at each other – Liv's face again asking the question and Maggie's shoulders once more shrugging a non-answer. By the time Liv had dropped them and headed off for a family dinner, leaving them to a quiet evening and another early night to ward off the jet lag, Maggie had had enough. They unpacked without speaking much, though Maggie was aware she was goading her daughter with questions and remarks about coat hangers and bathroom shelves. Maggie was spoiling for a fight and suspected Aly knew it, but Aly was stuck here with her and she couldn't think of how to head Maggie off. She tried silence, but she could see her mother getting quietly crosser and crosser, and she knew an eruption was probably inevitable.

And she was right. It took a couple of hours. Maggie took a long bath and Aly lay on the bed, flicking around the television channels with the remote control. Then Aly used the bathroom while Maggie dressed. It was strangely formal, like strangers sharing.

'Do you want to go down for dinner, love, or shall we see what they have in the way of room service?'

'I'm not hungry . . .' This was a red rag to a bull. It felt like punishment. She'd barely eaten when they'd pulled off the road for some lunch and she'd pushed around a bit of watery fruit for breakfast.

'Do you feel ill?' But the question sounded irritated, even to Maggie.

'I'm fine.' She so clearly was anything but. Maggie thought about Liv's abhorrence of the 'fine' response and felt tired.

'What in the hell is wrong with you, Aly? You've been so looking forward to this. I just don't understand you.'

'Oh, Mum . . .' Aly tried to turn away, but Maggie grabbed her upper arm and wouldn't let her. Aly's face contorted; she dissolved into tears, her shoulders shaking.

'Aly!' Maggie felt a rush of relief. Angry, sullen Aly had faded away in an instant. Aly cried so rarely. When she did – and this had always been the case, ever since she'd been really small – the tears were tortured, catastrophic, all consuming. She cracked open. Aly had crumbled, and now they might get somewhere. She took Aly into her arms. Aly let herself be held. 'What is it?'

Aly couldn't speak. Maggie stroked her back, peering anxiously into her face.

'Tell me. Please. You're frightening me. This is more than exams, isn't it? Much more. You have to tell me.'

Sniffing hard, Aly rubbed her eyes, trying desperately to bring herself under control.

'That's right, darling. Calm down. Breathe. In and out. That's it.' Maggie breathed in and out slowly and Aly found herself aping her mother.

'Calm right down, and then we're going to sit down and you're going to tell me what's wrong.'

Panic spread across Aly's face again.

'Sssh . . . Don't do that. In and out. Whatever it is, Aly. You're going to tell me and it's going to be okay.'

Maggie wished she believed that. The kind of promises that mothers make – she knew, since Jake, that they were just lies too. A mother couldn't protect her child. She hadn't seen Aly like this for a long, long time, and she realized she had no idea what was wrong, not the slightest clue as to what it might be.

When Aly's breathing had slowed, and tears were no longer rolling down her face, Maggie handed her a tissue and led her to the bed. She pulled two pillows out from under the quilt and laid them against the headboard, settling Aly into them. She took a bottle of Glenfiddich from the hotel mini bar and poured it into a glass, taking a big gulp before she handed it to Aly and watched her sip gingerly from it. 'Take a swig. Go on.' Walking round to the other side, she climbed on the bed and sat cross-legged in front of her daughter. She remembered reading something about talking to your teens in a car – that they found it much easier to confess to things if they didn't have to make eye contact with you because you were driving, but too bad. They weren't driving, and she needed to see Aly's face.

'When you're ready, talk to me, Aly . . .'

'You're going to hate me.'

'I could never hate you, silly girl. Little thing called unconditional love.'

Aly took two deep breaths, and then her words poured out on the exhalation. 'I think I might be pregnant.'

An hour or so later, once Aly was asleep, Maggie went into the bathroom, gave in to panic momentarily – gripping the marble, or faux marble more likely, sink surround and staring at herself in the mirror – and then she called Liv's mobile phone. She had thought about calling Bill, but only for a second. She couldn't cope with Bill right now. So much for making it Liv's week. That had lasted – how long? Five or six hours? But she didn't hesitate. She needed her and she knew Liv wouldn't mind. There were only three bars on her phone but she had to hope it would be enough. Liv answered on the third ring and her voice was miraculously clear, as though she were in the next room.

'Mags? Is that you?'

'It's me.'

'Hang on a moment. We're about to start eating dinner. Where are you? There are a squillion people here. I'll go out . . . wait a sec . . . That's better. Can you hear me now?' She heard Liv walking, and people chatting and laughing in the background.

'Yes. I could before. You hear me?'

'Barely. Why are you whispering? Are you in a cupboard or something?'

'Bathroom. Aly's asleep.'

'Okay. It's a bit early. Is she poorly? Is everything all right? You sound weird . . .' Maggie waited for a space, and hoped Liv hadn't been drinking. She needed her sober now.

'Aly thinks she might be pregnant.'

'Crikey.' A long pause. 'Shit. What?'

'Pregnant. I need you to bring me a pregnancy test . . .'

'Now?' There was no incredulity in Liv's tone, just matter-of-fact efficiency.

'Now. If that's okay? I don't want to leave her.'

'Okay. I'll do it. No one's going to miss the bride on the eve of the eve of the wedding. If I was going to do a runner, I'd wait until the day, right? The supermarket will still be open, I reckon. Let me tell Scott, and I'll be there in a few . . .'

'Don't tell Scott!'

'I won't tell him why, you daft bugger. I'll make something up. Why wouldn't I want to lie to my fiancé two days before our wedding? I'll say you've got the trots or cystitis or something . . .'

'Great.'

'You can't have it both ways. See you in a bit.'

'Liv?'

'Yep?'

'Thanks, sis.'

'You're welcome.' There had never been a question in either of their minds that Liv would do this. It was how they were. 'You okay, Maggie?'

'Not remotely.'

'Just hold on.'

She'd done the same thing – said the same thing – the day after the tsunami. Just hold on. Maggie remembered sitting in the big bay window of the Chiswick house, watching her cab pull up and Liv running up the steps, through the door Aly had opened, straight at her, arms open. Just hold on. Even though there was nothing to hold on to.

She brought two boxes. 'Better be sure . . .'

Aly was still asleep. Maggie opened the door with her

324

finger pressed to her lips. She grabbed the room key from the table and came out into the hall, closing the door gently behind her.

'I want to let her sleep a bit longer. I don't think she's slept properly in days, poor kid. And I need a drink. Another one. We already polished off a whisky from the mini bar.'

If a comment about foetal alcohol syndrome sprang to mind, Liv was sensible enough to suppress it.

At the hotel bar, Liv ordered a gin and tonic for Maggie and an orange juice for herself. Maggie stirred the ice around the glass then drank half of its contents in one gulp, her face grim. Liv mourned the passing of the peaceful, relaxed expression of earlier. Poor Maggie – there always seemed to be something.

'So what's the story?'

Maggie threw her hands up in the air. 'She thinks she might be pregnant.'

'I got that bit, Mags.'

'I'm glad you got it first time. I'm still struggling to process it . . .'

'I didn't even know she had a boyfriend. Did you?'

'I hadn't a clue.'

Liv exhaled loudly.

'Who is he? Did she say?'

'Ryan.'

Liv looked at her sister quizzically.

'Ryan. As in Jake's best friend Ryan.'

'My God . . . I didn't even know they were friends. Still, I mean.' Liv's mouth opened wide and then shut again, her cheeks puffed out with air.

'I know. I hadn't seen him in ages. I didn't know she had. Turns out they met up again, last summer, at some cricket match, she said.'

Liv wrinkled her nose. 'But isn't he at university?'

Maggie nodded. 'Yes, he is. Edinburgh. They've been writing to each other all this time. And she never said a word.' Liv caught the wistfulness in Maggie's voice. It was a big secret for Aly to have kept. She could see, in this moment, how shocked Maggie was, and she wondered how Aly could have got so far away from her mother, and from her, for that matter, in so short a period of time. Poor Maggie.

'You can't get pregnant writing . . .'

'Obviously not. They've been meeting up too, I suppose. I'm not crystal clear on the facts. I didn't want to stage a Spanish Inquisition.'

'And you didn't know, at all? Nothing?'

'Don't rub it in. Not a bloody clue. I feel bad enough already. No, I didn't know.'

'Meeting up much? For how long?'

'Not much, I don't think. Since Christmas. The party – the one she wore your dress to . . . ?'

'The little devil. I stuck up for her!'

'He invited her.'

'So it's been going on for months?'

'I don't know how long. Most of this spilt out in the hour just before I rang you. Between plenty of panic and copious weeping.'

'And why does she think she's pregnant?'

'She's skipped a period. And she never does that.'

'Don't tell me she wasn't using anything.'

'Liv.'

'She's smarter than that, Maggie. Come on . . . You know she is.'

'She said they were, that they did . . .'

'Then she's not pregnant. Finish that gin. We'll go up and

get this sorted out . . .' Liv slammed her glass down on the bar.

Maggie loved Liv for her practical calm. 'I'm sorry, Liv. You shouldn't be thinking about this now. You're about to get married, for God's sake. Not sitting here dealing with this. I promised I wasn't going to do this.'

'Do what?'

'Emotionally hijack the occasion.'

Liv snorted. 'Who'd you promise?'

'Myself.'

'Those ones are the hardest ones to keep.' Liv took her hand. 'Doesn't matter. Just a white dress and a big lunch. I already feel married. The rest is just the frosting.' Maggie knew, from their earlier conversation, that wasn't how it was but she loved her sister for saying so.

Aly was still asleep when Maggie let them back into the room. She perched on the edge of the bed and shook her daughter's shoulder gently. Aly opened her eyes.

'Liv's here, sweetheart.'

Aly rolled over to look at Liv, who was leaning against the chest of drawers.

'Hey, kiddo.'

'Oh, Auntie Liv.' Aly's face threatened to crumple again.

'Stop right there. No more crying.' She waved the pregnancy test she'd pulled from the box in the air. 'Let's find out, shall we?'

'I'm scared.'

'You'd be weird if you weren't. First time I took one of these, I was absolutely bloody petrified.'

'You've taken one?' Curiosity momentarily took over.

'God, yes. Show me the woman who hasn't and I'll show you the woman who needs to get out more.'

'Liv!'

'Sorry. But it's true. I was nineteen.'

'Was it negative?'

'Absolutely. Do you see any cousins?'

'I was seventeen. Did I teach you nothing, Liv?' Maggie was still sitting on the bed. 'But I think we all know how that turned out.'

Aly wailed dramatically . . .

Liv looked at Maggie and started to laugh. Maggie looked stricken at first, but then she too began to giggle. Soon the two of them were howling with contagious, absurd hilarity. Aly looked from her mother to her aunt, then back again, not understanding what the hell was so funny, but after a few seconds, it didn't matter that she didn't know what they were laughing at, she was just laughing with them, at them, laughing because it was the closest thing to crying . . .

Maggie had slid down to sit on the floor with her back against the mattress. Liv lay the box on Aly's lap and sat down next to her sister.

'Come on. Get on with it.'

Aly took the test and went into the bathroom, leaving the door open.

'Did you tell Scott?'

'Scott thinks your mum has a nasty bout of cystitis.'

That made Maggie start laughing again, for some reason. Liv joined in.

Sitting on the loo, Aly poked her head around the open door. 'Don't make me laugh. I'm trying to pee on a very narrow stick here . . .'

When she came out, Maggie and Liv had stopped laughing. Liv put out her hand and Aly handed her the test. Maggie scooted along the carpet and made room for her and she sat between her mother and her aunt, both of whom laid a head on her shoulder. They were sitting so closely together that their thighs were all touching.

'How long?'

'Two minutes, the box says.'

For two minutes they didn't speak. Each one was briefly lost in her own thoughts. Maggie was remembering discovering she was pregnant with Jake. She'd been alone when she'd taken her test. She hadn't even told Bill she was going to do it that day, though he'd known her period was late. She had a clear recollection of the shiny red face of the middle-aged Korean shopkeeper in the pharmacy where she'd bought the test, looking at her as if he knew all about her.

Liv was thinking about the boy she had been afraid had got her pregnant when she was still a teenager, and about how different her life might have been if he had. She hadn't loved him, not like Maggie and Bill. Maggie and Bill were always going to end up together – if her ten-year-old self had been a fair judge of something like that. The pregnancy speeded up their journey – it didn't fundamentally alter their path. Maybe Maggie hadn't been ready for a baby, but they'd made it work, the two of them. They'd made it work for a long time, and so far as Liv was concerned, it wasn't either of their faults that it had failed.

Aly was thinking about her A level exams. And her place at medical school. And, a little, about why she wasn't thinking about Ryan. He didn't know about this. It was weird, wasn't it, that you could have sex with a person, be naked in a bed that way, but be too – what was it, shy? – to tell them something like this.

Liv had laid the test on the carpet beside her, where the others couldn't see it.

'Do you two remember that episode of *Friends* where Rachel takes the pregnancy test at Monica's wedding, and

Phoebe's holding the test, and she lies about the result – she says Rachel isn't pregnant, because she wants her to be disappointed and thus to realize how much she did want to be pregnant, and then be thrilled when Phoebe tells her the truth – that she, in fact, is actually pregnant?'

'No,' said Maggie.

Aly's voice was shaky. 'Yes?'

'We're not doing that. Very cruel. You're not pregnant.'

'You're not mucking about?'

'I just said I wasn't. I always thought I'd have slapped Phoebe in the face, if I'd been Rachel. Mean trick to play.'

'So I'm not.'

'You're not. Not not not not pregnant. Not.'

'Give it to me.'

Liv passed her the test. Maggie had her head back and her eyes closed, but Liv could see that she was holding one of Aly's hands.

'I'm not. I'm not pregnant . . . Thank God!'

Liv patted her arm. 'I think you've killed your mother, though,' gesturing at Maggie.

Maggie opened her eyes and lifted her head. 'Not dead. Relieved.'

Liv stood up and put her hands on her hips.

'Right. So we're finished with this little drama, are we? Be all right with everyone if we got back to me now, would it? The little matter of my wedding, in . . .' she looked at her watch, 'a little over thirty-six hours' time, I'd say . . .'

'Yes, Auntie Liv.'

'And you'll both be on parade. Providing that cystitis clears up, right, sis? As if nothing happened. Which it hasn't, really. And friends? You'll be friends, right?

'Coming over tomorrow to help set the tables in the tents? I think you'll find it in the official job description for bridesmaid. I might kill one of Scott's cousins, if I don't have you two there. They mean well, but they've got no taste . . .'

After she'd gone, Maggie and Aly put their pyjamas on without speaking any more, brushed their teeth and got into the big bed in Maggie's room. Maggie propped herself up on one elbow and brushed the hair back from Aly's face.

'Do you really like him, sweetheart?'

'He's a nice guy, Mum.' Aly didn't look right at her as she replied.

Maggie smiled. 'He always was. I've missed him, to tell you the truth. He was almost a part of the family, wasn't he, when . . .'

'I think he's missed you too. Missed all of us, I suppose.'

'Do you two talk about Jake much?'

Aly shook her head. 'We did. At the beginning. When we started writing to each other. We don't so much any more.'

'Did it help?'

A single tear escaped from Aly's eye and Maggie caught it as it ran down her cheek.

'We never talked about him, Mum. You and me.'

'We did, Aly.'

She shook her head again, more emphatically this time. 'No, we didn't. Not right after it happened. You talked to Liv. You didn't talk to me. I don't think you talked to Dad much, either. I didn't have anyone to talk to. Do you know I spent more time talking to the matron at school about Jake than I did to you?'

'That's not true.'

'Stop telling me things aren't true, Mum. I was there. I wasn't a baby. I remember. I remember everything. You weren't there for me. Not really. I know you think it's a silly expression, "being there" for someone. I've heard you say it before. I was there. That's what you're thinking, right? I was there every day. I kept cooking and doing the laundry and driving to and from school and tennis and hockey. I was there. But it means more than that.'

Her face was utterly stricken. And Maggie knew that, really, she was right. It wasn't just the childlike spin. She hadn't been. She hadn't been able to be.

'I'm so sorry, Aly.' The weight of the apology was apparent to both of them.

'Don't be. You couldn't. I could see that. I tried so hard to be there for you, Mum. I really did. But it was so hard.' Aly's eyes were brimming now, with tears.

'My poor baby girl. I'm so, so sorry.'

'It's okay, Mum.'

For the first time in the longest time – since one or other of the kids had had a nasty bug, probably, when they were small – Maggie held her child close all night. Perhaps the last thought she had, before she closed her eyes and drifted off, was that these were what Bill called the breakthrough moments. Tonight, talking with Aly. Before, in the pool with Stan. Something was shifting. It had taken her too long, maybe, but she was here now.

Liv's day, thirty-six hours later, dawned bright and beautiful. A calm peacefulness had settled over Maggie and Aly by then. When Liv had shown up the night before, her dress in a white garment bag and her nerves frayed by a day of organization, the three of them had eaten a light supper on the hotel's terrace. Maggie had ordered a bottle of champagne and they'd toasted to the big day.

'No one got any last-minute dramas for me?'

Aly giggled. 'So sorry, Auntie Liv.'

'Sure? 'Cos I'm firing on all four cylinders, the day I've had. There's nothing I can't mediate, fix or brush under the carpet . . . Or just plain get over. Right now, ten miles north-west of here, there's an exquisite wedding cake – two layers, one a lemon vanilla sponge with a curd filling, the other a triple chocolate with a dark chocolate ganache. Both covered with an exquisite array of seasonal sugar flowers. Imported from Sydney in refrigerated transportation. With a cake topper stuck on the top that Scott's Auntie Mabel had on her cake in 1963. The bride looks like Elton John post hair transplant and the groom is a dead ringer for Lurch.'

Aly was taking a mouthful of champagne. She choked on a snigger, coughing into her napkin.

Maggie and Liv joined in, Liv still talking through her laughter. 'I wouldn't mind. I could cope with the hideous plastic couple leaving footprints in my icing. Just about. I mean, they're dreadful. Not even remotely retro groovy. But Auntie Mabel says they're for luck.'

'Aah . . . that's nice.' Aly's face was mock stern.

'It would be nicer if Auntie Mabel's husband Uncle Jack hadn't run off with a barmaid in 1975!'

'Luck!' Now they were howling like they had been the other night. Maggie wiped away a tear of mirth.

'I'll have to crop the wedding photos to cut off the top of the wretched cake.'

'We can airbrush them out.'

'Thank God.'

'What about your something borrowed?' Maggie asked.

'Yeah, what is that, again – borrowed, old, new . . . ?'

'Blue,' Liv completed.

'Do you believe in all that stuff?' Aly asked. Liv was so modern to her in every way that she couldn't imagine she did.

'Too right. Don't make that cynical face at me, Aly Barrett. You're too young. Wind'll change and you'll stay that way. You wait till you have a veil on your head. It does something

333

to you. Turns you all traditional. Even if you didn't know you had it in you.'

'So what have you got?'

Liv listed things off on her fingers. 'Something new – the dress, of course. Something borrowed – your mum's diamond-drop earrings. If she remembered to bring them . . .'

Maggie nodded, smiling. 'They're upstairs.'

'Something old – a hairgrip Dad gave me that Mum wore on her wedding day. Imagine him keeping that all these years. It's just got these three tiny crystals on it, and I'm going to tuck it in next to the comb that'll be holding my veil.'

'I never knew Dad was sentimental that way.' Maggie was amazed. Their dad was an undemonstrative, seemingly fairly unemotional man.

'I think he only pulls that quality out for weddings of the non-shotgun kind,' Liv smiled.

'Quite right. No diamante hairclip for me. I'd have remembered.'

'He came, Mags. That was a lot for him then.'

'And blue?' Aly didn't want the conversation to veer that way. She didn't want anyone to get maudlin tonight. Thinking about her mum's wedding to her dad all those years ago was a route to all thoughts sad. Bill, the separation, Jake, Gran not being around to see this. Grandad, who seemed older to all of them than he had the last time they'd been over to see him, his head sitting lower on his neck, like a tortoise, his hair thin and grey. No. Not tonight.

'Ah. I don't know what you had planned, but I wondered if you might want this . . . ?'

Maggie reached into her handbag, hanging on the back of her chair, and pulled something out. She opened her clenched palm into Liv's waiting hand, and Aly saw that it was a garter. Liv took it.

'I know – I know my marriage didn't work out. Maybe that makes it bad luck and you won't want to wear it. But you bought it for us, Liv. You gave it to me, on my wedding day. So it's special to me for that reason. And all I can tell you is that the day I wore it, I was happy. I was happy and in love and I believed it would last for ever. It's not the garter's fault it didn't.'

Aly looked from her mother to her aunt. 'For God's sake, you two. I'm not allowing this self-indulgent sentimental guff. Mum – order another bottle of champagne. And I swear to God, if either one of you starts blubbing, I'm going to bed!'

Under the table, Maggie squeezed Liv's hand – the one still holding the garter. Liv squeezed back.

'Okay. I'll wear it. Just so long as you promise Bill didn't take it off with his teeth . . .'

And she was wearing it under the narrow column of ivory gazar the next morning, as she walked down an outdoor aisle towards an arbour decorated with roses and greenery, to take her vows.

Sitting in the front row, watching her dad speak up as 'the man who giveth this woman to be married', the hand that held Liv's aloft trembling slightly with nerves, Maggie realized she wasn't holding on to any resentment about her own wedding, two decades earlier. Liv was right. Dad had come and that was the best he could do. And he was here now. Not tremendously close to her, not expressing much out loud, but she'd known, from his tight hug hello and the looks she caught him giving her, that he was sorry, about Bill, and that he was glad she was here.

Behind her sister and her father, a small posy of wild flowers in her hands and her hair pulled back in a loose bun, tendrils escaping down her neck, Aly took Maggie's breath away. She was acutely aware of wishing Bill were here so he could see how very beautiful and grown up she looked today. They'd always have that – the shared pride and love and interest. Aly seemed to float across the grass, her serene expression so transformed from the other night – the joy she'd initially expressed about Liv's marriage seemingly completely restored. Across from Maggie, Stan sat with his two new best friends – Angus and Kevin – stocky, tow-haired kids belonging to Scott's cousin, all three of them looking uncomfortable in their shirts and ties and unimpressed at the still, quiet solemnity of the occasion.

She missed Bill.

All around her were Australians, the country folk that were Scott's family and childhood friends and neighbours, and the city slickers who'd flown up from Sydney and arrived in a couple of minibuses that were parked around the back of the barns. They'd all milled happily together before the ceremony started. So had she. This was a good place to be. You could feel the love all around them. Scott and Liv didn't look anywhere but straight into each other's eyes as they made their vows. Maggie could see Scott's fingers stroking Liv's as they held hands and listened intently to the officiant. They were so sure and so happy. And for now, for Maggie, it was enough, just to share the space with them and to let herself feel it too.

Chapter Thirty-Three

Maggie scanned the labelled doorbells for Bill's name. She'd never been here before. She'd seen the plans for the renovation a couple of years ago – Bill used to bring her architect's drawings because she liked them – the precise, ordered neatness of them – and because she had a good eye, he said, for how spaces should be designed. She could have been an architect, he used to say. I could have been all kinds of things, she always thought in reply, but she never said it. Because the rest of the sentence was a reproach, and the rest of the sentence made a regret of Jake. I could have been all kinds of things if I hadn't fallen pregnant when I was still a child myself.

But she'd never been to the building once it was finished. She'd come tonight because he'd asked her to. At home, marvellous Kate – Kate who they'd all missed more than they had imagined they would, and had all been so, so happy to see when they got back – was dealing with the kids. Stan was due back at school in the morning and Kate was going through his bag with him, making sure he had what he needed. Aly was getting ready for her exams. The holiday was definitely over. The rest of their fortnight had passed in a blur of what Maggie might call contentment, if she had one adjective to describe it. After the drama, Aly had chilled out, and although she'd worked pretty hard some of the time, the rest of it she'd been lighter and easier. Stan had been beside himself with joy the whole time they'd been at the farm, and afterwards, when they'd stayed for a couple of days in the Blue Mountains and then back in Sydney. He had always been too young before, maybe, to appreciate everything that Maggie had loved so about the city, but this time, this trip, his eyes had been alight every day. He'd collected things to make a scrapbook of the trip and he'd itemized and explained every item to Kate the day they'd returned, before the kettle had even boiled. Maggie wished it had been nice to get home, but it hadn't been. She'd felt different while she was away – lighter and freer and more relaxed, somehow. It wasn't just the wedding – though Liv's incandescent joy had helped – it was everything. She and Aly had never felt closer. Stan was strong and healthy and golden, full of the farm. Being back had 'killed the buzz', as Aly would say.

Bill buzzed her in now. She took the lift to the top floor, and he was waiting for her in the doorway. He kissed her on both cheeks and ushered her in. The flat was very Bill, she thought, looking around. Neat to the point of anonymity – sleek and modern. He'd wanted to sell the Chiswick house for so long. And this was so the way he would have liked to live. Somewhere bigger, sure, but somewhere that looked like this inside. It would never suit her.

'How are you? You look really, really good.' She knew she did. Better than she'd looked for ages. The climate in Australia agreed with her – her olive skin could look ashy after an English winter, but now it was shiny and glowing again.

Bill looked good too, she acknowledged. Carrie obviously liked a stubbly look because he always seemed to have skipped a shave when she saw him these days. She wondered, briefly and uncomfortably, whether the whiskers left a rash on Carrie's skin when he kissed her. It was still strange, that he kissed her . . .

'Wine?'

She nodded. He'd already set out two glasses on the counter – the trendy kind that had no stem, just a thin bulb with a flattened base. 'White or red? I have both . . .'

'Red. Please.' He poured from a bottle he'd already opened and handed a glass to her.

'Good to see you, Maggie. How was the trip?'

'You haven't heard all about it by now from Stan?'

'Oh, I've heard from Stan. About the farmer. All about the animals and the machinery and the warm milk straight from the cow, and about the riding around chasing sheep . . .'

Maggie laughed. 'He loved the farm. Did he tell you we let him sleep there, while me and Aly were in the hotel?' Bill nodded, smiling. 'He was totally chuffed. He'd have stayed, given half the chance. A regular sheep-shearer in the making.'

'You can take the genes out of Australia, I guess, but . . .'

'I guess . . .'

'So how was the wedding? Stan was sketchy on the wedding itself.'

'Beautiful.' She pulled a camera out of her handbag. 'Haven't had a chance to download any of these yet, but I wondered . . . I thought you might like to see them. Not all of them, but maybe Aly . . . She looked so gorgeous, Bill. A real beauty.'

'I'd love to. That's really kind of you.' He took the camera from her.

She shrugged. 'It was weird that you weren't there. We missed you. Me and the kids. Liv too, I think.' He nodded acknowledgement of the compliment, and Maggie thought he looked sad for a moment.

They sat side by side on the sofa while Bill flicked through the photographs. Occasionally one or the other of them would comment, or Bill would ask a question about people he didn't recognize. He laughed at a picture of Stan, wearing an outback hat too big for him, milking a cow, his cheek pressed against its belly, his arms barely reaching around to grasp the teats. And waved his head in proud disbelief at a shot of Aly, taken with the sun setting behind her, glowing and willowy and pretty and grown up.

'He's a nice guy, right?' he asked, as he looked at a shot of Scott and Liv leaning on a gate, kissing. 'According to Stan, he may well be the second coming.'

'Don't know about that,' Maggie laughed. 'But yeah, he's a really nice guy.'

'So they've got a decent shot, then? At having something that lasts?'

'I hope so.'

Bill stood up and went to the window, his back to Maggie. 'How is Carrie?'

'Carrie is pregnant.' They couldn't see each other's faces. Bill hadn't known he would blurt it out like that, and he hadn't known until this second that he wasn't brave enough to say it to her face. He made himself turn around but didn't go any closer.

Maggie's face felt instantly hot, but her body was cold. She looked at her left hand, gripping the edge of the modern, square sofa. Her wedding ring was glinting at her. She covered it with her other hand. She should have taken it off by now. She should have taken it off months ago. She felt stupid and foolish.

'Say something.'

'What do you want me to say, Bill?'

'Whatever you want to say. Just something.'

'You're giving me a little too much credit if you think I'm going to say, "Congratulations. Good for you. I'm happy for you."'

'I wasn't expecting that. I'm not stupid.'

She snorted. 'What then, Bill?'

'I don't know.'

'Maybe you want me to ask questions. Huh? How far along is she? Boy or a girl? How do you think we should tell the kids? Our kids? Where are you going to live, after the baby comes? When is the baby coming, by the way? Autumn time? For Christmas?'

'Stop it.'

'I'm sorry, Bill. Just trying to figure out what you want me to say.'

'Summer. The baby is coming in the summer.'

'Christ.' Maggie did the sums in her head. 'You don't hang about, do you Bill?'

'It wasn't like that. It wasn't planned.'

She put up her hand, palm out, to stop him. 'Oh please, Bill. You sound like a teenager. Spare me.'

'We need to talk about this, Maggie. Sensibly.'

'I don't need to talk about it, Bill. It isn't happening to me. Our lives are not connected in this way any more. Or had you forgotten? Sometimes you don't seem all that sure. But they aren't. And this' – she waved her arms around her at the apartment and the news and the new, whiskery Bill – 'is not happening to me. I don't need to talk about it at all. I'm not staying here . . .'

She stood up, thrusting the camera back into her bag. Foolish. Bringing the photographs to show him. Telling him she'd missed him. Stupid.

'Maggie, please. This wasn't easy for me . . .'

'Christ, Bill. None of this has been easy for any of us. How dare you – how dare you say that to me? I don't want to stay here and listen to you explain it. You've "moved on".' Maggie carved big, angry speech marks in the air. 'I get it. So move the hell on and leave me alone. Leave. Me. Alone.'

She went to the door and out in the hall, pushing the lift button one, two, three times, hard and frantic. Bill came to stand in the doorway.

'Don't you dare follow me, Bill. I'm serious. Let me go.'

And he did. Once the lift doors had closed behind her, Maggie half collapsed against its cool metal wall and let out a sob which sounded inhuman, even to her.

Chapter Thirty-Four

Back in her room, surrounded by all the same textbooks, worksheets and Post-its, Aly sighed. This year had been endless, school-wise. She just wanted to get the damn exams out of the way. Even when you weren't working, you thought about them. And she had other things filling her head too . . .

Aly hadn't heard from Ryan so much since she'd told him there was no way she could come to Edinburgh. It was like an electronic sulk. Or maybe he was hurt. She wasn't sure she wanted to find out which.

Mum had been so brilliant that night in Australia. Liv too, but mostly it was her mum who had amazed her. It was so not how Aly had thought she would react. They'd broken down some high walls that night, the two of them. And now, it was nice. It was good. Mum was treating her more like an adult. But at the same time, she was kind of taking care of her more, too. Aly had been surprised by her mum's apology. She hadn't expected one, or even wanted one, but afterwards she realized how much she had needed to hear that Mum 'got it', and the apology proved that to her. It felt more like they were . . . equals . . . almost.

Mum hadn't pushed too much about Ryan, though Aly guessed she wasn't all that keen. Not on Ryan himself; she knew Maggie had always loved him. But on the situation. The practical stuff – him being older and so far away and everything. And the other stuff too. Mum had asked her, not that same night but on another one, when they'd been on their own, how Ryan made her feel. It had struck her as an odd question – she might have expected her to ask how Aly felt *about* him. But the second she gave her answer – 'anxious and sad' – she realized the point of the question.

'That's not how it should feel, is it?'

Maggie smiled at her, her lips tucked behind her teeth, and shook her head slowly.

'No. It's not, sweetheart.'

'So that stuff you see on the telly . . .'

'What stuff?'

'You know – the heart racing, butterflies in the stomach, I'll-die-if-I-can't-see-you-right-now stuff . . . that happens?'

Maggie laughed. 'Oh yeah. That happens. I remember one day, when I was meant to be meeting your dad after swimming practice, and I saw him, I suppose about a hundred yards away, just leaning against something, with his hands in his pockets and one leg back against the wall, you know, and he literally took my breath away. I couldn't believe – really couldn't believe – that he was mine.' Aly gazed at her, and Maggie smiled. 'Yes, I know. Weird when it's your parents, I suppose.'

'Your separated parents.'

Maggie was yanked back into the present – the one where Bill was having a baby with someone else and she didn't answer.

'I did feel that way about Ryan once . . .'

'When you were fourteen?'

Aly shrugged. 'Yeah. Absolutely then. But at the beginning, too – this time around – you know, after we met in the summer. And started writing . . .'

'What do you suppose changed?'

Aly thought about it. She was sitting curled into the sofa,

with a fringed blanket pulled over her. She picked at the fringe, separating the strands and braiding them into tiny plaits.

'I think it went a bit too fast.'

'Probably.'

'How long were you with Dad? Before you slept with him? I mean, I'm sorry – that's an incredibly personal question for me to ask. You don't have to tell me.'

Maggie put a hand up. 'It's okay. A few weeks. But we'd seen each other almost every day. All day, if we could swing it. He would come to swimming training and just wait for me. We couldn't stay away from each other. I'm telling you, we waited as long as was humanly possible . . .'

'Whereas we'd spent no more than a few hours together. God, I sound stupid, when you put it like that.' She couldn't bear to add the pregnancy scare to the mix – then she'd become so stupid in her own mind that she'd be unrecognizable to herself.

'Not stupid, no.' Maggie leant across and patted Aly's knee. Aly raised an eyebrow at her mother.

'I don't think that's all of it, though, Mum . . .'

'What do you mean?'

'Truthfully . . . I think it's because of Jake.'

'What do you mean, exactly? Try and explain it to me.'

'We both needed comfort. Jake was our common ground. I mean, I don't want to make it sound like we didn't have anything else in common. I really liked him. He was cool and funny and interesting. He *is* cool and funny and interesting – I don't know why I'm talking about him like he's dead. But it's like Jake was there, that night, between us. Ryan started talking about him. Telling me stuff. And he was there with us. And the sadness stuck. And it's ruined it a bit. I feel weird.'

'Because Ryan is part of your past?'

'Yeah. And the worst part. I don't mean that. Not about Jake. But do you get what I do mean? I'm always gonna see Jake when I look at Ryan. He's always gonna be there.'

'And you don't want him to be?'

'Not in that part of my life. I loved Jake. I never want to forget him or not be able to talk about him.'

'I get it, Aly.'

'You do? I feel like I explained it so crummily.'

'I think I do. You want your romantic life – falling in love and all of that – to be a part of your future.'

'That's exactly right.' Aly clapped her hands, relieved and thrilled that her mother could translate her teenage angst and so succinctly deliver it back to her in a sound bite. It made her feel they were on the same wavelength and that felt so good to her.

'I've been thinking about that so much, actually. Since we were in Australia.'

'About me and Ryan?'

Maggie shook her head. 'No. Not that. I mean, yes, obviously, but not in this context. I mean about the past and the present and the future, and how they overlap but they mustn't eclipse.'

'Deep, Mum.'

'Shut up. I tried to translate your barmy speak – the least you can do is try and return the favour.' She made a soft fist and gently pounded Aly's knee. 'That's what I've been doing. About Jake, but about your dad too. I'm sorry. Is this too near the knuckle for you?'

Aly shook her head. 'No. Go on.'

'Well, that's it really – that's most of it. Just that it's about a balance –you don't forget your past, but you have to keep it . . .' she gestured with a wide sweep of her arm '. . . you have to keep it where it belongs. Whatever it is. Behind you. So you face forward. Move forward . . .'

Aly thought about talking to Ryan. It felt like unfinished business, not telling him why she didn't want to see him. The whole thing was, and would always be, tinged with regret for her. She couldn't quite wish it hadn't happened, but she wished it hadn't happened the way it had. She knew it had no future. There'd be other boys, and other times, but it couldn't be Ryan. She understood it, though. Mum had helped her figure it out. But Ryan had gone quiet on her. Maybe he knew it was over – maybe he felt the same way. She'd rather see him face to face, anyway, so maybe . . . in the summer.

In the end, though, Aly wrote to him. So much of their relationship had happened on the computer – long emails she'd always remember. She didn't want to wait until the summer. She felt released by understanding and free to move forward, and she believed she owed Ryan the same. She'd never tell him about the pregnancy scare – what would be the point? The further away from that she got the sillier she felt about it, about Auntie Liv having to come away from her family dinner with pregnancy tests. It had done one good thing though – it had opened the door again with Mum, and she was glad of that. But there was still nothing to be gained from telling Ryan. The email took a whole evening to write – she saved it in draft form and kept coming back to it. She almost – almost – asked Mum or Kate to read it, but she didn't; it was still private. Eventually, just before she fell asleep, she read it through one more time, took a deep breath and pressed send. She slept better that night than she had in a week.

Dear Ryan,
I haven't heard from you for a while so maybe there is no need for this email, but I feel like there is, so I'm writing it.

I can't come to Edinburgh, and it isn't really because of my A
levels. I can't see you any more. It isn't right, and I think we both
know it, and I think one of us has to be brave enough to call it
before it goes any further.

I don't know how to write this and make it sound right. I will
always – and I mean this, I'm not just saying it – think of you and
what happened between us as a sweet and special thing. But it
was the end of something and not the beginning. I hope that
makes sense to you – and I kind of believe it will. I don't want
to regret it, and right now I don't. But I would . . . if we kept
going . . .

People always say let's keep in touch or let's stay friends. I'd like
that, but I feel like that time is some time away. I'm not closing
any doors.

Meanwhile, thank you. You know what for. Be happy, Ryan.

Aly

Something else was bothering her now. Maggie had told Aly
about Kate and her two husbands and the daughter she didn't
see, while they were in Australia, swapping confidences. At
first she'd felt duped – hadn't she and Kate talked about her
marriage to Philip? When she looked back, remembering
what she could of the conversation, she knew Kate hadn't
exactly lied to her – but she very deliberately hadn't told her
she'd been married before. Did she think Aly was too imma-
ture to understand? Maybe. But she'd told Maggie, and now
Aly did know. And she couldn't stop thinking about it. Suffused with relief and a new contentment about pulling her
own relationship with her mother back from the brink of
something that had felt very much like it could have become
an estrangement, Aly couldn't bear to think of Kate and this
daughter of hers not speaking or seeing each other. It felt so
wrong. How could you not want Kate in your life, apart from

anything else? Apart from Maggie, Aly couldn't think of anyone more nurturing and giving and good. It was something that Kate sort of radiated. Look at what she had done here, for them. For people she hadn't even known. It seemed to Aly that she and Stan and Maggie had been the beneficiaries of the well of maternal love that this daughter had knowingly rejected.

She wanted to make it better for Kate. Like Liv had made it better for her sister. The more she thought about it – how what Liv had done, contacting Kate and persuading them to have her come here, had changed their lives for the better – the more she wanted to do the same thing for Kate.

It became her default thought, when the studying got too much. It was an intense relief for her default to be, for a change, a thought not about herself – and Jake, or Mum and Dad, or Ryan. This was an altruistic thought, and much better for it, she reflected.

For weeks, she couldn't think how she might be able to help. What she needed to do was find this girl – well, this woman. She needed to talk to her. But she couldn't ask Kate. Kate didn't know that Aly knew. Maybe Kate didn't even know where her daughter was.

And that was how, one afternoon after school, when Kate had gone with Maggie in the car to watch Stan play cricket, she had found herself up in Kate's room at the top of the house. The room was neat and tidy, and smelt faintly, as Kate herself always did, of Chanel No. 5. There were very few things out on the surfaces. A picture of Philip in a small silver frame. Kate had brought that down one day to show Aly, when she'd been asking what he looked like. He looked nice. Not ridiculously handsome, but kindly, with twinkling eyes and really great hair, for an older guy. A box which contained her jewellery, and a small stand on which she hung the longer, bulkier necklaces she wore. A round hairbrush and a can of Elnett. Aly, her heart pounding, opened the door of the cupboard where Kate's clothes hung, but in there was nothing that might provide a clue. Maggie would be furious with her if she knew Aly was up here doing this. It was an outrageous invasion of privacy. Aly told herself that the ends justified the means – that she wasn't just snooping for curiosity's sake. But she felt a wave of what was probably shame when she opened the top drawer of the chest and saw Kate's bras, folded one cup in to the other, and her sensible Sloggi underwear, each pair halved and stacked. A second drawer held tights and slips – those shiny undergarments young people never wore. Aly was on the verge of giving up. There was nothing here. But after skipping the narrow drawers – she didn't want to see any more of Kate's intimate things – she opened just one more drawer, the deep sweater drawer at the bottom. In it, along with a couple of folded jumpers and two or three coiled belts, was a black plastic file – the envelope kind that fastened with an elastic pull. Aly slumped to the floor, her back against Kate's bed, and unfastened it. She thought she heard something from downstairs and froze for a minute to listen, but it was nothing. She glanced at her watch, though she knew she'd only been in here for a couple of minutes: 4.53 p.m. Mum had said the three of them wouldn't be back until six at the earliest and that they might well be later.

There were index headings inside the file, along the top. It was fat with papers, all neatly inserted. Aly knew Kate had had her post redirected, once she'd known she'd be staying a while with the Barretts – after a few weeks of having her live with them, she'd noticed official envelopes arriving with Kate's name on the front. Not much personal stuff, it looked like bills mostly. And that was what was here

– the utilities and other expenses on the house in Seven-oaks, arranged in alphabetical order in their sections: council tax; electricity; gas; a firm called Nice and Stripy, who obviously came in once a week now to mow her grass and tidy the garden; water rates. Another section held bank accounts – Aly didn't look at those, except to take in a Nat-West masthead. She didn't need to know how much money Kate had. Aly had, sometimes to Maggie's horror, an upper-middle-class child's attitude to money. It wasn't something she worried about. Nor did she check under the headings of 'accountant' or 'medical'. Even she, it seemed, had her limits. This was all making her feel quite queasy. Her heart rate was so fast – like she'd just been sprinting. At the very back was a section entitled 'lawyer'. This might be where she would find something. A clue. Aly didn't even know what she was looking for. She'd never done anything like this. All her searching was done on Google. But a search on Kate Miller had shown up surprisingly little. Philip's death announcement, but that hadn't told her anything she didn't know. There were a great many Kate Millers. She'd Goog-led Aly Barrett straight afterwards, to confirm that she was just as common, and she was – there were Aly Barretts on LinkedIn, waiting to make your business acquaintance, and Aly Barretts on the other side of the world, and an Aly Bar-rett who ran a wedding-dress resale business in Cardiff. She herself wasn't on there at all. But of course, she hadn't done anything, yet . . .

But a lawyer might know stuff. It was a bit of a leap to assume she could somehow get said lawyer to share what he knew with her – but Aly forced herself to go one step at a time. She carefully pulled out the whole section and laid it on the carpet, putting the file down on the other side of her, and began to look at each page, gently turning it face down before she moved on to the next one, to make sure things stayed in the right order. A bizarre thought about her naked finger-prints sprang into her mind – this search would leave forensic evidence . . . Too much late-night *CSI Las Vegas* on Channel 5. She shook the thought away. She'd have smiled at her daftness if she wasn't so tense.

But in the end, it was easier than she'd imagined. The law firm was based in Sevenoaks. Harman and Livingstone. All their details were on their letterhead, centred at the top and also printed neatly in the top left-hand corner of their envelopes. There were two or three of those. At first, Aly thought they were sealed, but then she saw that they'd been sliced open carefully with a letter opener, so that there was no torn, buckled edge to the flap. These were all dated ages ago – she held one up and checked the postmark. The year was 2000. She slipped the letter out and gingerly unfolded it.

She didn't understand all the legal stuff in the letter – something to do with some insurance policy with named beneficiaries – but the signature at the bottom was not that of the lawyer who had signed all the other letters. The first paragraph explained that Kate's lawyer – Nicholas Harman, the one who wrote to her in a warm and friendly tone, as though they might even be friends outside of this association – was on holiday and that the writer, someone else at the firm, obviously younger, and newer, had decided to write, since Mr Harman wouldn't be back for three weeks.

And there it was. The lawyer hadn't known, obviously, about Kate's estrangement from her daughter. She imagined Nicholas Harman himself had. The policy was in both their names, evidently, and there was a cc on the bottom: Rebecca Gardiner. Her name was Rebecca. She lived in London. At least she had done in 2000. There was an address, but no telephone number.

Now that she'd found what she had been looking for, and hadn't expected to find, Aly was shocked at herself. She dropped the letter as if it were hot, and sat with her head back and her eyes closed. After a minute or two, she stared at the address and then carefully folded the letter back into its envelope and returned the sheaf of legal letters back into their section. She refastened the file and put it back in the drawer, shutting it soundlessly, though she was still alone in the house and she could have been as noisy as she liked. She was paranoid about the details – checking and rechecking that she'd left everything as she'd found it.

Maggie had told her that Kate didn't know where her daughter was. Letters had come back marked 'Return to sender: not known at this address'. Both of them had been struck by the poignancy of that in particular. But that wasn't true. Unless this was an old address, Aly wondered – people did move, she knew, though she had lived here in this house almost her entire life, certainly as long as she could remember. Aly wondered why Kate would hide the truth from Maggie.

Back in her own room, she wrote the address down on a Post-it and stuck it in the front of a textbook. She looked at herself in the cheval mirror in the corner of her room – she was flushed and guilty-looking, and her chest was rising and falling too fast. She sat down on the rug and hugged her knees to her, rocking back and forth slowly, her face buried in her arms.

When Maggie and Kate came home, she had climbed under the duvet. When she didn't bound down the stairs to greet them, like she normally would have done, Maggie came up to find her. She couldn't face Kate that evening, so she feigned a stomachache. Her mother looked at her with concern, feeling her forehead and kissing her cheek.

'Will you come down and have some dinner with us? Kate made a goulash earlier today.'

'I can't face it, Mum. I'm so not hungry at all. Can't I just stay here?'

Maggie's eyes were worried. 'Shall I bring a tray up?'

'Nah. I really just want to sleep.'

'You're sure?'

'I'm sure. If I get hungry later on, I can go down and have some toast or something.'

'We'll put a bowl in the fridge for you. You could heat it up in the microwave.'

Aly nodded as though she didn't want to think about food, and closed her eyes so she wouldn't have to look at her mum. A snoop and a liar. A good evening's work, Aly, she told herself.

Maggie crept away, closing the door gently behind her. Aly lay in the dark as the light from outside faded. The sounds of the house were all around her – Stan haring up and down the stairs, the pump from the shower in the bathroom next to her bedroom wall, the theme tune from *Coronation Street*. No one else bothered her – Maggie must have asked them to leave her alone to sleep. At one point, she was sure her mother poked her head around the door, but Aly lay still, her face to the wall, and Maggie went away again.

But Aly didn't sleep. By 10.30, the house was quiet. Aly held her breath as she heard Kate's footfall on the top staircase and landing, but then the last narrow stripe of light at the bottom of her bedroom door went out, Kate's door closed and everything was silent. At 10.45, Aly switched on the bedside lamp on the table next to her and sat up against her pillows. She opened the textbook she'd had lying beside her and stared at the Post-it. Getting it might have been wrong. But doing something with it . . . how could that be?

In her room, safe at last, Maggie typed an email to Liv. She was trying to dial less and type more. That way Liv could respond if it was an okay time and not if it wasn't. She was trying to respect the new boundaries of Liv's marriage to Scott. Trying to come second in Liv's mind.

If the email was slightly dramatic, it wasn't her fault . . .

Bill and Carrie are having a baby. I have no idea how to feel about it. I was angry. Now I'm sad.

Liv rang her within ten minutes. Maggie felt almost weak with relief when she heard Liv's voice.

'He told you?'

'Yes. I went round, like a sap, with pictures of the wedding, and he told me then.'

'Bloody hell. Is there something in the water in your neighbourhood, or what?'

Maggie ignored the reference to Aly. 'And she's so pregnant already, Liv. The baby is coming in the summer, for Christ's sake.'

'Planned?'

'He says not. But I didn't hang around to chew the fat over the details.'

'Course not. Do the kids know?'

Maggie shook her head, though Liv couldn't see her. 'I've told him he's not to say a word – not while Aly's in the middle of these wretched exams.'

'Did you tell Kate?'

For a split second, Maggie wondered whether Liv would mind that she'd told Kate first. 'Yes.'

But Liv sounded relieved. 'Good.'

'What's good about it?'

'Good that you've told Kate. That someone knows. Apart from me.'

'I want to come home.'

'To Oz?'

'Yes. That's what I've wanted from the second I closed the door on his damn designer apartment. I have just wanted to run to the airport and get on the first flight and come home.'

'Running away?'

'Just running. I don't want to be here any more.'

Liv didn't know how to respond to this. Maggie sounded like a petulant child and that was new for her. She made a strange sound now, and Liv didn't immediately know whether it was a laugh or a cry or just an exasperated exhalation.

'You okay?'

'Yes. No. I don't bloody know. Is it funny that this has knocked me so much, do you think?'

'Not in the slightest. Why wouldn't it?' But Maggie had been knocked before; Liv realized it was the first time she'd ever heard Maggie talk about coming home.

Chapter Thirty-Five

It was a couple of days after her discovery that Aly had the chance to take the underground to Victoria and the overground train to Wandsworth and find the house that Kate's daughter lived in. Even now she should have been revising. The teachers seemed to think that was all you should be doing. 'The home straight,' they kept saying, in mock jolliness. 'You're almost there!' She'd never been to Wandsworth, so far as she could remember. She felt, on the train from Victoria, like she was heading towards suburbia, though in truth it took only a few minutes. The street was in what they called the 'toast rack' – one of a number of quite short, straight streets that ran between the Wandsworth and Clapham Commons. Number 14 was about halfway down. Now that she was here, Aly – previously so full of resolve, so sure of her purpose and her righteousness in this endeavour – didn't quite know what to do.

It was a nice-enough house – in a terrace, well maintained and ordinary-looking. Red brick and crisp white paintwork. There was an Audi A3 parked outside, but that didn't mean it belonged here. And a tiny garden – a narrow lavender border and a small patch of grass. Curtains hung half-closed across the bay window of what she presumed was the sitting room, and she couldn't make out much of the interior.

The car might mean Rebecca was home. Aly looked at her

phone. It was almost 6.15 p.m. She might be cooking dinner or watching the news. Maybe it was a bad time. On the other hand, Aly thought wryly, what might be a good time for this visit? She tried to imagine what Rebecca Gardiner might look like. And how she might react. She was almost forty. She'd been raised by Kate. She lived in this nice, smart neighbourhood. Surely someone like that wasn't going to shout and scream at her, chase her down the street with a broom or a stream of obscenities. She'd played out the scenarios in her head, over the last couple of nights. It made a welcome change from formulas and numbers. Maybe Rebecca Gardiner would slam the door in Aly's face, or perhaps she would sink to the doorstep in tearful relief, thrilled and grateful for Aly's intervention, entirely open to the possibility of reconciliation.

Most likely not. Because a) this was not a Danielle Steel made-for-TV movie and b) presumably, Rebecca Gardiner had known more or less where her mother was for the last umpteen years. If she'd wanted to find her, it wouldn't have been that hard. Kate had left her house but not the town. Philip had still worked at the practice he had been at when Rebecca was last at home. Pride had a lot to answer for, though, Aly told herself. It was one thing for Aly to attempt a reconciliation. But another thing entirely to respond to an attempt from someone else. To start with, Aly thought, she didn't need to tell Rebecca that Kate hadn't sent her. She wouldn't lie, she couldn't – but if it didn't come up it certainly wouldn't hurt, not at first, to have Rebecca think that she was Kate's agent in this endeavour, would it? What did she want out of it? Aly hadn't questioned herself too closely about this. She knew she wanted to fix this family. Because she couldn't fix her own. It was unmendable. But this one could be mended. Kate was alive. Rebecca was too.

Digging her fingernails into her palms, white-knuckled,

Aly opened the waist-high wrought-iron gate and strode up the narrow front path, ringing the doorbell before she could change her mind. It took ages – she was just thinking of ringing it again – before she heard a footfall. It sounded like someone coming downstairs. A light went on and the door opened, not fully, just a little, as though the occupant were cautious. The door only opened about four inches – there was a chain on it.

But it wasn't a woman. It was a boy. Aly judged him to be about nine years old, a bit younger than Stan.

'Yes?'

'Hello.' Aly was lost for words. Two big brown eyes were fixed on her questioningly.

'Can I help you?' So polite.

'Is this . . . are you . . . I mean, is this Rebecca Gardiner's house?'

'Yes.' He offered nothing else. Bull's-eye. Aly had expected, she realized, to find someone completely different. But Rebecca Gardiner still lived here.

'Is she in?'

'She'll be back any minute.' This answer sounded rehearsed. Was this a latch-key kid? Was he even supposed to answer the door when he was home alone, as he so clearly seemed to be? An image of Kate filled her head, sitting at the kitchen table with Stan after school, tea for her, milk for Stan and a cake tin between them, filled with Anzac biscuits and banana bread, the two of them chatting and laughing before Kate put the lid on the tin and Stan pulled out his schoolbooks.

'Is she your mum?' She made her voice kind and unthreatening.

The boy hesitated. 'Yes.' So Kate was his granny. It seemed ludicrous, then – rent-a-granny.

He made no move to close the door, but he didn't open it any wider either. He clearly wasn't going to speak again – she guessed he wasn't allowed to.

'She'll be home soon, though, you say?' She didn't want to make this little boy uncomfortable.

He nodded solemnly. 'She is always home around this time.'

Aly wasn't about to ask him if she could wait. Or tell him that she was going to. She'd seen a coffee shop on the street before this one, on the corner. She'd go there, maybe, and have a drink. Wait a while.

'Okay. Well, thank you then.'

'Aidan?' She heard a woman's voice and saw the boy's eyes dart left, with relief in them. Aly spun around and saw a woman closer to her than she'd expected. She must have walked up the street in the same direction, a minute or two behind Aly.

'Can I help you?' The boy had closed the door, but only to take the chain off. He opened it again and Aly saw a tiled hallway, a staircase at one end. A coat hanging on the banister.

'Hello.'

'Hello.' The woman looked at her quizzically but not unpleasantly. Now that she was nearer, Aly could see that she was Kate's daughter. Their colouring was different, and this woman was shorter and less slender than Kate, but it was Kate's nose, Kate's mouth, Kate's eyebrows that Aly was looking at. This woman wasn't as stylish. She was carrying a Tesco carrier bag and some kind of briefcase, and she had a thin-strapped leather handbag hung over her shoulder. She was wearing a trench coat, buttoned up. Kate would never button a trench coat. She'd tie the belt. But this was Kate's daughter.

Aly was blocking the woman's entryway into her house, so she stood back and Rebecca went inside. She kissed the boy's head and put her shopping down. When she turned back, she was unbuttoning the coat and still looking at Aly. The polite interest was being replaced with mild curiosity and maybe a flash of suspicion about the woman she'd seen quizzing her son through a chained door.

'Can I help you?'

Aly wanted to run away. To say she'd come to the wrong house, that she was sorry to disturb them. But her curiosity had the better of her now, piqued by the little boy she hadn't expected to see.

'Are you Rebecca Gardiner?'

The woman raised her eyebrow. 'Aidan? Why don't you go on through to the kitchen. I'll be there in a minute.'

The boy took a few steps down the hallway, but he stopped by the staircase and hovered.

'Who is asking, may I know?'

'You don't know me.'

'No, I don't.'

'My name is Aly Barrett.' No flicker of recognition, of course. Aly wanted the woman to ask her in. This wasn't a doorstep conversation. But that wasn't going to happen.

'I'm a friend of Kate Miller.'

Rebecca's head snapped back and her eyes flashed. She stepped forward and pulled the door behind her, so that Aly couldn't see Aidan any more and had to take a step back herself.

'Did she send you here?' The voice was quiet, almost a hiss.

'No. She doesn't know I'm here.'

'So why are you here?'

'I was hoping to talk to you.'

'I don't think I have anything to say about my mother to a complete stranger.'

'I'm not a complete stranger to your mother.'

'That really hasn't got anything to do with me.'

'I just want to talk to you.'

'I don't want to talk to you.'

'You're not curious? You don't want to know why I'm here?'

Aly was starting to feel indignant. Kate could be ill. She could be really ill. She could be in some kind of desperate need. This woman hadn't seen her in years and years, and someone had shown up who knew her – who knew where she was and how she was – and she didn't seem to care at all.

Now this Rebecca looked less like Kate. The features were the same, but the expression was nothing she had ever seen on Kate's face. She looked hard and mean. And angry, as though something toxic had been simmering beneath the surface for so long – for years – and it had taken only the mention of Kate's name for it to bubble over, erupt.

'I really don't. I'd like you to go.'

'Please!' Aly implored. 'I've come a long way . . .'

'Your problem, I'm afraid.' Rebecca was stepping backwards now, her hand tight on the edge of the front door.

Moments later, she'd slammed it, quite hard, in Aly's face and left her standing there alone.

Embarrassed and red-faced, though there was no one around to see what had happened, Aly paused only to push the index card she'd brought with her through the letter box, and then she turned and walked back down the street as fast as she could without breaking into a run. The card had been a last-minute thought – she'd pulled a fluorescent-pink one from the pile of revision detritus on her desk and written it on the way.

Just her phone number and her name. And at the bottom: 'IF YOU WANT TO TALK . . .'

Chapter Thirty-Six

Maggie sat at her dressing table, staring at herself in the mirror. It had been a long, long, long time since she'd done any of this. Tonight – and she mouthed it to herself in the mirror, making it real – tonight she was going out for dinner, to a smart restaurant with a man who wasn't her husband.

She hadn't heard from or spoken to Bill since that dreadful night at the flat. The little communication she and he had was through Stan and Aly. She'd sent him a single-line email.

You are not to bother Aly with this news before her exams are finished.

He hadn't replied and she didn't care. She veered between pure, hot rage and moments of deep despair. She'd been besieged, against her will, by her own memories. Falling pregnant with each of her children, their births – Bill at her bedside, holding her hand, whispering encouragements. Sleepless nights, milestones reached. She knew it wasn't logical and she knew it wasn't fair, but somehow Bill's news had made a lie of everything that had gone before. As if she'd found out he'd been sleeping with Carrie, impregnating Carrie, for twenty years.

Kate said it was the feeling of betrayal. For more than an

hour Maggie had sat in her car outside Bill's flat, crying and thinking. She'd stayed away from home until she guessed Stan would be asleep in bed and Aly secreted away with her books, and then she'd let herself in quietly, closing the door behind her gently so it made no noise. Kate had been in the living room, watching *Midsomer Murders*. Maggie had collapsed into her arms on the sofa, crying in a way Kate had never seen, spluttering out the news in breathless sobs. She hadn't slept properly for days, although the effort of keeping things on an even keel for the children was exhausting.

She wondered if dinner with Charlie wasn't, in part, revenge. She was going to dinner with Charlie. And she might not come home. This was their fifth date. After they'd gone out for the fourth time, a week ago, he'd parked his car a little down the street from her house when he'd brought her home and they'd snogged in the dark like a pair of teenagers, steaming up the windows of the BMW. She'd been wearing a silk blouse with tiny pearl buttons and when she got into the house, she realized two of the buttons were missing and there was a small tear where one had been, caused by his eager hand reaching in to touch her breast inside her lacy bra. He wanted her – that much was obvious. She wanted him too, didn't she? That's what she was trying to figure out as she stared at her reflection.

The trouble was, Bill was the only man she'd ever slept with. She'd been a virgin that New Year's Eve a million years ago when she'd met him in the sailing club. And she'd been with him her whole life. It might not be quite true, if you did a forensic examination of the previous decades, to say that she'd never looked at another man, but she'd certainly never laid her hands on another man or kissed one or even wanted one. Just silly crushes and random thoughts

– perfectly normal. But nothing had ever happened. It had been just Bill. Now he was gone. He was sleeping with someone else, with Carrie. And this man – Charlie – he actually liked her. And she might sleep with him. She wanted it too, she thought. She thought she should. She thought that too. And now she thought she actually might be going to. It was a very enormous thing to contemplate. She wanted to be wanted. She wanted a man to hold her and touch her and want to be doing it, with only her. Not someone younger, or fresher or without a past that made his heart hurt.

Earlier, she'd run a deep, hot bath, pouring in too much of the Jo Malone bath oil Liv had given her for Christmas and that she'd never used before, and sat in it for ages, thinking. She was part thrilled, part petrified, part bemused, and part just sad – as she always seemed to be, and she wondered if she always would. Thoroughly mixed up. She'd thought about calling Olivia, but she knew what Liv would say. And she'd be asleep, anyway. And this felt like a decision she should make on her own. Maggie Barrett, she thought to herself, are you up to this? She honestly didn't know. There was a vast mirror covering most of the wall behind the free-standing bath. It had been there for so long that she almost never looked in it these days. For a long time, she hadn't wanted to see herself. Now, standing to soap herself, she'd stopped and looked at her reflection, suds sliding down her wet skin – really looked at herself for the first time in a long time, trying to objectively decide how she might rate with someone seeing her naked for the first time. Bill had known her body when she was little more than a girl. He'd seen the shifts and changes. Charlie hadn't. What might he be expecting, she wondered? She'd never met Lia, Charlie's ex-wife – she never came to things at school, so far as Maggie remembered. But Amy looked nothing like her father, so perhaps Lia had had Amy's shape, her colouring. Lia wasn't seventeen though, any more than Maggie was.

Charlie himself was in good shape – she knew that much. He ran a couple of miles a few times a week, he'd said, and he liked things like mountain biking and windsurfing – they'd talked about that stuff. She'd never seen him undressed, of course, but you could tell, beneath the suit jackets and polo shirts, that he took care of himself. When they'd held each other, he had a good, solid manliness about him. Bill always had too, though she realized she hadn't given it a lot of thought over the years. In the last couple of years that they were together, that stuff had all fallen by the wayside. She felt guilty about that. She felt guilty about a lot of things. But that especially. He'd wanted her, Bill. She just couldn't.

What about me, though, she thought? How have the years treated me – the years that passed while I raised my babies and kept my house and grew desiccated and dried up and never once thought I'd be undressing for another man?

It wasn't terrible – her almost-forty body. She'd seen women – in swimming pool changing rooms and on beach holidays – women who'd let it all get a bit out of hand. She wasn't one of those. There was more of her than there had been, for sure, but not too much – more a thickening than a spreading. She still had the broad shoulders of her youth, the forgiving olive-toned skin. Her legs had never entirely lost the musculature of her youthful, swimmer's self. Her stomach was flat enough – no kangaroo pouch despite carrying three children – and although her bum was a bit flatter than it had once been, it wasn't too near her knees. Her boobs had never been big, so gravity and breastfeeding hadn't ravaged them too much.

It was a woman's body – not a girl's. But Charlie was a man, not a boy. He was fifty years old – quite a bit older than her. He liked her. She nodded defiantly at herself in the mirror and thought it again. *He liked her.*

She'd shaved her legs with a new blade in the razor. All the way up. Carefully. Twice. Moisturized with the stuff that matched the bath oil. Sprayed perfume into the air and walked through it. Put make-up on carefully. She tried to tame her curls in several different styles but gave up, exasperated, as she so often was, by the fact that her hair had so much more energy than she did, and elected to wear it loose. A matching bra and knickers, if you please, purchased last week in John Lewis when she was supposed to be looking at fabrics for new kitchen blinds. The kind of underwear that's meant to be seen: French and expensive. The lace was uncomfortable and scratchy compared to what she normally wore these days, but a glance in the mirror told her it was worth it, if she really thought she might later be taking off the red jersey wrap dress she was putting on over the top. They looked nice.

She was holding up different earrings and necklaces when Aly knocked briefly and came in without waiting for an answer.

'The gold ones.' She answered the unspoken question. Maggie put the silver ones back in the box and fastened a simple gold rope chain and matching hoops.

'Thanks. I think you're right.'

Aly smiled smugly. 'You look nice.'

'Do I?'

Aly nodded. She was eating an apple. She gave her mum a lingering once-over. 'Yep. Don't sound so surprised. Pretty good. Smelling good too.'

Maggie smiled shyly. God, this was weird.

'You going out with him tonight?'

She nodded. 'If by him you mean Charlie, then yes, I am.'

'Yes, I mean Charlie. There are others? What's this then . . . fourth date or fifth?'

Aly's eyebrows were raised as Maggie answered. 'Fifth.' Aly nodded, as though it were understood between them what that might mean.

Maggie laughed and turned back to put on her lipstick. 'You've watched far too much *Grey's Anatomy*.'

'What do you mean?' Aly feigned innocence.

'You know full well what I mean. You think you know things, but you don't know as much as you think, young lady.'

'Is that right?' Aly was almost laughing. What might her beautiful girl know, Maggie wondered.

'And you and I – we're not interns. We're not friends either.'

'You wound me.' Aly clutched her heart.

They were very new, these light-hearted conversations, the sense of fun between them. Each one left Maggie delighted and relieved, and grateful – to Kate, to Liv, to Aly . . .

'What are you up to this evening?'

'Stan and me are going out with Dad. Pizza and the cinema. Stan's choice, sadly. So it'll be something violent or just ridiculous. Still – it's a break. Had you forgotten? Or are you just too distracted!' But Aly wasn't reproaching her.

'And will Carrie be there?'

'I'm not sure. Dad didn't say.' That was true. Dad was trying to make it all laid back and normal, Aly knew. 'Would it matter if she was?'

'Of course not.' Maggie answered too quickly and too enthusiastically.

Aly looked at her hard. 'Are you sure?'

Maggie spun around on her stool. 'Yes, I'm sure, Aly.

Carrie is real. Carrie's been around for a while, and she's not going anywhere.'

'You don't have to like it, though.'

'It's not for me to like it or not like it. It is how it is.'

'Is that just mother speak?'

'Am I not the mother? Speaking of which, as the mother, can I just check – you are okay about Charlie, aren't you? It's not serious. I'm just "checking in" with you.'

'It's cool.' Aly brushed it off.

'Is that just daughter speak?'

'Am I not the daughter?'

Maggie laughed. 'Touché!'

Aly put her arms around her mother from behind. 'Have fun. You need to have fun. I want you to have fun. I love you.'

Maggie laid her head back on to Aly's shoulder for a moment.

Lobbing her apple core expertly into the wastepaper basket next to the dressing table, Aly threw her parting shot over her shoulder just as she shut the bedroom door behind her. 'Just don't go and get yourself pregnant, for Christ's sake . . . I am in the middle of my A levels, you know!'

They both drank a little too much at dinner. Maybe Aly had been right about the five-date rule, Maggie thought. The conversation was flirtier, less serious than before. They were a bit silly and a little giddy, and it felt very good. Over dessert, which she never normally ate, Charlie reached across the table, putting a finger under her chin, and lifted her face a little, so that he could see directly into her eyes.

'You look really pretty tonight, Maggie.' He was teetering on the verge of cheesy, but he looked so sincere.

She squirmed at the compliment. Charlie, still holding her face, looked at her reproachfully. 'No. Don't do that.'

'Do what?' She pulled herself away from his touch self-consciously, but she maintained eye contact and kept smiling.

'You always look uncomfortable when I pay you a compliment.'

'I'm not used to it, that's all.'

'You might like to get used to it. I want to say those things to you. I mean them, I think them, and I think it's okay to say them. If you don't want me to, you'd better say so.'

'I'm sorry. No. It's nice. God – nice is an awful word, isn't it? Talk about damning with faint praise. It's more than nice. It's lovely. Really lovely. I don't mean to be that way. It's just that I'm not used to any of this . . .'

'Me neither.'

Maggie lay her spoon down. 'Is that true?'

Charlie raised both hands in a gesture of surrender. 'True.'

'I've only ever slept with one man – my husband,' she blurted. She could feel her face colouring and her cheeks were instantly hot.

She stood up. 'Excuse me. Bathroom.' If she could have kicked herself all the way through the dining room to the cool cloakroom, she might have done.

Another mirror. Smooth, she told herself. You idiot.

When she came back five minutes later, having sat in the cubicle seriously contemplating climbing out of the tiny window and running far away, fast, Charlie was waiting. She sat down, with no clue of what to say next. Her last line had been a show-stopper.

As she sat, Charlie nodded and took a deep breath.

'I guess it's my turn, then.'

She put her hand up to stop him. 'I'm sorry, Charlie. I've over-shared. That's what Aly would call it.'

'It's fine. Imogen would call it a TMI situation.' They both laughed a little, and the tension eased. 'It's good, I think. I want to be honest with you too. So we both know where we are. I've slept with five people in my life. My wife, obviously. Three women before her and once since. The three before were one at school – just once, my fifteenth birthday, since we're over-sharing – one in sixth form and one at university. The whole time. We were *that* couple, I'm afraid.' Maggie didn't know which couple he meant – she hadn't, after all, been to university – but she didn't interrupt to say so. 'I think I thought we'd get married when we graduated, but we didn't. Not meant to be after all. I met Lia just after we broke up, so technically she was my rebound girlfriend, only she stuck. We were married a couple of years later. All pretty conventional stuff. Only slept with Lia the whole time we were married, which was almost twenty years, although sex was pretty thin on the ground for the last five or six years of that marriage. I guess you could call me a serial monogamist – though I really hate that expression. Never saw the point of sleeping with someone just for the sex. Not that I was beating them off with a stick through my teens and twenties, but I was okay – I could have slept with more girls than I did if I'd wanted to. The one woman since the divorce was a disaster. An embarrassing, humiliating fiasco. Not her fault, or mine, I don't think. We were both . . . a bit desperate. Trying to make something be there that just wasn't. That was about eighteen months ago. That's it. Full disclosure.'

Maggie, who'd been studiously pleating the edges of the tablecloth in her fingers and studying the weave of the cloth while Charlie spoke, looked up at him. 'A fine pair we are.'

Charlie laughed.

'Right! Coffee?' They were both laughing now.

'I don't want coffee. Can we get out of here?'

'Absolutely . . . I'll get the bill.' He gestured to their waitress, then turned back to her. 'But I've got one more thing to say, Maggie. Look – I'm glad. I'm glad I know about you and you know about me. I like you. I do. I fancy the arse off you, yes, but it's more than that. I really like being with you. I don't just want to . . . jump in your knickers. I'd like to try and . . . be together. Have a relationship. Don't get me wrong – at that level, I'm all about making you number six, and being your number two. I'm a guy, for Christ's sake! I'm just saying – it doesn't have to be tonight.'

Maggie leant across and gave him a lingering kiss, emboldened by all the red wine and honesty. He'd just said the magic words.

Charlie responded to the kiss in earnest, his hand hard on the back of her head. Maggie pulled back and smiled an invitation, surprised, in the end, by her own brazenness. 'But I think it probably ought to be . . .'

Charlie raised one hand like a kid desperate to answer a teacher's question. 'Bill . . . Please!'

It had been, she reflected afterwards, as she lay in Charlie's bed and he slept beside her, decent middle-aged people's sex. Quite reasonable, since she and Charlie were both decent middle-aged people. Which wasn't to say that it hadn't been good – it really had been. She'd absolutely been turned on – weak-kneed and trembly – by the time they made it to the bed, which was key, she thought. You couldn't have lain down and tried to go from nought to sixty – it would have felt contrived and ridiculous. And there'd been only the tiniest moments of awkwardness – easily ignored and overcome – as they undressed each other, found each other's warm skin in the darkness and began figuring out how they fit together, how they each liked to be touched. He had been turned on too, she knew. It just hadn't been . . . wild. Lights-off, one-position, 25-minute sex – not at all the stuff of porn, or even titillating 12+ films. Lovely, nonetheless. Healthy – her orgasm had spread its warmth from her fingers to her toes and suffused her with calm and a sense of physical well-being. You didn't get that when it was just you on your own – that was strangely unsatisfying, and often, for her now, ended with a wave of sharp sadness. Only with another person. A pretty good start? She wondered if that was what it was. Charlie had been thoughtful, and generous, and gentle, and then not that gentle – even quite thorough. She giggled at the word as she heard it in her own head. Thorough. He wouldn't be happy to hear it described that way. He'd tried really hard. He wouldn't like the sound of that much either. She didn't mean it disparagingly. She was . . . grateful that it had been so nice. Relieved.

Truthfully, though, it had felt strange too. Restricted to one adjective to describe the last half an hour or so, she might have to use that one. She'd never – never – had anyone but Bill touch her in those places, kiss her that way, be inside her, moving, and murmuring. And Bill had known her so well. Knew exactly what she liked, what worked – how to make it all happen in five minutes or last for hours, depending on what was required. Charlie had been finding out and, God knows, it had been fun to guide him. She'd even felt a bit brazen and slutty. No point getting older if you didn't get wiser. They had that over the kids, at least . . . for all their taut, hard flesh and endless staying power. He'd had a few tricks Bill hadn't, for sure, and she found herself looking forward to the next time. It was a riot in her head – the realization that, at nearly forty, she finally had someone to compare Bill to – he'd been her only notion of male sexuality, she suddenly realized, since she was seventeen years old, except what she had gleaned from books and TV and films, and the odd complaining or even celebratory confession made by a friend over a cappuccino and a Danish. The kind of stuff Aly – and evidently Imogen – would call TMI. Too much information. For just a second, an image of Bill with Carrie danced in her head, with all the inevitable questions she'd just had answered. But she resolutely pushed it from her mind. She wouldn't let them in – not now.

Right now, she had to decide whether to stay or not. She laid her palm on Charlie's naked shoulder. He didn't open his eyes but groaned softly and pulled her into him with one arm.

'Stay,' he murmured.

'I don't know.'

Now he opened his eyes. Maggie turned herself gently so that they were facing each other.

'I don't know if I should.'

'Are they waiting for you at home?'

She shook her head, no.

'Immy's not home tonight.'

They looked at each other, neither sure, suddenly, that they could read the other person.

'If you'd like to stay, Maggie, I'd like that.'

She didn't answer.

'But I won't get all bent out of shape if you want to go, either.'

'You won't?'

He smiled. 'No.'

'Promise?'

'Hey. I promise.'

Maggie sat up – pulling the sheet with her to cover her breasts. She didn't know. It might sound ludicrous, but staying seemed more intimate than the sex.

Charlie sat up too.

'Look – we slayed a dragon tonight, Maggie.' She giggled.

'Is that what you call it?' She tried to sound light and flirtatious, but even to her, it didn't entirely work.

'We don't have to do it all at once. I think it was a pretty good start.'

Her eyes widened. 'Exactly. That's what I think.'

He kissed her shoulder. 'Good. Then we're on the same page. I'd like to do it again. I'd like to keep seeing you. See where we're headed. No pressure. And if staying feels like pressure, then don't stay, Maggie. It's really, really okay.'

'Are you too good to be true?'

Charlie smiled. 'No. I'm just trying not to spook you.'

'You're succeeding. Officially unspooked.' Maggie picked up his hand and kissed it. 'But I'm going to go home.'

Charlie nodded. 'I'll take you.'

'There's no need for that. I'll call a cab.'

'It's two a.m.'

'It's fine. I have the number of a firm in my phone. They're pretty good.'

'No way. I'm taking you. No arguments. I'm not that guy.' He'd stood up with his back to her and was pulling his boxers on over a pretty good backside.

No, Maggie thought as she started to dress herself, no, you're not.

Chapter Thirty-Seven

Most other evenings, it would have been Stan who answered the phone. He usually dived at it from wherever in whichever room he was the moment it rang, eager to talk to anyone from the automated voice offering better interest rates than you were currently getting upwards. But Stan had a football match at school and Maggie had gone to watch. It was the last in the season and afterwards there was pizza and ice cream for the team and parents. Kate was sitting on the Penguin deck chair in the garden, reading a novel Maggie had recommended and drinking a large mug of Earl Grey tea. She had the feeling of domestic contentment that comes from a full basket of clean and ironed clothes, a fridge well stocked with food and an hour's peace between jobs. She was waiting for Aly to come home. As always, she was looking forward to the noise of a houseful – in Sevenoaks her days were largely unpunctuated, but here she had grown to love the breakfast chaos, how it gave way to quiet after the kids left, only to start again when they came home. Between times, she and Maggie might talk or just comfortably co-exist. And she loved performing the tasks she'd taken on for this family. In a way, it had brought her back to life. Now when she dressed each morning, she wanted to look nice, needed to put on her face and do her hair, to carefully choose her outfit. When she had an afternoon free, she was more likely than before to take the tube to the Portrait Gallery or the accessories hall of Selfridges. She was reading more, listening to more music. 'You're coming back to life,' Maggie had said the other day, and Kate knew she was right. 'Out of hibernation. Now we just need to get you a man . . .'

Kate had laughed.

'No, I'm serious. Aly was telling me . . . there's this website called My Single Friend. You write a profile of a friend and it gets posted . . .'

'What – a warts and all?'

'Not so much that – more like you toot the horn they're too shy to play.'

Kate was basking in the glow of Maggie calling her a friend, though she couldn't possibly be serious about this.

'I'm too old.'

'Bollocks. You're in your prime . . .'

But for now, Kate knew, this was enough. She didn't want a man. She'd had Philip and no one could ever . . . no one would ever replace him. Maggie hadn't pursued it – Kate hoped she would let it go.

In the absence of Stan, Kate was forced to get up from the deck chair and answer the phone herself.

'Aly?' The caller asked.

'Aly's not here, I'm afraid. I'm expecting her back soon, though . . . May I take a message?'

There was silence on the other end of the line.

'Hello? Are you still there?'

She was about to hang up. 'Hello?'

Some of Aly's friends had less than good manners, she thought.

Then, 'Mum?'

All the blood in Kate's head rushed to her feet, and she put her hand out to steady herself.

'Rebecca?'

A million questions ricocheted around her brain.

'What's going on, Mum?'

She hadn't a clue.

'How did you find me?' This was Rebecca.

'I didn't.'

'But you must have done. You sent that girl . . .'

'What girl?'

'Aly. You sent Aly to find me, right? This is Aly's number.'

'I don't understand.'

'So you weren't looking for me, then?'

'No. No, I wasn't . . .'

She wanted to say so much, but she was discombobulated. This made no sense.

'My mistake, then. Sorry.' Cold and monotone. And Rebecca had hung up.

Aly knew something was wrong the minute she came down the stairs into the kitchen. Kate had lost all her colour. She was sitting stock still at the table, with an untouched mug of tea clenched in her hands.

'What's happened? Are you okay, Kate?'

Kate looked up at her, and Aly's heart pounded with panic and guilt.

'I think you'd better tell me what happened, Aly.' Her voice wasn't angry, it was slow and far away. She was shocked, Aly could see that, and instantly she knew what it was about.

'Did she call?'

Kate nodded. God, what a cock-up, Aly thought. I should have told her. I should have guessed this might happen. She had questions, but Kate went first.

'How did you find her?'

Aly slumped into a chair across from her and laid her palms flat in front of her on the wood. She took a deep breath.

'I went snooping through your papers, Kate.'

'What?!'

'I know, I'm sorry. I'm really, really sorry. It was wrong of me, and I know that. Mum told me, when we were in Australia, about what had happened with you. And I couldn't bear it, Kate. I hated that you were estranged from your only child. It made no sense to me, when you'd been so good to us and you were so happy with us . . . I just couldn't bear it . . .'

'So you went to my room and rifled through my things?'

'Shit. It sounds so bad when you say it like that.' Because, Aly thought, it *is* that bad. I knew that while I was doing it.

'You never said a word.'

'I thought you wouldn't talk to me about it.'

'So snooping was your only recourse . . . ?'

Aly didn't reply and the two of them sat in silence for a while. Kate was still struggling to take it all in.

'Does your mum know?'

'God, no. She'd skin me.'

Kate didn't know whether to slap Aly or kiss her. She didn't know how to feel about any of this. Perhaps she should be angrier with Aly than she felt. She'd been way out of line. The invasion of privacy, the betrayal of trust, the meddling. The secrecy. It was all outrageous. The fixer. It had never occurred to Kate that she might go on Aly's list of people to fix. But she was a good kid, she knew, and, despite herself, Kate was touched, she realized, that Aly had wanted to try. Maybe she was being too soft on her. Maggie would, as Aly said, skin her.

'You've broken my trust, Aly.'

'I know. I know I have. I felt horrible while I was doing

it. But I told myself it would be worth it.' Aly was crying panicky tears now. This was all wrong. This wasn't how it was supposed to . . .

Aly realized she had no idea what had happened. Curiosity overcame her contrition.

'Did you see her?'

Kate shook her head. 'She called.'

'She called here?' Aly remembered the number on the pink index card.

'Asking for you. She got me.'

'Did you . . . did you talk?'

'She hung up on me.' Aly remembered the door closing on her.

'I'm so sorry, Kate.'

'If I'd had a warning . . .'

'I know . . . I know.' Aly's distress was evident now and Kate began to feel sorry for her, though she wanted to shake her too. 'But after I saw her . . .'

'You saw her?'

Aly sat back. This was getting worse.

She nodded. 'I saw her. I went to her house.'

Kate stood up. This was too big for sitting down.

'Aly!'

'I'm sorry.' That was all Aly had left. Her face was down now, and her voice was small.

Kate, her head in her hands, started to leave the room, too agitated to stay. She got up four stairs, then turned around and came back down.

'How was she? What did she say?'

They had to tell Maggie. Kate would have insisted but Aly knew, too, that her mother had to know. And the mess was too big to be contained now.

She sat at the table and told them both everything she had done and everything she remembered about the conversation she'd had with Rebecca. She tried not to look at Kate while she spoke, but she knew her words were raining down on Kate like blows. She almost left out the child, but she was afraid of making things worse and so she told them about Aidan, the little boy with the serious eyes.

'Is that everything, Aly?'

She nodded, sniffing hard and wiping her eyes with the back of her hand. 'Except that I'm sorry, Kate . . .'

Maggie put up a hand like a traffic policeman. She couldn't quite look right at her daughter. 'And you have an exam tomorrow?'

'Yes.'

'Did you eat dinner?'

Aly shrugged. 'I'm not hungry. I couldn't eat.'

'I'll bring you up some cereal and toast.' She was being dismissed.

Kate was wide-eyed.

'Go on. Off you go, Aly.'

Upstairs in her room, Aly got under the duvet with all her clothes on and faced the wall. What a mess.

Downstairs, Maggie poured a small tot of brandy into two shot glasses, and both women threw one back.

'Bloody hell.'

'Bloody hell indeed.'

'I'm sorry too, Kate. I told her.'

'You didn't know this would happen.'

'No. But I told her. I betrayed your trust too . . .'

'No.'

'Yes.'

'The trouble with secrets, huh?'

Maggie laid her hand across Kate's.

'Her heart was in the right place, Maggie.'

Maggie snorted. 'But her methods sucked, right?'

Kate would have laughed, if her heart weren't so heavy.

'You know, though, that she called, right?' Maggie said.

Kate hadn't thought much of that.

'What do you mean?'

'I mean, so okay, Aly doorstepped her, which was the sort of crazy, cretinous thing only a daft teenager would do, and she reacted badly, which I guess would be par for the course. And Aly left a number . . .'

'And she called . . .'

'Exactly. She must have been thinking about it – about you.'

'I told her I wasn't looking for her.'

'You were caught unawares, the same as she was . . .'

'But I wasn't looking for her.'

'I know that.'

'Oh God, Maggie. I've been such a stubborn, stupid woman.'

'You've both been stubborn.'

'And meanwhile years have passed. Years of our lives. There's a child. There's a grandson I don't even know . . .' Kate's voice was full of anguish now.

Maggie put an arm around her. 'We both know something about lost years, Kate. The way I figure it, you can lose more, or not. It's up to us, isn't it?'

'But what can I do?'

Maggie kissed the side of Kate's head, then sat down again . . .

'Well, I think we've established that cold calling and door-stepping aren't the way to go . . .' She smiled sideways at Kate, who sputtered into weak laughter.

Maggie held her arms aloft. 'Perhaps we should go

old-school . . . We've got an address, right? What about a letter?'

'I wouldn't know where to begin.'

'Maybe you'd let me help. If I'm not to be allowed to write the My Single Friend profile . . .'

Chapter Thirty-Eight

Kate was at Waitrose, Stan was on a school trip, learning to sail on Frensham Ponds, and Aly was sitting a biology A level paper. Maggie was home alone. It was warm, and the kitchen doors were concertinaed back to let the garden in. She'd made a huge mug of latte and taken it, with her kneeling pad and a small trowel, out on to the lawn, although so far all she had done was lie on the grass, her eyes closed against the sun. This was a great day, by English early-summer standards. But she was remembering the Australian light. She could vaguely hear Jenni Murray's voice from inside, where Radio 4 was playing. Sitting up, she gazed down at the bottom of the garden, where the wooden climbing frame they had bought when Jake was small still stood. It was still one of Stan's favourite things to do – to hang upside down by his feet on one of the bars. There was a trampoline too. They'd bought that for Jake's seventh birthday. Bill had asked a couple of mates around the night before, to build it while Jake was asleep. Then he'd tied red string around one of its legs and walked the string into the house, up all the stairs and into Jake's bedroom. He'd tied it loosely around Jake's ankle, pooling excess string on to the floor by the pine bed so that there was plenty of slack. Jake had woken them at 5 a.m., shouting his delight at the trick, and they'd all trooped down the stairs after him, her, Bill and Aly, all the way down to the kitchen. They'd all been laughing. He was watching the string so intently he hadn't looked up to see the big black trampoline clearly visible from inside. It had been Aly, squealing and pointing, who had seen it first, Bill clamping a hand over her mouth. The four of them had been jumping on it in their pyjamas before breakfast. Over the years, it must have been bounced on a million times. Used as a roof for a tea party on hot summer days. A place to sulk, scheme and tell secrets.

She heard the doorbell and sat up grudgingly. She didn't hurry back into the house or up the stairs to the front door. It didn't matter to her whether the caller waited or not – she wasn't expecting anyone or anything, except to say 'no, thanks', as politely as she could manage, to whatever someone was trying to sell her.

But it wasn't a salesman. Or a Jehovah's witness. It was a young woman, small and slim, blonde and pale, pregnant. It was Carrie. She knew immediately. From Aly's brief description, from the unmistakable swell of belly, from her own innate sense that this woman was the person her husband was sleeping with, living with, having this baby with.

She might have expected to feel rage. Rage was exactly what she had felt, in the moments after Bill had told her. About Carrie, all those months ago. And about the baby, more recently. But it had deserted her now, and the strength the anger had brought with it had evaporated too.

'Can I help you?' She was amazed by the façade of politeness. It came so easily, after all these years in England. God forbid that you should forget your manners.

'I'm Carrie.'

'I guessed.'

She had instinctively pulled the door to behind her – the two women stood awkwardly on the top step. It was too close for Maggie. She could see Carrie's pores. But to step back she would have to open the door to the home she did not want Carrie to see or be admitted to.

'I thought we should meet.'

There was nothing confrontational about Carrie's tone. If anything, she sounded timid, which she obviously couldn't be, not entirely, if she was brave enough to show up here.

'Does Bill . . . ?'

Carrie shook her head, and her straight hair swung like a curtain, falling back into place when she was still again. God, Maggie thought – we're as different as we could be. She touched her curls unconsciously, tucking one unruly sprig behind her ear.

'No. He'd be angry, I suspect. This was my idea.'

Maggie challenged her with silence and an expression she hoped dared her in some way. It was bolder than she felt.

'I mean . . . our lives – they overlap. Right? Look – I don't want to come in. I'm not trying to "do" anything. Here's the thing. I've been so curious about you. I figured maybe you had been about me too.'

Maggie thought of saying no, but it wouldn't be true. She'd like time to freeze them here, on the step, so she could study this person.

'I think at this point it would give Bill an aneurysm to think of us together.'

Maggie made a noise – even she didn't know what it signified.

'So . . . maybe it's ridiculous. But I thought . . . I mean, I was on the bus before I'd quite thought it through . . . but I suppose I thought we should get it over with. Set eyes on each other. If there's anything you want to ask me, you can ask me.'

Maggie didn't say anything. Part of her wanted to meet this girl halfway, but she couldn't quite bring herself to.

'It's an odd situation. I feel like the other woman. Like I've done something wrong. But I haven't. You two were separated. Before he met me. We didn't have an affair.' She sounded, if not exactly conciliatory, then slightly defensive.

'I didn't accuse you of that. Not either of you.'

'I know. It's something I've done to myself.'

'And you've come to prove to yourself that it isn't true?'

'I suppose I have.'

'Well, I don't think so. I know where you two met, and I know when. But I daresay you know more than that about me, and that makes me incredibly uncomfortable.'

'And I'm sorry.'

'About me being uncomfortable?'

'That, and about Jake.'

She didn't mean to be this way, but Carrie saying Jake's name was like a physical slap to Maggie.

She sat down heavily on the step. Carrie continued to stand, stepping down a step or two, moving further away. For a second, Maggie thought she might turn heel and flee. Something – resistance? Rage? Something flowed out of her. She gestured with her hand for Carrie to sit down beside her. And though she looked unsure, Carrie sat. She had to stretch her legs out in front of her – she had a tummy, and so she couldn't bend them up like Maggie had hers. Maggie liked her shoes. The two of them were quiet for a moment.

'You lost your husband, didn't you?'

'Yes. Jason.'

'Since Jake?'

'Yeah.' Carrie nodded.

'I'm sorry too.' Until very recently, Maggie might have thought her loss was greater. A mother – a wife. But Aly had turned all that on its head. It was like women in labour thinking they were braver than other women because they hadn't had an epidural. Who the hell knew how much things hurt other people. She'd been too lost in her own grief to think about Aly. She didn't know this woman. She didn't know how much she had hurt. It wasn't a contest. Not one anyone would want to win.

'Thank you.'

Maggie smiled. It wasn't a beam. It was weak, but it had a pulse.

'Are we really doing this?'

And Carrie smiled back.

Chapter Thirty-Nine

Dear Rebecca,

I'm writing for the first time in a long time because I hope that maybe there's a chance you feel a little differently about me and about what has happened between us. And I can't miss that chance.

I shouldn't have given up on you all those years ago. A mother should never give up on her child. I told myself it was what you wanted – that it was your decision. I was wrong. I was proud and hurt and sad, but I was wrong too. I let you go, and I have regretted it all these years, more profoundly than you can know.

The Aly who came to visit you is the daughter of a good friend, who knew about us and who wanted to help. It was entirely the wrong method, and for that I apologize, but I would ask you to believe her motives were pure. I did not send her, and I did not know, until after your phone call, that she had come.

But I can't bring myself to be sorry about it, Rebecca, if it gives me one more chance with you.

Aly told me you have a son. A little boy called Aidan. I wonder if you have a new understanding of the love between a mother and a child since he arrived. I thought I knew all about that, but I have had cause, in the last few months, to learn a great deal more about it from someone whose own child is far more lost to her than you are to me.

And nothing is more important, Rebecca. Nothing.

We can talk about what happened – between you and me or

between me and your father – if that is what you want. I have no
secrets, and believe me, most of the pride is long gone. But I think the
past belongs where it is – behind us.

I am your mother and you are my daughter. I love you more than I
could ever love anything or anyone. It is involuntary, unconscious and
total, and I cannot believe that I have lived in denial of that for so
long. It is the biggest single mistake of my life to have done so.

If you will give me another chance, I can promise you that I will
spend the rest of my life being a mother to you. A grandmother to
your child, if you will let me. A part of your life and your heart.

And if there is the tiniest part of you – however small – that
wants to be reconciled, I ask you, I beg you, listen to that part.
Your mum xoxo

Maggie gave up on her sleepless night at around 4.30 a.m.
She felt the sense of outrage at her wakefulness that pre-
dated Jake's death – afterwards, it had become her new
normality.

But this was a new sleeplessness. Her brain had been fizz-
ing with a hundred different thoughts, all zapping in and out
of her consciousness like laser beams. She couldn't lie in bed
a minute longer. Creeping downstairs, she put the kettle on
the Aga hotplate, removing the whistle carefully so she didn't
wake anyone else, and then paced up and down the wooden
floor while she waited to hear it boil.

She took her tea upstairs and closed herself into the front
room, sitting in her favourite armchair, facing the street.
Then she dialled Liv.

'How are you, newly-wed?'

'Loved up. Bow-legged from all of the lovely married
sex. Which is so much hotter than the unmarried kind, did I
mention?'

Maggie snorted. 'I think you're talking about honeymoon sex, honey. You get back to me about that five years in . . .'

'Ha! How are you? Up early?'

'Up early. Sleeping house.'

'How's Aly doing?'

'Good. Nearly there. She's only got a couple more papers, then she's done.'

'Bill manage to keep his trap shut?'

'So far. I think he will. He wants her to do well too.'

'Of course. Stan?'

'Gorgeous. He's got a cricket match this afternoon so I'll drive down to watch. He's really into it.'

'But who does he back for the Ashes – that's the question?'

'Don't! You know that would be an impossible question for him.'

'I can see him now – opening and closing his mouth like a fish trying to decide who to offend.'

'Poor Stan.'

'And Kate?'

'Want to be told one more time how right you were?'

'I wouldn't mind.'

'Kate continues to be pretty much the dream housemate. She's Nigella in the kitchen, our socks have never been so white, the kids are calm, clean and chatty, and we love Kate. Okay?' For the first time in a long time, Maggie withheld information from Liv. She didn't tell her about Aly and the visit to Rebecca. Or about the subsequent letter. When Kate had shown it to her, Maggie's eyes had filled with tears and she had held Kate in a long embrace. The letter had been perfect, and she hoped with all her heart that Rebecca would read it as she had and that there could be peace between them. She'd tell Liv, at some point. But not today.

'Okay. Just checkin'.' Her smugness came down the line loud and clear.

'And Scott. Apart from being a love god?'

'He's Fabio in the bedroom, John Torode in the kitchen, not much cop in the laundry . . .'

'Fabio?! Can he hear you?'

'He's out with his mates – playing five-a-side. Okay. Not Fabio. Brad Pitt . . .'

'Better.'

'He's just a doll. Love him more and more each minute.'

'Pass me the sick bag.'

'Sorry. Can't help it. Don't piss on my bonfire of joy.'

'You've gone weird. I might have to change my mind.'

'Change your mind about what?'

'Coming home.'

Liv's stunned silence.

'What?'

'Coming home.'

'Sorry. "What?" meant "please explain", not just repeat yourself.'

'When I got off the plane in Brisbane in April, I was glad to be home. I said those exact words to myself, in my head. I haven't done that in years. It felt like home.'

'And . . . ?'

'I've been thinking about it – most of the time – ever since. What's the point of me staying here?'

'Because it's where you've spent your adult life?'

'Don't you want me to come home?'

'Don't be stupid. How could you even ask me that?'

'I know. I know. Sorry. Look – I came because of Bill, right?'

'Yes?'

'And now Bill is with someone else. Not a fling or a

rebound – it's a real relationship. They're having a baby, for Christ's sake. They'll want to get married.'

'Has he asked?'

'No. But he will. Unless I do first. I met her, Liv.'

'Carrie?'

'Yep. Yesterday.'

'How?'

'She came to see me.'

'Bloody hell. Did Bill send her?'

'No way. I got the feeling he had no clue.'

'What did she want?'

'Nothing. For us to meet. That's all, I think.'

'What, so you all can be friends?'

'No. I don't think so. She may look like Pollyanna, but I think she's a bit more realistic than that. She was just the one brave enough to make the first move. She's met the kids. She's having his kid. I was the missing link. Like she was for me. We're going to be connected. Whether we like it or not.'

'Brave?'

'Yeah. Can't believe I'm defending her.'

'I'm not attacking her. I'm just trying to understand. But we digress . . . could we please get back to the bit about Australia?'

'That's my point. It's all about Carrie, in a way. She left, and I sat and I thought – well, Bill's moved on. He's done all right for himself.'

'And you have Charlie.'

'Charlie Farley. So not the same thing.'

'But couldn't it be?'

'A new lover isn't the answer for me, Liv. I mean, I'd love it if it happened. I don't want to be alone for the rest of my life. I would like another grand passion and I reckon I've still got one in me. But it isn't the answer. I have to fix myself first.'

'And how does Australia fit into that? You're not running away?'

'No. Absolutely not. I'm coming home.'

'The kids?'

'I'm going to bring Stan.'

'Bill will let you do that?'

'I don't think he'll stop me.'

Liv wasn't so sure. Not that Bill had many legs to stand on at this point.

'And Aly?'

'Aly is old enough to make up her own mind about what she wants. I've got to recognize that and I've got to loosen those apron strings a bit. Let her be grown up. She's been showing me the signs for a while, and I need to start reading them. My job is done, mostly. And I guess she'll want to take up her place at med school. Qualify here.'

'You're okay with being so far away from her?'

'She'll have Bill. And now, I rather think she'll have Kate too. They love each other.'

'But what about you?'

'I can do it. I'll miss her. A lot. But she'll visit. I'll visit.'

Liv didn't speak.

'And I'll have you and Scott. I'll have Dad. I'll have Stan. And I'll be home.'

'What will you do?'

'I haven't worked it all out, yet, Liv. There's a lot to sort out, I know that. I need to work, obviously. And you know I never have. I'm not trained to do anything. Yep. Hands up. Fell into that trap. So I'm nearly forty, no skills, no plan. I'll figure it all out.'

'I believe you.' Liv was already starting to think, her brain racing as fast as her sister's. She wouldn't have to worry that much about money, at least. She was lucky in that. Liv knew Bill had plenty, and she didn't doubt for a moment that he'd take care of Maggie and the kids. Wherever they were. Maggie said she had no skills but it wasn't true. She might not be qualified. But she had many gifts. For design, for art, for crafting . . . If she had some time to think, and some confidence, there was probably nothing she couldn't do.

'You're quiet, Liv. It's freaking me out.'

'Sorry, sis. Don't mean to do that. I'm just thinking . . . There's *so* much to think about.'

'Tell me about it – why do you think I'm pacing around the house like I'm on springs?'

'I'm not surprised.'

'I need to know if you're happy about this, Liv. I want to know if you think it's a good idea.'

Liv took a deep breath. 'I think it's a good idea, Maggie.'

And for me, Liv added, to herself. For me, it's wonderful. My sister is going to come home.

Chapter Forty

Bill stayed clear of Aly for the final week or so of her exams, mindful of Maggie's warning. He texted her every morning – brief, light-hearted messages of luck and love, so that she understood he was thinking of her – and she replied each evening in the same tone. On the morning of her last day, his text asked when she'd be free to eat supper with him, just with him, he said, to celebrate.

Not tonight, or tomorrow, she said. Tonight, Kate was cooking her favourite meal and they were eating at home. Tomorrow, when her friends with humanities exams had also finished, a whole bunch of them were going into the West End to party. But she'd be up for a pub lunch on the Sunday, she said, if he didn't mind her wearing dark glasses all day. Bill took the date she was offering and, meanwhile, ordered an elaborate bouquet of roses in sherbet colours to be delivered to Maggie's house from the florist, with a card that read: 'The final results could not make me any prouder of you, Aly. You're a star. All my love, Dad x'

He bought a bouquet for Carrie too, while he was in the florist, a small, tight arrangement of delicate white flowers, and took it home to her. She was curled up on the sofa, her handbag beside her and her kitten-heeled shoes still on her feet, as though she had walked in after work and been unable to get any further. At five and a half months, her bump was quite apparent now, neat but pronounced. Pregnancy suited her looks-wise – her face suited the small amount of extra weight, and she loved her new boobs. But she was exhausted at the end of every week day, and he often came in to find her like this. Bill didn't mind. In fact, he loved looking after someone this way. He was cooking more often now, and if the meals weren't as complex or quite as delicious as the ones she had cooked for him before, they were nonetheless gratefully received. This post-work sleep – an hour or so – meant she would wake refreshed to spend the evening with him. They hadn't exactly given up a hectic social life, so things were not so different.

They talked about the baby a lot. They had elected not to find out the sex, though Carrie hadn't been at all sure that the surly sonographer at the hospital – pointing out a heartbeat in a monotone that informed them she'd long since stopped being wowed by the miracle of birth – would have told them if they'd asked. It didn't matter. When he closed his eyes and tried to picture it, he didn't mind. Bill could see Carrie with a girl, and neither of them dreamt of a son for Bill. There was no replacement for Jake. He had Aly and Stan, so he already had a set. Their conversations stopped just short of thinking of another baby after this one. One step at a time, Bill thought. There were so many questions about their future. Marriage, children . . . For now it was enough that there *was* a future. And right now, it was co-existing as well as it could with their pasts – especially Bill's past. With Carrie, the physicality of the past had gone when Jason died. Bill's past was very much alive, living just a few miles down the road. Bill had tried hard, at first, not to talk about his other children as babies. Sometimes he would start to say something and then stop himself. Either Carrie was making a Herculean effort not to be jealous or she simply wasn't. He thought maybe it was the latter – there was something very simple and straightforward about Carrie and her emotions. He thought that if she felt it, she'd have said it. If they talked about Aly and Stan, Jake even, in the context of this new baby, it was almost always because Carrie raised them – asked a question. She had a copy of *What to Expect When You're Expecting*, which she was dutifully reading, but Bill was an interactive reference. He was surprised at how much he remembered of his children's infanthoods, in truth. He thought Maggie had done all of the practical things. He'd been working so hard, particularly when Jake and Aly were small – long hours, bringing paperwork home at night. He'd been so young, for Jake. But he did remember.

Of all the things he loved more and more about Carrie, he realized, her refusal to get twisted up about Maggie and the kids was one of the things he loved the most. He was incredibly grateful. He didn't necessarily think he would be that tolerant and understanding, if the situation were reversed. Look at the stupid way he reacted to the home Carrie and Jason had shared.

That home was on the market now. They'd started to make the big decisions. This wasn't necessarily where they would stay, but it would do fine for now. There was underground parking for the car, and an elevator to bring them and all the baby paraphernalia up and down easily. They had room. It was clean and comfortable. In time they would move – a toddler needed a garden. A young mother needed friends with babies. There was time for all that. But it would never be Carrie's house. That had just gone up for sale, with two agents, who thought it would sell quickly. Bill could see that the pregnancy was helping Carrie as much as it was helping him, now that he'd grown used to the idea. Before, he had an inkling that selling the house – severing that last physical tie to Jason – would have been hard. Really hard. Now it was relegated to a practical decision, a moving on. It wasn't that Jason had gone away entirely. Bill knew he never would. At the biggest, and sometimes at the smallest, or the most random moments of her life, for the rest of her life, Jason's face would appear in her mind. He knew that. And he could understand that. Carrie loved Jason and he had died. And now she loved him. Not more, or even differently. Just then and now. And now was better because it was real. And they were having a baby together. Sometimes excitement bubbled in him, obscuring all the rest of the questions that needed to be answered.

Carrie stirred and rubbed her eyes.

'God – how long was I out?'

'Don't know, honey. You were like that when I got in.'

'I'm sorry. What a bore.'

Bill came over to where she was, and knelt on the floor in front of her. He put both his big hands across the bump – easily spanning it. 'Boring? I don't think so.'

She ruffled his hair. 'Good day?'

'It was okay. I missed you.'

She laughed. 'You're soppy. I never knew you were so soppy.'

'I wasn't.' He was telling the truth now.

'Well, I quite like it, so don't stop on my account.' She kissed the top of his head. 'Ooh.'

'What?'

'Kick.'

'Where?' She took his hand and moved it downwards and to the left. 'Do it again, baby,' she murmured, but nothing happened.

Bill kissed the top of her hand on top of his hand and closed his eyes. These were good days.

*

Aly was sitting on the front step of the house when he pulled up on Sunday morning, and he was grateful to her for not making him ring the doorbell and face her mother.

She wasn't, in fact, wearing dark glasses across her eyes, though they were perched in readiness on the top of her head. She looked fresh and pretty and happy to be free.

'Hey, you!'

'Hi, Dad.' She climbed in, and they hugged awkwardly across the gear stick. 'Got the top down.'

'Gorgeous day. We only get about ten of those in the average English summer, so I thought I'd make the most of it. Okay with you?'

'Fabulous with me . . . hung way over, I'm afraid, and glad of the fresh air.'

'You don't look hung over. There's no bloody justice.'

'I know, I know . . . youth is wasted on the young. I've heard it, Dad.'

'Sorry. Terribly predictable, am I?'

'Not too bad. Anyhow, where are we going?'

'I thought we'd go out to Surrey – somewhere off the A3, find a nice pub by a river.'

'A pootle. Sounds perfect.'

They set off. 'So, darling – congratulations.' He patted her knee. 'How does it feel to be finished?'

'Brilliant. Amazing. I feel like the weight of the world has been lifted off my shoulders, you know?'

'I just about remember.'

'I can just forget all about it for a few months.'

'Do you think you did enough, for the marks for Imperial?'

Aly shrugged happily, the attitude of a girl who was pretty confident she had. 'Who knows? Have to wait and see.' He looked at her archly. 'But I think so, Dad. I hope so.'

He put his hand across and squeezed her knee again.

'How's your mum?'

'She's okay. You guys haven't spoken in a while, right?'

'Not for a while, no.'

'I think she's trying to take a step back, Dad.'

'You do?'

Aly nodded. 'You've got your new life, haven't you? She's just trying to get hers together. That's all. We're getting on really well. Really well. Better than in years. Long story. Long story I'm not sure you need to hear. In fact, pretty sure you don't need to. But she's good. Don't worry about her.'

Bill nodded. So easily said.

The traffic cleared after Richmond, and Bill sped up, effectively stopping conversation for a while. For a few miles, the two of them just enjoyed sitting there. Aly put the radio on, and turned Capital up too loud, but Bill didn't turn it down.

They found a pub by a weir somewhere quiet and green, and took a table by the water. Bill bought drinks, and ordered two ploughman's.

'A toast. To my brilliant daughter. No longer an A level student.'

They clinked glasses. She laughed. 'Thanks, Dad. Thanks for the stunning flowers too.'

'Not too showy? I wanted to send you something.'

'Not too showy at all. Well, actually, pretty showy. But lovely. I loved them.'

'Good.'

'How is Carrie, Dad?'

His courage deserted him. 'She's really well.'

'And things are good, with you two?'

'We're good, yeah. Really good.'

'Happy?'

'I am happy, Aly. That's the truth. She makes me very happy.'

Aly nodded her head. 'I'm glad.'

'You are? It isn't weird for you?'

Aly thought for a moment. 'Not really.' She shrugged. She looked almost surprised as she said it.

'You're amazing.'

'I'm not, Dad. Not really. I love you both. I want you both to be happy. Simple. Better happy apart than making each other miserable.'

'Is that how you saw it? That we were making each other miserable?'

'Course not. Extenuating circumstances, call it.'

Bill nodded into his beer.

'I mean – I don't remember you being unhappy when I was a kid.' Now she was reassuring him. He loved her for it. He wished he remembered more clearly.

Again, he didn't answer.

'Were you? Unhappy?'

'No.' He shook his head emphatically. 'No, we weren't. I'm not sure we were always quite as gildedly, blissfully happy as maybe we could have been, but that's not the same as unhappy.'

'Isn't that just marriage?' No one as young as Aly should be so cynical, Bill thought. If he'd been that cynical, when he'd been her age, would he ever have fallen in love with Maggie? Married her? He wished Aly many things, but he wished her love maybe more than anything else. He hoped the cynicism wouldn't get in the way. He hoped the cynicism wasn't his fault.

'I don't know. I hope not. I'm not so sure about anything any more.' He searched for a way of explaining it that would make sense to both of them. 'You stop seeing each other. You stop trying, a bit. We did, at least, I think. We grew up and we grew a bit different, I think. Doesn't help. But are you saying you don't believe a marriage can be really, really happy, all the time?'

'I don't know, do I? You're the one who's been through it all – you tell me.'

'Tell you what – I'll cure cancer, find Osama bin Laden and discover a green renewable energy source first, shall I, and then I'll pontificate on how marriage ought to be . . .'

Aly laughed. 'Fair enough. But you and Carrie, you're happy today?'

He nodded and smiled. Easier to answer. Maybe a day at a time was the most you could ask. 'We are.'

'Well, good. I think I could like Carrie.' Aly felt a brief shiver of what was probably guilt – she maybe hadn't tried as hard as she could. But she didn't want Bill to see that. She only wanted her dad to see the good in her. 'I mean, of course it's a bit strange – seeing your dad with someone else. And she's so completely the opposite of Mum – so that's odd too, although I suppose it would be weirder if she was a carbon copy. But I like her, I do. She's nice. Really nice. Honest and straight and quite ballsy. I even don't mind she's so young. You two don't look funny together or anything – like you're her sugar daddy, or something.'

'That's a relief!' Bill laughed ruefully, and Aly laughed with him, an easy, spontaneous sound he loved, and that he had missed.

'She's all right.'

He hadn't known for sure he was going to tell Aly today, or even if he knew how. Today was about her, he'd reasoned. A celebration. He wasn't sure how she would take this and he didn't want to upset her. Truthfully, he'd driven her out here so she couldn't storm off, he realized, if it came up.

He'd been so shaken by Maggie's reaction – and the ugliness of that scene between them. Not that he blamed her. But he was frightened that Aly would be upset. And things seemed so good lately, between them.

But he had to now.

'Actually, Aly . . . there's something I need to tell you, about me and Carrie.'

'You want to get married, and you've asked Mum for a divorce?'

Bill was taken aback.

'What makes you think that?'

'Just a guess.'

'No.' Yes, he thought. I suppose at some point we do. And I will.

'Sorry, go ahead. I'll stop interrupting. It's all this study-ing – I'm desocialized. Go ahead.' She laid her hands on the table and he looked right into her lovely, open face.

'Well. This isn't that easy to say. So I'm just going to say it. Carrie and me – we're going to have a baby. She's pregnant. Carrie's pregnant. With my baby.'

Shut up, he thought to himself. How many ways can you say the same thing, you garbling fool? She's not an idiot.

'Wow.' He couldn't read the wow. And now, sitting facing the sun, he couldn't read anything on her face. But at least she hadn't thrown her drink in his face yet.

'Wow.' She said it again and pulled her sunglasses down. Bill didn't know if it was the news or the bright sun that made her do it. It felt like she was hiding and that the moment of closeness between them from just before was gone.

'And she's quite pregnant. Almost six months.' This had poured salt in Maggie's fresh wound, he remembered. He wanted to be up front with Aly. 'The baby is due at the end of the summer.'

'Okay.' She was nodding and breathing.

She must just be trying to absorb it. Bill needed to fill the spaces of silence.

'I should tell you we weren't exactly planning it.' Saw Aly

wince just a little, behind the glasses. 'And I was shocked. Like you are now. But I've had time to get used to it . . .'

'You've known for ages, obviously?'

'A while. Your mum asked me not to tell you until your exams were finished.'

'She knows, then?'

'Yeah. Of course.'

'When? When did you tell her?'

'After you guys came back from Australia. Why?'

Aly nodded slowly. 'Because it makes sense of some stuff . . .'

'What do you mean?'

She waved his question away. 'Nothing. Doesn't matter.'

'I would have told you sooner, Aly. But your mum was right . . . You didn't need that kind of distraction.'

'It's okay, Dad.'

'Is it?'

'It really is.' She took his hand. 'It's good. It's a good thing.' With her eyes still obscured, it was the small break in her voice that gave her away.

Chapter Forty-One

Maggie waited until the morning after Bill had taken Aly out to celebrate her finishing her A levels to talk to her. She had guessed he'd tell her and she'd hoped Aly would come to her with it, but she didn't. Not for the first time, Maggie was torn. She was too . . . too something to want to call Bill and ask him how the conversation had gone. Proud, angry, hurt . . . ? Whichever it was, it stopped her picking up the phone.

She'd chosen a quiet time and knocked on Aly's door, and gone in, and sat on the edge of Aly's bed and chatted about inconsequential things and tried to do what Kate was so good at – to make the space for Aly to tell her. Eventually, she did.

'So, I suppose you've figured out that Dad told me?'

'I thought he would, yes.'

'Thank you for asking him not to, before the exams.'

'It seemed like the sensible thing.'

'It wouldn't have helped, that's for sure . . . with the concentration and stuff . . .'

'Indeed.' Maggie smiled at her conspiratorially. 'And how do you feel about it?'

'I should be asking you that, Mum . . .'

'I asked first.'

Aly shrugged. 'I told him I thought it was a good thing.'

Maggie tried not to register shock on her face.

'But I don't know if I mean it. I was trying to make him feel okay about it.'

Typical Aly, Maggie thought.

'I don't know if there is a prescribed way to feel about it.'

'I mean . . . I'm not threatened by it. I know Dad loves me and loves Stan. I don't feel like this baby will be replacing . . .' Her voice shook on the word replacing, and Maggie knew exactly what she was thinking about. She was thinking about Jake.

'Of course not.'

'Did you ever think about having another baby, after Jake?' Maggie shook her head.

'Why not, Mum? You were young enough. Maybe if you had . . .'

'I don't think like that, Aly, and I don't think you should either. It never came up – it honestly didn't – after Jake. It wasn't like it was something your Dad wanted that I wouldn't go along with.'

'Truly?'

'Truly . . . Where's this coming from, Aly?'

'I don't know. It's just . . . it's just made me think, you know.' Aly's eyes filled with tears. 'Everything is different now, isn't it? Everything's changed. And I suppose I thought it might change back. And now, I see that it isn't going to.'

'Your dad and I aren't not getting back together because there's a baby, Aly. It's so much more complicated than that.'

'What about you though, Mum? Dad's going to be all right, isn't he? He's found his new family . . . What about you?'

Aly was sitting with her back against the bed Maggie was sitting on. Maggie slid down to sit beside her, like they had in Australia when they'd been waiting with Liv for the results of the pregnancy test, and laid her head on her shoulder.

Maggie didn't know if now was a good time to talk to her about what she was planning, but it was a time and Aly was listening and so she talked.

'I think I have a plan, Aly . . .'

'What do you mean?'

'I've had a bit of an epiphany.'

Everything Carrie believed she may have started to achieve with Aly had been undone by the revelation of the baby. They hadn't exactly been friendly, but there had been cordiality and, Carrie believed, the beginning of something, in their conversations after that first time they'd met. She'd wondered whether Bill had said something to her after that – the second time she was warmer, less brittle, even if Carrie could see it was partly forced. It wasn't much to get excited about, but it was, she hoped, the beginning of something.

Since Bill had taken her out and told her about the baby, Aly had gone three steps backwards. He'd reported a conversation full of positivity, but that wasn't borne out in the way Aly was with Carrie, when Bill wasn't looking and listening. Carrie had tried –she really had – to put herself in Aly's position and to see the threat posed by a new baby. See the loyalty she must feel towards her mother. But she was losing patience. The baby was something wonderful to her. Magical, even. A healing, good, exciting, wonderful thing. She and Bill were closer than they'd ever been. The excitement she saw in him sometimes moved her deeply. She knew he'd found it hard, telling Maggie. She knew Maggie had reacted badly, angrily. She didn't blame her, she supposed. At least she'd done her name calling and door slamming and backed off and away. But Aly was different . . . Aly was quietly undermining her happiness. Without saying a word.

And she'd had enough. She seized her moment, when the two of them were alone in the car. Bill had bowed to Stan's pressure to stop at Starbucks and buy everyone a drink. She'd watched Bill amble along, with Stan bouncing beside him, and she'd decided it was as good a time as any to say something to Aly.

'Aly?'

'What?'

'How long do you think you're going to keep this up for?'

'What do you mean?'

'This angry teenager thing.'

Aly didn't answer.

'I mean, you've obviously made your peace with your dad, but now I'm the Wicked Witch of the West.'

Aly snorted.

'You're acting like this was all me.' Carrie gestured at her bump.

'And wasn't it?'

Carrie fought the urge to say that if Aly believed that, perhaps she wasn't such a great candidate for medical school.

'That's a nasty thing to say, Aly.' She turned around and looked right at her. 'Listen to me, Aly. I see you.'

'What's that supposed to mean?'

'I mean that you've been acting like this with me ever since you found out, and I'm starting to wonder whether it's more of an act than how you actually feel . . .'

'Really?' Aly's voice dripped with sarcasm. Bill wouldn't recognize this Aly.

'Really.' Carrie's voice was cross now, loud with indignation. 'And it's exhausting for me, and for your dad too – because don't think he doesn't notice. He does. And he feels stuck in the middle, Aly. It must be even more tiring for you.'

'Hmm.'

'And I think it's unfair.'

'How?'

'It's unfair on your dad. You don't need me to tell you how much he loves you.'

'That's for sure. I don't.'

'And so why do you want to make him suffer?'

'Who says he's suffering?'

'Aly!' Her tone was exasperated. 'You're smarter than that. I don't get it, I really don't. From what your dad has told me, you're this completely different woman.' Her use of the word woman surprised Aly. 'You've been the one who has tried to take care of everyone. Since Jake. You've tried to fix every-thing . . .'

Aly squirmed. She was sort of shocked that Carrie would go there. At the same time, she was amazed her dad had said that about her. Amazed and grateful. But she wasn't quite ready to let Carrie in.

'I don't want to fix your dad, Aly. I don't want to replace your mum, for him or for you and Stan. We'll never be parent and child – whatever happens between me and your dad. But we can have whatever relationship you want. Stay relative strangers or be friends. Your choice. I'm not threatening you and I'd never for one moment imagine that if this was a contest you couldn't easily beat me. I'm just asking you to think about it. I was your age once. Not that long ago. My parents didn't get divorced or split up, but I know how much I would have hated it if they had. It isn't what any kid wants. I know that. But it's happened. And it didn't happen because of me. Isn't it better that they be happy apart, if they can't be happy together? Don't you want them both to be happy? And don't you see that I might be his best chance of that? Me and the baby?'

Carrie's voice was quieter now. 'I don't want to fix him,' she repeated, and it seemed to Aly then that she was talking to herself as much as to her. 'I just want to love him.'

The two of them sat in silence for another couple of min-utes, with Carrie's words hanging heavily in the air. Aly wanted to say something but she was caught like a rabbit in the headlights between guilt and righteous rage, between tears and screams. Bill and Stan came out with a cardboard tray bearing the lattes and frappuccinos they'd ordered, and Bill smiled towards the car.

Carrie turned to her one more time. 'Please, Aly,' she implored. 'Please . . . just think about it.'

Mrs Schilling rang Maggie one Wednesday afternoon to tell her that Stan had been in trouble that morning for 'shoving' a class-mate in science. A number of test tubes had fallen off the bench and smashed as a result of the shove. The boy in question was unharmed. Mrs Schilling said that the science teacher had been in a different part of the lab with some other children, and that neither Stan nor the other boy involved had been forthcoming on the subject of their argument. Mrs Schilling wanted Maggie to know – it was so unlike Stan. Punishment had been meted out at school in the form of detentions and a letter of apology to the teacher for the damage caused, but Mrs Schilling was concerned. He'd been belligerent for several other teachers, it transpired, and that was not like Stan either.

Maggie promised to talk to Stan and put the phone down with a sigh and a heavy heart. And a slight flutter of panic. She was frightened of this kind of trouble. She was exhausted before she even began dealing with it, and she hated herself for that – it was normal stuff, wasn't it, that every kid and every parent went through. Stan had been her Achilles heel for so long that she knew she heard the news differently than she would have done if it were Aly, or Jake. She worried more, panicked more quickly, over-analysed and over-thought . . . She knew it, she saw it, but she couldn't control it. And Stan had been so good lately. So worry-free. It was alarming how quickly all her negative feelings flooded back, like toxic adrenalin, with Mrs Schilling's call.

When Stan came home that afternoon, instead of running down to the basement kitchen like he normally did, he disappeared upstairs, his bedroom door slamming hard behind him. Downstairs, Maggie and Kate heard. Maggie stood up. 'I better go and talk to him.'

'Unless . . .' Kate almost stopped.

'You think I should leave him for a while?'

Kate shook her head. 'I wasn't going to say that. I wondered if you'd like me to go and talk to him . . .' She was afraid she'd overstepped.

'Would you? He might talk to you, mightn't he?' Maggie seemed, if anything, grateful to her, and Kate was relieved. She stood up and, in synchronicity, Maggie sank back down into her seat.

'You must think I'm pathetic . . .' She half-smiled, ruefully.

'Not at all. I think you're tired of doing all this by yourself. And I'm here so you don't have to.' She squeezed Maggie's shoulder as she passed.

Upstairs, when her knock went unanswered, Kate spoke loudly enough so he could hear her on the other side of the door. 'Stan? I'm coming in, okay?'

Stan was lying on his bed, facing the wall, and when he didn't turn to greet her, she sat down on the swivel chair he kept at his desk, being very careful not to disturb the array of models and ornaments he kept so meticulously there.

'I suppose you've heard . . .'

'Mrs Schilling called.'

'She said she was going to.'

'Well, she did, Stan. But more out of concern than anger.'

'She was pretty cross.'

'I daresay she was. Shoving? That's not like you.'

'That's what she said.'

'Well, if we both think it, then maybe you'll agree that it was out of character.'

Stan's shoulders moved up and down on the duvet, in what might have been a shrug. Resigned or defensive, Kate found it hard to tell.

'I'm sure you had a reason. Not that that makes it okay. But I'd like to hear it, if you'd like to tell me.'

'I didn't really. He said something. But it wasn't much of anything, not really.'

'What did he say?'

Stan sat up and clutched a stuffed bear called, bizarrely, Fernando, to his chest. His arms were around his knees.

'We were talking about . . . just stuff. Someone else's mum is getting married again at the weekend. She was divorced. And he said his dad had kids before he married his mum, but he didn't care about them any more because now he had him and his brother.'

'Ah.'

'And he said his dad might as well not have had the first lot, because he never saw them or took them on holiday or spent any money on them or anything like that.'

Bloody child. Kate would quite like to shove him herself.

'And did this child . . . what's his name?'

'Archie. Archie Fellowes.'

'Did this Archie Fellowes know about your dad?'

Stan shook his head. 'Nobody does. I haven't told anyone at school.'

At least, Kate reflected, Archie Fellowes was just a moron and not, it appeared, a malicious one.

'Well then, Stan, I have to tell you – Archie Fellowes is a blithering idiot.'

Stan smiled. This was not what he had been expecting. Not at all.

'Not that it is okay to shove him. Or anyone else. But I know you've been punished for that already, at school. Listen to me carefully, Stan.'

Stan leant forward conspiratorially.

'The love between a mother and her child, or between a father and his child, cannot ever, ever be changed. Not by anything – a new wife or husband, a new baby, a new home . . . nothing. Do you understand?'

'I think so.' His face belied the words.

'Nothing will change how your dad feels about you, Stan. Ever.'

'But everything changes all the time, doesn't it?'

'What do you mean?'

'We used to be a family of five – me, Mum, Dad, Jake and Aly. Now we're a family of three. Jake went first, then Dad went. What about when Aly goes – she's nearly grown up . . . ?'

Kate's heart ached for him.

'People are sometimes in other places, Stan . . .'

'Like heaven and college and Roehampton.'

'Like heaven and college and Roehampton.' Kate smiled. 'But love doesn't change. I promise you that, darling. Dad will always love you, no matter what.'

Stan held Fernando aloft and then swung him around by his teddy arms.

'Even if I was a bank robber or a murderer?'

'Yes, Stan. Even then.'

Chapter Forty-Two

It was early – a few minutes after 4 a.m. and not yet beginning to get light – on a Sunday morning when Carrie woke him. He'd had a few glasses of wine with his dinner the night before and was sleeping far, far away when she touched his shoulder – in a surreal unremembered dream, it took him a moment to differentiate between that dream and this wakefulness. Carrie was already dressed in a white shirt and one of the stretchy skirts that had become the last clothes she owned that would stretch over her vast bump. The expression on her face was an almost unimaginable combination of fear, panic and excited joy. His eyes focused, at last. Seeing her, he was instantly jolted awake, from nought to sixty. Adrenalin surged around his body.

'It's time to go. To the hospital. At least, I think it's time. This time I think it's time.'

This had happened before. Last week, they'd made another mad dash to the maternity unit of their local hospital in the middle of the night. Carrie had been sure then that it was starting. It was early – the baby's due date wasn't for another five weeks at that point, but then they'd both been warned throughout the pregnancy that it might be. She'd woken with fairly persistent intermittent pains – Braxton Hicks, of course. Bill had thought they might be. He remembered Maggie having them the first time, mistaking them for labour the same way Carrie did now. But it was one of the many pieces of long-forgotten pregnancy trivia that had resurfaced in his mind and which he'd chosen not to share: if Carrie needed to go to the hospital for reassurance that this wasn't labour, just a practice, then he would gladly take her. Reassurance worked for him too. She'd been embarrassed, then, but the midwife had been sweet to her. She'd told Carrie it happened all the time with first pregnancies – women coming rushing in long before the system wanted to deal with them. It wouldn't be long now, she said, eyeing Carrie's tummy. Carrie wouldn't get to term, she was certain; the baby had already dropped right down, and she was such a tiny thing. 'He's getting ready,' she'd said. 'Is it a boy?' They'd both shaken their heads. 'We don't know – we decided to be surprised,' Bill supplied. 'Good for you,' the midwife had smiled broadly. She was a kind-faced, stout woman, in her fifties, Bill guessed. 'Not enough of that, these days. Not many real surprises left in life, I say, eh?'

They'd had to wait for what felt like ages to finally be officially sent home, and by then it had been starting to get light so they'd stopped at a transport café for a fry-up, then gone back home, to bed, to sleep off the adventure. The pains had subsided and then stopped entirely, and Carrie had eventually been able to relax. Bill had spooned her in their bed, his hand spread on the swell of her stomach. '*You've* been my surprise, Carrie Stiles. It's been you.' She didn't answer, too close to sleep for words, just put her hand on top of his, on top of the baby, sleeping now, and squeezed his fingers.

She didn't look so relaxed now. 'I think my waters have broken. I mean, there's definitely water. Pretty sure it isn't pee.' Carrie grimaced. 'Sorry.' Bill shook his head. There was no need. She was swaying slightly on wide-apart legs, her hands either side of the bump.

Bill jumped up. 'Are you having contractions? Different from last week? D'you have any idea how far apart?'

Carrie rubbed her tummy through the shirt. 'Not sure. Something's happening though. I definitely feel weird. My tum is all tight. I feel . . . different. Scared. Weird. Not like last week.'

'Give me a minute.' Bill ran his fingers through his hair and scanned the chair in the corner of the room to see what clothes he had discarded there the previous night. 'We'll go and find out. I need two minutes.'

'I don't know if we should go now. What if we get sent back again . . . what if it's all in my head again . . . ?'

'Then we'll come home again. It's fine. I can do this every day.'

'I'll feel stupid.' Carrie pouted. Bill smiled in a way he hoped was reassuring.

'Not as stupid as you'll feel if we don't go and you end up giving birth in the car park because you've run out of time. We'll go.'

She looked distraught at the suggestion and he wished he hadn't said anything. There was something about this whole business that made men feel like clumsy, insensitive oafs. There should be a handbook, a script. He stopped frantically pulling his clothes on and went over to where she was standing. Putting his arms around her, he dropped his head on to her shoulder for a moment. 'It's going to be okay, Carrie. I'm here. I'm going to look after you. I promise.'

Their eyes met. 'Do you?'

And in that moment, he meant it when he nodded and gently kissed her mouth.

She was right this time. This time she was a magical, viable, wonderfully 'normal' thirty-six weeks and she was in labour. She was already three centimetres dilated by the time they'd filled in her forms, put her in a room, and a gown, and someone had come to check her. Carrie had hoped the same midwife as last time would be on, but this woman was young – in her early thirties – and more briskly efficient and emotionally detached. She kept calling Carrie 'mum' in a weird, discombobulating, third-person kind of way. Carrie and Bill grimaced at each other behind her straight, busy back. The primary care trust promised continuity of care, and wrote in all their literature with great enthusiasm about 'teams' and the high percentage likelihood of being delivered by someone who'd overseen your obstetric care throughout the pregnancy, but they'd never seen this midwife before and both, independently, hoped her shift would finish soon and bring them another, different total stranger to help deliver the baby.

Carrie looked tiny and almost ethereal in the big, high hospital bed. In the last few weeks her bump had grown to a disproportionate, almost grotesque size for her frame, and though she hadn't complained, it was painfully obvious how uncomfortable it must have been for her. She'd had enough. Bill was glad she wasn't going to last forty weeks. The midwives thought the baby was a decent weight at thirty-six weeks, and, though he or she would most likely go to the special care baby unit straight after delivery, it would almost certainly be a formality.

Carrie's size – her childlike hips and tiny pelvis – might pose a problem for her in labour, they'd been warned. But so far, apparently, things seemed good with both mother and baby. Watching her lying there, though, Bill felt an all-too-familiar sense of impotence. And something else. A hot and cold, ever-widening ribbon of terror pulsing down his spine. An anxiety he had never felt at the births of his other children. With Jake, everything had been frightening, of course –

it was all new and unexpected, and messy and bloody and loud – but he had never, somehow, doubted that all would be well. Once Jake was born safely, and relatively easily, he didn't remember ever questioning that Aly and then Stan would come the same way, slithering out in a bloody, violent rush, their shocked cries mingling quickly with Maggie's animalistic grunt as she delivered them. Each time had been tense, of course – he clearly remembered being anxious and tired, and that useless feeling, and then there was huge relief, mingling with the joy, when the babies appeared. But no terror.

Now, he was petrified. The effort required to hide it from Carrie was exhausting – not just now. Over the preceding months, it had come in fits and starts, puncturing the happiness – dark clouds across the sun. He didn't know if it was Carrie or if it was Jake making him feel this way. She was so fragile – compared to Maggie. And he really couldn't help but compare, though it left him with the feeling that doing so was disloyal to both women. But really he knew that this was about Jake. Bill hated that this was a part of his son's legacy, but it was. Jake's death had, in an instant, removed every ounce of certainty and complacency he had ever had. It took away any sense of safety or entitlement. It made planning seem futile and counting on things impossible. Statistics were meaningless now. Luck and fate had stopped being forces that had been good to him and become malevolent, brooding ghouls that haunted him. How could he assume anything? How could he believe it would be all right? Jake had died. All bets with the universe were off. That dark force – he could hold at bay most of the time. Today, it hung around him like a mist. The feeling disorientated and nauseated him.

Did Carrie feel it too?

Progress was slow but steady for the next few hours. They were largely left alone between checks. He'd brought music, but Carrie didn't want it. She wanted quiet. She dozed or simply closed her eyes, her head back against the pillows, between contractions. When the pains came, she opened her eyes wide with alarm and sucked at the Entenox pipe the midwives had set up for her like a dying man would suck at a straw in a puddle, but once they'd passed, she was calm again. She was concentrating, he could see, and she'd removed herself a little, from the room, from the pain and from him. Bill held her hand when she let him, read articles out loud to her from the newspaper, willed himself to stay calm. By lunchtime, she was six centimeters dilated. Each one hard won, but she didn't seem too tired yet.

'I don't think I want to do it today.'

Bill smiled. 'I don't think it works like that, sweetie.'

'Really? We can't just go home? I'll do it tomorrow. I'm so tired . . .'

'I'd do it for you if I could.'

'Oh, good idea. Yes please.'

He leant over and kissed her lightly. 'I'm here, Carrie.' She kissed him back.

'That's *it*?!'

At Carrie's suggestion, Bill went off to get a cup of tea and a sandwich he couldn't eat and returned to find that last week's midwife had taken over and that Carrie was beaming at her between contractions. She'd visibly relaxed in the presence of this new carer, though everything was getting stronger as Carrie's labour moved towards its inevitable conclusion. This midwife was Maddy, she said. She remembered them well, winked at Bill. 'For real today, huh?'

Bill nodded. 'How's she doing?'

'She's doing marvellous. So far, so textbook. We had a little talk, while you were gone, about the pain relief. She wants to keep going. What do you think?'

She was asking him whether Carrie would cope. Whether she could do the rest without anything stronger than the gas and air. Bill realized he'd no idea of her physical pain threshold. He looked at her. Her hair was tucked behind her ears, she wore no make-up and she looked about eighteen years old. He didn't know how she was with physical pain, but he knew he had sure as hell watched her grapple with pain that went far beyond what a body could endure.

'I think she's fantastic. I think she's a lion.'

Carrie beamed at him, understanding what he meant, and that glance was the most connected to her that he had felt since they'd arrived here. 'Here comes another one . . .' Carrie suddenly bit her lip and reached for the pipe, shoulders hunching forward.

'Right then, lioness. Let's see how you roar . . .' Maddy laughed gently and took Carrie's free hand. She looked sharply at Bill – and he knew she saw on his face what he'd been trying so intently to shield Carrie from. 'And you? You okay?'

'I will be.'

'We'll be all right, Carrie and me, if you need to step out for a moment.'

She was smart, this woman. An offer and a warning.

'I'm fine. I'm not going anywhere.'

'Well, all right then.' Maddy nodded her head decisively.

By mid afternoon, Carrie was declared ready to push. Up on her knees, gripping the back of the bed, she rotated her hips and focused, like the books told her to and with Maddy's gentle encouragement, on staying relaxed, open. Working with her body and not against it. Visualizing the baby's passage downwards. Bill held her two hands, linked in the middle of the headboard, and watched in awe. How women could ever be described as the weaker sex . . . He knew he could not do this. Now Carrie was more vocal than before – small, guttural sounds of effort and strain. But she was never loud, never uncontrolled. If she was scared, she didn't seem it – until the point when the baby's head was crowning. 'I see the baby, Carrie. I see your baby,' Maddy smiled encouragingly. 'Stop. Wait a moment. Don't push.'

Then Carrie's eyes widened in fear. 'I have to. I have to. I need . . .'

'Go now. Push with all your might.' Released by Maddy's voice, Carrie blew her cheeks right out, squeezed her eyes tightly shut and pushed.

And then, within a minute, the baby was out. Carrie rolled over and flopped on to her back. And Maddy lifted his child from between Carrie's legs.

Bill remembered – or he thought he remembered – red-faced babies with mad-professor curls, unctuous with a sheath of slimy white vernix, mouths moving like hungry birds, fists pumping a desperate rhythm by their faces. By comparison, this baby was almost clean. And this baby was still and serene, and very, very beautiful. A network of tiny blue veins beneath a translucent pale skin covered a tiny, pointed head; the merest peach fuzz of strawberry blonde topped it. Its eyes were closed. And it was silent. The mid-wife held it aloft in her hand, gently working the knuckles of two fingers into the child's miniscule sternum. 'Come on, baby – come on. We want to hear you. What have you got to tell us, eh?' Her tone was light, unconcerned, sing-songy, but Bill's heart stopped. A splutter, a Lilliputian cough, and then a cry. Weak and reedy, but all that was needed. 'That's it. Well done. Welcome, baby. Here's your momma,' and Maddy laid the baby on Carrie's bare breast.

Carrie was sobbing, and Bill felt his own throat constricting, his eyes suddenly wet. They both stared at the baby.

'What is it?'

Bill hadn't looked. Hadn't cared. Hadn't thought.

'You've got a little girl. A beautiful little girl. Congratulations!'

Maddy stood back for a moment and observed the tableau with a tear in her eye that had been her consistent response since she'd delivered her first baby, almost thirty years earlier. Best job in the world. 'There's lovely.'

Carrie looked up at him, tears running down her face. 'A girl! We've got a girl.'

The lump in Bill's throat made speech impossible. He took Carrie's face in his hands and kissed her hard. Then bent over her and kissed the impossibly soft, earthy-smelling top of his daughter's head.

Chapter Forty-Three

The post dropped on to the mat at the same time every morning. It was the usual assortment of pizza flyers, bills in brown envelopes and unsolicited catalogues of clothes no one would wear. And one white envelope, addressed to Kate. Not stamped with the redirection mark most of Kate's post carried. This one had been sent here.

Maggie went downstairs, with the post in her hand, to where Kate was finishing a boiled egg. Chris Evans was talking about the gorgeous day ahead and introducing a Fairground Attraction song Maggie hadn't heard in years.

She smiled at Kate and slipped the letter between her egg cup and her mug, then leant against the cupboard and watched her.

'Something for you . . .'

Kate picked up the envelope gingerly.

'Recognize the handwriting?'

'No.' But they both knew who they hoped it was from.

'It's probably something completely different.'

'Only one way to find out.'

Kate used her toast knife to open it and pulled out a single sheet of paper. Before she unfolded it to read it, she looked at Maggie, fear and excitement etched on her face.

'Go on. Read it . . .' Maggie realized she was holding her breath.

Kate read out loud.

Dear Mum,

Thank you for your letter. I'm sorry all the wires got crossed with that girl Aly – I was shocked and I wasn't nice to her. I find myself glad you've got someone who cares about you. I had read that your husband had died.

Kate's voice faltered. Maggie moved a little closer and slid into a chair.

I don't want to be estranged, Mum. It all seems so stupid and pointless. I don't know how it got to this point, except that I must have all the same foolish pride you do. I know it wasn't all your fault, but mine too.

I need a little time to get used to it. I'm not ready to meet just yet, but I know I will be soon. I need to sit with it a while.

You were right about one thing. When my son was born, I wanted you to be there. I don't know why I didn't do anything about it. It was like I understood something then that I hadn't before.

Just give me some time, Mum.

Love, Rebecca.

She put the letter down on the table and smoothed it out carefully. Her eyes were shining.

'I can't believe it.'

'Believe it. It's there in black and white.'

'She needs more time.'

'That's understandable. You both had a big shock. She'll get there. It won't take long, I don't reckon.'

'You don't?'

Maggie squeezed her arm. 'No way. And then how could she not love you? *We* love you, don't we?'

Maggie had telephoned Charlie earlier in the morning and asked him whether he was free for lunch. He'd sounded thrilled to be asked and said he could be – he had an internal meeting he'd need to move, but she'd be saving him, he laughed, from a very dull lunch. He'd love to meet, he said. Would she like to pick a restaurant or leave it to him? Maggie had said that it was a beautiful day and that she'd rather meet outside – she'd stop off at the deli and pick up some stuff and meet him in St James's Park, near his office. Charlie agreed happily. The forecast was for sun and temperatures in the seventies. This was the English weather Maggie loved the most. What could be nicer than a picnic in the park?

But she was dreading it. She stopped at Carluccio's and picked up pasta salads and salamis, some perfectly ripe apricots and cherry tomatoes, and two bottles of Limonata. At 12.45 p.m. she was sitting on a bench outside Charlie's office. She hadn't wanted to go in and ask for him. The fewer people in Charlie's world who knew of her the better, it felt to her.

She told herself it had only been a couple of months. They'd gone on their first date – when was it? – in March. Hadn't slept together until May. It had only been a couple of months. How much could he be invested in it? They hadn't made promises to each other, they hadn't made any declarations. She wondered, not for the first time, whether, if she wasn't going to Australia, she and Charlie might have a future. Bill was gone, and he wasn't coming back. She didn't know . . . the truth was, she hadn't thought about it. And maybe that was the most telling part of all – that she hadn't daydreamed of it. That Charlie had figured so little in her decision-making process. She certainly didn't love him – nothing close to it. She knew that. Whether she could have done, eventually, or not was irrelevant now. It was what he was thinking about her that was bothering Maggie today.

He'd taken off his tie and left his jacket in his office. He beamed at her.

'Hello. What a treat! I'm so glad you called.' He kissed her cheek, near her mouth, lightly. Stepping back, he kept his hand on her elbow. 'You look fantastic. Tanned already. It's been sunny for what . . . three days, and you're golden already. Damn. Love this dress . . .'

Oh, God. Maggie wondered if she'd done the right thing. What else could she have done? Sent him an email. Texted him. She owed him a face to face, at least. She hadn't thought ahead about how romantic the suggestion of a picnic may have struck him as being – she'd thought of open spaces and privacy. Better to have this conversation on grass with space around them than crammed cheek by jowl into a table at the Wolseley where every word would be overheard.

'You even thought of a blanket. A professional picnicker!'

They chatted – small talk about his day, and almost polite questions and chitchat about the kids, the exams – while Maggie spread the plaid blanket on the ground and arranged the plastic containers of food on it. Charlie twisted the metal tops off the Limonata and took a long drink from his, before clinking his glass bottle against hers.

'Cheers.' He leant in for a kiss. Maggie let him kiss her on the mouth, but when his lips became harder and his hand came up to hold her shoulder, she pulled back just a little.

He affected to ignore the rejection, or just didn't notice it, she wasn't sure which, and busied himself forking pasta salad into his plastic bowl, making appreciative noises about her choices. She'd thought – if she'd thought that far – that she might wait until they'd eaten, but sitting here now that seemed unfair.

'Charlie . . . I need to tell you something?'

'Okay.' He stopped loading his bowl and put it down.

'There isn't really an easy way to say this.' His face grew

428

serious, and he put his fork down slowly too. 'So I'm just going to say it.'

'You don't want to see me any more?' He didn't wait for her to say it.

'Charlie!'

'It's okay, Maggie.'

His voice made her sad, passive and accepting. 'That's not it, Charlie. Let me finish, will you?'

'Sorry. Sorry. Go ahead. I'm listening.'

'I can't see you any more. It isn't that I don't want to.'

'I don't really understand.'

'I'm going away, Charlie. I'm going to Australia for a while.' She realized that didn't clarify things accurately. It was more than that, wasn't it? Not another extended holiday. 'To live. With Stan.'

Charlie was staring at the blanket. 'I see . . .' He so clearly didn't.

Maggie reached across and took his hand, but although he didn't move away, he didn't respond.

'I don't know if you do, Charlie. I'd like to make you see . . .'

'You don't owe me an explanation, Maggie. Really, you don't.'

'I certainly do. We've been . . . something to each other. We've been seeing each other for a while. And I would like you to understand.'

He didn't speak.

'It isn't you. It's me.' It was official – she hated herself. Who said that? A vision of Aly rolling her eyes in exasperation swam before her.

Charlie looked at her now. His eyes were dull.

'That came out wrong. Sounded like bollocks – even to me, and I said it . . .' She forced a small half-laugh. 'I'm making a mess of this . . . and I so didn't want to do that.'

'I don't know if you can break up with someone in a non-messy way, in fairness . . .'

He was trying to meet her halfway and she appreciated him for that. He was smiling weakly, which was better than the clubbed-seal look of a few seconds earlier, and she appreciated that too.

She nodded her head two or three times, composing herself. 'I need to make a change. I've been living this awful kind of half-life since my son died. Three years. My child has died, my marriage has ended, my relationships, with my children, with other people – they've all suffered. And I need to make a change.'

'And that change is geography?' Now he was Paxman, pushing to the heart of the matter.

'Not just geography. Australia was my home for the first twenty years of my life. It might still be. I feel a bit like I'm going home. But I might be wrong. It's about a change. It's about taking charge of things. I don't want things to just happen to me any more. Enough. I want to make things happen. So I'm going to try. I'm not running away. That's not it. I'm *doing* something.'

'I thought we were *doing* something.'

'We were. Charlie. You have to know how much I like you. How much I've appreciated you.'

'Hmm. Appreciated me.' He rolled the compliment around his mouth, and Maggie knew what he meant.

'That sounds wrong too. You've been a part of what has happened to me in the last few months that's been good. You showed me something.'

'What did I show you?'

'You showed me that I can have another life. That my life's not over.'

'But your life isn't with me, right?'

430

'It was too soon for that. You weren't thinking that, were you?'

'I like you, Maggie. I liked you. Really, a lot. I wasn't about to propose marriage, or even moving in together or anything. I just thought . . . I just thought we were maybe moving in that direction. For the first time since my divorce, I thought there was just a shadow of a possibility that I might have found a person to move in that direction with. You're telling me you weren't ever feeling that?'

'I'm not saying that.'

'But not enough to stay.' It wasn't a question.

'Please try to understand, Charlie.' And she knew she needed to understand too. This meant more to him than it did to her – that was just the way it was.

He was quiet for a moment. 'I do, I think. It hurts. I can't lie. I feel like an idiot.'

'You're not an idiot. You're a good man. A really good man.'

'And some girl will be really lucky to have me, right?' He smiled weakly at her again.

Maggie nodded. 'Abso-bloody-lutely!'

She leant forward, resting her hands on his crossed knees, and kissed him. This time, she didn't pull away, and they kissed for a long minute, a tender, sad kiss, tinged with long-ing and regret.

'I suppose a goodbye shag is completely out of the question . . . ?'

He broke the tension, and in that second she loved him for it.

'Are you serious?'

'Abso-bloody-lutely.' He wasn't, though, and she knew it. That would never happen again. 'Just tell me one thing?'

'Anything.'

'If you weren't going to Australia, if you were staying here . . . would you keep seeing me?'

'You know I would.'

'So if you come back, if it doesn't work . . . Would you call me?'

'In a second.' It might not be true but it didn't matter. Not to either of them, she supposed. Right now, that was what Charlie needed to hear to make him okay, and she was going to do that for him.

Outside his office, after a slightly awkward, melancholy picnic which neither of them had an appetite for, while the young couples smooching and hand-holding around them on the grass and the paths of the park seemed to have been ordered up to humiliate them, he pulled her into a hug – real and warm and fond.

'If you decide you'd like a more . . . personal goodbye, you call me.'

Maggie laughed. 'I promise.'

'And Maggie? I hope – I really, really hope that this works for you. I do. Please know that. I would like you to be happy. I might prefer that you try to be happy with me, but if somewhere else might be the answer, then I hope it is. I do.'

She took his face in her hands and looked into his eyes. Kissed him once more, lightly, on the lips. 'Thank you, Charlie.'

On the tube, heading home, Maggie thought about Charlie – how he let her break up with him with the same gentle, polite kindness with which he had conducted the whole relationship – the dinners, the sex, all the conversations. And she saw that it could never have worked. She needed something more fiery than that. She needed passion. She and Bill had had it. She could close her eyes and summon up the feelings she'd had for Bill, within a ridiculously short time of meeting him, and she could remember it exactly, and she knew she had never had anything like that with Charlie. And it surprised her, somewhere between West Kensington and Ravenscourt Park on the District Line, to realize that she wanted to find it again.

Chapter Forty-Four

Bill called quite early one morning mid week and asked if he could come by. He usually gave her more notice, and they usually met on neutral ground. But Maggie had been avoiding him, she knew, and so she'd agreed. Stan was at school and Aly had stayed the night with a friend before a whole gang of them headed to Thorpe Park. She had put it off long enough and it was time to tell him. The kids knew. Kate knew. Liv and Scott knew. Even Charlie knew. It was getting ridiculous. She had to tell him. She had never thought of it as asking him. Until now. She needed him to let her take Stan away. She needed him to give Stan up. Not entirely, but enough to be devastating. The magnitude of it hit her now. The idea had seemed so blissfully simple. She hung up the phone and stared at herself in the hall mirror.

Downstairs in the kitchen, Kate was folding laundry she'd brought in off the line. The glass doors to the garden were pushed wide open and bright sunlight was streaming into the room on a soft breeze. Radio 4 was playing on the Roberts radio; Jenni Murray's earthy voice was the only sound in the room. Kate looked up and smiled. Walking over, Maggie pulled a few of Stan's school socks out of the basket and began pairing them up.

'That was Bill. On the phone.' Kate nodded, as though she'd been expecting it to be Bill.

'He wants to come round and talk, he says.'

'This morning?'

Maggie nodded, then sank into a chair. She felt exhausted before the conversation had even taken place. 'He'll be here in an hour or so.'

'I'll go out once I've put this lot away. Give the two of you some space.'

'There's no need.'

'I think there is, Maggie. The two of you have things to say to each other.'

'That's true.' Maggie blew a long breath out through pursed lips – it was almost a whistle. How was she going to live without Kate? Who could have guessed, after twenty years in this country, that the person she'd miss most was someone she hadn't even known this time last year? Life was a strange thing.

Kate put the basket on the chair next to her and sat down beside Maggie. 'You've been avoiding him, haven't you?'

'Of course I have. It's going to be hard to tell him. Really hard.'

'So . . . now he's made it easier – he's coming to you. Do you think he knows?'

'No. I don't think so. Stan and Aly know I wanted him to hear it from me.'

'But something might have slipped out . . . This is Stan we're talking about!'

Maggie smirked. 'Stan is entirely capable of letting something slip out. But you know him. He'd also be crippled with remorse. There's no way he could keep it to himself – if he'd done that.'

'True. So why is he coming, do you think?'

Maggie looked at her with her eyebrows raised.

The penny dropped. Kate's mouth formed a round O. 'The baby . . . !'

Before she went, Kate squeezed Maggie's shoulder and put the palm of her hand on Maggie's cheek briefly.

'In an hour, you're going to feel better.'

'Do you think?'

'I know. Whatever he says, however he reacts – it's going to be better when he knows. The minute you've said it, saying it won't be hanging over your head any more. There's a relief in that, for sure. Whatever he says.'

Maggie leant against the door frame, her arms folded.

'I don't know Bill, Maggie. But something tells me he's going to understand.'

Maggie showered and dressed once Kate had gone, wondering if she was right.

Bill looked rough. He had what looked to be two or three days' stubble on his cheeks and chin – and she was surprised to see that his beard was coming through tinged with grey; she hadn't noticed that before. His hair was a mess, like he'd dressed and left home without looking in a mirror. But his eyes – his eyes were shining bright. Maggie instantly knew, when she opened the door to him, that she'd been right about what he had come to say.

And it didn't hurt. For a silly, overcomplicated moment, Maggie wondered if it hurt that it didn't hurt. She almost laughed at herself. Enough with the endless, endless self-analysis. She was tired of it, tired of living with this filter that made her question how everything made her feel the moment she'd felt it. For a moment, this moment, it was enough to be happy for him – there was a simplicity and a purity in it. And she wanted to make it easy for him, like Charlie had wanted to make it easy for her the other day in the park. Liv's face appeared in her mind's eye. What would George Bailey do?

She smiled at him. 'Your baby came?'

Bill nodded, his face surprised, then it crumpled and his

eyes filled with instant tears. Maggie instinctively opened her arms to him and he stepped towards her and let her hold him. They were two people who had loved each other long and well.

'Wow. It came. Early, no?'

He rubbed his eyes and pushed his fingers through his hair. 'A month early.'

'Is everything okay?'

Bill looked amazed. New-father face. She remembered it well. 'Yeah. She's little but she's fine. Totally fine.'

'Congratulations, Bill!'

His eyes searched her face and she nodded encouragingly. 'Really. Congratulations. I'm happy for you. Both of you.'

He had no words.

'Come in . . . What say we wet the baby's head with a cup of tea?'

Down in the basement kitchen, she put the kettle on the Aga plate and took mugs from the cupboard. Bill sat at the kitchen table and watched her.

'This is so odd. You're amazing.'

'I'm so not amazing. I'm a bit amazed. I'm not amazing.'

'Amazed?'

'I'm amazed that this is okay. This being okay is really, really new for me.'

He nodded. 'I know. For me too.'

'Tell me about it. She's a girl?'

'Yes, a little girl. Four pounds, two ounces. Seventeen inches' long. Strawberry blonde. Beautiful.'

'With a name?'

'She's Jemima.'

Maggie's breath caught in her throat, just for a second, and she smiled through lips pressed tightly together. 'That's a very pretty name.'

She looked at him and he held her gaze for a long moment. The kettle rescued them with its strident whistle. Maggie busied herself making the tea.

'She came to see me, you know, a while back.'

'Carrie?' It was obvious from his expression that he didn't. 'I'm sorry. I wish she hadn't.'

'Don't be. I'm sort of glad she did.'

'You are?'

'She was right – we had to meet at some point. Probably better to get it over with. Now I can't imagine her any prettier and sweeter than she actually is.'

Bill searched her face to see if she was making fun or being snide, but she wasn't, he didn't think.

'She didn't say.'

'I think she sort of thought it was between the two of us.'

'And was it okay?'

'Bill . . . what did you think might happen – that I'd slap her or shout at her?'

'I don't know.'

'We just talked a bit. We're not going to be best friends – don't get me wrong. But I'm . . . I'm glad we met. And I'm glad the baby is fine. I honestly am.'

She brought the mugs to the table and took the top off a cake tin.

'Coffee and walnut? Or chocolate? We have both. There's always cake now. Kate is a demon cake-baker. I think I've put on ten pounds since she came.'

'That isn't true, and you know it . . .'

She waved away the compliment. 'So, do you have a photograph of this little girl that I could see . . . ?'

His eyes narrowed quizzically. 'Are you sure?'

'I'm asking, aren't I?'

Bill took his phone out of his jacket pocket and scrolled

through the icons for a moment, then handed her the phone.

It was a picture of him holding Jemima. It must have been taken almost as soon as she was born; she was swaddled in the striped hospital blanket. The baby's face was tiny, almost obscured. She'd seen Bill's expression before – three times. That mix of relief, joy, excitement and exhaustion. Her memories were visceral – she could smell her own delivery rooms, hear his voice encouraging and praising her. Her stomach contracted. She handed the phone back to him.

'She's lovely.'

'Thank you, Maggie. She really is.'

'And thank you for coming to tell me yourself. That can't have been easy.'

'I couldn't let anyone else tell you.'

'The kids don't know?'

'Not yet. How do you think they'll be?'

'I think it'll be fine. Stan will be disappointed it's a girl.'

Bill smiled. 'And Aly?'

'I think Aly is okay, Bill. She's used to the idea.' Aly amazes me, Maggie thought. She'd almost forgotten that Bill didn't know about Ryan. There was no need, now. It wasn't the time to tell him. In this new life, she realized, there was no obligation either. It was his relationship with Aly – she didn't need to be a middleman or a go-between for them any more.

'Do you think she'll want to be involved?'

'I don't know. It might be weird for her at first. But I'm sure she'll love Jemima. Once she gets the chance to know her. They're sisters.'

Bill leant forward, his hands on his knees. 'Thank you.'

'You've got to stop saying that.'

'I can't. You've been extraordinary, Maggie. You could have made all this so much harder for me.'

'Why would I do that?'

'Because you could. Because I know how hard it's got to have been for you.'

'I want all of us to be okay. You. The kids. Even Carrie and this little girl. We've all been so unhappy for so long.'

'And you?'

'I want to be okay too. I want to be happy. I don't know if I ever can be, not completely. This changes you. My life has been ruined, and I don't think I'll ever be totally happy again because I don't think you can be, after what's happened to us. But I can be happier.'

'That's what I want for you, Maggie. So much. I'll always love you, you know?'

'I know. I'm glad you feel that way. I've got something to tell you too.'

He sat back again in his chair. 'Okay. I'm listening.' And at last, he knew, he was.

She took a deep, deep breath.

'I'm going to Australia, Bill.'

'Another holiday? Is everything all right with Liv . . . ?'

'Liv's fine. No. Not a holiday. I'm going to go . . . and I'm going to stay.'

'For ever?'

'I don't think in terms of for ever any more, Bill. I can't. That's stopped. I'm going for now.'

Bill couldn't immediately digest this information. Maggie leant forward.

'I need to take Stan, Bill. I need you to let me take Stan.'

Bill pictured Stan's face.

'Aly?'

'Aly wants to come, just until she takes up her place at

Imperial. If she gets the results she needs. I think she will. She worked really hard. She'd be back in September, October maybe.'

'But not you?'

'I don't think so. No.'

'Stan's so settled. He's been so much happier.'

'I know. He has. But I've found this amazing place in Sydney. A great school.'

'Christ, Maggie.'

'I know. I know it's a lot.'

'Seems like you've been planning this for ages. You're just telling me now?'

'Not for ages.'

'When?'

'When I was over for Liv's wedding at Easter, I started to think about it.'

'Was it her idea?' He didn't mean to sound hostile.

'No! No, Bill. It was mine.'

'Why?'

'Because I can't do it here.'

'Do what?'

'I can't start again. Not in this house. Not in London.'

'I understand about the house. But Australia. It's so far away . . .'

'I know it is. I know what I'm asking, Bill. Believe me, I know. But I'm asking something else too. I'm asking you to let me do this. Let me go.'

He didn't say anything.

Maggie needed to make him understand.

'Listen to me. I was wrong, okay. I did it wrong. I thought I was dealing with my feelings differently. But I wasn't dealing with them at all. I wasn't coping. I was – it was like I was dead too. I was wrong.'

Bill shook his head. 'There's no wrong or right . . .'

'Maybe not. But look at us now. You're so far ahead of where I am. You let yourself feel it all, Bill. You never switched any of it off. Do you know, when you went back to Thailand the second time – I almost hated you for it?'

'Because I left you behind.'

Now she shook her head vigorously. 'No. No. That's not it. You've always thought that, and maybe I let you feel that, and that was wrong too. It was because you could face it. You were strong enough to let it all hit you.'

'I didn't feel strong.'

'But you were. You ran at it. I ran from it.'

'We both did what we did, Maggie.'

'And you were more honest about it.'

'I don't know.'

'I do. I was so bloody rude and dismissive of what you were doing when you were reading all that stuff about grief. When you started going to counselling. I thought it was non-sense. I didn't want to read about it. Or talk about it. I wanted to hug it to myself.'

'Maggie . . .'

She put her hand up. 'And I blame myself for all of it.'

'That's not right.'

'I do. I shut you out. I shut Aly out. I shut myself down.'

'It wasn't your fault.'

'It was. I should have listened.'

'So what changed?'

'Oh . . . I don't know where to start. Everything changed. This was my year of facing up, I think. Kate helped. She helped a lot. I never could have guessed how much difference a stranger could have made to our lives. If you'd told me six months ago, I'd have said you were crazy. Really. But having her with us, I could suddenly see more clearly. Like I was seeing us through her eyes, if that makes any sense. And what I saw was a mess . . .

'And you – Bill – you changed too. You met Carrie. You met someone. And as much as that hurt, it needed to happen. It made me realize we weren't going to be getting back together.'

'Did you think we were?'

'While I thought we were apart just because of Jake, I did, yes. I suppose I did. But it wasn't just because of Jake, was it? Not if we're honest. Jake put us under a microscope. Losing him put us under inhuman strain. So many marriages don't survive that kind of stress. Much less stress, for that matter.

'But it wasn't just that. It feels like it's not fair to Jake to keep believing that was why. There were cracks there already. We were different. With each other and with the world.'

'What do you mean?'

Maggie shrugged.

'We were just kids, Bill, when we started. You know – just like I don't have an answer for you when you ask me whether we'd still be together if Jake hadn't died, I can't honestly give you an answer to the question whether we'd ever have been together – married together, I mean – if Jake hadn't been born.'

'Wow.'

'Don't say it like that. Be honest with yourself. Think about it. That's what I've done. If Jake hadn't been born – I mean if I hadn't got pregnant when I did, and you hadn't married me when you did because he was coming . . .'

'I loved you desperately.'

She put her hand on his. 'And I loved you desperately too. And I don't know the answer to the question – not for sure. I just wonder . . .'

'You think we wouldn't have ended up together.'

'I think we *might* not. That's all I'm saying. You'd have come home and gone to university. I'd have stayed and kept swimming. We'd have tried to make it work, I expect – letters and phone calls and visits. And maybe it would have done. But maybe we'd have grown apart. Like we did, in fact, even when we were living in the same house . . .'

'Don't make a lie of the last twenty years, Maggie. Please don't do that.'

'That's not what I mean to do, Bill. Honestly. We have loved each other well. We had three beautiful children and we made a life together and we tried.'

'Did you love me, all that time?'

'Of course I did.'

'Because I loved you.'

'I know.'

For a moment they were both quiet. They both sensed that it didn't matter. Unravelling the past, painstakingly and painfully, wasn't where either of their energies should lie now. There was no conclusion to draw. No right or wrong answer. Only where they both found themselves now. Bill knew that he would let her go to Australia with Stan, though he would miss his boy more than he felt he could bear maybe – but probably not, since he already knew what he could bear, and it was more, much more, than this.

'And now you love Carrie.'

'Yes.'

'And all I know, sitting here with you now, whatever went before, is that hearing you say that doesn't kill me. It doesn't kill me, Bill. It's a surface wound, and I know now that it's going to heal.'

Bill came round for spaghetti bolognese a few nights later, and they talked to the kids about Australia and about

444

Jemima together. It was the most normal and close they had been as a family in no one remembered how long, and the irony of that was lost on no one, except perhaps Stan, whose brain moved at its usual million miles an hour in all directions. Aly already knew, of course. But Stan needed to hear it from both of them. He needed to hear from Bill, and see on his face, that it was okay for him to go. He was easy to reassure. He accepted everything at face value, which was his gift.

Kate was there with them – a part of the conversation. It didn't feel right for her not to be, not any more, not even to Bill, who had come to understand how much she had meant to his family in these last few months. How much she had done for them.

He helped her clear the table, while Aly got ready to meet her mates at the pub and tell them what was happening, now that it was official, and Maggie tucked Stan into bed. He stacked the dishwasher like he always had, more methodical and organized than Maggie had ever been – all the knives and forks together and facing the same way in the cutlery section at the top, while Kate wiped the table mats and cleared away the Parmesan cheese sprinkled liberally around Stan's place.

'I'm grateful to you, Kate, for what you've done. I want you to know that.'

'I haven't done so much.'

'I think you know as well as I do that isn't true.' Bill smiled. 'You've done things I'd tried so hard and not been able to . . .'

'I love them all.' Kate stated it simply and quietly, and Bill knew that he believed her.

Upstairs, afterwards, once she'd washed her face clean of make-up and moisturized and brushed her hair and put on

Chapter Forty-Five

They kept Jemima in for a few days in the end, just to make sure. She was a 36-weeker and a decent weight, but she had a touch of jaundice and they wanted to make sure she took to feeding okay, and put on a few ounces, before they let her go home. Bill got Carrie a private room, so she could be near her, and he went back and forth, trying to be there as much as he could and also getting the flat ready for their imminent release. Carrie was tired – exhausted – and frustrated by trying to feed Jemima, who had what the midwife called a 'lazy suckle', and to express milk between times. She'd needed a few stitches after Jemima was born, and the tear didn't heal as straightforwardly as it might and it was sore. Bill admired her stoicism now as he had during labour; she hardly complained. She was wonderfully, quietly sleepily happy, despite the problems, and spent hours wrapped in a white dressing gown, her hair loose across her shoulders, sitting with Jemima on her shoulder, rocking gently and whispering to her. They were incredibly beautiful to him in those moments, the two of them, and each time he caught them that way a wave of tenderness and a peculiar, and unfamiliar, sense of well-being washed over him.

'I didn't understand it before.' Carrie was holding Jemima, who was asleep in a pink blanket, snuffling gently. Carrie didn't look up as she spoke – she just stared down at the child in her lap.

'Understand what?'

'How this love feels. I mean, I've felt all kinds of love in my life. I thought I understood it. And maybe that's the wrong word – you can understand the love a parent has for a child, I guess, but you can't feel it, you can't appreciate the breadth and depth and force of it, can you, until you have your own child . . .'

'I suppose not.'

'And I'm so sorry, Bill. I'm so sorry about Jake. Sorrier than I've been before . . .' Now Carrie was crying.

'Sssh. Don't. Don't cry.' He stroked her beautiful face. 'It's okay. It's going to be okay.'

It was a Wednesday when Bill eventually drove to collect them with the new car seat fixed securely in the back seat. He couldn't believe how all things baby had changed since Stan. It was all more high tech. The young girl from the baby warehouse – a cavernous behemoth of a shop on the South Circular, where he'd felt utterly bewildered – had shown him how to click it in and out of its station, which was fixed permanently in the back seat. When Jake had come home from the hospital, they'd brought him in the back of a black taxi in a hand-me-down seat his mother had bought for them at an NCT sale. Jemima's was brand new – a smart black and hot-pink affair, with a matching pushchair frame. When the car seat was clicked into that, she'd sit high up, facing forwards or backwards at the flick of a switch. The girl assured him it was simple to use, although he wasn't convinced.

She'd been a month early, and she'd still caught them unawares, as ridiculous as that sounded. The baby warehouse had also provided dozens of newborn nappies and plastic paraphernalia he knew he should remember the function of but didn't, in his sleep-deprived, euphoric fog. Bags of improbably small clothes, tiny scratch mittens and cardigans with buttons far too small for his big fingers to ever fasten. He sometimes marvelled that he'd done this all before – it seemed so alien.

Aly had delighted him by asking if she could help get the nursery (the second, sleek, minimalist bedroom in the Roehampton flat) ready. She'd come to the hospital the evening Maggie had told her – Bill thought Maggie must have driven her, though his wife didn't come in. Stan didn't like hospitals – he said he'd wait until the baby was home at Dad's place, although he'd sent a card with Aly, with felt-tip flowers and stars scrawled on it, and Jemima's name spelt with four 'm's.

Carrie had been sleeping when Aly arrived, so Bill had taken her down to the special care baby unit and watched her carefully wash her hands in the deep medical trough of a sink. With her arms bent at the elbow, hands held up, she looked like the doctor he knew she would one day be, and his heart swelled at the sight. Jemima was in the 'warm' room – the section of this ward reserved for the least-at-risk babies, and visitors – family members only – were allowed to hold her. She wasn't connected to any wires or monitors.

'Oh my God, Dad – she's so tiny!' Aly exclaimed. 'I don't know if I even want to hold her – she looks so fragile . . .'

'You don't have to hold her . . .'

'I'm kidding, Dad. Hand her over . . .'

Bill leant into the crib and lifted Jemima out gently, her head easily fitting into the palm of one hand and her bottom the other. She curled like a question mark. Aly sat down in the rocker in the corner and held out her arms to receive her sister. Bill laid Jemima on her and stood back. For the first minute or so, she didn't say a word, or look at Bill, completely absorbed by the body she held. When she looked up at her father, there were tears in her eyes.

'She's perfect, Dad.'

And so are you, he thought. My big girl.

He didn't need to mention the connection – he could see from her face that Aly already felt it. This *was* her sister. And he was so grateful, then, again, to Maggie. To Aly. To Stan, with his felt-tip greeting. To Carrie, sleeping down the hall, knowing that he was here with his other daughter and wanting that to happen. He was going to be allowed to have this bigger, more complex, blended family. And in that moment, standing watching his two daughters together, he couldn't believe his luck.

Aly had sent him to B&Q, where he felt infinitely more at home than he did in the baby warehouse, with a list of paint colours from the exhaustive Farrow and Ball colour chart she'd always loved. While he was gone, she sketched out in pencil a simple design on the far wall of what would be Jemima's room – large, graphic flowers with rounded petals and leaves. For the remaining three days that the hospital kept Jemima and Carrie, she worked alone in the room, refusing to show Bill her progress. Bill and Stan assembled the white cot and changing table, Stan studying the instructions and Bill deciphering Stan's instructions, and left them standing in the living room, along with the bags of clothes Bill had bought.

The day he went to collect his girls, Aly finally let him in to the second bedroom. She'd worked long after he'd slunk off to sleep the previous night, and she looked exhausted but triumphant as she opened the door with a theatrical flourish and a 'Ta-dah!'

And she'd done something beautiful. Bill was amazed. She had Maggie's creative knack. The nursery was like an exotic fairytale garden, blooms painted all around it at different heights and in different sizes, all in a muted, almost pastel palate that was restful and pretty. On one wall, she'd written

Jemima's name in coral-pink letters about twelve inches high, and on the opposite wall, she'd painted several evenly spaced frames made up of tiny multi-coloured flowers, each a little larger than eight by ten inches. 'They're for photographs,' she explained. 'When you've had some taken. And for this . . . Mum's present.' From behind her back, she pulled out a white shadow box frame, with a flax-coloured linen backing on to which Maggie had pinned a note written in her distinctive handwriting: 'For new memories, with my love to you all. X'

'We all had one – remember? You have to put her little hospital bracelet in it, a photo of the three of you, a copy of her birth certificate, stuff like that . . .'

He didn't know if he could. The shadow boxes were such a part of the fabric of the Chiswick house and of his family with Maggie. He took the box from Aly and laid it carefully on the carpet, leaning against the freshly painted wall, his throat full of emotion.

'It's stunning.'

'Not very minimalist, I'm afraid. I don't think babies are into clean lines. Apparently they're into black and white, but that seemed like a dull old way to decorate a baby's room. So I went for colour . . .'

'I don't know what to say, Aly.'

'Say thank you. It's my gift. For you and Carrie, but mostly for Jemima.'

He pulled his daughter to him and squeezed her hard, murmuring his thanks into her hair.

'And then get the furniture in here quick, because you've got to go . . .'

'Will you stay and wait for me to bring them home? I'd love you to show Carrie what you did . . .'

'No way. That's for you and Carrie, Dad. I don't belong at

that moment – when you bring your new baby home for the first time . . .'

'How did you get to be so wise?'

She looked at him and her face answered the question. She didn't need to say anything out loud.

He knew she was right. He hoped she'd be there, with him and Carrie and the baby, often. But she was right about right now.

'You'll come soon, though . . . You'll come often – before you leave?'

'Course I will. Don't get all soppy on me, Dad. You've got things to do . . .'

He took her lovely face in both his hands and kissed her.

'I love you, Aly Barrett.'

Bill took Stan to Stamford Bridge, to say goodbye to him. He couldn't really concentrate on the game, though Chelsea scored early and Stan was exultant. At half-time, he turned to him, wondering if it would be possible to get his full attention now, even when there was no one on the pitch.

'Stan?'

'Yes, Dad.'

'I'm going to miss you, when you go to Australia. You know that, don't you?'

'Sure. I'll miss you too, Dad. You know that, right?' Stan was mimicking his father but his face was sincere, his big eyes wide.

'But you know that I'm not far away.'

Stan snorted. 'Twenty-four hours . . .'

'I don't mean that – not physically. Although I could jump on a plane any time I wanted. Or you wanted . . . I mean there's the phone and email, and we can Skype and even write actual letters . . . I mean there are lots of ways for you and me to stay close. And I want us to use them. Okay? I never want you to forget, while you're gone. That I'm thinking about you and loving you and that I'm here for you. Always. If you need me . . .'

Stan wasn't really concentrating. His eyes were darting about the crowd, staring with a childish intensity at people coming and going from their seats.

'You listening, buddy?'

'Sure, Dad. I'm going to email you every day. Can I get Facebook? Then I could post every day. Put pictures up and stuff . . .'

'We'll talk about that, Stan.' Over his dead body, Bill thought. The idea of Stan with unfettered access to the internet in that way sent chills down his spine, and he knew Maggie felt the same way. 'But email, yes.'

'Right. An email a day . . .'

Bill didn't believe that for a moment. Stan was a whirlwind. But he nodded and smiled.

Now Stan didn't even look at him as he spoke. 'And you can come and visit us, right, Dad? I'd love that. We can go to Scott's family's farm. Yeah . . . You'd love that, wouldn't you?'

Bill didn't know how to answer. But Stan turned to him and held his gaze. 'I'll show you how to milk one of the cows. I got pretty good at it by the end. I'll show you . . .'

He smoothed Stan's already smooth pelt of hair back from his forehead.

'That'd be great, Stan. Great.'

That was all Stan needed. He turned back to whatever or whoever he'd been watching before, checking his watch every thirty seconds to see when his beloved players would be back on the pitch. Bill watched his darting glance, and his ever-turning head, and felt a huge lump in his throat.

*

The plans came together fast, then. Kate would stay in the house for a few days. She'd hold the keys and come in every couple of weeks to deal with the post and make sure everything was all right. A cleaning company Bill worked with would come in once a month to deal with the cobwebs and the dust, and the firm of gardeners who had always dealt with the lawns and beds in the back would continue to do so. It wasn't a long-term solution, but everyone involved knew and accepted that, at this point, no one was dealing in long-term solutions. This was what was happening now. Bill wasn't worried, he said. The house could sit empty as long as Maggie was gone. It was Maggie's house now – not his.

Kate could have stayed in it, Maggie said so – but she knew the house would feel odd without the rest of them there. She'd go back to Sevenoaks, and the thought didn't frighten her so much now. Because now everything was different. This had become a second home for her, more quickly than she would ever have thought it could. Aly and Stan and Maggie were a second family. She felt very certain that the connection they had made wasn't ephemeral. People who needed things from each other as badly as all of them had needed things didn't have time to waste. They had to get straight to it. Aly would feel even more Kate's over the coming months, and maybe even years. She imagined weekend visits, Aly laden with loads of laundry and a vast appetite. Aly sitting at the round kitchen table she and Philip had eaten breakfast at, eating cake and talking about the course, and the boys and the nights out.

Aly and Kate were watching the local part of the ten o'clock news. Kate could see Aly was dog tired, though she wasn't sure why – she was on holiday. Maybe it was the cumulative effect of the weeks and months of exams and studying . . . all that pressure. The two of them had sat, not really watching but not quite having the energy or the will to get up and go to bed, for the last forty-five minutes really. Now Aly sat forward and something in her hair caught the light.

'You've got paint in your hair!'

Aly pulled a strand forward and examined it closely. 'Have I?'

'Here . . .' Kate touched another part of Aly's head. 'It's a pretty colour.'

Aly stood up and went over to the mirror, peering at herself. 'Yeah. Cook's Blue, I think that one is.'

'It's lovely. What are you up to?'

'Up to?'

'What are you painting? I haven't noticed an easel anywhere. And when I put your laundry in your room this afternoon, it was the same colour it's always been. So you're painting somewhere else . . . Are you the new Banksy?'

Aly turned and smiled shyly. 'I'm painting my little sister's nursery.'

'Really?'

Aly pulled a notebook out of her bag and slid back into the chair next to Kate. She pushed her mug away and opened the book to a page painted with sample stripes of perhaps a dozen different colours, with a pencil drawing. She pushed it towards Kate, who took it and looked at it carefully.

'Wow. That's really beautiful, Aly.'

'D'you think so? Thanks.' Aly flushed with pride and pleasure. 'I'm not sure it looks quite like this on the wall, but . . .'

'I bet it's gorgeous. Your dad must be pleased.'

Aly shrugged her narrow shoulders. 'He hasn't seen it yet. I won't let him in until it's finished.'

'He'll love it. Carrie too, I'm sure. Not to mention the baby . . . It's a lovely thing to do, Aly.'

'It's sort of a penance, really.'

'A penance?'

'For being a bit of a bitch to Carrie.'

'I didn't know you had been.'

'I was very clever and quiet about it.' Aly paused. 'But I was.'

Kate put her hand across Aly's. 'It can't have been easy . . .'

'Of course it hasn't. None of this has. For any of us. But none of it was Carrie's fault, was it? I was taking it out on her because it was easier than being mad at Dad for leaving, or Mum for letting him, or myself . . .'

'And now you're not mad any more?'

Aly nodded her head. 'New leaf. New me.'

Kate put an arm around her shoulder. 'Don't be too new a you. I'm rather keen on the old you . . .'

To her surprise, Aly put both arms around her and held on tightly in a hug full of sudden emotion. 'I'm going to miss you so much, Kate.'

'There, there.' Kate stroked Aly's back. 'It isn't for long.'

'But you're . . . you're . . . It's like – and I feel a bit soppy saying it – but it's like you're part of this family, part of my family.'

Kate's eyes filled with tears.

'I know you've got . . . I know there's Rebecca and Aiden . . .' Kate wished she did have them. She hoped. That was all she had, so far as the two of them were concerned. Hope.

'But . . .' Words failed Aly at that point, so she just clung on.

'I know, lovely girl. I know . . .'

'But do you?' Aly pulled back and looked earnestly into Kate's face. 'Do you know what you've done for us? Really?

You've done so much. You've done all this . . .' She held her arms up. 'I don't know how, but you made it start.'

Kate didn't know what to say. She wanted to tell Aly that she had done something extraordinary for her too – that she, only she, had brought the possibility of that relationship back to life – but it was too big; the feelings were too big for this moment. It would all keep. They had a future, and she would have her chance to say it.

'And I'll be so looking forward to coming back – to uni and everything, to Dad and Jemima, but to you too. Especially to you.'

After the last conversation Maggie and Bill had at the house, Maggie had gone, at last, to a solicitor. She'd told Bill she was going to.

'It's time. For the ostriches to take their heads out of the sand and look around. You need to be free,' she'd said, thinking of Carrie and Jemima. 'And so do I.' She'd asked him to do the same.

Bill had asked if they might consider going to the same firm, telling them there was no acrimony in this divorce, and Maggie had agreed, relieved. He didn't feel anything close to acrimony or resentment. The money mattered less than anything else. He'd give her the house and he'd pay for the kids, and he'd be more than generous with Maggie, for the rest of her life. There need be no questions about how important she had been in the growth of his successful business – no pettiness and no antagonistic toing and froing over who had worked harder during their marriage. Who had given more? They'd both given everything, for so long. She'd been more than pivotal. She'd never stopped working. The paperwork they'd both been dodging for a long time started to get done in the days before Maggie left and, like lots of things that summer, it didn't hurt as much as either of them had thought it would.

The day before they flew, Maggie asked Bill if he would go with her to Jake's grave. She asked almost apologetically, anxious that Carrie wouldn't mind. A subtle, almost imperceptible shift had taken place with Jemima's birth, and Maggie had started to defer to Carrie. A new order existed, without anyone having to say so.

But how could Carrie mind? When Bill asked her, or told her – he wasn't sure which, she was holding Jemima in the garden nursery Aly had painted, and which Carrie had loved, because it was pretty and more because Aly had done it. She closed her eyes and buried her nose in the side of the little girl's powdery, soft neck, feeling her wriggle in her arms, tiny fists raining fairy blows on her mother's cheek and head. Hormones swarmed. Jake had been Maggie's Jemima. The thought of what had happened to him, and what might happen to this little girl, was too enormous and too dreadful and too terrifying to be allowed into this flat, this nursery, this rocking chair where she held her child.

Jake was buried in the churchyard of the church where he, and indeed Bill before him, had been christened, out near the house Bill's mother had lived in when Maggie and Bill had first arrived from Australia. Maggie didn't like graveyards – the spooky feeling that you were walking over bodies. Or coffins. But she'd been an automaton when they'd got Jake's body back. And she remembered that there'd been some absurd thought process – at the time: it had been so complicated for Bill to bring him home, once he'd found him in the makeshift mortuary, that it seemed daft to cremate him. After all that trouble. It seemed ridiculous now. People had said she would need a grave to visit – a place to go to remember him and to think about him. Bill had seemed to want it, or at least to be too dazed to proffer an alternative. It was all a bit fuzzy. The people who'd said that couldn't have been people who had lost a child. Who were those people? The people with all the wisdom and experience and advice back then? She couldn't see their faces. You didn't need a special place. The love between a mother and her child was bigger and grander than that – it stretched across everything and seeped in everywhere. She remembered him and thought about him in every place she ever went. She didn't go to the graveyard often. That was where she felt him least, it sometimes seemed to her.

But still, it didn't feel right to go so far away, for who knew how long, without coming to see it. Bill drove, and they were quiet in the car. It was a beautiful day, the sun strong, but tempered by a light breeze. A cloudless, turquoise sky.

Jake's headstone was simple, light-coloured granite, squared cleanly at the corners:

Jake William Barrett

April 19th 1986 – December 26th 2004

Beloved son, brother and friend

Always with us

And he was. Everywhere. The grave to his left was covered in a gaudy display of silk flowers in colours never found in nature, piled so that you couldn't read the name of the person buried there – although Maggie knew by heart that it was a beloved wife and mother called Susan, who had died in her sixties exactly a month before Jake. She'd come once, in the spring of the first year – when she came mostly because she thought people expected her to – and seen a small crowd of people at the grave, crying and arranging the pots of flowers.

She'd gone away without 'seeing' Jake – their grief was too raw and too awful to be near.

To the right of Jake's grave, there was a small expanse of grass and a tree with one of those circular benches that curved around the trunk.

They sat on the bench, close but not touching. Maggie began to cry, gentle, quiet tears, and Bill took her hand. He raised it to his cheek and held it there for a moment. When she looked at him, she saw that he was noiselessly crying too, and in another moment her hand was wet with his tears. For a long time, they didn't speak. Their living children would always bind them together – for the rest of their lives. But this dead child – their first-born – he tied them with stronger ropes. They had known what it was like both to love him and to lose him.

Eventually, Maggie spoke.

'Do you think he needs flowers? Like Susan?'

'I think he'd think what we've given him is nice.'

'I think he'd have told us to cremate him. Or stick him under a tree in a willow basket. That boy was not into church, as I remember. More spiritual than religious.'

'And more practical than spiritual, sometimes. He'd want us to donate his organs first. Do you remember that card he carried – after they had some talk in assembly or something? He was rabid about it, do you remember?'

Maggie nodded, smiling. 'He was so cross that they'd still have to get our permission, while he was a child, even though he had the card.'

'That's right.' Bill remembered a militant young Jake, sur-prisingly eloquent. 'He made us all get one.'

'So we got the whole thing wrong, then?' As if they'd had any choice.

'Maybe. But since we didn't cremate him and we couldn't

donate his organs, I think he'd agree with us about the neon-blue and yellow flowers.'

'And you don't think he'd feel . . . neglected? I hardly ever come. I don't think you do much more often . . .'

'I don't. I don't like it here.'

She looked at him sharply. 'Me neither. It never feels to me like Jake is here.'

'I know what you mean. Me neither. I have a kid's hard hat hanging behind the door at the office – the one he used to wear on site – that makes me think of him more than I can when I'm here.'

'And songs – that just come on the radio. Not songs you choose. Just . . . Jake songs.' Sometimes, in the car, a song would come on and she would be racked by sudden sobs so strong she'd have to pull the car over and wait for them to pass. As if Jake had had a soundtrack, and when you played a part of it, he was there, in your field of vision, acting out his life. Not a haunting, but a memory so vivid that you could almost reach out and touch him, smell him.

'Exactly.' She wondered if songs on the radio ever made Bill have to pull over in the car.

'You never said that to me before. I always thought this was what you wanted.'

'I didn't know what I wanted then, Maggie.'

They stayed for an hour or so, sitting in the dappled shade of the tree, talking about their son. Life is a strange, strange thing, Maggie thought. We are going through a divorce, I am about to move to the other side of the world, and Bill has just had a child with another woman, someone he has fallen in love with. Our family is shattered. But sitting here, we're closer than we've been in – God knows how long.

'It's never going to go away, is it? This feeling.'

'No. Not completely. We've been changed.'

'But it's going to recede.'

'Yes.'

'For the longest time, I longed for that. And now I'm frightened of that. Does it make any sense to you?'

'All kinds of sense. It's like forgetting him.'

'How could we?'

'We couldn't and we won't. We're just going to live.'

'That's what he'd want.'

And it was, they both knew. And it wasn't so frightening any more.

And in the end, it was Bill who drove the three of them to Heathrow, parked the car in the short stay at Terminal Four and helped them wheel the two trolleys heaving with suitcases, too heavy even for Stan to push on his own, into the huge departures hall.

Kate had waved them off from the steps of the Chiswick house. Each one of them in turn had clung to her, and she to them, holding tight. He hadn't heard what Kate had said to Maggie, but it had made Maggie's eyes fill with tears, and she had held Kate's face in her hands and said something back and a look of pure understanding and affection had passed between the two women. He hardly knew Kate, but he was grateful to her. Stan held on for dear life, eyes squeezed shut, and she stroked his cheek. She'd gripped Aly's shoulders and kissed both cheeks. They laughed.

The timing, Kate thought later, was extraordinary. If it had happened that way in a film, you'd be irritated by how unlikely and implausible it was. But life could be that way.

Maggie, Aly and Stan had been gone barely an hour. They'd just about be getting to the front of the line at check-in, perhaps. As she'd closed the door of their home, Kate had hugged herself and tried to ward off an almost overwhelming feeling of desertion and loneliness that she didn't think she could bear. The house was still and quiet around her. Kate bent down and straightened an abandoned pair of Stan's trainers, a single tear running down the side of her nose and into her mouth as she bent. His feet grew so fast – these were too small but still perfectly good. She'd take them to Oxfam later. She sniffed hard and rubbed at her eye. Damn it, she wasn't going to cry. She wasn't going to let this feeling win. She wasn't going to start fading back into black and white. This wasn't goodbye.

Kate shook herself and went into the front room to switch on the radio, turning the dial hard to the right so that the music was really loud. She looked around. She started thumping the feather cushions from the giant sofa in time to the music. She loved Maggie and Aly and Stan, but she bloody hated this sofa. It looked like an unmade bed the moment anyone sat on it, and she was the only person who ever puffed the cushions back up. She bet Bill had done it, when he'd lived here. He wasn't an unmade-bed sofa kind of a guy. Thumping turned to punching, and it felt good. The next song was Aretha Franklin, and suddenly Kate was singing and dancing and thumping the cushions. She'd look like a crazy person to anyone passing on the street who happened to look up, but she didn't care. She was fighting.

She almost didn't hear the phone. The shrill rings eventually broke through the soul singer's demand for R-E-S-P-E-C-T, and she suddenly heard them and dropped the cushion she'd been pummelling. She knew it wasn't a forgotten passport, because Maggie had been holding them when she left, but maybe it was a last-minute instruction – maybe something had been left behind that needed to be posted . . .

'Hi.' She hadn't realized she was so breathless.

'Mum?' She'd expected it to be Maggie's voice. Maybe one of the kids. She hadn't expected this.

'Rebecca?' Kate slumped against the wall.

There was a long pause, and for a moment Kate thought she'd been cut off or that she'd hung up. But she could hear traffic noise, other voices speaking. Rebecca was still there.

'Are you all right?'

'I'm fine. Mum. Mum. I know what I said. About needing time, and everything.'

'Yes?' Kate held her breath. She scarcely dared hope.

'I don't need time. I need to see you.'

'Oh.' A sob caught in Kate's throat.

'And the thing is, Mum, I'm here.'

'Where?' Kate didn't immediately understand.

'I'm at the end of your road, I think. I don't know what I was thinking. I just, I woke up today, and I couldn't stop thinking that it was all so stupid. What happened between us. It shouldn't have done. That it was all so bloody ridiculous. And that I didn't need time. I needed you. And I just got on the tube. And I'm here.' She was laughing.

'Rebecca.' Kate's voice broke as she said her daughter's name.

'It's probably a really bad time or something. I should have called . . .'

'Can you see the post office?'

'It's just across the road.'

'Give me two minutes. Stay there, Rebecca. Stay right there . . .'

It was more like ninety seconds. Kate grabbed her key off the hall table, from in front of a picture of Jake, who would never again call Maggie, and ran, as fast as she could, as fast as she ever had towards her daughter.

*

Maggie – always in command – had always kept all five family passports in a battered old leather document holder her dad had given her. It had been a bit of a family joke – not trusting anyone else, even Bill, to keep the documents safe. With reason, to be fair: Bill had left his loose once, on a security conveyor belt, and it had become stuck in the mechanism for a few minutes – causing a bout of indignant sputtering and heavy sighs from the impatient travellers in the long line behind him. Bill remembered joking with Jake, before he left on the big trip, that he'd probably lose it the first chance he got, having never had to look after it before. He'd taken a photocopy of each page, and written down all the numbers, anticipating a panicked phone call from the other side of the world and endless conversations with a far-flung embassy. There was no room for the leather pouch in Jake's rucksack, though Maggie had offered it to him. He'd tucked the passport into a front pocket that he'd bought a small padlock for. They'd never found it – the passport or the padlocked rucksack – after the wave had washed away the contents of the shack he and the boys had been sleeping in. So then there'd been four passports.

Now she had just three passports to look after – and yet it was still his family, standing, unconsciously, in height order at the check-in desk, answering the routine security questions, Stan as serious as a heretic in the Spanish Inquisition ('What do you mean, could someone have interfered with my case?'). They always would be. At home, waiting for him, and making this next part bearable, was his new family.

They were early, and yet there was nothing for it but to go through passport control, into the snaking line for the security check. Bill eyed up the café on the corner and for a moment contemplated asking them to come for a drink, but he knew there was no point, really, in prolonging this.

Stan and Aly hugged him as one, Aly leaning in above Stan's head. She drew back first – she would be home in a couple of months. He'd pick her up from this terminal, he'd already agreed. Stan held on much longer and much harder.

'Don't forget me, Dad,' he implored melodramatically.

'Don't be daft, Stan. He's your dad. Dads don't forget their children.' This was Aly, placating as always.

'No, we don't. We can't. I won't.' He kissed Stan hard.

Maggie was watching them, guilt etched on her face for the first time, although she had always known and understood what this would cost Bill. Aly took Stan by the shoulders, asking him to help her decant her lip gloss and his Rescue Remedy into the small plastic bags the security man was handing out. And Bill turned to Maggie.

'I hope it works out, Mags. I really do.'

She didn't speak, just bit her lip and nodded her head a little.

'You call me, you hear? If you need anything at all . . .'

They both knew she was making the kind of break, and he would be making the kind of life, where she wouldn't, couldn't keep doing that. But she nodded and smiled. 'Thanks.'

'I'll always love you, Maggie. You know that, don't you?'

'And I you.'

Suddenly, almost violently, he pulled her towards him, knocking the shoulder bag she was carrying so that it fell off her arm on to the ground. They held each other for a minute, as tightly as it was possible to hold another person, almost painfully tight, without any words at all. For that minute, they were unaware entirely of everything around them – in this airport building and in the world beyond each other. But reality lapped back at them eventually. Stan and Aly were watching. Other people were too – clustered in their own small groups, saying their own goodbyes. He stroked her curls and stepped consciously back from her.

'Be happy, Maggie.'

He blew kisses then, at Stan and Aly, standing a few feet further away, Stan waving his plastic bag of liquids enthusiastically, and then backed away, two, three, four steps, before he turned, so that they wouldn't see his tears, and walked fast towards the door, his right hand held aloft in a wave.

Maggie watched him for a few seconds, with the old familiar ache in her chest and sternum. This was it.

Then she turned, picked the bag up off the floor and scooped her children up, one under each arm, leading them towards the gruff-looking passport inspector and their futures . . .

Acknowledgements

I am, as ever, incredibly grateful to my editor, Mari Evans, and to everyone else at Penguin, to my agent Jonathan Lloyd, and all at Curtis Brown, to my careful copy-editor and eagle-eyed proofreaders, and to my publicist, Annabel Robinson. This book is better because all of you have had a hand in it, and the comfort of having such great teams of people behind me is invaluable, and special.

Thank you, David, Tallulah and Ottilie Young, and David and Sandy Noble. I know you all know what for.

And finally, I have written a fictional story about an event which actually happened and I felt the responsibility that brings. I have to acknowledge that many, many people had direct experience of the 2004 tsunami and its aftermath, and that for some of them, my imagined sorrows reflect very real ones. If I have made mistakes in telling my story, I apologize.

Read an extract of

Things
I want my
Daughters
to
Know

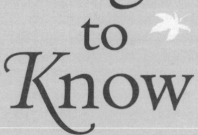

Elizabeth Noble

June 12th

Dear All of You,

Despite my controlling streak, there aren't too many rules, so far as the funeral goes. Do it as soon as you can, won't you? Good to get it over with. Lisa knows about the music, if you can bear to go with what I've chosen. We've talked about the committal – you know I only want you lot there, and you know which coffin, and which fabulous outfit. I'd like this poem – which, by the way, I love. Thank God for insomnia and the internet – I'd never have found it otherwise, and you'd be stuck reading something yucky. It should be read by whoever thinks they can do it without crying, because that is my biggest rule. No crying, please. If you can manage it. Oh, and no black. Wear the brightest thing you can find in your wardrobe. Both are clichés, I know, but better the colourful one than the sombre. And try and make the sun shine (although I recognize that this last one might be outside of your control). I'm not saying anything mushy in this letter – strictly business – but I daresay there will be other letters. I have other things to say, she says ominously – if I last long enough to write them . . . (don't you just love terminal illness humour?).

I'm sorry you all have to do this; I really am.

So, never ever-ending love, as always . . .

Mum

Do not stand at my grave and weep
I am not there, I do not sleep
I am a thousand winds that blow
I am the diamond light on snow
I am the sunlight on the ripened grain
I am the gently falling autumn rain

When you wake in the morning hush
I am the swift uplighting rush
Of quiet birds in circling flight
I am the soft starlight at night
Do not stand at my grave and cry
I am not there, I did not die.

(Isn't that perfect for a funeral in a field?!)

Lisa

Lisa lay back gingerly in her deep aromatherapy bubble bath and looked at the 8" x 10" picture she had taken from the top of the piano downstairs and brought up there with her. She'd propped it behind the taps so that she could see it clearly from where she lay in the steamy water, and now she was trying not to splash it. It was a black-and-white shot of her mother, Barbara and it was taken on her sister Jennifer's wedding day, eight years earlier. Mum looked desperately glamorous, with her salon-fresh hair and artfully artless outfit. No mother-of-the-bride peach suit with matching hat for her. Lisa remembered the hat – three feet wide, floppy brimmed espresso coloured straw. No one sitting in the four pews behind her saw a thing of the ceremony. You couldn't see why, and she no longer remembered, but Mum was laughing her big, loud laugh. Her head was thrown back, the ungainly hat long abandoned, the auburn waves of her hair blown messily across her face by the summer breeze. Her large, expressive mouth was open and wide, so that you could see a filling on the top row of her teeth, and her hazel eyes had almost disappeared into the crinkles of her face. It was an especially great picture of her mother, although Barbara had always been photogenic. Lisa could almost hear it when she looked at the picture, deep and throaty, and so, so alive. It was Mum's raucous laugh she would miss the most – that, and the smell of Fracas.

She thought about the last big belly laugh they had

shared. It was the day Lisa had helped her mother plan her own funeral. She couldn't bear to do it with Mark, she had said. He would keep crying, and she so badly didn't want to cry. She was almost obsessed by not crying, towards the end. Hannah was too young, obviously. Amanda wasn't around. Off doing whatever Amanda was doing right now. And Jennifer ... well, Jenny Wren wasn't exactly the person that sprang to mind for the task, she said, making a stupid grimacing face and rolling her eyes. No, she wasn't – Lisa could see that. Part of her was horrified, and part flattered, of course.

She hadn't expected it to be hilarious, but now that she thought about it, she didn't know why not. The two of them had done a great deal of laughing together, through all of Lisa's life. Mum had been quite well that week. She was thin, and a bit of a funny colour – a sort of translucent pale lavender – but she was still mobile, and almost energetic. She'd had all these brochures and computer printouts spread across the dining-room table. Coffins, hearses, wreaths ... She always said life was a retail opportunity, but now, obviously, so was death. The last great party you got to go to, they said, if you planned it right. It was macabre and weird for about the first twenty minutes, and then they both just got silly, because that made it easier. Mum had even got prices for those horse-drawn affairs – but they decided that people weren't really ready for a purple crushed velvet, Kray-style East End send-off. She'd planned the clothes, though. She wanted to wear her Millennium Eve party dress, although it was a bit big for her right now. Which was a minor cause for celebration, and almost the justification for an open-coffin ceremony, since she'd eaten cabbage soup for a week and had one of those ridiculous lymphatic wrap things in order to squeeze into it on December 31st, 1999, and it hadn't been near her since January 1st, 2000, when the wrap wore off and all the cellulite flooded back. Lisa remembered the dress – it was emerald green, lithe and silky, and her mum had looked amazing in it. The kind of good that almost makes adult daughters a little bit resentful. There'd been an underwear issue – she'd talked Mum into the first and last thong of her life, convincing her it was the only acceptable option under the dress bar going commando. Mum had rung, on New Year's Day, to say it was so uncomfortable she'd taken it off after about an hour and seen the New Year in knickerless – with a Magistrate and a headmaster at the table, if you please. More laughing.

'Isn't that a bit of a waste of a perfectly lovely Ben de Lisi? I was hoping I might have that,' she had joked. Actually joked. Jennifer would have been fulminating. 'Too bad,' said her mum, winking. 'There'll be a bit of money. Use it to buy one of your own.'

What really did them in was the music. Mum said she couldn't bear to have something miserable – no 'Abide With Me' ('no one can ever make the high notes – you can always hear the tear in their voice'); no 'Nearer My God to Thee' ('Too *Titanic.*') 'Lord of the Dance' was nixed because it reminded her of Michael Flatley, and who the hell wanted to think of that daft prancer as they were shuffling off their mortal coil? And 'He's Got the Whole World' was far too tambourine-y. She'd got a fondness for 'Jerusalem', which was more wedding than funeral, but who cared? And definitely, definitely 'Be Thou My Vision', although preferably the Van Morrison version, piped in, even if it sounded tinny in the high-ceilinged church. She had also surfed the net for a website recommending popular non-religious music choices, however, and it was this list that finally had them shedding tears of mirth. Frank Sinatra's 'My Way': 'As if dying at 60 would ever be *my* way!' Gloria Gaynor's 'Never Can Say Goodbye': 'Well, I suppose it's more appropriate than "I Will Survive,"' she spat out through the chortles, 'but who the hell *are* these people, and why have I never been invited to one of their funerals?' Imagining the coffin being carried out to the saccharine strains of Doris Day's 'Que Sera Sera' made their ribs hurt, and the idea of quietly listening to Vera Lynn's 'We'll Meet Again' sounded like the funniest thing ever to the pair of them. When they'd regained their breath and dried their wet faces, they'd settled on Louis Armstrong's 'Wonderful World'. But the moment her mum nodded decisively and wrote it down on the A4 pad in her round, girlish handwriting, Lisa heard it playing in her head, imagined the scene and had to turn her face away so her mum didn't identify the fresh tears she refused to see.

Now that day – the day they had meticulously planned, but that, somehow, found her so very unprepared, was here. Van Morrison and Louis Armstrong were lined up in the portable CD player and the organist had his sheet music open at 'Jerusalem'. Just that now it wasn't funny any more. Lisa sank down into the hot water so that it splashed around her nostrils and squeezed her eyes shut. If only, if only, if only Andy was here.

Jennifer

Stephen said he was parking the car, but he'd done that. The driveway was full: Mark's car, and Mum's Polo. Lisa's VW beetle – she'd said, when they'd spoken the previous morning, that she was going to stay the night. So he'd driven a little down the street and expertly parallel parked. She could see him, for God's sake. He'd switched off the ignition and wound the window down a little. Now he'd picked up his BlackBerry and was staring at it intently. Today was terribly inconvenient for him. She'd gotten that message. He had these clients, passing through London on some trip from somewhere. They'd only had today to see him; they were important. He'd made sure she understood that. Not more important than her, obviously, since he was here, and not there but it was close. And he hadn't been gracious about it. She hadn't needed to know, after all, anything about any clients, or meetings, or power lunches. She was burying her mother today. It shouldn't have mattered. He was her husband. Everything about his demeanour, all the way here, had been irritated. The reception got fuzzy on the radio. He'd switched if off viciously. The line for a coffee at the service station was too long. He'd sighed dramatically, and bought a Coke. And now it was too hot. He'd hung the jacket of his black suit on the hook of the back passenger door, unbuttoned the neck of his shirt and loosened the black knitted tie. She stood at the end of the driveway for a few minutes, realizing she was too embarrassed to go into the house without him. They should be together. He should *want* to be with her, shouldn't he, today of all days?

Stephen hated funerals. He'd confessed to her, once,

long ago, that coffins terrified him. He couldn't stop thinking about the body inside. Wondering how it looked, how it smelt, how it would feel to the touch. He remembered losing it completely, when he was about 8 years old, at his grandfather's funeral – having to be taken out of the crematorium, screaming.

He was right about the weather, at least. It was too sunny for this. It was what Mum would have wanted, but to Jennifer it seemed wrong. It was like the day those two planes flew into the World Trade Center. As they made their final descent into hell the sky behind them was too impossibly, perfectly blue. It wasn't the right backdrop. She wanted a slate-grey sky and drizzle; she wanted to shiver with the chill. Not this beautiful day, not today.

The door opened and Mark stood on the doorstep. 'Jen?' Jennifer shuffled from one foot to the other, feeling like she'd been caught out. She waved and gestured towards Stephen. 'We'll be there in a minute. Stephen's just . . .' but Mark was coming towards her. He wasn't dressed – not for the funeral. He had on a pair of linen shorts and a scruffy pink T-shirt, and he was barefoot. He didn't speak when he got to her, just opened his arms and drew her into a tight embrace. Jennifer felt herself stiffen momentarily, then relax and lean into the man who had been her stepfather for the last sixteen years. God knows she needed the hug.

When he drew back, he put his hands on either cheek and looked intently into her face. He smelt of soap and coffee. 'How are you doing?'

'I'm okay. You?'

'I'm trying.' He shrugged his shoulders. 'She got the weather she ordered, hey?' Jennifer nodded, and smiled weakly.

Mark looked behind her, at Stephen. 'He coming in?'

'He's just got to check a few things . . . There's a lot going on, you know, at work, and . . .'

Mark took her hand and the squeeze he gave it said 'Don't explain him, don't defend him.' Out loud, he just said, 'Don't worry, no hurry. Amanda's not here yet. Show doesn't start for a couple of hours. Come on in – I've got some coffee going, and muffins and croissants . . .' Jennifer gave the back of Stephen's head one more sad, reproachful glance, and went into the house with Mark.

Hannah

Hannah stared at her face in the mirror and wondered whether it was okay to wear mascara. She couldn't wear it to school, but she could at the weekends and on holidays. To Church? There'd never been a rule that she'd known of. Maybe if she wore it she wouldn't cry, because she'd know that then it would run. Maybe wearing it would help her not do it.

'No one was with her when she died.' That was a line from *Charlotte's Web*. It had been one of her favourite books when she was young. And that was one of her best bits, the line when Charlotte the spider had finished her web-making, egg-laying mission, and gently slipped away into oblivion. 'No one was with her when she died.' It was so deliciously sad. You could revel in it, in the small dry ache it caused at the back of your throat and the little sting in your ribs. When she was younger, Hannah liked to feel sad, so long as it was 'artificial' sad; that was what she called it when the sadness was about something that wasn't real. Like when Leonardo

DiCaprio slips beneath the icy waves at the end of *Titanic*, with Kate Winslet hoarsely whispering her promise never to forget him. Or when Charlotte died. Well, this was different. This sad was real; the ache wasn't fun. Trying not to cry was a huge effort, one she made all the time, all day, until she got into bed at night, and didn't have to try not to any more. Especially today. They'd all promised that they wouldn't. They'd promised Mum, although Hannah didn't think it was fair of her to ask for that. Still, none of it was fair, was it? She tried not to think about Charlotte anymore. Unhelpful bloody spider! There'd been loads of people around when Mum died, anyway. She'd died in a crowd scene. All of them there, around that horrible high hospital bed they'd brought in, so incongruous in the pretty room. Her sisters, Jen and Lisa . . . Dad. And the vicar, and the doctor – both more by accident than design, she thought. It made her think of a Philip Larkin poem she'd learnt at school – something about the priest and the doctor running across the fields in their long coats trying to figure out all the answers to all the questions. The doctor came every other day, checking up on Mum. The vicar came because Mum had asked for him, which was slightly odd, since Hannah only really ever remembered seeing him before this year on Christmas morning, once every three hundred and sixty-five days, belting out 'O Little Town of Bethlehem', the tip of his nose perpetually bright red and dripping with a winter cold. She told Dad she was hedging her bets. Not in front of the vicar, of course. And even more people downstairs, Mum's friends, in and out on a rota, making tea that no one wanted to drink and sandwiches no one wanted to eat and taking phone calls no one else wanted to answer.

She decided against the mascara, and picked up the

hairbrush, running it through her long auburn hair. Mum's hair. Dad's hair was silvery above the ears, and still pretty dark on the top. That would have been okay too – the dark, not the silver. But she had Mum's hair. When she'd finished, she sat on the end of her bed, with her hands folded in her lap, squeezed tight together. And waited.

Jennifer didn't want coffee, but she took a mug for something to do with her hands, and wandered across the large living room. The house was immaculate. It was a great house for the summer. Mark had built it. Not with his own hands – he was an architect, and he'd designed it for him and Mum the year they married, just before Hannah was born. They'd bought a hideous bungalow with peeling, custard-yellow paint, on a lovely three-acre plot, and immediately knocked it down, even as the neighbours watched, open-mouthed, muttering to each other about how the elderly couple who had sold it to them had bothered to remove every picture hook and filled every crack in the place. It had taken six months to build the new place, and they'd lived in a caravan on the site the summer it went up. Jennifer remembered her mother standing on the steps of the van, pregnant with Hannah, offering cups of tea made on a camping stove. She remembered how obscene it had looked to her then. Jennifer had been 22. She hadn't lived at home since she was 18, and she felt like she barely knew Mark. It was all wrong – her mother, 45 years old, with her vast, fertile baby-belly. Living in this temporary squalor with a man ten years younger than she was. Jennifer had been embarrassed for her then, or for herself.

Now she stood staring at the garden out of the tall glass doors that ran the entire length of the back of the house downstairs and wondered whether she'd just been jealous. She'd never lived here; she'd never really been a part of the family that happened here, the happy, laughing life they'd had before Mum got ill. Each corner showed her a different memory. Baby Hannah, with her smooth, round arms and legs kicking contentedly on a plaid blanket under that apple tree. Her mother, kneeling at her beloved herb garden, tending the fragrant plants. Mark flipping burgers on the barbeque; Mum, radiant with happiness and contentment. She'd always been just a visitor.

Stephen loved the house. He'd spent hours, the first time he'd come, wandering around with Mark, looking at details Jennifer had never really taken in. His questions, and examinations, had gone way beyond flattery, although Mark was always happy to show it off. She knew he wanted something like it for himself, one day. They couldn't afford it now, of course. Their flat was a good start – right area, high ceilings, great light. It was modern and fashionable, all dark wenge wood and stainless steel. But it was nothing like this, and it had nothing to do with money. It just didn't have the heart.

Mark came and stood by her, gazing into the garden. 'Needs a damn good water. Everything's dying.' He didn't seem to realize what he had said.

She smiled at him. 'You've been busy. Cut yourself some slack.'

'She'd be cross.'

'No, she wouldn't.'

Mark smiled his half-smile at her, and she smiled back. 'Okay, maybe a bit cross.'

Then, 'Where's Hannah?'

'Upstairs. Lisa was having a bath – I think Hannah's in her room.'

'No Andy?'

'No. Haven't asked her about it. She came last night. We had a curry and too much red wine. But she hasn't mentioned him.'

Jennifer nodded. She wondered if she ought to offer to go and see Hannah. She didn't want to. 'How is Hannah doing?'

'She's quiet. She's been quiet for days. No crap music blaring out of her room. She hasn't been on the phone much to her mates, and no one's been round. I expect they'd like to come, some of them, but I don't think she's spoken to any of them. I'm not even sure she's told them, although they must know by now. She hasn't even watched *Coronation Street*, which has me *really* worried.' He was trying to sound lighthearted, but he was failing.

'It's early days, Mark. She's lost her mum. She's only 15.'

'I know. It's . . . it's hard. I'm trying, but I don't have a lot of juice left in my tank, you know? I know she needs me. But I need . . . I need Barbara. I need her to help me. And she's not here.'

Upstairs, someone knocked gently on Hannah's door.

'C'mon in.'

It was Lisa, still damp from the bath, wrapped in a bath sheet.

'You got any make-up, Hannah? I forgot mine. Can you believe it? Can I come in?'

Hannah nodded, and pointed to her dressing table. 'Not much. Some – mascara and lip gloss and stuff. You can borrow whatever you want.'

'Cheers.' Lisa closed the door again behind her, and let the towel fall to the ground. She was wearing a strapless bra, and she had a thong on. They were beige, with lace, and they looked expensive, and nice. Hannah felt shy, and Lisa saw her glance away.

'Excuse the blatant semi-nudity but I'm so hot. That bath was boiling, and it must be 90 degrees out there already. I should have had a cold shower, really.' She was pretty red, and her legs were blotchy. 'I forget you're not really used to sisters running around naked. Me and Jen did it all the time when we were younger.' That didn't sound like Jennifer. 'It's fine, really.' Lisa caught her sister's glance. 'Okay . . . not Jennifer. Just me. I ran around naked all the time when we were younger. Jen just tolerated it.'

Lisa sat down in front of the dressing table and started applying make-up, although Hannah didn't think she really needed it. She was dead pretty. Lisa's hair was much lighter than her own – strawberry blonde, with really light bits in it. And she had all these freckles, tiny ones, across her nose and cheeks. But her lashes and eyebrows were surprisingly dark (maybe she did something to them?), above eyes that were more green than hazel most of the time, and almond shaped. Hannah didn't think Lisa had had spots when she was young – if she had, there was no photographic evidence in the albums Mum kept. She was slim and tall, with great skin and hair that just looked nice, without you spending ages on it – the kind you could just put up in a ponytail, and the ponytail didn't make you look like you hadn't had time to wash it – it looked pretty and natural. Hannah felt a stab of envy and misery. She wasn't spotty, or fat, or ugly, or anything. She knew that much, at least. She just didn't feel comfortable in her own skin like Lisa seemed to. She wasn't easy like her sister was. She'd rather die than have anyone see her in her bra and knickers.

'What are you wearing?' she asked Lisa.

'Well . . . Mum really did a number on me with her "brights and primaries only" thing. I'm more of a black and beige girl, myself; neutrals all the way. I found something in the summer sales. Don't you hate how they have those in July – it's like summer's over before it even starts, don't you think? It's bright yellow. A bit Jackie O, I thought. A sundress, thank God! I doubtless look like a giant banana in it. But it fits the bill. You?'

'I've got this pink dress from last summer. I wore it to a wedding – my friend Amy's sister got married and she was allowed to invite one friend, and she took me. Mum got it for me, so I think she liked it. It's a bit sparkly, is all . . .' Hannah's voice tailed off.

Lisa looked at her in the mirror, through narrowed eyes. 'She'd love that even more,' she said, as gently as she could. She swivelled around on the stool.

'Hannah?'

Hannah stood up. 'Don't be nice to me, Lisa. You'll make me cry. Please don't, okay? Let's just get it over with; I just want to get it over with. Doesn't matter what we're wearing, does it? It's a stupid, stupid rule.'

Lisa nodded, and when she spoke again, she made her tone jokey. 'Well, you and Jennifer have that opinion in common, at least. She was bitching about it the other night on the phone. Said that Stephen would refuse to wear anything but black; said she was thinking about it. I said she could compromise – black dress, red shoes, you know. God knows what she'll be wearing when she turns up.'

'What about Amanda?'

'God knows if *she'll* even turn up . . .'

They smiled hopefully at each other. That was how Amanda was – you wouldn't exactly count on her in a crisis, although neither of them really doubted that she would be here today.

'Is someone coming with you?'

'No.' Lisa looked at her quizzically. Hannah shrugged. 'Didn't ask anyone. I don't really want anyone to come. How about you? Andy isn't coming?'

'No, he's not.'

'How come?'

That was a good question . . .

The sound of a car stopping outside the house saved Lisa from further questions. The engine idled, doors were opened and closed again. Hannah ran to the window.

'It's Amanda.' Until she heard the words, and felt the relief, Lisa hadn't realized how much she needed to hear that her sister had arrived.

Amanda

Amanda paid the taxi driver and thanked him, as he heaved her rucksack out of the boot of his car.

'Blimey, girl, are you telling me that you lug this thing halfway around the world?'

'Someone has to!'

'What the hell have you got in it? Bricks?'

'No bricks, no. My entire life.'

'That explains it!' He doffed an imaginary cap at her, like Dick van Dyke in *Mary Poppins*, and opened the driver's door. 'Good luck to you, then, girl. And welcome home.'

'Thanks.'

Home.

She'd been 8 years old when they'd come to live here, in the house that Mark built. She'd lived here for eleven years. And then she'd left. Not permanently, of course. She'd been back. Sometimes for months at a time, sometimes just for the night. And she'd had other places to live. Flatshares, rented flats, rooms in houses, university halls . . . But this was still the place she thought of as home; still the address she wrote in the boxes on the forms.

This time she hadn't been back for nearly three months. She hadn't seen Mum when it was really bad, and she hadn't been here when she died. That was deliberate, and, at the time, she believed, or so she told herself, that Mum understood, and that it was okay. But now she didn't know whether or not she was glad that she had missed it. She looked back down the road to where the taxi was driving away, and felt a familiar flight impulse, and then she turned back to the house. With some effort she hoisted her backpack onto her shoulder and trudged up the path. Mark saw her and came to the front door. Behind him, she saw her three sisters. When she reached her stepfather, Amanda put the rucksack down beside her and almost fell into his arms, and the two of them stood there for a long time, without speaking, holding each other. After a minute, Hannah pushed past Jennifer and Lisa on the threshold, and wrapped her arms around her father and her sister. 'You're home!'

Stephen, presumably having finished whatever crucial business he had been conducting in the car, was coming up the path to the front door, adjusting his tie. He sidestepped the emotional scene and went into the welcome cool of the entrance hall. 'I see the Prodigal Daughter has returned,' he remarked wryly as he passed his wife. Jennifer threw him a withering look. 'Sssh!'

Behind him, a few other people were starting to arrive now. Mark's brother Vince and his wife Sophie were parking behind Stephen, and more cars behind them. These were the prime spaces – you could walk to the church from here. Mark remembered strolling back, flanked by friends and family, one beautiful May morning, after Hannah's christening, as she slept in his arms. Some of the same cast would be here today. Looking at them, he groaned quietly. 'Christ, should have got my trousers on earlier!' He released Amanda, and went out into the front to say hello, and be hugged, and answer inane questions about parking.

Hannah and Lisa took the rucksack between them and set it down at the bottom of the stairs.

'You cut that a bit bloody fine, didn't you?' Jennifer didn't mean it to sound as harsh as it did.

'Don't start on her,' Lisa chided. 'Not now.'

'I'm sorry.'

'No, *I'm* sorry. I didn't mean to make you worry.'

'You never do.' Jennifer said this quietly, and under her breath. Lisa was the only one who heard.

'Go and make her a cup of tea, or coffee, or something, will you?' Looking Amanda up and down, she asked, 'I assume you've come straight from somewhere, right?'

'From Stansted. Yes, please. I'm parched.' Jennifer sniffed into flared nostrils and went to the kitchen.

'Come upstairs. We've got to get out of these dressing gowns. Why the hell are people arriving early? It's not like you need a great seat – she's in a bloody basket! Is that what you're wearing? *Please* say it isn't. Hannah, can you manage the rucksack . . . ?'

'Where the *hell* have you been?'

They were in Hannah's room now, with the door closed behind the three of them. Lisa was climbing into her startlingly yellow dress, not looking straight at her.

'You sound like Jennifer. And I thought you'd rescued me from her wrath downstairs.'

'I did, but only so I could subject you to mine up here. And my wrath might be less frequent, but it's not less scary. Where the hell have you been, Mand? Mark's got to have been going nuts.'

'*Has* Mark been going nuts, Hannah?'

Amanda looked to her little sister for support. Hannah shrugged. 'He just said you'd be here if you could.'

Amanda looked at Lisa, who gesticulated in exasperation.

'That's not the point, Mand. *I've* been going nuts, okay. *I've* been going nuts.'

'I wrote, in that email, that I'd be here.'

'Almost a week ago.'

'And I'm here.'

'Just.'

'But I'm here.' Lisa threw her hands out in exasperation, then turned to the mirror, saw her big yellow self and snorted.

Amanda was rummaging in her rucksack. She had, of

course, been wearing what she thought might do for the church. She just didn't want to admit it.

'Bright, right?' she now asked Hannah.

'Bright.' Hannah shrugged. 'Mum's wishes.'

'Right . . . Bright.' She opened another flap, and started pulling creased clothes out of the pack's dark recesses. 'She'd be lucky to get clean, let alone bright. Even the stuff that started out life bright isn't so bright now . . .' Her voice cracked. Lisa softened. She put a hand on Amanda's back, as she bent over a pile of her stuff. 'Are you okay?'

Amanda's eyes had filled with tears. 'I'm fine.'

She wasn't fine. Of course she wasn't fine. Had it been a week? It could have been a month, or just two minutes. Time had stopped, there in the internet café. The world had gone weird. She'd sat, for ten minutes, looking at the screen. Mark's address . . . the red exclamation mark flashing urgency at her. The email was dated with yesterday's date; no heading – it didn't need one. She knew, before she pushed the button that opened the text and made it real: Mum was dead.

She hadn't gone far, this time. She'd been in Spain. Working at a beach bar on the Costa Calida, near Murcia. Staying with some friends of friends whose parents had a little villa out there near the sea. It wasn't somewhere she would normally have stayed for long. But she couldn't have gone further. She'd been waiting, waiting for this email.

When it finally came, she sent a one-line reply, saying she'd be home. And now she was. In the five days between, she had drunk too much tequila, taken long walks along the beach and resisted the urge to change her tickets home to somewhere else, *anywhere* else.

But it wasn't because of the trouble she would inevitably be in with her sisters. She found the idea of other people's grief far more frightening, far harder to cope with than her own. She had come home to immerse herself in it, and she was afraid it would feel like drowning. It wasn't going to be like some film – *Steel Magnolias* or *Terms of Endearment*, where the funeral marked the end of the really bad time, and the start of everyone getting better. It wasn't going to be like that at all: it was going to be the beginning.

Hannah took her hand. 'I'm glad you're here now. I don't really care where you've been.'

'Thanks, Hannah.' Amanda let herself be held. It wasn't something that happened often. Mum had always said she was a wriggly cuddler – unwilling to sit still and be embraced. Mum once said she'd almost enjoyed it when Amanda was poorly as a young child – it was the only time she allowed her to put her arms around her and stroke her hair.

Jennifer came in without knocking. Amanda readied herself for round two.

'Listen, Jen. I know you're mad at me, and you probably have every right. I'm sorry I took off and left it to all of you. I know it was selfish and cowardly, and all that. And I'm sorry if you thought I would be back sooner. I just needed a bit of time, that's all, to let it sort of sink in. I know – selfish again. That's me, hey? But I really am sorry. And I really am here now. Can we leave the flagellation out, just for today. Hey?'

'What's flagellation, anyway?' Hannah asked.

'Beating. Brought on by guilt.'

'No one wants to beat you up, Amanda.' Jennifer tried

to sound less like a teacher. 'I just thought we should be together for this. For *all* of this.'

She was biting back. Amanda was right. She *was* mad. It wasn't fair – she'd buggered off, and left it all to the rest of them. And now she was crying, damn her, and that just wasn't supposed to happen.

Hannah stepped between the two of them, facing Jennifer. 'Please, Jennifer. Don't be angry at her, not today.' She held her gaze, and Jennifer was shocked, as she often had been in the last couple of years, at how grown up she looked and seemed. 'Today is about Mum: our mum.' And she was right.

Amanda and Jennifer joined hands on either side of Hannah's hips, and pulled her into a hug, which Lisa joined, her arms encompassing all three of them, and squeezing tight.

Like sisters throughout time, whatever battles raged between them, it was always, always, all four of them against the rest of the world. They emerged from Hannah's room a few minutes later, holding hands, Amanda dressed in something Hannah had found in her wardrobe, her hair pulled back from her face, her tears dried.

The church wasn't too bad. Amanda said they looked like extras from some cheesy musical, or a girl band scoring nil points at the Eurovision Song Contest, all dressed in their bright colours – Lisa in yellow, Hannah in pink, Amanda wrapped in orange and red – and even Jennifer, in a sky-blue shift dress. They stood ramrod straight in the front pew, flanked by Mark – now changed into a purple linen shirt – and Stephen, who remained resolutely and ostentatiously dressed in black, but at least he had left his BlackBerry in the car. They got there early, so they wouldn't have to watch everybody else file in, and they didn't turn around. They knew it would be full. Mum had a lot of friends; friends they would eventually have to talk to, they knew, at the wake. But not now.

It was the committal that made them break 'the big rule'. Barbara had chosen a humanist site, about three miles from the church where they held the service. She said she couldn't bear to be cremated, with that supermarket conveyor belt effect, and the vaguely comical curtain that opened and closed, and that she didn't want to be put in the ground in a churchyard. So she was going to decompose gently, in a biodegradable coffin, and go back to the earth. And eventually have a tree growing on top of her that they could come to, if they wanted to, and visit her. In an expanse of green with grass and butterflies, she said, instead of some depressing grey field of marble and granite. She said it would save them a fortune in flowers. Jennifer remembered the night she had told them that, remembered being jealous that she'd sorted everything out with Lisa. Why not her? Mark had squeezed Barbara's hand, all serious and po-faced. Then he'd whispered to her, 'Christ, you want flowers as well! Is there no end to the demands?'

Which was how the four of them, along with Mark and Stephen, came to be standing alone except for the officiant, on a hot August afternoon, with the heat haze shimmering all around them, in a field, in front of a strange and beautiful woven willow casket containing their mother, reputedly resplendent in emerald green Ben de Lisi, listening to Van Morrison sing 'In the Garden' on a tinny tape recorder. Where every one of them cried exactly as much and for as long as their broken hearts dictated.

'God, Mark, you're going to be eating Coronation Chicken for the rest of the month!' A bunch of Barbara's local friends had catered the wake, and cleaned up, storing leftovers in clear Tupperware containers. They'd done a beautiful job. It had looked for all the world like a party – a wedding, maybe, or some family reunion. There were trestle tables set out on the lawn, draped in yellow crêpe paper, and jugs and vases with roses cut from the garden dotted between the large bowls of rice and potato salads, French bread and heirloom tomatoes. There were trays of oatmeal biscuits, and small bowls of strawberries, with dishes of clotted cream, sweaty in the heat. People had drunk Pimms and real lemonade. It had all been beautiful. Instead of the low, respectful hum usually heard at funerals, there had been laughter, and stories, and a soundtrack from inside the house of Simon and Garfunkel and the Mamas and the Papas. The men were not shifting uncomfortably from foot to foot, hands in pockets; the women did not have red-rimmed eyes. It was exactly how she would have wanted it to be – good friends, good food, good weather. Just no good reason.

Barbara's friends had cleared up too, graciously and more cheerfully than they felt, and now they had gone and the family was alone, sat in the living room, staring at the vast Tupperware offerings on the kitchen counter.

'Looks that way.'

The music was switched off now. Lisa had kicked off her shoes, and was curled into the corner of the sofa, her legs beneath her. Hannah was almost dozing, her head on her sister's lap. Amanda was cross-legged on the floor, her back against a stool.

At the front door, Jennifer was being hugged goodbye by Stephen. Barely. His lips were dry against her cheek, and his arms had no squeeze in them as he held her. He'd tried to take her hand, walking back from the burial to their car, and she'd let him take it for a minute or two. She was irrationally angry with him about the black suit and tie, and the BlackBerry. And, of course, mostly about the one thing totally beyond his control. She knew that too; she knew work was busy at the moment. She knew he'd missed too much, really, in the weeks before Barbara's death. But she was still mad at him. When he put his arms around her, she held herself a little stiff, and wouldn't relax into the embrace.

'Are you sure that you want to stay?'

'Yeah. I haven't seen Amanda in a long time, Hannah is a mess and I don't want Mark to be by himself . . .'

'Aren't Amanda, Hannah and Lisa here to look after him?' His tone was almost sarcastic, almost amused. 'You look exhausted.'

'I just buried my mum, Stephen . . . How do you expect me to look?' She didn't want to go home with him, that was the truth of it. She wanted to stay here.

'I didn't mean that.' He knew it, whether she told him or not. He knew she'd rather be with all of them tonight. He tried not to let it hurt him.

'I know. Sorry.'

'I'm sorry.' God, this politeness.

'I'll be back tomorrow, by the time you get home from work. Lisa'll drop me off, I'm sure. Or maybe I'll take a train . . .'

Stephen raised his hands in a gesture of unnecessary surrender. 'Fine, fine . . . Seems to me, to be honest, like you haven't really needed me all day.'

'Is that what you want to feel – like I need you?'

He rubbed his eyes impatiently with one hand. 'You know what, Jen? It's fine that you stay; it's fine.' He kissed her again, the same dry lips skimming her skin. 'I'll see you tomorrow.'

She leant against the doorframe and watched him walk to the car, get in, drive away. He looked back at her, and called out that he loved her, not waiting for an answer. But once again, it felt as if they were on opposite sides of a big hole, a chasm they both made attempts to cross, just never at the same time.

When she got back to the others, Mark was making tea: the national pastime. She got the milk from the fridge and poured some into each mug. He put them on a tray and carried them back to the sofa.

'How mangled are you all feeling?'

Lisa laughed weakly. 'Scale of one to ten? A good nine.'

Hannah raised a limp hand from her reclining position. 'Eleven over here.'

'Why?' Jennifer asked.

'Because there's more,' replied Mark. 'Not the official stuff – we'll sort that out at the lawyers. This is your Mum. She did manage to write a few more letters, like she said. I have them. I was supposed to give them to you all after this was finished. I'd have waited until tomorrow, but Jen's not going to be here . . .'

'I am, actually. Stephen just left . . .'

Lisa raised an eyebrow quizzically at her sister.

'He's got an early start tomorrow. I just thought . . .'

Mark put a hand on her shoulder. 'I'm glad you're here. Your Mum would be pleased – to know that all her girls were here together.'

They didn't open them right away. It wasn't Christmas morning, after all. Each of them held their letter in their lap. Amanda tried to remember what her mum's hands looked like, imagining them holding the envelope. They chatted until they were too tired. Hannah fell asleep, and had to be gently shaken. They peeled off one by one, a subdued chorus of Waltonesque goodnights issuing forth on the upstairs landing, and went to bed, glad, at least, to have put the day behind them.

A conversation with ELIZABETH NOBLE

How do you draw on personal experience to write your emotive books?

Every writer does this differently, but my way is to put myself in my characters' shoes. I'm not, ever, writing straight autobiography, but I am definitely imagining myself going through every experience I write about. The tricky part is to then reimagine that experience through the eyes and mind of the character I've created – twisting, if you like, how I feel into how they might feel.

Do you have a favourite of your books? Or a favourite character?

My favourite is always the one I am about to write. I love the blank-page moment, when the story and the characters are brimming in me, and I am about to start spilling them out. (My least favourite, predicatably enough, is always the one I've just finished – because by then I am in the neurotic, self-doubting stage, and that's no fun!)

I am proudest of *Things I Want My Daughters to Know*, because, of my seven novels, it is the one that has most connected me to my readers. It created a huge response at the time of publication, and I really felt I'd tapped into something profound. The mother-daughter relationship is, I believe, the most complicated relationship most women experience in their lifetime. I wanted to write about a flawed, very real mother, and her fear of leaving her daughters before she feels they are ready to be without her . . .

And *Alphabet Weekends* is the most fun. I long for it to be made into a film because I think it has the makings of a classic rom com … I play a little game of fantasy casting with that one, and daydream about wearing a posh frock at the LA premiere … or the Oscars …!!

Which authors did you read when you were growing up? Has anyone inspired you?

I read for pleasure voraciously from the age of about seven until the time I went to university – and I read everything, from the classics through to the books I borrowed from my mum. I was devoted to Laura Ingalls Wilder as a girl, and devoured the *Little House on the Prairie* series. I was reading adult novels from quite a precocious age, and had a pretentious few years in my early teens where I read prize winners. The only genres I never cared for were crime and fantasy. I suppose I'd say that as a young person I was inspired by pretty much everyone who'd been published, because it seemed such an unachievable dream.

Long-distance relationships with family is a theme central to *Between a Mother and Her Child*. Did you draw on your experience of living in New York to write around that theme?

To some extent I did. I wrote *Things I Want My Daughters to Know* and *The Girl Next Door* when I was living in New York, thousands of miles from friends and family, and I can see the emotion of that situation when I reread those books. When I was a teenager, my parents and my younger brother lived in Sydney, Australia for several years, while my older sister and I stayed behind to continue our education in the UK (our choice, incidentally – how much do I regret that decision!). Much of Maggie's feeling for Australia comes from that experience too. Living abroad affects people differently – in my case, it has always made me acutely homesick.

You write evocatively about the death of a loved one in a number of your books. Do you feel a responsibility to people who have suffered a similar trauma when you're writing about that kind of loss? How do you ensure you stay faithful to that experience?

Of course I feel a responsibility – it would be awful to get it horribly wrong. I haven't been bereaved in that way, thank God, although my own life and family have been through health scares, near misses and vicarious experiences that have given me some real life insight into some of the situations I write about. But I try to remember that I am, respectfully, writing fiction, from imagination. And I know that, actually, in terms of grief, there is no right, wrong or universal way in which it is experienced or handled by people going through it. What matters most to me is making sure that each character responds to his or her situation authentically. I'm not telling anyone else how they should respond to anything similar.

How has your writing changed (if at all) since you started writing?

I think you get more confident as you write more – things like structuring a novel, and moving a plot along at the right pace become easier. Conversely, I feel more nervous with each new book than I did with the last in terms of how it will be received in the world. That anxious feeling gets worse each time!

In terms of what I write, I think I've become more relaxed about slightly messier endings – with my first few novels, I felt compelled to tie up all the ends neatly, and to leave every character completely 'sorted'. But life, of course, is not like that, and so novels about life shouldn't be either . . .

What kind of response do you get from fans for your books?

Usually a lovely one. I am always touched and moved by people who want to tell me that they've loved or been touched by something I've written. That, to me, represents success. Because so much of my soul is laid bare in what I write, the publicity part of the process makes me feel intensely vulnerable. I have learnt to care far less what reviewers say, because they often have agendas. Readers just love to read, and if they love to read what I have written, that is completely thrilling to me, and I'm grateful to every one of them.

What do you want readers to take away from your books?

That's a simple question to answer. I want them to feel satisfied – that they've been on a journey, if you like, with characters they have come to care about, and that they are, if not pleased, then at least satisfied with the ending of that journey. I want to write characters that are believable and relatable, and situations that resonate with readers. I'd like my reader to want to switch off the telly and go to bed early to read, to see what's going to happen next . . .

Psst

want the latest gossip on all your favourite writers?

Then come and join us in . . .

THE BOOK BOUTIQUE

. . . the **exclusive club** for anyone who loves to curl up with the latest reads in women's fiction.

- All the latest news on the best authors.
- Early copies of the latest reads months before they're out.
- Chat with like-minded readers as well as bestselling writers.
- Excellent recommendations for new books to read.
- Exclusive competitions to get your hands on stylish prizes.

SIGN UP for our regular newsletter by emailing
thebookboutique@uk.penguingroup.com
or if you really can't wait, get over to
www.facebook.com/TheBookBoutique